W9-BMY-379

		DATE DUE	

TRINITY: MILITARY WAR DOG

This Large Print Book carries the
Seal of Approval of N.A.V.H.

TRINITY: MILITARY WAR DOG

RONIE KENDIG

THORNDIKE PRESS

A part of Gale, Cengage Learning

GALE
CENGAGE Learning˙

Detroit • New York • San Francisco • New Haven, Conn • Waterville, Maine • London

GALE
CENGAGE Learning·

Thorndike Press, a part of Gale, Cengage Learning.

Thorndike Press® Large Print Christian Mystery
The text of this Large Print edition is unabridged.
Other aspects of the book may vary from the original edition.
Set in 16 pt. Plantin.

LIBRARY OF CONGRESS CATALOGING-IN-PUBLICATION DATA

Kendig, Ronie.
  Trinity : military war dog / by Ronie Kendig. — Large Print edition.
    pages cm. — (Thorndike Press Large Print Christian Mystery)
    ISBN 978-1-4104-5414-0 (hardcover) — ISBN 1-4104-5414-2 (hardcover) 1.
Dogs—War use—Fiction. 2. Life change events—Fiction. 3. Large type books.
I. Title.
PS3611.E5344T75 2013
813'.6—dc23   2012037191

Published in 2013 by arrangement with Barbour Publishing, Inc.

Printed in Mexico
3 4 5 6 7 17 16 15 14

*To a special breed of heroes —
military working dogs
and their two-legged handlers.
Thank you for your grueling
work and heroism, which often
goes unnoticed or unthanked!*

ACKNOWLEDGMENTS

Brian, you will forever be my hero! Ciara, Keighley, Ryan, and Reagan — thank you for enduring fast food, on-your-own nights, and even forgotten meals as I vanished into foreign countries and other people's lives. Thanks to my amazing in-laws, whose support is unending! I love you, Mom and Dad!

To Al Speegle — Thank you for sending me that e-mail that launched the idea for this series. You are a gentleman with razor-sharp wit. It is an honor to count you as a friend!

Various MWD handlers and military "experts" who have replied via e-mail or in person to my plethora of questions, including John Burnam, Richard Deggans, Elgin Shaw.

My agent, Steve Laube, who believed in this series from the first bone I threw his way. Without your encouragement, things would've been — are you ready for it? —

ruff!

Jaime Wright Sundsmo — Thanks for your help and expertise regarding climbing. Hopefully I didn't inadvertently kill a character with a climbing mistake (which would be my fault, not yours, LOL).

Julee Schwarzburg, editor extraordinaire. I am so humbled by you, sweet lady. THANK YOU for your sacrifice of time/wisdom, your calming and encouraging guidance, and your genius!

My dear writing friends, without whom I could not survive this journey: Dineen Miller, Robin Miller, Shannon McNear, Rel Mollet, Jim Rubart, Kellie Gilbert, Lynn Dean, MaryLu Tyndall, Kimberley Woodhouse, Becky Yauger.

The amazing Burnett Sisters — I hope General Burnett does you proud. I hear he has amazing daughters. Thank you for such incredible encouragement!

Thanks to my Audience of One, who has gifted me with this writing dream, enabling me to follow in His Son's steps by telling stories to impact His kingdom. What a joy and treasure!

LITERARY LICENSE

In writing about unique settings, specific locations, and invariably the people residing there, a certain level of risk is involved, including the possibility of dishonoring the very people an author intends to honor. With that in mind, I have taken some literary license in *Trinity: Military War Dog*, including renaming some bases within the U.S. military establishment and creating a new order of warriors within the Chinese Army. I have done this so the book and/or my writing will not negatively reflect on any soldier or officer. With the quickly changing landscape of a combat theater, this seemed imperative and prudent.

GLOSSARY OF TERMS/ACRONYMS

ACUs — Army Combat Uniforms

AFB — Air Force Base

AHOD — All Hands On Deck

BAMC — Brooke Army Medical Center, San Antonio

CJSOTF-A — Combined Joint Special Operations Task Force-Afghanistan

DD214 — Official Discharge from Active Duty

DEFCON — Defense readiness Condition

DIA — Defense Intelligence Agency

FOB — Forward Operating Base

Glock — a semiautomatic handgun

HK 9mm, HK USP — Heckler & Koch semi-automatic handgun

HPT — High-Priority Target

HUMINT — Human Intelligence

IED — Improvised Explosive Device

klicks — military jargon for kilometers

lat-long — latitude and longitude

M4, M4A1, M16 — military assault rifles

MRAP — Mine Resistant Ambush Protected vehicle

MWD — Military War Dog

ODA — Operational Detachment Alpha (Special Forces A-Team)

PLA — People's Liberation Army of the People's Republic of China

PTSD — Post-Traumatic Stress Disorder

RPG — Rocket-Propelled Grenade

RTB — Return To Base

SIS — United Kingdom's Secret Intelligence Service, otherwise known as MI6

SOCOM — Special Operations Command

SureFire — a tactical flashlight

tango — military slang for target or enemy

TBI — Traumatic Brain Injury

UAV — Unmanned Aerial Vehicle

PROLOGUE

Body rigid, ears trained on the sound coming from the dilapidated structure, she waited. Breaths came in staccato pants, the heat of a brutal Afghan summer beating down on her. While the Kevlar vest provided protection, it also created a thermal blanket that amplified the heat. She panted again and strained with resolute focus on the building. This wasn't her first tour of duty. It wasn't even her second. She'd completed three tours and outranked the Green Berets huddled behind her on the dusty road. Trinity lowered herself to the ground, waiting.

When she took her next breath, drool plopped onto the gritty sand.

"Easy, girl." Staff Sergeant Heath "Ghost" Daniels knelt beside his Special Forces-trained military war dog, his M4 aimed at the building where three men had disappeared. This so-called security mission for the sweep team in prep for an HPT convoy had taken a turn toward interesting. So much for intel that said the area was clean.

"Ghost, what's she got?"

At the sound of team leader Dean "Watterboy" Watters's voice, Heath assessed his sixty-pound Belgian Malinois again. "Nothing," he called to the side, noting Trinity's stance and keen focus.

With the sun at high noon, they would blister out here if they didn't get this road cleared before the general's pack came through at thirteen hundred.

Trinity came up off her hindquarters, muscles rippling beneath her dark, silky coat.

Heath's pulse kicked up a notch as his gaze darted over the nearly monochrome terrain. What had she detected? Sometimes he wished he had the sharp hearing inherent in dogs.

Having taken cover behind a half-blown wall, Heath peered around the peeling plaster and stared down the sights of his weapon. He let the crosshairs of the reticle trace the structure in which the rebels had taken refuge, but he didn't see anything. No trace of the men who'd scurried away from the sweep team. Men who'd raised the hackles of every member of the team, including Trin.

Snapping and barking, Trinity lunged. For a split second, her paws rose off the ground as she bolted forward. A plume of dust concealed her movement.

In a bound-and-cover movement, Heath and Watterboy hurried after her, making sure they didn't expose themselves to gunfire or RPGs. As they came up on the house, Heath flattened himself against the sun-heated wall.

A scream hurtled through the now-dusty day.

At the telltale sign of Trinity's hit, Heath hoofed it around the corner.

Screaming, an Afghan male bent toward the snarling dog who held his arm tight and jerked it back and forth. Five hundred pounds of pressure per square inch guaranteed submission. Trained not to rip the guy to shreds from head to toe, she maintained her lock on the target.

Heath came up on the guy's right, noting Watterboy on the left. "Down!" he shouted in Pashto. "On your knees."

More screams, this time mingled with tears as the guy warred with his instinct to fight and the order to kneel. Blood streaming down his arm, he dropped to the ground.

"Out!" Heath gave the release command to his canine partner.

Obediently, Trinity disengaged and trotted to his side as Heath maintained control. "My dog is trained to kill," he said in the man's native tongue. "Do not make any sudden moves or she will attack. Do you understand?"

Master Sergeant Tiller nodded his intention to enter the building, and with Sergeant First Class James "Candyman" VanAllen, they led the rest of the team into the structure.

Cradling his arm, the man frantically bobbed his head and whimpered.

Watterboy moved in to search the man while Heath kept watch. Once they cleared the man of dangerous weapons or materials, Heath led Trinity to the shade where he squirted water into her mouth from the CamelBak bite straw. She lapped it up, then turned in a circle.

"Good girl." He smoothed his hands over her body, assuring himself she hadn't been injured during the encounter.

As he straightened, the others streamed back out of the house, faces smeared with dirt and sweat — and frustration. No way.

"Empty?"

"One hundred percent."

Their medic hurried, bandaging the rebel's wound.

Watterboy faced the rebel. "Where'd they go?"

The tearstained face of the rebel rose to the Special Forces unit. He gave a slow nod behind him.

As Heath glanced over his shoulder, his gut knotted.

A new enemy rose, proud and majestic. With his M4 against his chest, Heath gazed up at the forbidding terrain of the Hindu Kush. He'd flown over them dozens of times, each time grateful they didn't have to comb through the rugged mountain terrain. The sun bathed the rocky slopes in an orange glow.

He removed his sunglasses and swiped his sleeve across his damp face. He wanted to curse, knowing they'd probably lost the Taliban fighters.

"Ghost, what's Trinity hit on?"

At the sound of Watterboy's voice, Heath snapped his gaze to his furry partner. Nose to the ground, she sniffed and maneuvered around a pile of rubble. She immediately sat down, ears perked and trained on the wood and cement.

Like a volcanic eruption, wood and cement shot upward and outward. Two men darted across the road.

Trinity streaked after them, her black-and-amber fur rippling beneath her muscular body. He pitied the idiots. Her snapping echoed through the narrow valley that ensconced them.

"Go!" Watterboy shouted.

Heath sprinted after his partner. In fact, she was his superior by one rank. If anything happened to her, it was his head on the platter. But that's not what had him sprinting in seventy-pound gear across the singed terrain. It was Trinity. His girl. His only girl.

Heath homed in on the sound of her barking that helped them navigate the brutal terrain. Rocks and twigs shifted beneath their thick boots. Trees and shrubs reached over the footpath, as if trying to distract the team with the lure of shade and a slight breeze.

Undeterred, Heath hauled butt up the side of the mountain. As he moved, he glanced up —

There!

Trinity sailed over a crevice and disappeared. A klick up, the path widened. Heath pushed onward, determined to find Trinity. She'd been more loyal and faithful than any friend or girlfriend. She had put her life on the line more times than he could count. He owed it to her to get there and interdict before things went bad.

"Whoa. Hold up," Watterboy mumbled.

Heath hesitated, one boot higher than the other as he glanced at his friend.

Watterboy's face glistened beneath the stifling heat. "I don't like it."

"I second the motion." Candyman took a knee, surveying.

For a split second, Heath took in the terrain he'd vaulted up. Like a sharp V, two sides dropped toward the team. An avalanche would bury them alive. The outcroppings were perfect for snipers.

"SOCOM suspects this area is crawling with Taliban," Tiller announced as he joined them. "Eyes out."

Which meant the real possibility of an ambush. Or an IED. Or both. But Heath knew one thing — due to their extreme effectiveness, military war dogs were high-priority targets with obscene bounties. He wasn't letting anyone get a bounty on Trinity.

Barking reverberated through the canyon. A shot rang out, followed by a yelp. Then . . . silence.

Heath burst into a run. His foot slipped on the rocky incline. The thin air pressed on him. Heavy. He felt heavy. But he wasn't stopping. Not till he found Trinity.

As he came up over a rise, a pebble-strewn path stretched out and around a crest in the rugged mountains. And two dozen yards away — Trinity. Pacing, her right back leg dragging. She'd broken behavior.

Something was wrong.

Thinking past the drumming of his pulse, he eased closer, his nerves prickling with anticipation of an attack. He darted a glance around without moving his head and advanced. "Trinity, down."

She turned, her gold eyes boring into him. Started to sit but rose and paced again, this time slower.

"Trin—" That's when he saw the dark streaks on her hindquarters. *She's shot!*

Instinct shoved him into a crouch, gauging the steep slopes towering over them, knowing the enemy had shot her from some hiding spot. He keyed his mic. "They've hit her — wounded her. She's broken behavior, not responding."

He inched along the crevice, fixing his gaze on Trinity. Her leg. Hopefully they hadn't done permanent damage. If he could get an IV in her, she'd have a chance.

A quick check to his six showed him the team, weapons trained as they slunk through the rocky edifice. Fluid, stealthy, the best — pride infused him. Confidence that they'd cover his six enabled him to turn back to his partner. He crouch-ran the last few feet to Trinity. Dropped to his knees.

That's when he noticed her vest. It lay a dozen feet away. How on earth did that happen? He pushed to his feet and started for it.

Trinity moved in front of him, snarling.

He'd seen the damage those teeth could deliver. "Easy, girl. It's okay." After rubbing her tall ears, he moved around her.

She lunged. Snapped. And again, snarled.

Heart in his throat, Heath stilled and drew back. Swallowed against his desert-dry mouth. He noticed the foam at the corners of her mouth. From his CamelBak he loosened the bite grip and squirted some liquid refreshment down to her.

Stance rigid, she stood off with him.

Concerned, he stroked her head. "It's okay, girl. We've got it." Again, he tried to retrieve her vest.

She lunged. Trapped his hand between her jaws. Five hundred pounds of pressure per square inch clamped through his flesh. Shock insulated the pain — at first. *What're you doing . . . ?*

Blood slid down across his thumb. This

should hurt. Bad. *Real* bad. Thoughts became reality. White-hot fire tore through his muscles and veins, shoving him to his knees. His pulse pounded in his temples. He growled the command, "Out!"

With a whimper, she released him.

Agony pulsed as he cradled his hand. "Down," he growled.

"What's happening?" Tiller shouted as he came up on Heath's nine.

"Her vest is off," Heath hissed.

"Think that wound they gave her is messing with her mind?" Watterboy asked as he caught up.

With his uninjured hand on her, Heath held up his other to stem the flow of blood. "Nah . . ." That wasn't like her. It took a lot to wig her out.

"Let's get her vest and clear out. This place is ambush central." Tiller jogged around them.

A growl rumbled through Trinity's belly. Her upper lip curled into a snarl —

"No!"

BooOOOom!

Wicked and thick, a concoction of haziness and pain pinned him down. His eyes wouldn't obey his command to open. He felt heavier than the time he leapt from that bridge and blacked out as a kid. He'd come to as a friend hauled him, unconscious, to the surface. That same feeling, heavy but weightless . . .

A voice . . . sweet and soft.

Heath stilled his mind and followed the voice from the void. What . . . she — it was a woman, right? He hadn't lost that much touch with reality, had he? — what was she saying?

As if his ears broke the water's lip, her voice became clear.

". . . all anxiety or pain you might be feeling. Finally, I pray you'd be uplifted by His grace and feel yourself enfolded in the peace of His embrace."

Peace . . . drifting . . . away . . . so quiet.

Wait. No. Trinity! Where was she? His arms resisted the plea to lift. Fire lit down the side of his neck. He moaned.

At least, he thought he moaned. Maybe his voice wasn't working —

A gasp nearby.

Still, Heath couldn't move or respond.

"What are you doing here?" Male, older, gruffer. Who . . . ?

"Shh," she said. "You'll wake him."

"This" — warbling in Heath's head garbled the words — "bring him back."

"This isn't about *him*," she hissed. "And

he won't remember I'm here."

"What if he does? That's a problem —"

"He won't!"

Heath's hearing closed up, his mind drowned in the words that struggled to find purchase against the pain and emptiness devouring him. He struggled. Tried to focus on her voice. That sweet, soft, angelic voice.

Please . . . God, don't let me forget.

Quiet descended and pushed him back into the depths.

Wakhan Corridor
Hindu Kush, Afghanistan
One Year Later

"*Opportunities multiply as they are seized.*" The words of the ancient warrior Sun Tzu held fast in the mind of Wu Jianyu as he hauled himself up over a steep incline, hands digging into the sharp edifice. Weakness meant failure.

He could afford neither weakness nor failure. Not again.

Squatting, he let his gaze take in the breathtaking view. Hazy under the taunt of dawn's first light, the rugged terrain was terrifyingly beautiful. Already, he and his men had hiked for two weeks, having left the province of Xinjiang, which lay more than a hundred kilometers behind.

When he'd spied the worn path traders, including Marco Polo and the Jesuit priest Benedict Goëz, had used for centuries, he ordered his men away from it and away from prying eyes. To the north rose the formidable land of Tajikistan. Behind him, to the south, stretched the borders of Pakistan. West lay Xinjiang, and east . . . Afghanistan.

His path to honor.

Then there was his path: A central branch that ran through the southern portion of Little Pamir to the Murghab River.

That assumed, of course, one was trying to get into China.

He was not.

Twisting in his crouched position, he drew in a long breath of crisp, cold air. Invigorated, he rose, allowing the mountains and valleys, the rivers that snaked and sparkled beneath the touch of vanishing moonlight, to speak to him. Remind him that he alone had been chosen for this mission. And it was his alone to fail. Or succeed.

Two more days would deliver them to the province where he could do what was asked of him. And regain what was rightfully his. What had been stolen, ripped from his line of ancestors.

I will not dishonor you again, Father. In fact, to distance his father from the disgrace that

25

had become Jianyu's alone, he'd taken his mother's surname. Thus Wu Jianyu was born. And Zheng Jianyu died. For now.

With one fist closed and one resting atop it, he bowed his head. Closed his eyes. After many minutes of silence and meditation, he once again reached for that which had always been his — emptiness. The chant of the Heart Sutra drifted through his mind and on the wind. It would work. The monk had told him. "*. . . indifferent to any kind of attainment whatsoever but dwelling in Prajna wisdom, is freed of any thought covering, get rid of the fear bred by it, has overcome what can upset and in the end reaches utmost Nirvana.*"

He needed the hope. To fill the empty places.

No, no. That's not what the monk said. Jianyu ground his teeth.

"*There is only one place you will find peace, Jianyu.*" The voice, soft and silky like a lotus petal, seeped past his barriers. His anger. His brokenness. And melted over him like honey.

"No!" He lowered himself to the ground, bent his legs, and rested his hands, palms upward on his knees. Focused on the Heart Sutra. Repeated the words he'd memorized in the years since she vanished and left him with nothing but dishonor.

ONE

Chinese Tea House, Maryland

Darci pushed through the heavy red door with the brass dragon handle. On the soft carpet she paused and removed her coat. The hostess looked up from her podium. Her face, with a practiced smile and faked cheeriness, exploded into a genuine welcome. "Darci, so good to see you!"

"And you, Lily."

The hostess motioned toward the back. "He's waiting."

Of course he was. Darci had seen his car in the parking lot. Not that she needed that to know he'd arrived before her. In fact, she was sure he came at least a half hour ahead of schedule every time. He was as cast in his ways as was the porcelain shrine of Buddha sitting behind the central fountain.

Even now, through the opaque rice paper sliding door, she could see her father's shadowed form. Though she relished their

29

lunches, this would be one she would regret. As she always did when her job took her out of town, away from her father.

Hand on the small handle, Darci took a steadying breath. *Be strong. He loves you. He just doesn't know how to show it.*

With a quick smile to Lily, who watched with a furrowed brow, Darci slid back the paper door. As she closed it behind her, she slipped off her shoes. The bamboo mat beneath her feet sent a chill up her spine. Afraid to meet his disapproving scowl, she eased onto the empty pillow at the table across from her father.

Darci inclined her head, gaze down as expected. "Sorry I am late, *Ba*." She wasn't late, but apologizing seemed to smooth out his frustrations that had taken such strong root in the last few years. Even more so on days like today.

She poured some tea and sipped it, using the little black handleless cup like a shield as she peeked over it to see his face. Hard lines. Burdened lines. The whiskers that framed his mouth were streaked with the paleness of wisdom. Too much for a man his age. There were secrets, family secrets, that he would not share with her. She'd tried to talk of her mother and brother, but they were forbidden subjects.

"You should trim that beard. It makes you look like a grumpy, old Chinese man."

"That" — his sad eyes met hers for the first time as he lifted his shoulders — "is because I *am* a grumpy, old Chinese man."

"Li Yung-fa is a kind, gentle soul." She smiled. "I know. I'm his daughter." With her spoon, she lifted some rice from the bowl in the middle of the table, her stomach clenching as she watched her father.

The mirth around his eyes faded, the rich brown of his irises seemingly lost in another time. She ached for what he'd lost twenty years ago. What she'd lost. She refused to let their lunch once again take a turn for the depressing. She pushed onward with safer topics.

"How was work this morning?" After setting the pile on her plate, she spooned sauce over it, then chose some beef and broccoli.

"As usual." His graying goatee flicked as he talked. "Same paperwork. Same mindless games. They waste my abilities. If they would just use me . . ."

So much for safer topics. Darci gave a slow nod. His mood was not encouraging, and when agitated, his already-heavy accent would thicken. No doubt, he would soon spin into full Mandarin, especially with the news she had to deliver. Squeezing some meat and rice between the chopsticks, she lifted the bowl closer.

"Where?"

Darci aimed the first mouthwatering bite toward her lips. "Excuse me?"

The slant in his eyelids pulled taut. "In your eyes rests the weight of the message I see you withhold."

All these years in America and still he held to the old ways of speaking, as if he were Yoda. She'd teased him without mercy as a teenager, hoping he would be more American . . . less Chinese. Anything to ply a smile out of the rigid face. There had been few smiles then, and as of late, even fewer.

Darci set down the bowl and sticks, cupping her hands in her lap, eyes downcast. "I leave tomorrow." She sighed. "I am sorry, Baba. I know this upsets you that I am gone so much."

Shoulders squared, he looked every bit the general he had once been. "Where?"

There was no use lying to him or trying to deceive him. The man worked with some of the highest-ranking officials in the government. If he doubted the veracity of her information, he'd hunt down the truth. Direct, strong, relentless . . . She'd gained a lot of her mother's American features with the fair skin, the European nose, but her father's strong Chinese heritage rang through her long black hair, slightly slanted eyes, and fire-like tenacity.

Which often left her wondering why he had not searched harder for her brother.

An eyebrow bobbed, as if demanding her answer.

"Afghanistan."

A tic jounced in his cheek as it often did when he tried to rein in his emotions. "That is very far."

"More like 'too close to China,' is that it?"

Like a provoked dragon, fire spat from his eyes. His fisted hand pounded the table. "Too far — from here." He thumped his chest. "From me."

Darci lowered her head. "He won't find me, Ba. I will be caref—"

"Like last time?" Fury erupted. "He nearly killed you!"

She would not let this happen again. "*He* is in China. I will be in the mountains . . . nowhere near him or any Chinese." Darci wanted one thing from her father. "Trust me. Believe in me. Yes?"

His whiskers shimmered — twitched. Was his chin bouncing? "I do not want to lose you, Jia!"

Her breath snatched from her lungs. So

afraid someone would find them, he had not used her birth name in twenty years. Her superiors had chosen the name for this mission, one she feared would be her last.

Darci placed a hand over his as she crawled around the small square table to his side. She touched his back. "You will not lose me. Not before my time."

His chest rose and fell unevenly. Hands resting on either side of his bowl, he drew back his hands and uncoiled them. After a few seconds, he pulled in a long, quiet breath. Then gave an almost imperceptible nod.

"I should only be gone a few weeks."

Another nod. "What you are doing is good. You serve your country." His lip trembled.

An invisible fist reached into her chest and squeezed the organ pumping hard and frantic as she took in all that had just transpired. He'd never been open about his feelings, about his fears. Was it a bad omen?

Two

Texas Hill Country
"You'll be tempted to ignore this opportunity, but those marks on your hand have shown you trust that beautiful animal who saved your life. Bring her out. Let her decide if this is right for your team."

Nerves on end, Heath climbed from his truck. Trinity bounded from the bench seat onto the grass that collided with a ten-foot chain-link fence. He pushed the door closed and took in the property that rolled out on each side, as well as the white luxury SUV he'd parked beside.

Trees, some barren of their leaves and others thickly outfitted, and brambles lined the east. A half mile west, a rocky edifice rose a good thirty feet straight up. Twenty feet from his position, within the fenced area, sat training equipment. A complete agility and tactical course set up. Cedar trees hogged the perimeter of the fence. But not

a person in sight. He'd half expected someone to emerge from the ranch house
perched at the top of the slight incline, but
that hadn't happened either.

What on earth?

Rubbing his knuckles along his lips, he
hesitated at the unlocked gate. He glanced
back down the almost mile-long dirt road
that led to the black wrought-iron gate. Sun
streamed through the lettering in the arch:
A BREED APART. Who was behind this
elaborate setup?

"Hello? Anyone here?"

A bitter January wind answered, creaking
the branches.

The training facility held too much draw.
He let Trinity take in the settings, her attention also focused on the training field. She
sniffed along the fence line. "What do you
think, Trin?"

She returned to him. Trinity swiveled her
head back to the front, her black-and-amber
coat sparkling in the sun. He smoothed a
hand along her dense fur. Her ears perked
and her body went rigid.

Heath slanted a look in the direction in
which she'd made a hit. A mass of white-
blond curls dipped into a beam of sunlight
streaming through the cedars as a woman
emerged from one of the house-shaped

training structures. She glanced back inside and stalled. After much coaxing, a yellow Labrador lumbered from the building.

Anticipation rippled through Trinity's coat, her muscles taut, all but begging for permission to meet the new dog.

"I know you?" Heath asked. This woman with her gun-shy dog didn't seem the type to know much about training, let alone his past.

She straightened and came toward the gate. "No, do I know you?" She glanced down at her yellow Lab, who sat off to the side facing away from them, his expressive eyes conveying his skittishness. He hung his head, then flattened himself to the ground.

"You're the one who invited me here?"

"No, actually," she said with a smile. "I'm not. My friend Khat lives here with her brother. They invited me." At the gate, she slipped through and waited for her dog, who had given up about halfway across the yard and lain down. She let out a sigh and turned to Heath with an extended hand. "Aspen Courtland."

"Heath Daniels. You say you know who owns this place?"

Clap!

Heath jerked toward the wraparound porch and stilled at the figure that emerged from the shadows. "Khouri? No way."

The low, slow chuckle of a man he knew in the Army rolled through the air as the man strode off the porch. With two legs. How . . . how was that possible? Heath had been there when a Coke-can-turned-IED shattered the guy's leg and career beyond repair. Just a few months before Heath lost his career, too.

"Hello, Aspen. Khaterah got called out. She's sorry she couldn't be here to greet you."

"No problem," Courtland said.

Wearing a red knit cap over long brown hair and sporting a thick beard as if he'd never left the field, Jibril Khouri grinned as he met Heath's gaze again. "I wasn't sure you'd come."

Pulling the guy into a half hug, half back-patting embrace, Heath scrambled to get his bearings. "You always knew how to get my attention."

"Yes, but you always got the girls. We had to distract you so the rest of us would have a chance."

Heath shirked the tease and ran a hand over the back of his head, across the scar that changed everything. "Yeah, well, things change."

"So they do." Sobered, Jibril stepped back

with another pat on Heath's shoulder, then bent and offered a hand to Trinity. "Hello, girl. Remember me?"

Trinity sniffed his hand, then turned in a circle, her focus locked on the yellow Lab.

"Ah, Trinity has the right idea," Jibril said with a laugh. "Let's go into the training area while we wait for our last recruit."

Uncertainty rooted Heath to the ground. Too many unexplained variables. Too many unknowns. "Khouri, what is this?"

"Now is not the time to be skittish, my friend." Jibril smiled. "Trust me, just as I trusted you the day Trinity saved my life. Yes?"

Stuffing his frustration and uneasiness, Heath gave a curt nod and followed Jibril, Aspen, and Trinity into the fenced-off area.

"Ah, this is Talon." Jibril squatted beside the Lab, who lifted his head and cast furtive glances at Jibril. "All the dogs and handlers invited to the ranch today are former military war or working dogs. Talon here has seen more combat than I have. You'll meet Beowulf and Timbrel Hogan soon — they're former Navy."

With a huff, Talon slid down to the ground, propped his lower jaw on his front paws, and let his gaze bounce over the yard. Those eyebrows did more work than his

39

whole body, tracking Trinity around the training grounds. He looked like he was as through with the military as it was with him.

You and me both, buddy.

Tension bunched at the base of Heath's neck. He stretched it. "So." He shifted his attention to Aspen. "You've seen combat?" That was hard to believe.

"I was Air Force, but no, I haven't seen combat." She must've seen his confusion. "My brother was his handler. He went MIA and Talon was declared 'excess.' "

MIA often meant dead. Not enough body parts to ship home. Heath now understood the Lab's reaction. Trinity had pretty much done the same thing when they'd been separated, well, except she became border-line aggressive and noncompliant. Talon was . . . gone. As if he'd checked out.

"So you adopted him?" Heath and every handler before and since sent up shouts of praise at a new resolution signed into law by President Clinton a few years back, which allowed dogs to live out the remainder of their years rather than being euthanized after the military decided they were done with the dogs. "I know your brother would be glad if he were alive."

"Austin's not dead." Blue eyes flamed. "He's *missing*."

Heath took about five mental steps away from her and that volley of anger.

Trinity nosed Talon's ears, walked circles around him, sniffed, investigated, sized up the new guy. He showed neither aggression — via a low growl to tell Trin to stand down — nor did he move away.

Arms folded, Aspen studied him. "What happened to you?"

"IED in the mountains." Heath held up the right hand Trinity had permanently marked. "Trinity saved my life, but the concussion from the blast and the shrapnel that sliced my thick skull put me out."

Squinting against the sun, Aspen nodded to Trinity. "And her?"

That was a story he didn't deserve, the undying loyalty and devotion of a creature with a pure heart. "When they sent me stateside, she refused to work with other handlers. So they retired her — gave me first dibs."

Aspen wrinkled her nose and looked at Jibril. "I'll be honest. I'm not sure about this."

"It will take time, but I think it will help him, and you."

"I'm not sure Talon —" Aspen froze as the yellow Lab ducked at the mention of his name. "Oh, I'm sorry, boy." She rushed to

41

his side and knelt. "It's okay," she crooned as she stroked his head.

"Don't baby him."

Aspen looked up at Heath. "What?"

"He's going to read your soft voice as a reward for cowering. He's a trained soldier, a warrior, a killer. Even though some people don't like the sound of that, it's true. He's trained to take down terrorists, men with bad intentions, and rout explosives from hot spots. He's not a pampered pet. Don't treat him like one. Give him some respect."

"But he's scared."

"I guarantee while your brother loved that animal, he didn't baby him. They were partners in combat, not out for a playdate."

She let out a small grunt with a smile. "Point taken."

A dog bounded out of a Jeep and through the gate. *Crap, that isn't a dog. It's the Hound of Hell.*

"Ah, Timbrel. Welcome! I am Jibril Khouri."

Dressed in jeans, a long-sleeved black shirt, and hiking boots, the woman exuded attitude as she tugged down the brim of her baseball cap. The wind teased the brown ponytail dangling out the back. "I never miss a party."

Something in Heath's stomach churned.

Young. Immature. What was she doing with a beast of a dog like that? Hadn't Jibril said all dogs were former MWDs? This one, too?

"Beowulf is as handsome as ever," Aspen said.

"I wouldn't have any other man." Miss Jeep sauntered through and latched the gate.

Heath shoved his attention back to the drool-bombing dog. No wonder the woman named him Beowulf. Or maybe it was because of the dog's good looks. Trinity, ears flattened, had her hackles up as the beast let out a bark that seemed to send ripples through the fabric of time and space. Lip curled, canines exposed, Trinity held her ground as she watched the beast out of the corner of her eye.

"Hey," Heath called to the owner. "Get your dog under control."

"Relax, Prince Charming. He's just having fun." Timbrel laughed. "I sure hope your girl is fixed."

Heath's heart pounded. "Don't blame me if your dog goes home with a chunk of his throat missing."

Timbrel seemed to feed off his warning. "May the best dog win, eh?"

"Timmy," Aspen said, her voice soft but reproachful.

"Okay, fine." With one snap of her fingers,

Timbrel brought her mountain of a brown-brindled mutt to her side. She bounced her shoulders with a smirk. "If only I could control men with such ease."

Heath wanted to laugh, but something about this chick grated on him. "If you approach relationships the way you do him, I bet you're single."

"Men have two things on their minds: money, which they're not getting from me, and sex, which they're also not getting from me." She crouched and kissed the mutt, whose jowls were coated in slobber. With a slurping noise that made Heath cringe from six feet away, Beowulf returned the love. "Beo wants nothing but to be with me. He protects me and won't leave me, unless" — she stood and gave a flick of her wrist at thigh level — "I tell him to."

Despite his broad, stocky build, indicating strength not speed, Beowulf sprinted down the field and skidded to a stop, waiting. "Now, see? If getting rid of guys could be as easy . . ."

Heath shook his head. "No wonder they put you out of the Navy."

Her eyes flamed but she didn't miss a beat. "Want to see what he does to men I don't like?"

Heath chuckled. "No thanks. My girl

would take your dog down, and I'd hate to see you lose the only 'guy' willing to kiss you."

Her eyebrow arched, challenge scratched into her expression. "Oh, Prince Charming." Her caustic, hollow laugh bounced off the obstacle course equipment. "I think you're going to eat those words and beg for mercy."

Heath flared his nostrils. "I never beg."

"Game on, Hot Snot."

Jibril laughed. "That's quite the introduction. But, let me tell you why we're here." He motioned everyone closer. "I've invited the three of you here for a business proposition."

Aspen leaned against one of the ramps. "And what is that?"

"Train your dogs."

"Look," Miss Jeep snipped. "I came out here because Aspen knows your sister and said I could trust her, but . . . this just reeks."

"Like your attitude," Heath muttered. He'd dealt with worse. Heath pointed to the man he'd served in combat with. "Jibril is one of the best men I know. He doesn't talk often, but when he does, it's worth listening to."

"Miss Hogan," Jibril said. "I bought this

45

property so handlers like yourself, Miss Courtland, and Ghost could continue training your dogs, and possibly others."

"To what end?"

"Once you are comfortable with your dog's training and progress, I would ask that you allow me to place each dog-handler team on the grid."

"Grid?" Heath couldn't stop the frown. *Grid* sounded too much like combat. Being messed up the way he was with traumatic brain injury, he wasn't looking to press his luck.

"Yes, make your services available to others who might need your help." Jibril's smile this time hung an inch from genuine. "My sister, Khaterah, is a veterinarian. She's agreed to treat your dogs."

"Then . . . why do you seem like you aren't happy?" Heath had known Jibril long enough to see through that.

His friend's face fell for a fraction, but when his gaze hit Heath's, he shrugged. "We have a difference of opinion on a few things."

Aspen offered a smile. "Khat is one of the most beautiful women I know — inside and out. She loves animals and hates violence."

"Who likes it?"

"You." Jibril's green eyes held Heath's.

"Me — according to her. Since we were in the military, since you train your dogs to protect, she believes it breeds violence."

Heath raised his hands. "Okay. Got it. So, who would be hiring us?"

"It would all be contract work. I've seen interest from companies who have contractors on the ground in Iraq and Afghanistan. I've even seen interest from our own military. They've seen the great benefit of war dogs and will pay nice fees to have a for-hire availability."

Heath pursed his lips, considering the info. "HPT and VIP escorts, etcetera?"

"Roger." Jibril grinned.

"I like the idea," Hogan said. "But what's this to you? Why are you doing it?"

Though tempted to roll his eyes again, Heath remained neutral as Jibril moved toward a central position among the four of them — *is he limping?* — and bent down.

"Two years ago, I was a Green Beret." He tugged up his right pant leg . . . up . . . up. Until shiny black and silver metal glinted in the sun. A prosthesis. "Were it not for Trinity and Ghost, I would not have just lost my leg that day. I would have lost my life."

THREE

Hindu Kush, Afghanistan
One Week Later

A cool breeze slid across Darci's shoulders, swirled around her bare neck, and trailed down her spine. She drew her legs closer as she sat on a small outcropping and laid aside her field notebook and pencil. Though she'd climbed higher mountains than the one that cradled her now, there was something forbidding, ominous about the Hindu Kush. Rugged, brutal beauty towered over her, as if daring her to carry out the mission. Her most dangerous to date. But she was up for it. She had to be.

Glancing at her field book, she groaned. A week of field mapping and field checking the Russian geologic maps for validity amounted to seven days of backbreaking hammering, measuring, sketching . . .

"In other words, mind-numbingly boring." She freed her jet-black hair from the elastic and rubbed her scalp, letting the wind whip it free and loose.

Though she'd gone out each night searching, she'd found nothing. No sign of her targets. If she didn't find something soon, she'd have to go back a failure.

She'd never failed a mission or her commanding officer. Her dedication and commitment to her country and its foundations forbade her from allowing defeat.

A yawn tugged at her, and she rubbed a hand over her face, trying to shake off the sleepiness. As she did, a striation in the rock below caught her attention. Darci tilted her head, then brought herself forward onto all fours. Gingerly, she peeked over the lip of the outcropping. Straight down — more than seventy feet. She grinned at the challenge.

But no — her focus. The lighter striation. With care, she dug her fingers into the rocks and wedged her toes into the lateral clefts running along the cliff face. Air rushed up at her. Gravity pulled at her limbs. She smiled as her pulse ramped.

"*What* are you doing?"

The gruff voice struck Darci. Her foot slipped. Rocks dribbled down.

She bit down on a curse as she caught herself, palms sweating against the adrenaline jolt. Peeking up and over to her left, she spied Peter Toque glaring at her. "Tempting fate."

"You've got to be the stupidest, most pig-headed . . ."

Darci blew out a breath and inched away from the ledge. She'd have to check out the striation later — it looked like a hidden path, popular among terrorists to scurry from one location to another. And if that was true, it could lead her to the targets. It fit, didn't it? Well hidden. High in the mountains.

Definitely.

But she'd given bad intel once before, and it had cost . . . too much. She wouldn't make that mistake again if she could help it. She'd verify her suspicions later. Courage rose on the bitter wind, steeling her against fear that had threatened to overtake her earlier.

"Aren't you supposed to be on the other side of this rock?" She glared back as she lifted her field notebook and pencil.

"We finished an hour ago."

"Wow, and you already turned in your field slips and sketches to Dr. Colsen?" Darci would not let this wad of muscle and testosterone get to her. He'd shadowed her every move since they'd landed at Bagram

Airfield last week.

"I was on my way back."

"Right." She aimed herself in the direction where her field partner, Alice Ward, worked.

"Hey."

A jerk on her arm spun her around — straight into Toque. If she didn't find him so irritating, she might be willing to admit he had the looks most girls wanted. Angular jawline. Height. Muscle. Blue eyes. But then there was his arrogance.

"What you were doing is dangerous."

She flared her nostrils. "So is touching me."

He released her arm. "Look, I'm just —"

"Save it."

"You're not the only one here. And this isn't exactly Central Park."

"If you'd put as much effort into your job in the field as you do in trailing me like a lovesick puppy, maybe we'd be done and back at Bagram, analyzing the maps and able to figure out our next steps."

"Lovesi—" Toque clamped down on the words and shook his head.

She rounded a bend in the path and almost collided with Alice. Despite the jet-black hair — dyed, not natural like Darci's Asian-black — nose ring, and kohl-lined eyes, the girl was as sweet as they came. And she had a Texas-sized crush on the cad behind Darci.

"Jia." The girl's voice and gaze dropped when she saw Toque. "Are you done?"

Darci nodded to the red streaks in the sky. "Night's coming. We should head back."

When they stepped into the cluster of tents set up on the plain central to the area they were testing for lithium deposits, Darci stomped toward her tent. Five tents formed a circular perimeter with a fire pit in the middle. One half of the larger tents served as the communications hub, replete with computers and equipment Darci could barely spit out the names for, while the other half sported a long table with two benches used for conferences and meals.

"Hey, Jaekus. You missed all the fun." Toque grabbed a tin cup and poured himself a hot drink from the large steel drum. "Jia there was scaling the cliff when I found her — should've been there with her."

Something about Peter Toque unsettled her and left her guessing. Darci couldn't put her finger on it, but she would. Soon enough.

Perched atop one of the field chests, Jaekus raised an eyebrow at Darci. "Rock climbing again, eh?"

Darci shrugged. "I saw some unusual striations in the rock. Wanted to check it out."

"*You have killer instincts, Darci. Trust them.*" The general's admonishment years ago had come at a high cost — her first and only training failure.

"Well, no more of that." Dr. Colsen ducked as he stepped out of his tent. His muddy brown eyes glared as he dropped into a chair around the hub of chairs and makeshift tables. "I won't be responsible — or have this expedition canceled — because someone took unnecessary risks and got herself hurt or killed."

"It was *necessary*, and remember? I'm a certified rock climber." She might not have the alphabet soup behind her name that he did, but the crash course the general had secured for her enabled her to perform on a level regarding geology with those around her — at least enough to buy time. Dr. Richard Colsen objected to her overseeing the lead on the team, but the man objected to just about everything that wasn't his idea.

"I don't care what you are — except a member of this survey team. If you —"

"All right, all right, old man." Toque pushed off the chest. "Give it a rest."

"You listen here," Colsen said, his face

reddening. "This is my project and my name. If I say —"

"Dr. Colsen," Darci said as she joined the team, resting an arm around him. "What results have you found about the samples we brought back already? Are they showing significance?"

The ruddiness bled from his face until the normal, pale color returned. "No." He looked like a grumpy, old man right now. The professor's failing health relegated him to rock analysis instead of the rigorous workout required to carry out the research. Just shy of seventy, how long would he last up here with the thinner air, the rigorous hiking? Maybe it was a good thing he'd elected to remain at the camp while they hiked to check out the terrain today.

It also allowed her time to recon.

"However," he said, snapping her attention to him. "One of the samples Jia brought back from the northeastern grid does show promising signs." His gaze rose to hers, and she saw the approval and thanks for rescuing yet another souring conversation among the team. "We'll look into it further back at the base. When we return in a week, hopefully we can map it out and get the full scope of what's out there."

That worked in Darci's favor. She needed

to report in, gather her thoughts, and figure out a contingency plan. That odd striation in the rock plucked at her conscience again. If she could get to the path — *it has to be a path!* — she was certain she'd find a gold mine. She needed to collect samples while she collected information. But Toque was on her back 24/7.

Which meant when they returned, she'd have to ditch the shadow.

A Breed Apart Ranch
Texas Hill Country

Swaying as if urging Heath onward, the branches shook their limbs at him, void of leaves and weight in the cold February morning. Heath hit the trail that snaked through the trees. The path coiled up and around A Breed Apart's beautiful, expansive setting. Jogging cleared his mind and strengthened his body — and Trinity's. She kept pace without a hint of complaint.

A month. They'd been at this a month, running and training, pushing as he pressed toward the goal of shedding his weakness, headaches, blackouts. The Army had severed his career with the Green Berets because headaches and subsequent blackouts, which occurred when the exercise became too strenuous, left him unreliable. A danger. To

55

himself. To his buddies.

But thirty-two days of fresh outdoor exercise and stress-free workouts in the hills had brought about a significant difference in his stamina and nudged his body toward health. His mind toward all he had to be thankful for these days.

With each foot he planted, Heath felt closer to victory, to "normal."

As he ran the trail, going higher and longer each time, he couldn't escape the irony. First, he and Trinity had been paired up, put through the dog-handler program at Lackland Air Force Base. Nearly five months of training spent there in San Antonio with brutal, suffocating heat, then further training for Special Operations Command. All so they were there that day to save Jibril, who came home — alive. Started A Breed Apart, which gave Heath hope that he hadn't reached the end of his usefulness.

Who was saving whom?

Because of his PTSD and TBI diagnoses, he wouldn't be cleared to return to his Special Forces unit, but maybe he and Trinity could provide some benefit if the chaplaincy fell through. That was his first goal — make chaplain so they'd send him back to the action. To the adrenaline. Serve with the guys. Be one of them again.

At the summit, Heath stood on a ledge that protruded from the cliff, noting the throb at the base of his skull. In recent days, the effects were much reduced.

Lowering himself to the rocky lip brought Trinity to his side. He wrapped his arm around her, the sun glistening across her tan hues, making the amber color richer. Around her broad chest, shoulders, and hindquarters, it looked as if an artist had shaded her coat with charcoal. But what made him fall in love with the Belgian Malinois was her almost completely black mask. At times, when the sun set just right on her coat, it almost seemed as if her black mask were the burned sections, indicative of the fire brimming beneath. And man, was there ever fire in this dog's belly that streamed out through her amber eyes.

"Hey, beautiful," he mumbled as her keen gaze locked on the wilderness. Legs dangling over the ledge, Heath tugged the bite valve from the CamelBak and took three long drags from it. As the cool water swirled around his mouth, he aimed the valve at Trinity and squirted her.

Her head snapped around, and she lap-licked at the water. Sated, she shook out her fur.

"Hey." He shielded himself as water sprayed him. "Payback, huh?"

She nudged the paper sticking out of his waistband.

"Can't ignore the inevitable, huh?" Heath plucked the white envelope and stared at it. The U.S. Army logo stamped in the left-hand corner. Inside, words that formed his future. They had to let him in. It made sense, having been a Green Beret, to get assigned to SOCOM as a chaplain. It was his dream. His yearning.

What if they rejected him? He should've had his new stats sent to them. That would have given him his clear shot. They didn't know, though, how much better he was doing. How improved he was.

Trinity sniffed the envelope.

"Yeah, yeah," he grumbled as he shoved his finger between the flap and the envelope, ripping it open. The wind tapped against the paper, crinkling it in his hand. Heart in his throat, Heath scanned the words, his courage slipping, pebble by pebble like the dirt on the ledge.

"We regret to inform you . . ." Lips moving with no sound, Heath shook his head. "Augh!" He balled up the letter. What? Even God was rejecting him? Telling him he wasn't even good enough for the chaplaincy program?

How could that be? He grew up Baptist. Knew scripture — he'd won every Bible drill in youth group! Faithful and Christian. How could he get denied?

Just like everything else. Shut off. Cut off. Closed off.

He punched to his feet, paced. What type of person got rejected from the chaplaincy? With a growl, he kicked the dirt off the ledge. Trinity stared at him, ears perked. He ran a hand over his face and the back of his neck. "Unbelievable!"

A few minutes later he returned to Trinity's side and they sat in quiet solitude. It brought back so many memories of doing the same — in combat. Sitting for hours on end, watching a settlement. Waiting for a target. Climbing into heavy air as they tracked down Taliban rebels in the brutal hills and mountains, where the fighters had the advantage over the team but not over Trinity, who'd seized many a bad guy.

Expelling a long breath, Heath stared out over the land. Those days were long gone but maybe not as much as he'd feared. The chaplaincy . . .

But isn't it hard to preach what you don't believe?

Heath shook off the thought. "Why are

You doing this to me, God? You keep closing doors. . . ."

A sparkle snagged Trinity's attention. She craned her neck forward, watching the sun glint off a windshield. Digging his fingers into her coat, Heath watched Jibril's SUV lumber up the drive to the house. He'd worked with the guy for less than a year, but even then, Heath figured out Jibril was made of steel inside. Now, with this ranch, Heath knew he'd been right. Now that he didn't have the chaplaincy, this ranch, these gigs, were his only chance to feel like he had a purpose.

Heath patted Trinity's side. "C'mon, girl. Let's see how he's doing." The jog down was no less treacherous, but it was less arduous. They cleared the trees and made their way to the fenced-off arena.

Jibril stood at the gate waiting. "Morning!"

Panting and mouth dry, Heath nodded as he let Trinity inside. "You're here early."

Trinity trotted to a small trough, where he lifted a hose and provided the water. She lapped as he sipped from his bite valve.

"You must like the ranch," Jibril said. "You've been here every day for the last four weeks."

Heath eyed his friend.

Jibril shrugged. "The security logs show you accessed the gate every morning at the same time — except on Sundays, when you come earlier."

Retrieving Trinity's ball, Heath tried not to read into Jibril's happiness — or nosiness. What was the guy doing tracking his movements? His buddy was a dichotomy at best. On the phone or through e-mail, you'd never guess he'd grown up in a home with an Iranian father. Or that his first language was Farsi. And you'd never pick him out of a lineup as a terrorist with those green eyes and light brown hair, unlike his sister who had most of their father's features with black hair, brown eyes, and an exotic look. Heath had to admit she was a beauty.

The anger over the rejection needled him. He was stuck here. With them. As a nobody. He whipped the ball down the arena.

"Are you well?"

Trinity bolted, her body streamlined as she tore up the ground getting to it.

Heath jerked a glance toward Jibril. "No. Not really. They refused me for the chaplaincy. Said my last eval rated too low." Tail wagging, pleasure squinting her amber eyes, Trinity trotted back to him. "Trinity, out."

After a few more chomps on the ball, her teeth squeaking over the rubberized toy, she deposited it at his feet.

"Good girl," he said, rubbing her ear. He shifted in front of her and held out a hand to her. "Trinity, stay." He backed up several paces, then shifted and flung the ball down the grassy stretch. "Trinity, seek."

Again, she launched after it, her gait firm and purposeful.

Heath let her get about halfway, then called, "Trinity, down."

She went down, her nails clicking on the pebbles as she flattened against the ground. It seemed her body trembled with the broken anticipation of retrieving her toy. But her attention never wavered from her target that lay so close yet out of reach.

"Good girl." He waited and let a few seconds fall off the clock. "Trinity, seek."

She lunged into the air and closed the distance, seizing her toy.

"Trinity, heel!"

At his side within seconds, she kept the ball.

"She's magnificent," Jibril said.

Heath ate up the praise. He loved his dog and knew she was an impressive animal. She made him proud.

"Will you take her through the course?"

"Yep. You wanna put the bite suit on?"

Jibril's eyes widened. He swallowed. "Uh,

sure." A fake smile. "She won't hurt me, will she?"

"You just said she's magnificent."

Arm held out, Jibril rotated it. "So is my arm! I'd like to keep this limb."

Heath's intestines cinched. *Smooth move, ex-lax.* "Aw, man. I'm sorry." The guy already lost his leg and Heath wanted to put him in a bite suit so Trinity could attack him? "I didn't —"

"No," Jibril said with a stern expression, gaze darkening. "We're friends. Don't do this. I'm very grateful for my life." The light returned to his eyes. "I just make it with one skin-and-bone leg and one micro-processor-and-noble-anthracite leg."

"Microprocessor?" Okay, it sounded space-age just saying it. Something like the movie *I, Robot.*

"It senses my full body movement and compensates."

"No kidding?"

"Nope." Jibril crossed the yard and re-trieved the padded bite suit that made him look like a trimmed-down Michelin Man. "Just remember —"

"Ya know, this may not be a good idea, you getting in that suit. You'll have to run, and she'll chase you."

Jibril laughed. "I know how to run." He

stepped into the thick suit.

Something seemed inherently wrong with this. Heath had been trained to protect guys like Jibril, who might think they knew what they were doing but really had no idea what they were getting into. "Okay, listen, just hold your arm out — she's trained to go for the part that's sticking out the farthest. We won't have her chase you."

"Are we doing this or not?"

"Trinity, heel." Heath waited as she sat beside him. Eyebrows bobbing as she peeked at Heath, then back to Jibril, she seemed to ask, "Now? Can I? He's getting too far away . . . you'd better hurry or he'll get away."

Anticipation rippled through her coat as she awaited the command.

Jibril held out his arm and nodded to Heath.

"Trinity, seek!"

With a bark, she burst into action, straight for the would-be attacker. Sailed through the air with a grace and elegance that belied her purpose.

Her jaws clamped on the suited arm.

Jibril grunted but pulled away, making sure she had a good bite. He turned a circle, Trinity tugging and growling. Whipping her head side to side.

Heath jogged over to them. "Trinity, out!"

After another test bite, she released and unhooked her teeth from the material and returned to her handler.

"Good girl, Trinity. Good girl. Heel." On the other side, he rewarded her by tossing her ball. She sprinted after it, tackling the thing, then chomped it before returning.

Jibril laughed as he shed the extra heat. "She's amazing. You both are. I've always admired how well you work together."

Heath grinned, an arm hooked over a training window. "She's my girl."

After Jibril returned the suit to a hook, he joined Heath, all seriousness and business. "I was contacted about you and Trinity."

Stilled by the news, Heath waited. More bad news? Did someone else say he wasn't good enough?

"The PAO would like you to go over and speak to the troops. Show them what Trinity can do. Tell them your story."

Public Affairs Office. Great. They wanted his story — a sob story. "I don't know . . ." He'd hated the people who came over acting like they knew all about military life, knew what it was like to be soldiers in combat. In some of them, he saw the judgment. The thinly veiled belief that he was a killer. In most, he saw fear mixed with awe.

"They know you, Heath. You've been there, done that. You got hurt but came back stronger."

"Stronger?" Heath snorted, hands planted on his belt, gaze on the field, on the emptiness before him. "I don't think so."

"It's true. They need to see that if something happens, if they lose something — a piece of their heart, mind, or" — Jibril tapped his prosthesis — "body, it's not over."

Yeah, you'd have to believe that to dish it out.

"Will you go?"

It'd all be a sick reminder that he could never be the man he wanted to be. But he couldn't say that to Jibril. *Especially* not Jibril. Mr. MicroKnee.

"Yeah, I'll go."

FOUR

"I'm going back," Heath whispered into the semidarkened room. Bent forward, elbows on his knees, he threaded his fingers and stared at the form lying on the bed.

Crisp white sheets tucked in around the once-strong body peeked out from a gray wool blanket. Hall light stretched across the darkened room and snaked over the safety bars and myriad tubes and cables surrounding the hospital-style bed. The silent feed of oxygen pumped the vital air into the lungs of the sixty-two-year-old man.

General Robert Daniels.

His uncle. More like a father. The man who'd raised him, loved him, nurtured him after his parents' deaths in a car accident when he was two. Uncle Bobby was Heath's hero. He'd served more than thirty-five years in the Army, a short stint in 'Nam,

67

Panama, the Gulf War, and the War on Terror — the war that ended his career and trimmed a year or two off his life.

Well, if you could call breathing through a machine and being fed by someone else a life. It wasn't much by normal standards, but it enabled Heath to hang on to his uncle a little longer. Clinging to the hope that Uncle Bob might come out of this. They told him it wasn't possible. It'd take a miracle.

And Heath was too aware of how rare those were.

"Not to war — well, yeah, to the combat zone, but not as a soldier." He snorted. "They wouldn't even let me be a chaplain." The wound over those words was still raw. He rubbed his knuckles, aching for the man who'd guided him through many a bad decision to speak up, tell him if this was the stupidest thing he'd ever done. "Trin's goin', too — I know how much you like her, got a kick out of her."

A cool, wet nose nudged his arm.

Heath slid his hand around Trinity's shoulder and patted her chest, massaging his fingers into her dense fur. The staff at the home allowed her as long as he let her "perform" for the veterans and wounded. It was a small highlight in their day, and seeing those faces light up after, no doubt, hours of boredom, made his day, too.

He sighed and rubbed his hands over his face as he slumped back in the chair. Head against the wall, he looked at his uncle. Two years like this. Moments of amazing clarity suffocated by long stretches of comatose-like absence. More gone than not in recent days.

If Heath went back in this condition, would he end up like Uncle Bobby? What if he *wasn't* better, improved? Just because Heath wasn't with the military in an official capacity didn't stop attacks. Americans were Americans — prime targets. War dogs and specialized search dogs were high-value targets. Terrorists paid big for dead military working dogs. Couldn't exactly explain to an RPG that you had peaceful intentions.

Then again, hadn't he wanted to be like Uncle Bobby all his life? Wasn't that why he joined up in the first place?

"Heath, live your own life. You don't have to follow in my boots, son."

That willingness to let Heath pursue any career, that care and advice, was the reason Heath joined at seventeen, with Uncle Bobby's approval and signature for an early sign-up. Heath walked the stage at his high school graduation with honors, skipped the parties, and flew to Fort Benning Monday morning.

Leaving his uncle now, after vowing to take care of him for the rest of his life — he felt a deep conflict. He owed his uncle. Owed him the respect of seeing him live out his remaining days with dignity after all the hours he'd invested in Heath, in the nation. What if something went wrong — if the Old Dawg finally gave it up after all this time? What if the doctors needed Heath to sign off on something?

Dude, chill.

He was overreacting. It wasn't like his missions with Special Forces where he didn't have contact with his family for months at a time. This was a PAO gig. Two weeks over, then back home.

No big. No worries.

A shadow broke the stream of light and Heath's concentration. Straightening, he glanced to the side and smiled at the brunette leaning against the door.

"I thought I could smell wet dog. Oh, and you brought Trinity."

Her tease pulled a smile from Heath. "Hey, Claire. How's it going?"

Nails clacking against the vinyl, Trinity sauntered over to Claire Benedict and nosed her hand.

Heath pushed out of the chair.

The fiftysomething woman smiled. "Good." She tossed her chin toward the bed. "Has he been awake at all?"

Surprise lit through him. "Awake?"

"Yep, the Old Dawg woke up this morning when I was here." Her voice, always filled with honey, held a fondness that made Heath ache. If his uncle had been . . . well, not been laid up, would he have remarried after Auntie Margaret died ten years ago? Maybe married Claire? She'd entered his life right before the general headed over for his final tour.

Heath grinned. "He always was partial to you."

"That's only because I didn't let him treat me like one of his recruits, nor did I let his bark scare me off."

He laughed. "There is that."

Eyebrow arched, she gave him a look. "You okay?"

"Yeah, sure."

"You'll have to do better than that if you want to convince me." Always ready with cheese cubes, Claire tossed one to Trinity. "So, what's eating you, Heath?"

He leaned back against the wall. "I have a gig for me and Trinity. It's a morale-boosting thing."

"For you or them?" Wariness crowded her mature but attractive features. "Where?"

"Northern Afghanistan for a week, then heading south."

She sighed and tossed another cube to Trinity. Standing, Claire folded her arms. "He'd tell you to go, that you have a warrior's heart." Her gaze drifted to his uncle's bed, and her lips twisted and tightened. "War didn't scare him. Being weak did." Her eyebrow arched again. "That's what you're thinking, isn't it? That because you're not over there, you're somehow weak, or less?"

Heath stared at his boots. "Wasn't thinking anything of the sort." Though it might seem odd, him talking to a woman not related to him, they'd both spent many hours watching over his uncle. She had leverage in his life not many did. "Besides, I wasn't looking for it. This gig came to me."

"How?"

Still . . . talking to this woman always made him want to close up. Claire had an uncanny ability to read him, to cut open his heart and expose things he hadn't seen or didn't want to see. But he told her about A Breed Apart, about Jibril, about his new training regimen that had helped him overcome most of the TBI effects.

"I feel good, focused, for the first time in eighteen months."

Quiet draped the room, punctuated by the bleeping and hissing machines. When seconds turned into minutes and he felt the bore of her gaze drilling him, he finally closed his eyes. "Go on. Get it out. I know you want to say something."

"You're not weak, Heath."

His attention snapped to hers.

"Going back, doing this — it may be a good thing — but it's not going to give you back what you think you lost. You're a strong, amazing young man. Bobby always said that. He was very proud of you."

But Uncle Bobby didn't know today from ten years ago. He didn't know that Heath had lost all he'd worked for, all the general had lauded and clapped him on the back for.

"Yeah, he *was*." Heat and pressure built in his chest. He rolled it up and stuffed it away with his humiliation and shattered pride. "I'd better get going." He called Trinity and started down the quiet hall.

"Heath." Her voice chased him.

He hesitated at the juncture that led to the elevators as he met her soft gaze.

"The man Robert loved is the man whose character got him where he was. Not the

73

career he chose or the uniform he wore —
or doesn't wear." That tone again, the one
that slipped past his barriers — like a slick
coating on a sour pill that made it go down
easier — forced him to listen. "No matter
what you do or where you go, your character
is what will always make your uncle proud."

"Claire, he's not even conscious. When
he's awake, the doctors aren't sure if he's
lucid. He believes I'm a soldier, an elite
soldier. That's what he remembers." His
throat thickened. "I'm not that man anymore."

Lackland AFB
San Antonio, Texas
"It's not personal."

"Bull!" Heath's temples throbbed as he
faced off with Jibril.

When a uniformed presence made itself
known shifting into his periphery, Heath
lowered his voice so the MP would leave
off. "You and I both know this is very
personal. Two days ago, this was *my* gig.
The PAO asked for me. I agreed. Now,
everyone's going?"

"Heath, please — it's not —"

"Don't lie to me, Jibril." Heath cocked his
head. "We're too good of friends to go
there."

74

Jibril held his gaze but didn't look away. Silence hung rank and rancid between them as they stood on the tarmac, the C-130 engines ramping up with a whinnying screech. The jumbo plane would ferry them halfway across the world so Heath could begin the speaking engagements.

Heath glanced down at the crate that held Trinity. Just like his partner, he felt caged by the TBI. Would he ever be free? What was this, some enormous lesson on trust? *Is that what this is, God? Because I think I already wrote the book on this with the surgery.*

Jibril broke the silence after a jet roared into the sky from another runway. "It makes sense, Ghost. This is the first mission for the organization. I was coming anyway, and it's logical to bring Timbrel and Aspen. We all need to feel this out. Their dogs aren't coming though."

Pulse whooshing through his ears, Heath reared up. "This. Isn't. About. The. Dogs." If only it were. It wouldn't feel like such a colossal ambush. He took long, deep breaths, trying to calm himself, head off the thumping that warned of a migraine. "It's about me." He poked a finger against his own chest. "You don't think I can handle this. I'm not a cripple."

Calm and ever serene, Jibril said, "No."

Swallowing hard, Heath felt like a heel. The man before him was missing a limb. Before his prosthesis, he'd been a "cripple."

"But you are diagnosed with TBI. And I have a responsibility — especially with regard to insurance and protecting the organization — to make sure you arrive alive and return in the same condition."

"This is bunk." Heath wanted to spit. "Would you be sending all of us if it was Hogan?"

Hesitation provided the answer.

"I don't believe this." He spun around.

"Please, Ghost —"

"Whatever. Forget it." Heath raked a hand through his short crop. Despite the affront, despite the intense feeling of failure, of not having his friend believe in him, Heath held his anger in check. Anger would only ignite the TBI. It'd inflame an already tense situation. And what if he got so upset he blacked out? Yeah, that would help.

A car rolled to a stop near the private jet waiting.

"Heath, please. Understand my situation —"

"I do." Man, he hated to admit that. Because admitting it tanked the frustration. Tanked the anger. And right now he wanted to be angry. As much as he didn't want to face it, as much as it angered him to almost be called a liability . . . Heath understood the position this put his friend in.

Time to suck it up. To look at the flip side of this coin. "Thanks."

Mouth agape, Jibril blinked. "For what?"

"For believing in me. I know you wouldn't let me go, you wouldn't put ABA at risk if you didn't believe in me." Swallowing his pride, Heath sighed. "Thank you."

Two thuds stamped through the air.

Heath glanced at the car where Hogan and Courtland waited. Aspen wore guilt like a neon *chador*. Hogan on the other hand held her ground. She must've had the world handed to her and didn't care who she ran over getting to the top. Spoiled brat.

"I'll meet you on board," he said to Jibril, then headed up the ramp into the plane. He made his way past the cargo hold stacked with equipment. Techs anchored the pallets with straps.

Getting out of the Army, he thought he'd escaped the looks of pity and actions that bespoke hesitation and concern about his ability to perform his duties. So much for that idea. The truth was spelled out on the three faces of the other ABA members: They didn't trust him to do his job. They expected him to fail.

Heath entered the small cabin area and stuffed himself into one of the seats. After fastening his belt, he pressed the back of his skull into the headrest with his eyes closed. God just wouldn't give him a break. Strip the beret from him. Strip the chaplaincy from his hands. Strip the respect for him from his own team. Anything was better than facing the team he had already failed. Failed with a capital *F*.

Because that's what it boiled down to, wasn't it? If they already felt they had to protect him, then they'd hover over him on the trip. Nobody would be productive. Everyone would be stressed. Especially him.

Why had he agreed to this again?

Oh yeah. Because he thought he could bury the past. Be of help to others.

Hard to do when failure is your middle name.

"Commit your actions to the Lord, and your plans will succeed."

Heath groaned. "I tried that. It didn't work!" He'd made plans. God shut them down. Where was the verse for that?

"We can make our plans, but the Lord determines our steps."

Frustration tangled his retort. Heath pinched the bridge of his nose, letting the agitation and — yes, he had to admit —

hurt leech out. He groaned again. *Enough with the verse tug-of-war, God.*

Cool air swirled around him as a light floral perfume intermingled with the treated air. "It was concern that pushed us to talk to Jibril."

Heath shifted but said nothing to Aspen. At least she sounded contrite.

"Heath, look at me."

Jaw clenched, he rolled his head to the right and met clear blue eyes.

Dull lights from the cabin ceiling bathed Aspen's porcelain features in a somber glow, adding to the look already in her gaze. "I lost a brother over there." White-blond curls tumbled around her face as a gust of wind carried into the small seating area. "Please understand that I didn't want to lose anyone else. That's the only reason I went along with Timbrel."

Heath leaned forward, anger roiling through his body like an undammed river. "You don't control who is lost and who isn't."

Unfazed, she remained stoic. "Perhaps, but there's safety in numbers."

"Bigger numbers also mean easier targets. Easier to find."

Aspen sighed. "We care. Is that a crime?"

"No, it's not." He adjusted in the seat so

he faced her. "But I need you guys to trust me. I wouldn't go over there if I thought I'd put anyone in danger." The words tugged at his conscience. He hadn't even considered anyone else when Jibril mentioned the speaking gig. He'd been so anxious to have a purpose for existing, to bail on boredom and leap headfirst into the action. "Don't say your going is about concern for me. Tell me you wouldn't like to take a look around and maybe find out what happened to your brother."

Her face flushed.

"So, don't put this off on me, okay? I'm healing."

Then why was his vision graying? What was the hollow roar in his ears? Heath dropped against the seat as the world went black.

FIVE

Bagram AFB, Afghanistan
Look him in the face. Tell him the truth. It would hurt for the first few seconds.

Darci nodded to the MP guarding the door, and he turned the knob to General Lance Burnett's office. The door swung open to reveal the stuffy interior. Salt-and-pepper hair highlighted by the overhead lamp, the general looked up from his desk. She snapped a salute.

He acknowledged with one of his own. "Kintz! Why do you look like someone killed your cat?"

"I hate cats, sir."

He let out a booming laugh and motioned to the steel chair in front of his metal desk as she heard a click from behind and knew they were alone. "What do you have?"

Seated, Darci let out a long breath. "Nothing, sir." The words were bitter and sour at the same time. She hated bringing back

81

nothing. Hated the very taste of failure.

The wheels on his chair squeaked as he leaned back. "Not what I'd hoped to hear."

She wasn't sure what was more painful — her father who would never let her into his heart because she was a reminder of the wife he'd lost, or the general she would never be able to please after a near failure on one of the biggest missions of her career.

Darci put on her confident facade. "I know, sir. I'll have more for you after our next run. We've only been out there a few days, and that netted me about six hours to reconnoiter alone."

General Burnett stared at her for several long minutes, then narrowed his blue eyes as he dropped forward in his chair. He moved to the small portable fridge that sat beneath a table and pulled out a Dr Pepper. Imported straight from the factory in Waco by his wife, Marilyn. The tiny carbonation combustion hissed through the room. He took a slurp as he turned — his eyes hitting hers. "I'd share, but these are pure gold."

"Of course, sir."

Can cradled in his hands, he sat on the chair beside her. Took another sip, then set the burgundy can on his desk. Clasping his hands together, he took a breath and let it out. "Darci, I need to ask a question."

Oh boy. Here it comes.

"And I want the truth." His blue eyes probed hers. He'd always seen to the truth of things. Which worried her. Especially now. "Is this mission, this location, too . . . close?"

Her nerves fidgeted under his scrutiny. "Sir?"

"Darci," he said, his warning clear: Don't play dumb.

Darci swallowed and darted a glance to his soda. She sure had a lot in common with that sweating can. "No, sir. It's fine."

He roughed a hand over his jaw. Youth clung to his chiseled features — angled jaw, slightly hooked nose that was masculine and strong. Gray streaks in his hair hinted at his midfifties age.

With a growl, he plucked his soda from the desk and returned to his chair. "Look, fine. I won't bring up the past —"

"Thank you, sir."

He hesitated, then plowed on. "But if you don't get me something, I've got to yank you and send you home. Bring in someone who can find what we're looking for."

She wet her lips. "I —"

"Lieutenant."

Pulled up straight by his use of her rank and his "general" voice, Darci stilled.

"This area has seen unprecedented violence in the last few months, and yet we can't figure out where they're coming from. The Chinese are here setting up that mine, and while I'm ticked so much I can't see straight that US research efforts regarding the ores in those mountains on behalf of the Afghans are lost and sold to the Chinese, I need this wave of violence over. Stabilization is the key. We can't do that if we can't find these terrorists." His battle-worn face hardened. "Am I clear?"

Defeat clung to her like the sand out here that seeped into every pore. But she'd brought this on herself. Now she had to fix it. "Sir, yes, sir." She wouldn't look down. She'd withstood much worse interrogations. She'd been beaten within an inch of her life by a man she thought she'd fallen in love with.

But General Burnett . . . he'd plucked her from the mind-numbing boredom of analyzing reports back at DIA. Chosen her for her ability to see what others missed, for her ability to speak Mandarin as fluently as she spoke English. He'd believed in her and recruited her into the covert field she now worked. He'd mentored her, invested his best in her training.

And she'd let him down.

Again.

"I'll find something, sir." If it took her last, dying breath.

Smile lines crinkled at the corners of his eyes. "I know you will, Darci. You're just like your father. That's why I put you on this." He studied her for a minute, then nodded. "That's all."

Weighted by the disappointment in his expression, Darci rose. "Thank you, sir." Why on earth were her eyes stinging? She blinked and rolled her eyes, trying to ward off the tears.

"Darci."

Door open, she stopped. Bolstered her courage. Glanced back. "Yes, sir?"

"You look tired. Take a couple of days off. Check out the entertainment tonight? Might do you some good."

"Thank you, sir, but the geology team heads out in the morning."

He scribbled something on a notepad, called in his MP, handed him the slip of paper, then grinned at Darci as the young specialist slipped past her. "Not anymore. Departure delayed due to activity in the area."

Entertainment was the last thing she wanted. "Yes, sir."

"Lieutenant." He scowled. "That's an order."

Irritation skidded through her. "Understood, sir." Was he trying to butter her up? Soften his blow? Or was he trying to tell her something by ordering her to the entertainment show tonight?

"You okay, ma'am?"

Darci jerked her head to the side, surprised to find another specialist in place. "Fine."

Just fine. He'd grounded her. Again.

She strode from the building, muscles tense, mind buzzing. Why did it feel like her entire career was on the line? She had to ramp things up. Quit playing it safe. She'd avoided a couple of opportunities while in the mountains with the geology team, afraid of being discovered. Well, she'd connived her way out of many a situation. She'd been gifted with a quick mind and tongue. But she hadn't completed her mission — yet.

Her boots crunched on the dirt road between Command and the mess hall. She'd grab a bite for dinner, then head over to the field for the entertainment. She'd be there in body but not in mind — she'd be tracking routes and exploring possibilities.

Movement collided with the clap of a bark, pulling Darci up short as a large dog bolted into her path. It jumped and pegged Darci with its front paws — almost knocking the breath and life from her — then dropped back and barked twice. Alarm died down as Darci stared at the dog. Tail wagging, the canine seemed to have something on its mind.

"Hey" — Darci craned her neck to the side and peered at the dog's underside — "girl. What's up?" She bent toward her, noticing the tattoo on the left ear. Darci jerked back up. MWD. Which meant no petting. "So, you're not just a stray."

The dog sat on its haunches, pink tongue dangling out the side of her mouth. Gorgeous coloring, rippling with power and yet restraint. On all fours again, she backed up, prancing and tossing her head as she barked. Wagged her tail. As if she recognized —

Darci sucked in a hard breath. This couldn't be happening . . . She leaned closer to make out the dog's identification numbers.

It was him — her.

Darci took a step back, feeling the heat and nausea of fear spiral through her veins.

The dog tensed.

I am dead meat.

A beast of a Mine Resistant Ambush Protected vehicle towed a Humvee, severing Heath's visual cue seconds after seeing Trinity's spine go rigid. He slapped the MRAP and scurried down its line. "Move!" Between the two, Heath saw a lithe woman bend toward Trinity. "No! Don't touch her." The brakes of the larger vehicle ground, suffocating his words. Heath tightened his lips. If Trinity saw her as a threat —

He hit the back of the MRAP again and rushed through the two steel hulks, his gaze locked on the woman and his partner. "Trinity, out!" He doubted she could hear him with the noise of the compound, but he had to try. He threw himself over the hitch and beelined toward her.

The woman took a step back.

"No, don't move!" Heath slid to a stop, his boots stirring dust plumes. "Trinity, out!"

His girl stood down and trotted to his side. He eyed the woman as he clipped Trinity back under his control. "Sorry." He straightened, holding the lead taut so there was no give for her to take off again. "She broke behavior. That's unusual for her. Sorry."

Pretty almond-shaped eyes stared back. What was that? Fear? No, not fear. Sluggish movements. Dazed eyes. Open mouth, as if words hung frozen. Shock? What . . . ?

Heath scanned her body to make sure Trinity hadn't bitten her. The woman wore black tactical pants like his, and that gray-on-black North Face jacket wasn't military issue. Long, black, silky hair pulled away from her face. Pink lips. Attractive — *very*. But no wounds as far as he could tell. And no words.

Heath signaled for Trinity to heel. "Did she hurt you?"

As if he'd thrown a bucket of water over her, she hauled in a breath. "What?"

A protective instinct rose within him. He touched her elbow. "Hey, you okay?" Man, if Trinity shook her up this bad — what was she doing out here in a combat zone? Who was she? Civilian?

She shook her head again and pulled away. "Fine." Her gaze flicked to Trinity. "She . . . she seemed to want to play."

"Yeah, sorry about that." He looked back the way he'd come. "Can't believe she did that. She never breaks behavior like that." She was trained not to. This could spell out a disaster, especially on a base where there was constant action and threats. "We need to work on proofing. I guess she's out of practice."

"Aren't we all?"

Her words caught him by surprise, considering her toned physique and confidence that surged to the front all of a sudden. At her transformation, he didn't believe for a second she was out of practice. But he was. He stopped his hand midair — subconsciously reaching for the scars that had shaken the confidence he'd once had in approaching women. "Maybe so."

Though her eyes slanted a bit, she looked half Asian. But she was all beautiful. Her skin — one word came to mind: alabaster.

Okay, now he was losing it. Who even used words like that anymore?

He extended his hand. "Heath Daniels."

"Jia."

Her fingers were cold and small in his, yet strong. "Nice handshake." He liked that. A lot. "My uncle says you can tell a lot about a person by the strength of the handshake."

A subtle tinge of pink hit her cheeks. Was she blushing? Man, when was the last time he'd done that to a woman? Maybe he hadn't lost his touch.

"Yeah?" She folded her arms over her chest. "And what does mine say?"

"Confident." Heath nodded, as if agreeing with his own assessment. Yeah, now that she shook off the shock of meeting Trinity close up and personal, this woman had confidence oozing out of her pores. "You aren't afraid to try something new."

"Interesting." That wasn't quite an affirmation, but the way her lips quirked told him she wanted to smile. But wouldn't.

Why? Could she see his scar? He adjusted the black A Breed Apart ball cap, smoothing his hand down his shorn hair. She hadn't seen the back of his skull, so she couldn't have seen the scar. Right?

Shift gears. Don't obsess or stress.

Laughter billowed on the cool wind as the sun set. Heath glanced toward the building guarded by sandbags at least six feet high and deep. Hogan, Aspen, and Jibril disappeared around the door. Chow time.

"We're heading to the mess hall. Want to join us?" It seemed logical, and maybe it'd give him a chance to unwrap the mystery before him. She'd given almost all one-word answers. Was she always this stiff? Or had Trinity rattled her?

Nah. She wasn't the type easily rattled.

Which meant something else was behind her standoffish behavior. The training in him made him want to find out what she was hiding. Or maybe it was the soft brown eyes against that fair skin that tricked him into inviting her to dinner.

Heath took a step toward the building and

91

away from those thoughts.

"I . . ." She wet her lips.

"It's a nice quiet dinner with . . . about five hundred grunts and bad food." He chuckled, trying to ease her nerves. Heath coiled his hand around Trin's lead, noting his partner full at ease so he didn't have anything to be worried about. "I promise, Trinity won't drool on your food tray" — he paused for a smile — "much."

"Sorry, I've got to get to work."

Yeah, should've known a pretty woman wouldn't want to hang out with a washed-up wannabe when there were men around who had all their well-muscled pieces in the right places.

"No worries." He tugged open the door and stepped into the mess hall. Why he even created that personal invitation to rejection he didn't know. He rubbed the back of his neck and entered the cafeteria. Something about her . . . he couldn't put his finger on it. But she seemed . . . familiar.

Six

The whumping of rotors had nothing on her pulse. Darci stalked back into the command building and down the hall. Did the general know? If he knew and hadn't told her . . . How could this happen? Breathing hard, she hurried around the corner. And skidded to a stop.

No guard.

Meant no general.

Darci spun. What was she going to do? She darted her gaze around the narrow hall, as if the gray cement and walls would provide the solution.

The general would tell her if he'd known Daniels would be here, right? Had the Green Beret returned to duty? He had his dog. He looked fit. Into her mind flitted the image of his black performance shirt stretching over his chest and biceps — *definitely fit.*

Had he been cleared to return to duty?

Okay, this wasn't a big deal. He was here.

She was here. But they were on different missions. It wasn't like she'd be working with him or anything.

Then again, little missteps could blow her entire cover.

"Why don't you check out the entertainment tonight? I think it might do you some good."

The general's order pushed her back outside and to the activities building. Inside, she headed to the bulletin board where schedules were posted. A wave of heat rushed through Darci as she stared at an eleven-by-thirteen poster with a handler and his dog. The headline seemed lit in neon lights: FORMER GREEN BERET TO SHARE HIS STORY. There, along with the time and date was an image of Daniels and his Belgian Malinois.

No no no. Darci stepped back, mouth dry. This couldn't be happening.

Okay, calm down. He doesn't remember. According to the doctors and experts, he should have no recollection of her or the first few days after that incident. So, there wasn't a problem. Right? She wet her lips and trudged back into the darkening evening.

But what if he *did* remember?

"One way to find out," Darci mumbled as she pivoted and entered the mess. Then stopped. If he was in there, he was with friends. She wouldn't be able to direct the conversation.

Okay, so . . . then what?

Maybe if she showed up at the activities arena ahead of the scheduled time, she'd catch him before he went onstage. Waiting around wouldn't work because they were flying out first thing in the morning to dig in for the next week for more work. And her only chance to get back to the site and figure out what those striations meant. If her instincts were right . . .

Two hours. She'd have to kill two hours. And she knew just how to do it. In the activities building, she snatched the poster and went to her cot. There she retrieved her laptop, powered up, and while she waited, let her gaze sweep the poster again. He was good-looking, but that wasn't why she had to know about his background.

She typed in the organization *A Breed Apart*. The first page of results provided a link to the website. After scanning the mission statement, she clicked on *Teams* and found a close-up of Heath and Trinity at the very top with a link to his bio. Energy surged through her. This was what she wanted.

A highly decorated Green Beret, Heath

Daniels and his military war dog, Trinity, served several tours in Afghanistan, Iraq, and Somalia. Two weeks before returning home for some R&R, Heath and Trinity were involved in a mission that received bad intel. Trinity hit on explosives and stopped Heath, leaving him with permanent scarring on his right hand, but the soldier who tripped the bomb died in the blast.

Never one to give up, Heath fought his way out of the hospital. Diagnosed with traumatic brain injury, he battled excruciating headaches and occasional blackouts. As a result, Heath was medically discharged.

Darci stared at the words, choked up. He'd been discharged. She'd heard the men on his team saying he'd rather be dead than not serve. Is that why he'd joined the private contracting dog team?

She scanned down a little more and read about their journey toward a civilian partnership. Impressive that the dog had become too attached to be reassigned to another handler.

He was a hero. One of the real ones. And even though she had more information on him now, she still didn't know what he remembered of the incident or the days after.

A distant noise — no, barking! Darci

punched to her feet. Outside, she spotted Heath and his dog crossing the compound. Heath flung a ball down the road, and Trinity bolted after it.

Back at her cot, Darci powered down and stowed her laptop. She snatched a clean shirt and stuffed it on, then brushed out her hair. As she checked her teeth, she stopped. *What're you doing? It's not a date.*

True, but maybe if she was a little refreshed, she'd be more on her toes.

Yeah, go with it.

Within minutes, she entered the outdoor "theater," if one could call it that. It amounted to a field where chairs had been set up and a black stage that stretched the width of the front. The two times she'd been here before had been for celebrities. Once with country crooner Craig Morgan, and the next time she had the privilege of witnessing the genius that was the Lt. Dan Band with cofounder Gary Sinise.

Darci edged around the fenced-in area, careful to cling to the shadows at first.

Onstage, Heath walked back and forth with Trinity on a lead. They made it to stage right, and he released her lead. Though he said something to the dog, Darci couldn't make it out. Then he walked to the middle and lay down.

Trinity watched him, 100 percent focused on her handler. In the spotlights of the stage, the amber shading of her coat seemed more vibrant than usual. Her black nose all but vanished against the black curtain.

Trinity launched forward and raced to Heath's side in what looked like two large bounds and heeled at his side. Incredible. What signal had he given? Darci hadn't noticed one.

Heath sat up and rubbed her ears. She licked his face.

"Daniels!"

Darci flinched as someone came up on her six, glanced at her, then continued toward the stage.

Heath squinted at them, apparently blinded by the glare of the lights.

"They're moving your show up," the man announced. "You've got thirty. You good with that?"

"Sounds like the choice was made for me."

The man laughed. "You got it." He spun and stalked away. Darci eased out of sight.

"Jia?" With one hand on the ledge, Heath hopped down from the stage and Trinity with him. The guy's muscles rippled and stretched his shirt taut.

Those were things she should notice as a part of her job. Because it told her he had the muscle power to take her down. Of course, it shouldn't elicit a traitorous, involuntary reaction from her body. But it did. How crazy was that?

She stepped into the open. "Hi."

His cockeyed grin made her heart skip a beat. *Grow up, Darci!*

"You checkin' up on me?"

"Actually, yes."

He raised an eyebrow. "Yeah?" Why did he seem so pleased? It was meant to put him on the defensive, not make him happy.

"Saw the poster in the activities building, so I looked up A Breed Apart." She walked with him to the side of the outdoor theater. "And your bio."

"Ah." Heath's smile faded as he looked down.

"I'm glad Trinity came home to you."

He shot a sidelong glance to her, then to Trinity. "Yeah, I was lost without her. When they called and said she was declared 'excess,' I flew into action. Paid to bring her back and picked her up after the vet cleared her."

"You're a good team." Thank goodness, her mistake in the field hadn't created a permanent separation.

From his pocket, he produced a ball. Trinity pranced, turned, scurried a few feet, then glanced back. Heath flung it down the aisle of the seats. Trinity tore off after it.

He leaned against the platform that formed the soundstage. Hands resting on the wood on either side of him, he looked at her. "So, you know my story —"

"Not all of it."

He cracked another smile, then tossed his chin at her. "What's your story?" He slumped back and folded his arms over his chest. "What're you doing out here on a military base? I mean, I have yet to see you in ACUs or battle dress, and you don't salute the officers."

Wow, he hadn't missed much. Although she did salute General Burnett. But him alone.

"Geology. I'm with a geological survey team." Why did that lie feel like a mouthful of the rocks they'd been studying? "We've been here a few weeks already, and we head out first thing in the morning."

Soldiers trickled into the arena as Trinity trotted back with her ball. Heath retrieved it and tucked it in his pocket. Trinity paced, then sat back on her haunches at Heath's side.

"What are you surveying?"

"Rocks."

"Wow, I never would've guessed."

Darci laughed and relented with the information. "There are reports of lithium up in the mountains, so we're trying to determine if mining will be lucrative or a waste of time and resources."

He shrugged. "Yeah, but the Chinese are stealing all our gigs. Why do the work for them again?"

Darci eyed him. He'd paid attention to what was happening here. She couldn't say the same for many of the soldiers or most people she knew. "Thankfully, my job is just to determine if the deposits are large enough to warrant mining. I'll let the politicians argue out their differences."

He nodded, watching the men and women filter in.

"But I would hope that no matter who mines the lithium, Afghanistan can become a stable, formidable country."

"Amen."

"Religion?" She kept the curiosity from her tone.

His smile twisted to the side. "Sort of bred into me. Grew up in church, my uncle dragging my angry teen butt in every Sunday." He glanced at his watch. "Hey, I need to head backstage." He took a step away, his gaze on hers. "Are you staying for the show?"

Darci saw it all over his face. Expectation. Hope. What was even stranger was she felt it. A hunger within her to be wanted, to have someone who cared, gnawed at her defenses. "I wouldn't miss Trinity in action for the world."

Amusement twinkled in his pale gray eyes. "Good. Would you . . . ?" He checked the crowds again, then hauled his attention back to her. "Up for a walk afterward?"

Her chest squeezed. "I . . ." She had to get some sleep. They were heading out early. "Sure."

"Great." He looked down at the lead in his hand, then peeked at her again. "I know this will sound crazy since we just met, but I like hearing you talk. Your voice sounds familiar."

"The men and women beside you are your friends, your partners. You're on the same team," Heath said at the close of his presentation as he stepped off the stage, walking the center aisle, pleased that he hadn't fainted, blacked out, or choked up. "You hang out, you grab rec and rack time together — well, no coed, or you'll have officers breathing down your neck."

Laughter rippled through the packed-out area.

"But you're there for each other. You've got each other's backs."

Beside him, Jibril — dressed in full practice gear — stood and lunged at him.

He heard the collective gasp and knew the plan had worked. Turning, he saw Trinity sail off the stage, over the heads of a half dozen soldiers and right into Jibril's back. Which shoved Heath — and his head — straight into a chair.

Whack. His teeth vibrated against his skull. Pain speared his head and neck.

But he regrouped. Shoved aside the pain. Focused on Jibril, who'd gone down beneath the weight of Trinity, who'd chomped on the heavily padded arm.

Heath hauled himself upright. "Trinity, out!"

Disengaging, she shook her head to release her teeth from the fabric, then trotted to his side.

The crowd erupted in applause as he helped Jibril to his feet and out of the suit. Concern clouded Jibril's eyes as he whispered, "You okay? Your head hit —"

Heath winked, about all he could do with the searing fire in his neck and back. Afterward, he'd down a few ibuprofen and be fine.

He returned to the stage as the applause

died down. "As you can see, Trinity is trained to protect me with or without commands, with or without a lead. She's got my back. The funny thing is — that fateful day, she warned me." Man, he hated to admit that. "Told me there was something bad, and I didn't listen — that day, *I* broke behavior. Another guy on my team hadn't noticed Trinity's warning. He lost his life, and I almost did, too."

Heath looked down, remembering Tiller. "Sometimes, we do that to God." The words served as a gong against his conscience. "He prods us, gives us warnings, and we just ignore it. Do life our way." The truth clogged in his throat.

Heath swallowed and went on. "Then when things go bad, we blame Him. Get angry." *Oh yeah. Definitely.* "In fact, I'd bet someone in this crowd is ticked at me right now for even bringing this up." He held up his hand with the scars from Trinity. "Don't put God in a position where He has to scar your sorry carcass. I did that. Then I was ticked. Beyond ticked!" *Still am!* "I hated God, hated life. Laid up with TBI and discharged from the one thing I wanted in life — being a Green Beret — I blamed God for everything."

Shame gripped him, thinking of Jia listening to him. What would she think? He had this overwhelming need to see her reaction, yet as he scanned the crowd, he couldn't see her. Or worse, what if she learned he still felt that way? Not as much . . . but the aftereffects lingered.

He shared how he'd begged God for a miracle — to heal him. When it was obvious that wouldn't happen, he sunk even lower. In his darkest hour, he'd begged God for one good thing to happen. When nothing happened, he vowed his days of begging were over. Never again. But then a ray of sunlight struck his storm-riddled world — he got the call that the Army had decided to retire Trinity.

"God has your back." Toes dangling off the edge of the stage, Heath stared out at the faces of those who put their lives on the line. "You aren't alone. He's there. Always. And I pray you find the strength to reach out to Him." He drew in a long breath and smiled. "Just because things don't go the way *you* planned, doesn't mean God left you. He may have just put you on a new course. Follow the adventure!" He held up a hand. "Thanks for listening to me tonight. I'll be around to talk if you have questions."

Jibril took the stage to explain A Breed Apart a little more, then turned over the stage and night to one of the soldiers, who dismissed everyone.

A steady stream of admirers walked by Trinity, but — thank goodness — they remembered he'd warned them not to mistake her for a domestic dog they could pet. Trinity was working. Always.

He shook hands, signed some miniature scrapbooks, and took pictures with others. All the while, he searched the crowds for Jia. Where had she gone? Heath hoped he hadn't said something from the stage that scared her off. Being brutal-honest with the audience opened himself up to ridicule. But . . . the thought of her thinking worse of him rankled.

Weird. Why would he care what some chick thought? He never had before.

Yeah, and you've never tried to soften up a woman since your life wrecked.

Man, his head felt like someone drove a tent stake through it. What happened? Maybe it was just all the excitement of the night. Or that collision with the chair. He pinched the bridge of his nose.

"Great job," Jibril said as the crowd petered out. "You're a natural." His smile rivaled the lights on the stage. "I knew I picked the right man."

"Thanks. Hey, have you seen — ?"

"Your Chinese friend?"

Heath jerked, stunned.

"I saw you two talking before the show." Smoothing his beard, Jibril studied him. "Is she stationed here?"

Heath clipped Trinity's lead on. "She's not military. Civilian with military contract to scout for minerals. She's leaving in the morning."

"I am sorry," Jibril said, his expression somber. "I saw her leave about halfway through your presentation."

"Oh." What did that mean? "Maybe she got a call."

"It is possible." Jibril patted his shoulder. "Are you okay? Your head is hurting?"

"Just too much excitement, I guess."

Jibril looked unconvinced. "This has been a long but good day. Now, I must rest. We head south tomorrow, so be sure to rest up. I'll see you in the morning."

"Right. Okay." But Heath's brain cells were engaged on wondering why Jia had left.

He tugged Trinity's lead toward the tents where contractors bunked. Maybe Jia wasn't feeling well. As he stared down what looked like an endless row of tents, he realized the futility of his personal mission.

Gutting up the disappointment, he headed for his own tent. He rounded a corner and almost stopped, but his old training kicked in and kept him moving. Jia stood with a general, hovering in deep conversation. Jia, a contractor with a *geology* team. With a general. He'd like to hear the explanation for that.

The general's face darkened beneath the large, powerful lamps that shattered darkness in the compound. He stabbed a finger at her, his voice loud but unintelligible.

What's up with that?

Trinity pulled taut, watching the showdown, too. Heath didn't like it, and apparently Trinity didn't either. She stopped short, as if she'd gotten a hit — on Jia. Good thing he'd tethered her, or Trinity would've taken off.

"Trinity, come."

Jia glanced over her shoulder and saw him. She said something to the general, then walked toward Heath. She let out a long sigh as she approached. "Sorry I missed the last part of your presentation."

Heath shrugged. "No worries." He nodded to the general who disappeared into the command building. "What's with that? He looked ticked."

"They're giving us grief over our paperwork again. And I think Dr. Colsen, who's the lead geologist, is being less than gracious — again." She smiled, but it didn't reach her eyes. "So, still up for that walk?"

"Absolutely." Heath headed toward the canine practice field, knowing they'd have the area to themselves. But her story didn't sit straight with him. Why would the military hassle them over paperwork if the team already had been here for three weeks? And why did she seem buttery-sweet all of a sudden?

What was she trying to divert his attention from?

SEVEN

Copper Mine, Jalrez Valley
Wardak Province, Afghanistan
Hear no evil, speak no evil, do no evil.

Carved out of stone, the statue before him epitomized the old proverb, since its head and hands had crumbled and disappeared with time beneath the harsh elements in which its temple sat. And yet, some might think the armless and headless condition of the statue indicated the broken power of the gods.

To the left, another broken stone figure stood on the other side of an entrance. Through that opening lay the mine China had begun to excavate copper from. Frustrating China, the mine bore the great tragedy of being situated at a 2,600-year-old Buddhist temple. What should have been a quick insertion of Chinese progress through mining ore morphed into a nightmare in preserving the reputation of the

People's Republic of China by protecting the Afghans' history through archaeology.

Colonel Zheng Haur glanced once more at the crumbling relics. Was it a bad omen?

"So much for the power of their god." Captain Bai smirked.

"No god has power. Only man." How many times had General Zheng said that?

"Colonel." A Chinese lieutenant rushed into the open. The sun struck him as if illuminating his presence. Was that a sign as well — was a god shining on this man who saluted him? "I did not know you were coming. What can I — ?"

"I am here to speak with Colonel Wu." Haur kept his focus like steel.

The man's gaze darted around the area as he frowned. "I . . . so sorry, sir. But the colonel left a week ago."

Cold spread across Haur's shoulders. "What do you mean he left?" The orders given to Jianyu had been to remain here till the general sent for him. "His orders were to oversee this mine."

The man nodded and half bowed. "Yes, sir, but he said he was recalled to China."

Haur raised his gaze once more to the stone god. What secrets lay beneath his lap besides archaeological finds? Did Jianyu send this errand boy up here to deceive Haur?

He glanced to his left, where Captain Bai stood ready. The look in the eyes of the man he'd trained and worked with bespoke the suspicion Haur felt. "Search it."

In Chinese, the captain shouted, "Search it!"

A dozen men climbed out of the deuce-and-a-half and trotted through the narrow opening with their weapons in hand.

"You will not find him, Colonel. He is not here." The man shifted nervously. "Please — this site is very old. Your soldiers will disturb the relics and archaeologists."

"We respect your work here, but we have our orders." Haur considered the implications if Jianyu actually had left.

As Haur's men returned to the truck, tension rose.

"When did Colonel Wu leave?"

"I told you, one week —"

Impatience snapped through Haur. "Date? Time? What direction?"

The lieutenant cowered. "I . . . I don't —"

Captain Bai lunged. "Do not —"

"No!" Haur held up a hand to his captain, then redirected his focus on the lieutenant. "A week ago. Was it Thursday? Or Friday —

right before the holiday?" Chinese New Year had always been important to Jianyu.

The man's eyes widened. "Yes, yes. He said he was going home just in time to celebrate with his father."

Haur studied the man. There was more to this story, but whether the old man knew it or not was another thing. "Morning or evening?"

"As soon as the sky lightened."

"Let us both hope you are telling the truth." Haur would prefer that this man was not telling the truth, because the implications were too great otherwise. If Wu Jianyu was not here, where was he? What was he doing? And with a group of China's elite, the Yanjingshe warriors?

Haur returned to the Lexus SUV and closed the door. He pulled out his phone and dialed. When it connected he said, "General Zheng, he is not here."

The long pause stretched painfully. "Explain."

"Jianyu left a week ago. He told the miners you called him back."

Silence choked the connection, but as the car pulled over the dirt road, Haur thought he heard hard breathing. No doubt his brother had yet again disappointed the general. He ached for the pain that stretched through the silence. "Should I return — ?"

"Find him!"

Haur's chest tightened at the rage in the general's voice.

"Find him and bring him back to me."

"Of course." Haur ended the call and slid the phone back into his pocket. Hand fisted, he pressed it to his mouth and propped his elbow on the window ledge. Staring out over the rugged landscape, he probed the possibilities of where Jianyu had gone. What intention did he have in this game he had begun?

Watching Jianyu collapse beneath the weight of the general's scorn after the spy had been discovered —

Haur diverted his gaze. Even though the incident was in the past, the general refused to discuss the breach and the records had been sealed. Beyond their building at Taipei City, nobody knew of the American spy who had penetrated their so-called secure and advanced systems.

And Jianyu's heart. Something Haur never thought possible. He had wished to have met this spy, the one who broke his brother.

Since the day she had fled back from wherever she had come, Jianyu had become a stranger. His father refused to speak to him. Refused to acknowledge he had a biological son. In the last thirty-six months, *son* became a term applied not to Jianyu but to Haur.

And Jianyu despised him for it.

"This is bad. Here, so close to American and British soldiers . . ."

Plucked from the past, Haur nodded at Captain Bai.

"The general will kill him."

The words hung ominous and true. There was no wrath like that of the enraged General Zheng. Ruthlessly powerful. Yet . . . so gentle and kind — to Haur.

"What do you think he is doing?"

There could only be one reason for Jianyu's disappearance: He wanted to restore his name and honor to his family. To do that, he would of course need some great plan to win his father back. "Whatever he is planning, it is not good."

"Where should we start?"

A glint in the sky lured his attention back out the window. Two small, dark shapes glided along the horizon. Black Hawks. Americans.

Inspiration floated down from those helicopters. Haur straightened. "There. Stop." He pointed to a clearing and snatched the GPS from the dash. As the plan congealed in his mind, so did a horrible certainty.

To see it through, he would not live.

Conversation with Heath had been easy and comfortable. More than it had ever been with any other man besides her father. Hands stuffed in the pockets of her North Face jacket, Darci eyed the man. About six-two, well-built, sandy blond hair cropped short. The guy had a subtle charm that drew its strength not from a cocky attitude, as she'd seen in other men like Jianyu, but a quiet presence that ensnared her curiosity worse than heat-seeking missiles to infrared radiation.

Now he jogged the course with Trinity, leading her up, over, and through the various obstacles. The Belgian Malinois moved with grace and speed, at ease as if she did it every day.

It wasn't Darci's smartest move, seeking him out. Researching him. The whole thing just made her ache. As an operative, she couldn't have the kind of life she dreamed about. A husband, two-point-five kids, and a house in a suburban location.

Even if she could, she didn't deserve it. Not after what she'd done. Not after what her father had done. Darci wrapped her fingers around the cold wire of the chain link, as if holding on to that would somehow enable her to hold on to her dream. Hadn't she spent the last eight years working to regain some honor for her family, for her father? He couldn't have stopped her mother's death. Darci wasn't angry at him. She just wished things could've been . . . different.

A thunderous clap snapped her attention back to Heath.

He and Trinity trotted back into the triangle of light from the lone field lamp. Heath slowed, his feet dragging on the hard-packed ground as he rubbed his temple. But then, as if he hadn't just looked like he was in pain, he lifted the ball and in a fluid move spun around and threw it back into the darkness. Arm swinging around, Heath's gaze locked onto Darci.

Trinity burst after the ball.

As he came toward her, Heath gave a smile that warmed her all the way to her toes. It was more than a friendly hello smile. It was one that showed pleasure in her presence, pleasure that she'd come to him.

"Bored?"

"Tired," she said as she joined him, leaning against the fence. "It's been a long day."

"I'm sure the general's tirade took its toll."

Darci preferred to keep that conversation

tucked away. "So, you said you head out for another base?"

"Yep. We'll head out around sixteen hundred tomorrow." He clapped at Trinity, who trotted back into the light in a lazy run and pranced around them, as if to taunt them with "Ha! I caught the ball." She dropped it at Darci's feet.

Wow, wasn't that like breaking some dog-handler code? Darci checked with Heath. "May I?"

Another approving smile shaded his jaw in the uneven lighting. "Sure, I'll deal with the traitor later."

She lifted the slobbery ball from the ground, took a practice step, then sent it sailing through the air.

"Whoa! Nice arm. Where'd you learn that?"

Reveling in his praise, Darci turned as Heath moved away from the fence, stunned. "I played softball in high school and college. Shortstop."

His gaze skated over her with an appreciative nod. "Remind me to never get in your line of fire."

Darci laughed. When was the last time someone made her feel this special? Probably too long, but there wasn't anything to lose here. They would go in opposite directions soon, so no loss, no gain. Well, maybe a small gain. When she was out in the mountains, she could remember Heath's smile. Or the way the sinews in his arms rippled as he threw the ball for Trinity. Or his approving smile. Fantasize that he was the man filling the role that could never happen — husband.

Okay, way too weird.

She needed to be careful. There were certain pieces of classified info that would tank any chance at a relationship — not that there was one . . .

The slower pace of the last twenty-four hours and being with Heath kneaded out some of the kinks in her neck and shoulders. Trinity returned, made her way to the trough, and dropped her ball in the water, then lapped up some refreshment.

"So, you going to tell me?"

They both started toward the gate as if communicating on some hidden signal. The camp had quieted but still bustled with activity as was the MO during wartime operations.

Darci wrinkled her brow as he linked up with Trinity. "Tell you what?"

At five-ten, she appreciated the height on Heath. And his soulful gray eyes. The almost bashful way he behaved.

Hands in his pockets, the lead looped around his wrist, he looked down at her as they walked across the camp. "Whatever it is you're not telling me."

Ouch. Never think a Green Beret is bashful. They were trained to ferret out inconsistencies and get to the heart of the matter. But this was a matter and a heart he couldn't intrude upon. Not this time. As much as she'd wished otherwise.

As her tent came into view, she slowed, then turned to him. "You were a Green Beret long enough to know if I'm not telling you, then I can't." Why did she go and say that?

"Thought so." His gaze raked the blackened sky, disappointment lurking in his eyes.

Time to cut this rendezvous short before she gave in. "Look, it's been nice hanging out with you. Talking. But . . ." She hated this part. But it was necessary. Wasn't it? "You're going on tour, and I'm going into the mountains." She shrugged and shook her head. "Let's not ruin a great friendship with complications."

Despite the creaking of axles and rumbling engines and shouts, the only sound she heard around them was the rhythmic panting of his dog. Though she looked up to read his emotions, she stopped at the one that affected her the most: hurt. It was hard to remember that hardened grunts like him could have soft hearts.

"Complications." He pursed his lips, his chin dimpling. "Right. Yeah." With a quiet, disgusted snort, Heath caught the lead and drew Trinity up. "Well, good night — and good-bye — Jia." He did not wear disappointment well. In fact, it weighted his shoulders. "Hope things go well for you."

She'd taken the abrasive, aggressive road of telling him they'd never see each other again, and he wished her *well*. He the hero, she the villain.

As his form hulked through the darkness, Darci told herself to stay put. Or better yet — go into the tent.

Instead, her feet carried her after the war-dog team. It took a stretch, but she caught his arm. "Hey, wait."

In a lightning fast move, Heath spun around, his eyes bright beneath the flood-light as he flipped their grips so his hand wrapped around her wrist.

Frozen in time and shock, she stared up at him as his fingers slid along her forearm, then back to her wrist until he entwined his fingers with hers. He grinned down at her. "Thought so."

Stunned, Darci mentally pushed him

back . . . a dozen feet. But she clung to the husky words. Two simple words that outted her. Strangest thing was, she didn't mind.

Standing toe-to-toe with him did crazy things to her stomach. Though she couldn't resist, she should stop staring at their intertwined hands. She'd *never* reacted like this with a guy. And in those time-warped seconds with their gazes locked, it dawned on her that he'd known she wasn't immune to his charm.

"Just give me a chance, Jia."

Oh, but she didn't like that name on his lips. Darci. She wanted him to call her Darci. "To what?"

His gaze darted around her face, as if studying a political map. "To prove I'm not like whoever hurt you so bad."

Beneath the teasing caress of his husky works, her brain caught up with her stupidity. She freed her hand and swallowed — hard. "It won't work." She wanted to punch him. How had he gotten through her defensive perimeter?

He smirked. "You haven't tried yet."

"Look, it's not that I don't want to . . ."

"Hey. I'm interested. You're interested, but . . ." Heath shrugged, his high-powered smile gleaming as he held up his hands as if in surrender. "I won't beg."

Darci took a step back, her stomach clenched. "I'll e-mail you."

"Cheater."

"Excuse me?"

"It's your get-out-of-jail-free card. You walk away under that ruse, I'll never hear from you again."

It was her turn to smile. A sad, heavy smile. "RockGirl@rkmail.com." With that lie, she pivoted and hurried into her tent. At least he knew the truth.

EIGHT

Last night had been the best night of his life . . . but it'd also been the worst.

Had Jia blown him off because of the scar? Or because he just wasn't good enough? Like everything in his life he didn't measure up for?

"What happened?"

Heath shot a look at Aspen as they strode into the workout room. "What do you mean?"

Hair pulled back with sprigs of curls framing her face, she rolled her eyes. "You've got more bite than Trinity this morning. What happened?"

Oh. That. "Nothing."

"Did she turn you down?"

Heath ripped open the zipper of his gym bag and grabbed the hand wraps. He straightened and looked toward the corner. "Speed bag."

Aspen's wry grin needled his mood. "Hey, Ghost."

Wrapping his hands, Heath tried to ignore the woman. The yellow roll slipped out of his hand. He grunted.

Aspen stepped in, rolled it back up, then used care in wrapping his hand. Tight. She knew how to do this. "Heath, she's a smart girl. When she realizes what she's missing out on, she'll be back."

He tugged free. "She gave me the kiss-off. Besides, she headed out this morning."

Aspen made quick work of prepping his other hand, too. Heath grabbed his boxing glove and tugged it on using his teeth. She smirked. "I guess that explains why she just came in."

Aspen was looking over his shoulder, and he followed her gaze.

Oh, man. Jia. Black workout pants. A red tank. Hair pulled back. Donning gloves.

Unexpected impact against his gloves jerked his attention back to Aspen. "Free the oppressed, right, Hot Shot?" Aspen nodded. "She looks oppressed."

He wasn't a Green Beret anymore, but the ingrained motto guided him regardless. Still, Heath's courage slipped through the slick gloves. If Jia didn't want something to work between them, then "freeing" her wouldn't make a difference.

But what if she *did* want it to work? Heath considered that possibility as he made his way to the universal punching bag. Warming up, he threw some light punches, bouncing back and forth for a good cardio workout but also good boxing posture.

A few right hooks, an uppercut, and he shifted to his left, jabbing.

Since his career change, Heath had steered clear of female involvement. A few thought it was cool that he'd taken a hit during an ambush. But the cool factor waned at the headaches and depression. More and more, he felt himself turning into Uncle Bobby.

That scared him. Right out of dating.

Not that he thought less of his uncle, but the man had lost his will to live when the chopper he'd been in went down and left him paralyzed in both legs. Strong military hero reduced to a wheelchair. How many times had his uncle groused about that?

Left-right-left. Heath moved around the bag, blocking. Punching. Blocking.

He took a step back and shook out his arms and stretched his neck.

She was beautiful. Light brown eyes. Sweet smile.

"It won't work."

Heath led with his right foot and nailed a

hook. The impact rippled through his arm and up into his shoulder. Felt good. Strong. The days of grueling physical therapy reminded him that anything worth having — getting back on his feet — was worth fighting for.

Jia.

A left uppercut. A right cross. *Whoosh. Thud. Whoosh-whoosh. Thud.* He repeated it.

As he bounced on his toes and hung his head back, staring at the ceiling, he sensed someone at the bag beside him. He took a step to the side. Jia had a wicked throwing arm. Nice figure. A laugh that embedded itself into his memory and made him want to hear that sound a lot more. He had a feeling she didn't laugh nearly enough.

Argh! Why wouldn't she get out of his head? Heath ducked, blocked with his left, and threw a hard right. A left hook. A right. *Whoosh. Thud. Whoosh.*

The echo of his movement registered. He started to look to the side, but he had enough distractions. This workout would be his last for a while. After this, he'd retrieve Trinity from the kennel and take a run.

Left up, he jabbed several times with his right. He'd hit a nerve when he took that leap, mentioning someone had hurt her. In fact . . . that was when her defenses went to the highest state of alert. He toed his way around to the other side, out of the line of fire from the other boxer. So, who had hurt her?

He slammed a left hook into the bag.

The person boxing beside him came around the back. Heath angled, using the challenge to slip between their bags without getting hit.

Thud! At the impact against the back of his head, Heath blinked away stars. Resisted the urge to tell the guy to bring it down a notch. But he wasn't in charge here. Not anymore.

Right. Left. Left uppercut. Right hook.

The movements were echoed again. To his left.

Heath cocked his head slightly. What was with this person?

A foot flew toward his face.

Heath jerked away, arching backward. "Hey!" He straightened and found himself staring at those perfect brown eyes.

"Sorry." Without another word, Jia threw jabs and hooks into the leather-padded column.

Uncertainty slowed him as he returned to his workout. He moved through his routine, one he'd established while doing PT. But as he worked, he noticed his movements mimicked. What, was she challenging him? He did the regimen faster.

So did she.

Heath stretched his neck and moved to the side farthest away from her. What was she doing here anyway? She said they were bugging out. Did she lie? Or did the plans change?

His bag lurched toward his face.

He angled right, narrowly avoiding a faceplant with leather. *That* wasn't an accident. Jia tracked him to the back. He threw a right. So did she.

Right. Left upper. Right hook. Right jab.

Heath moved around, gaining the front and Jia trailing — banging into his back.

"Sorry."

"Sloppy work, RockGirl."

If he'd figured out her little game, then after another left hook —

Her foot swung out.

Heath ducked and stifled his smile. "Let's hope your work in the field is better." He took himself through the routine again. Waited for her foot. Heath dropped and swung his leg around, catching her foot and sweeping her off her feet.

Jia flipped back. Her body thudded against the mat, yanking a grunt from her chest.

Heath bent, his arms resting on his knees. "If you need boxing lessons, I'm available. Anytime."

She shook her head, chest heaving from the workout as she fought a smile. But it fought back. Won. And pried a laugh out of her.

Heath liked what he saw. The healthy flush on her cheeks. A girl not afraid to take him on. Able to laugh at herself. And at him.

"Train me?" She angled a look at him. "It took you ten minutes to figure out I was next to you."

"Five." He extended a hand as an olive branch. As she stood, Heath steadied her. "And I was distracted."

Jia's smile was warm. Like the rest of her in his arms. "Yeah? What could distract a former Green Beret?"

"A beautiful woman who said it wouldn't work."

Her smile slipped. She took a step back. Lifted a gloved hand to her forehead where she swiped loose hair from her face.

Man, she was more skittish than Aspen's Lab. What had her on the run? The real question, did he have the stamina to pursue?

"Want to shower up and grab some chow?"

She laughed. He could get used to that

sound. "You don't let up, do you?"

"Not on you."

Jia stared at him. Then looked around, which was when he noticed a few spectators. She yanked off her glove. "Okay." Jia eased back, her eyes darting everywhere but his face.

"Out front, fifteen."

Sweat sliding down her temples, she gave a curt nod, then strode out of the main workout room toward the showers.

Heath's heart pounded as he used his teeth to pry off the Velcro band of his gloves. What was he doing? The scar ... the TBI ...

Jia.

He spun, grabbed his bag, and wrangled out of the wraps as he headed to the showers.

"One joy scatters a hundred griefs."

Darci stared at herself in the mirror of the showers. One joy. Heath definitely qualified. It'd been stupid, really, to goad him. She felt foolish, as if she'd returned to junior high.

But his expression ...

A giggle slipped past her tough facade. Covering her mouth with her hand, she used the other to brace herself against the porcelain sink. *What are you doing?*

131

"Crows everywhere are equally black."

What was this? War of the ancient Chinese proverbs? Darci tucked her chin. The point was — just as crows were black in China and in America, men were . . .

No. There was a world of difference between Jianyu and Heath. She saw it. *Felt* it. Heath's character had a moral base. He didn't even know her, and already she felt challenged. How did he know? She searched the mirror for signs of distress on her face. How did he know someone had hurt her?

Heath wanted the chance to prove he wasn't like Jianyu.

But that meant being vulnerable.

She squeezed her eyes tight. She wanted it. Wanted a family. Wanted to *not* be alone anymore. What he said, what he did . . . it was what she wanted. *Yearned* for.

But you don't deserve that. You sold your soul in Taipei City.

Heath would never understand. Darci straightened, then blew out a breath. Enough pining over the hunky dog handler. Time to return to reality.

Her gaze struck the Exit sign. She pivoted, tugged her pack off the bench, and strode out the door. Grief and regret nipped at her heels, but she stomped onward. She made the right decision, no matter how much it yanked out her heart.

Icy wind slapped her face, hard and un-welcoming.

"Ready?"

Darci stopped cold as Heath came off the back wall of the building, sporting a field jacket. "What are you — ?"

"Come on. I've got two hours to change your mind."

Mortar rounds in the distance echoed those in her chest. "About?" He knew she would try to skip out on him. The guilt felt a thousand times worse than if he hadn't. She was an absolute heel.

He winked and eased her pack from her hands. He slung it over his arm and guided her down Route Disney, the main thorough-fare through Bagram.

"Where, exactly, are we headed?"

"There's a Thai restaurant down by the shops." He stuffed his hands in his jeans.

"How'd you know I like Thai?"

"I didn't." He grinned. "It's my favorite. Sorry — being selfish here. Last good meal for a while."

Why did she not believe that? Because Heath seemed to anticipate every move. Every thought. It hit her like the bitter wind roiling through the base: if he'd known, she probably would've gotten more nervous.

Would've backed out.

Which is what she needed to do.

Darci stopped and turned. "Heath."

With his lightning-fast reflexes, he slid an arm around her waist and pulled her close, his jacket gaping and forcing her to press against his T-shirt. Warmth tingled against her fingertips. Awareness flared through her. That hunger . . . *No no no.* It roared for prominence, for satiation.

"Jia." Every morsel of lightheartedness vanished as he looked down at her. "It's one date — lunch, if that makes you more comfortable."

Her throat constricted. She lifted her hands from his chest, from feeling the rhythm of his heart beneath her right palm, then let them rest again. "Why . . . ? Why can't you just let it alone?"

"Because." He craned his neck to the side to look into her eyes.

At that moment, she was lost. Lost to her own mechanisms that kept her safe. That suffocated her lone dream.

A slow smile slid across Heath's face as he smoothed his knuckles along her cheek. "Because of what's happening right here . . ." He lowered his head toward hers, eyes on her lips.

Swirls of warmth and cold, exhilaration

and dread, spiked simultaneously. *I can't.*

But she couldn't move.

Heath's breath caressed her cheek.

She lifted her head, pulse thudding against her own inner warnings. If she did this, if she let this happen . . .

A face ignited from the past.

Darci shoved Heath back. Blinked. Shook her head. "No." She spun on her heels and started away.

Heath hooked her arm. "Jia."

She stopped. "Please . . ." It hurt. To hope. To feel what she felt with him. It scared her. Beyond any imagining.

"I'm sorry." He ran a hand over the back of his neck. "You're right. That was too fast. I just . . ."

"What?" She didn't want to ask that, but she needed to regain her fortitude against his stealth romance.

"I want this to work."

Her heart misfired. "Why?" Vulnerability skated along that single syllable, but if he was going to pull out the stops and be blunt, so was she. "Why do you want this to work?"

"Because I've never felt anything like this. I can't stop thinking about you. I want to kill the guy who hurt you, and my dog likes you."

A chuckle leaped up her throat. "Your dog?"

"Hey, Trinity's a very discerning animal."

She couldn't help the laugh. Because she knew he was right. She'd seen those dogs in action. Knew their loyalty rested with their handlers and no one else.

The muscle along his strong, angular jaw bounced. "If you want to take it slow, we will. But don't shut me out. I see it in your face, hear it in your words, Jia."

Darci.

"You want 'us,' too. So let's figure it out, RockGirl."

Her lips tweaked in a smile all their own. "I'll never live that down, will I?"

"And lose one of the ways I can make you smile?"

She swung her gaze to him. He wanted to make her smile? Willing to take things at a different pace just for her? "Are you for real?"

"Let me kiss you, and then you tell me."

"Ha." Darci laughed harder, too pleased with the attention and determination of Heath Daniels, and started walking. "Are we going to eat or what?"

NINE

Dawn cracked the day with a splinter of blue. That lone sliver of light through the dark sky allowed Heath to take in the bustling base. Teams gearing up to head out for patrol. Others in formation for drill. Beyond the barricade that held in the patriots and kept out the terrorists — in theory — loomed the mountains. In the distance to the north, he saw the same shape that had stolen his career.

No, a bad intel decision and an ambush stole it. Not some innocuous scrap of land. God shut the door on his career and his hopes.

Heath slowed to a lazy jog as he and Trinity skirted the airfield on their third circuit. A stream of people crossed the sand to a waiting Black Hawk. Among them — Jia.

Impulse stopped Heath. Trinity sat, but her panting and a small whimper indicated she had spotted her, too. Stretching his arms over his head, he watched the team board. Yesterday had defined things for him. He wasn't so sure about her. More accurately, she wasn't sure what she felt. Probably too tangled up in the past, tangled up in who-ever had hurt her that she was terrified to risk a relationship again.

A guy about the same size as Heath spoke to Jia. She glanced over her shoulder to him, the backwash from the rotors whipping her hair into her face. Across those eyes. A smile, shy and still uncertain, flickered across the distance.

Why did he care? She wouldn't commit to save her life. And he'd pulled out all the stops. When was the last time — *never*. He'd never been that bold or direct. He was messed up.

And yet . . . he stood here, like a lost puppy, wishing she'd been willing to try.

The desire was there, buried deep in her past. It was okay. He wasn't going to rush it. Wasn't going to stress. Something in him said this wasn't the last time he'd see her.

But that didn't stop the desperate feeling that she was getting away.

She strapped into the chopper, her back to the pilots and facing Heath.

Trinity barked.

A smile slid into Jia's face. Her hand lifted an inch.

So. That's it: good-bye.

Why was he acting like a chump? He had her figured out, really. That inch of a raised hand was a mile for her, which meant she *was* trying. He could live with that. For now.

He ruffled the top of Trinity's head. "C'mon." He made his final circuit, passing several other choppers. Lucky ducks would get a fast trip to wherever they were going. Of course, they were twenty-million-dollar targets for RPGs. Then again, the MRAP and Humvees that would ferry him and the A Breed Apart team to their next gig, though not as expensive, were just as vulnerable.

Vulnerable . . . yeah, he'd exposed his backside to Jia for a nuke of a rejection.

But then he'd pushed it back into her court, cornered her as best as he could. Convincing her not to repel what she felt for him was like trying to get a cat to take a bath.

At his tent, Heath placed Trinity in her crate with some fresh water and headed to the showers, ready to wash the dirt, grime, and frustration from his body. It was okay. He wasn't in a place where he could nurture a relationship — or more important, where he wanted to. They had time. And his life was screwed up enough with his uncle in the soldier's home and his own failings, thanks to the TBI. He hadn't even told Jibril about blacking out on the way over. Thankfully, it was a short one.

Most people who weren't familiar with the blackouts would never realize what happened because they came and went in seconds. It'd seem as if he was just disoriented or lost in his thoughts. Still, it was a problem. But if he stressed about it, the symptoms would grow worse.

Back at the tent he shared with the other ABA members, he noted all of Jibril's belongings packed and gone. Heath double-checked his watch. Not late. But he should get his ruck and head to the rec building to meet up with the team.

He let Trinity out, and she jumped up on his cot and stretched out. "Spoiled." Pink tongue hanging out, she squinted beneath the rising sun as if to say, "Yeah, so?"

Ten minutes later, he and Trinity ambled across the base to the main gate where two MRAPS idled. Four soldiers stood around talking. The others were already assembled. "Did I miss an earlier rollout time?"

"No," Jibril said.

"What's the matter? Lose track of time

after your hot lunch date?" Hogan smirked. "She seemed to be into you."

If Hogan didn't have such a stinking attitude, he might find her attractive. She was as annoying as a kid sister.

A swirl of rushed movement from the side severed his biting retort. A dozen men rushed toward a chopper, armed to the teeth, determination carved into their faces. Heath took a step in their direction. Saw their patches. Heat zapped through his shoulders, the familiar *tsing* of adrenaline. It was —

Couldn't be.

He took a few quick steps.

One of the SOCOM guys, eyes shielded by Oakleys, looked his way — and slowed.

Watters!

Heath's body lurched into action two steps before he told himself to stay put. The pounding of the helo's rotors thudded against his chest. The wind whipped and tore at his face. He offered a two-fingered salute to the man.

The skids lifted, and Heath stepped back as the chopper rose. Its nose dipped down, then leveled and rushed forward to save the troops.

That used to be me.

And what was he now? Comedic relief.

Entertainment. The thought burned and scraped as he swallowed the painful dose of truth. He gulped adrenaline and disappointment by the liters, very aware of the emptiness in his chest. First, Jia . . . now . . .

If only they hadn't gotten bad intel on his last mission. He'd love to wrap his fingers around the neck of the person who had cost him his career.

"Hey, Prince Charming, you coming, or do I inherit your beautiful dog now?"

Heath dropped his gaze, regrouped, and dumped the depression that had swooped in once again. He turned to Hogan. "I'd like to see you try." Because Heath knew that even if he died, Trinity would never leave him. Her training was now as inbred as her instincts.

Jibril and Hogan headed into the second MRAP, while Heath and Aspen climbed the three steps into the first one. As they settled, the driver became immersed in radio chatter.

"Yes, sir. We'll wait, sir." Over his shoulder, he hollered to Heath and Aspen, "We've been ordered to hold."

Heath slumped into a seat, Trinity on the seat next to him, and looked at Aspen, who shrugged.

Ten minutes later, the driver cursed and

muttered something to the soldier in the seat next to him. Heath rose and peered out the front heavily fortified window. Two generals and at least a dozen special-ops guys jogged toward them.

Noise drew Heath's attention to the rear, where the door sat open so he could see another MRAP pulling up behind. Heath leaned in and patted the driver. "What's happening?"

"Hanged if I know. They told me to wait, so I wait."

Heath glanced at the guy. He looked young. Too young. "How long you been here?"

"Yesterday."

Something strange twisted in Heath's gut. "You ever been off this base?"

"No, sir, but I'm ready."

Heath choked back his groan as he bent in half, swung around, and threaded his way around Aspen and Trinity to the rear door. "I'll be right back."

"Heath —"

A man appeared in the doorway. "Make a hole!"

Heath eased back into his seat. With only four seats in the vehicle, he wasn't sure where this guy was going, but the authority with which he spoke pushed Heath back down. In his seat, he gripped Trinity's collar and lured her to a spot between his legs.

The soldier dropped into the seat next to Aspen. Another flipped down the spare jump seat. As he did, Heath noted the trident on the guy's arm. A SEAL. Interesting. That swung Heath's attention back to the guy next to Aspen.

His gaze hit the rank on the man's vest, then ricocheted to the man's face — eyes burning holes into his own. It was the same general who chewed out Jia last night.

He took in the lettering on his chest. Burnett.

The general paused as he stared down Heath. "Of all the . . ." He muttered something about being cursed, then banged on the hull. "Get it moving, Specialist!"

The back door clanged shut and they lurched into motion.

Though the four-star might want to play the silent game, Heath didn't. "Is this a personal escort to our next site?"

Blue eyes met Heath's. "If you want it to be."

Placating him. Heath would have to dig a little harder without ticking him off. "You and I both know those stars on your chest are more of a homing beacon for trouble than a shield."

Gaping, Aspen sucked in a breath but said nothing. Her own military training probably dumbed her into submission.

But like Trinity, his training was as much instinct now as ever. He didn't play dumb. He got info and made a plan. His experience told him something big was happening if two generals were added last-minute to an entertainment convoy.

Heath nudged Aspen's boots. "This should make an interesting addition to my talk with the troops tonight, don't you think, Aspen?"

"Don't drag me down this hole." Her pale cheeks went pink.

"Oh, c'mon. You know the troops would get a kick out of hearing how two four-stars hitched a ride with us."

General Burnett leaned in.

In a heartbeat, Trinity read the aggressive move and leapt to all fours. Had her side not pressed against his leg, Heath might've missed the low growl of warning that rumbled through her chest.

Burnett was undeterred as the SEAL aimed his weapon at Trinity.

"Hey!" Heath shouted, throwing his hand into the line of fire. "Trinity, out!"

"Unless you want a personal escort to a detainment cell, Mr. Daniels," the general said with his own snarl, "I'd suggest you keep this little endeavor to yourself."

Heath's head pounded as he coaxed Trinity down, just as he did his own pulse. Seeing that SEAL take a bead on his partner . . . He looked to the general. "Understood. Sir." As he eased back, Trinity once again relaxing on the steel floor, Heath closed his eyes. Focused on calming down. *What was that, Daniels? Getting info is one thing, but getting stupid's another.*

In the back of his mind, he wondered if his aggression toward the general wasn't some reaction to the way the man had treated Jia.

The generals were making a secret trip. Where? Why? Was Air Force One in the area? Dignitaries meant to bring peace and unity often brought death and destruction — to their own troops with the invisible target painted on their heads.

Heath settled in, wishing for all he was worth for an M4A1 to level the playing field. The general had a sidearm. And the SEAL an M4, an M16, and a modified handgun.

Prepared. Armed to the teeth. *What's going on?*

Whatever drew them out, it was big. And Heath hoped they lived through it.

Dead stop.

In the second he heard the driver mumbling about something in the road, Heath went for the weapon he didn't have. His gaze struck the general, who was in motion, too.

"Why did we stop?" Burnett demanded.

"Back up!" Heath shouted at the same time the general spoke. He locked gazes with the steely-eyed general.

"Not sure, sir. Something about a road-block."

"Back up, back up!" The general's face reddened. "Get us out —"

The vehicle lurched. Shoved Heath out of his seat. Into Aspen. Her blue eyes went wild as the MRAP dropped down and bounced. He stood and pushed himself back, mind racing.

"Go, go, go!" Heath shouted to the driver.

BoooOOOOOooomm!

Whipped into the air, Heath tensed. His hearing hollowed. His vision went black.

Coughing, Heath snapped awake. A sweet, metallic taste filled his mouth. He couldn't breathe. He dropped his head back and coughed again. Again.

A warbling sound came from his right.

There, the general knelt, his mouth moving in hollow shouts.

Heath blinked. Shook his head — and the whole world spun. Man, why couldn't he breathe? It felt like something was on his chest. He craned his neck — and let out a soft grunt. Stretched across him in a defensive posture, hackles raised, teeth bared, Trinity snapped. Growled — he felt it rumble across his ribs. He rested a hand on her flank and dropped his head back. With another cough, his head cleared. Trinity snapped at the general, who attempted to get closer.

Aspen's fair skin was smudged with black. "She won't let us help."

"Trinity, out," Heath said with another cough.

She ceased aggression and licked his face.

"Good girl." He scooted to the others, throat burning. "What's happening?" Wiping the grit out of his eyes, Heath tried to get his bearings. By the way things were playing out, he hadn't been out more than a few minutes. Was it the TBI? Or had he hit his head?

Aspen swiped a hand across her forehead, smearing black over her pale complexion but looked otherwise unscathed.

A streak of blood ran down the general's temple, but it seemed his helmet absorbed most of the impact. "RPGs. Got our driver. Backup's en route. But we still have a shooter out there. Idiot about took my head off."

The MRAP sat on its side, having been divested of passengers. The SEAL knelt at the front, staring out in the direction from which they'd been hit. Heath sidled up next to Aspen.

"You okay?" His throat burned as if he'd swallowed a blowtorch.

She nodded, the helmet cockeyed on her head.

Heath rubbed Trinity's ear, letting her know she'd done a good job protecting him, as he scanned the area. In front of him a cement wall lined the road they'd been ambushed on. Following it to the far side, he recalled the zigzag at the corner. Two shops sat at the end, then the row of apartments, in which the shooter had taken refuge.

As he scoped it, a man rushed from the side of the building, glanced in their direction, then tossed something aside.

"Target! Give me a gun!" Heath shouted.

"Are you crazy?"

"Completely."

The general grinned and tapped the SEAL, who passed him the small fully automatic. "You're not authorized to engage the enemy, Mr. Daniels."

Heath jerked toward him. "Trinity and I can find him. Take him down. Or do you want this punk to kill more of your men?"

"Lieutenant Wilson, go with Daniels." Fierce eyes probed Heath. "Temporarily activated."

Heath rose and Trinity with him. Using the dilapidated wall as cover, he sprinted down the street with Trinity a full length ahead of him. "Trinity, seek!"

The command fueled her desire. She surged ahead and barked. Across the intersection, which was ominously empty, and into the building.

Heath raced after her, knowing that while she was trained only to attack those in an aggressive posture, she hadn't done this in a while. The doubts were new. She had her vest — one thing he'd insisted on, knowing how much terrorists wanted MWDs dead.

Snapping and barking ahead pushed him faster. "She hit on something," he shouted to the SEAL behind him.

"Let's hope it's a *someone*," Wilson retorted.

They hustled up to a corner, and their actions were seamless. The SEAL eased around and cleared it. Heath rushed into the room and pied out. Nothing. *Where is she?*

Paint curled off the walls, reaching for them, as if looking for escape from the neglect. Plaster pocked with holes seemed as dejected as it looked. This place bore the marks of abandonment. *Years* of abandonment. But the carpet, table, pillows, and, in particular, the steaming cup of tea told him someone had been in here recently. Very recently.

"Tea." His single word alerted Wilson to trouble.

Another bark.

"She's close." Heath sidestepped and eased into the hall. The tip of Trinity's tail was low and flicking. Back legs spread, she snarled.

Heath rushed forward. Took point, then let the SEAL again clear it.

The guy stepped into view.

Tat-tat-tat.

Wilson jerked back, stumbled. Went down.

Trinity vanished.

A feral scream stabbed the tension and replaced the gunfire.

Heath rushed the room, weapon aimed,

knowing Trinity had taken the tango down. The assailant lay on the floor, screaming, his arm between Trinity's powerful jaws. Heath hurried to her side, Wilson rushing the combatant. "Trinity, out!"

With a stretch of her jaw, she released her quarry and came to his side.

Cowering and simpering, the man held his arm.

In Pashto, Heath said, "Down on your knees. Do not make any sudden moves. My dog is trained to attack on or off lead. Do you understand?"

A frantic nod.

"Hands behind your head." Wilson grunted and held his side. "Slow."

As he complied, the man darted looks to Trinity and tears streamed down his cheeks.

Weapon trained on the terrorist, Heath backed up. A half-dozen shapes swooned to his left. This was it. He'd die. Never see Jia, make her face what she felt for him. If that was possible. They were all going down. Heath swung his weapon to them.

"Friendly, friendly," one shouted.

Standing down, Heath indicated to the room. "We need a medic."

"We've got it from here," a SEAL said as his team went to work securing the prisoner and aiding their comrade, whose vest had intercepted the bullets that would've put him six feet under in Arlington.

As Heath waited in the forward room, he took a knee and smoothed a hand along Trinity's coat. Panting, she smiled up at him, her amber eyes sparkling. If she had a voice, she would be thanking him for letting her get back in action. He wasn't as glad.

"Good girl." He smoothed a hand over her head and rubbed her ears. "You're a top-notch soldier, Trinity."

"Wow," Hogan said as they regrouped. "If you had talked to that Asian chick as nice, I bet she wouldn't have left. Or maybe that was the problem — you were too nice."

A retort was on the tip of his tongue, but as Heath came to his feet, he spotted General Burnett. The man seethed.

The SEALs came through, Wilson with a hand over his side, his face knotted in pain. No doubt the bullets had left a bruise. The last two warriors brought out the attacker.

"Did he do it?" General Burnett asked.

"Yes, sir," a SEAL said.

The general's brow furrowed as he considered the man. "Did he know *who* he was hitting?"

The SEAL shook his head. "Only that he was hitting Americans."

A disgusted look washed over the general's

face, replacing the worry that had been there seconds earlier. "We'll have to hunker down till nightfall. Choppers are on a rescue op south of here and can't get to us till then."

Aspen handed Heath a water bottle. He took a swig, then held the bottle out for Trinity, who lapped it so fast, half of it missed her mouth. She shook out her fur as if to shake off the attack itself. Heath crouched in front of his partner and stroked her fur.

"See you got our man."

Heath looked up at the general. "Let's hope so, sir." Some Afghans hated Americans and would make any claim that made them look like a hero when the real villains could still be lurking on the rooftop.

"They cleared the roof. Found the tube." Gruff and to the point as always. Without a "thank you" or "job well done," the general pivoted.

Jibril frowned as he moved into Heath's path. "Are you okay?"

"Yeah, sure." He gave the answer everyone wanted. But there was something in him, something deep and forbidding, digging into his brain. A thought he never imagined he'd have. Maybe he was just out of practice. Maybe it was the general's attitude.

But Heath couldn't evade the warning that something was very wrong here. And that if he stayed in this country that had tried to snatch his life once, he would die.

Ten

Parwan Province, Afghanistan

Night descended with a wolfish devour. Cold and biting, all the winds of Asia seemed to roll over her, ripping at her jacket. Burrowing against the bitterness, Darci pressed her body into an elongated, cuplike formation. Rock and twigs poked into her belly as she settled. She tugged the wool hat down over her ears and lowered her chin so she could recirculate the air she breathed in the hopes of keeping herself warm.

From her small pack, she retrieved the night-vision goggles. Cold against her face, the goggles morphed the darkness into a monochromatic mural of greens and whites. Rocks. Trees. Slopes and rises. All spilling down toward the valley guarded by the mountain range.

The howling wind snapped at her cheeks, but she focused on the distance.

She'd seen them.

Zooming with the NVGs brought the image into sharper focus. Good. She scanned left and counted eight . . . no, nine — ten! A cluster of ten tents straddling the valley floor near a mud-brick home. Here the two-story structure with a perimeter wall would be considered a mansion. The wealthiest of —

Her lens hit something. Darci hesitated. Retraced the wall. Portions were missing. In a normal village, the wall would've been repaired, their "noble" taken care of by the people. Farther down, she could see diagonally from one side of the house through to the other side . . . and out. Crumbling and spitting mud and plaster from a hole, the wall mocked the white tents flapping outside.

Interesting that there was no rubble pile from the missing section. Which meant it had either been cleaned up — unlikely if they were willing to let the hole go unrepaired — or it had blown. Like from an RPG. Or high-powered rifle.

The thought traced an icy finger down her spine. To make that shot, the attacker would've been . . . *Right where I am.*

If that was true, then the Afghans would've had sentries monitoring this spot.

Darci froze and listened. The roar of the wind and the defiant rustle of her coat made it impossible to hear anything. If someone wanted to sneak up on her, she'd be dead and never know. Then she'd never have to feel the guilt again of giving Heath the fake e-mail address.

Swallowing, she pushed her thoughts to the dilapidated "fortress." No light twinkled through a curtain or blanketed opening.

Abandoned?

She flicked her gaze to the tents. When a glare of white burst through the lens, she resisted the urge to tense. More than a hundred yards from the camp, there was no way they would know she was here. But it still left her feeling naked, more so with the unusually cold night.

The men wore *qmis*, loose-fitting shirts that reached their knees, and *shalwar*, full trousers tied at the waist with a string. Heavy jackets concealed whether or not the men wore vests, but she was sure their *chap-lay*, the thick leather shoes, provided little protection against the cold night. At least not the same protection her Columbias provided.

What made her hesitate was the *pagray*. The turbans were not worn high off the forehead as normal — necessitated for

touching of the forehead during prayers —
but instead they were low and pressed
against their brows.

Odd.

Move on. It was cold, and she'd been gone
too long already. Someone — Toque — was
bound to notice.

She dragged the NVGs over the camp,
counted heads and tents, memorized the
layout. Another odd thing. It wasn't set up
like a village, with clusters of tents close
together for families. They were all huddled
together. Not family-like. More . . . like the
military.

Well, they were Taliban. And she had their
numbers and location. Which was what her
CO wanted to know. But did a small cluster
like this justify the great increase?

Tugging the jacket hood up over her head,
she dug down into her coat and retrieved
the phone. Capitalizing on the protection of
cover from her hood to shield the blue glow
from the night and sentries, she turned it
on. Punched in her lat-long, her data, and
the date and time. Sent it spiraling to the
satellite somewhere overhead. Then powered
it down, tucked it back in her pocket, and
nudged the hood out of the way.

Once again, she used her NVGs to study
the valley. The people. The layout. Learn

everything she could. Trailing the neon-green along the upper portions of the valley, she traced the hills. The plateaus. Searching for caves and other possible groupings of fighters.

Small for a Taliban camp, this settlement broke too many molds and unsettled her. But analysis wasn't her job. Recon and reporting were.

"Just tell me what you see." Burnett had been adamant that she not put herself in danger. Darci cringed every time he warned her to be careful. She and danger had a love-hate relationship: She loved to avoid it. It hated to miss her. Invariably, it not only found her, but hunted her down. Sort of like Heath.

No, no. Can't go there. Not now. Not ever.

"If you don't go into the cave of the tiger, how are you going to get its cub?"

Darci ordered the voice to shut up, to leave her alone. Going into that camp — or going there with Heath — would not bring trouble to her doorstep. She'd walk into its den!

But if she didn't, the little inconsistencies about what was happening out here wouldn't be answered. What if something was going on down there? They were less than two hours from Bagram. From thousands of American troops and their allies.

Darci pushed onto her knees. "Don't do this." She tucked the NVGs into her coat and zipped it as she started down the side of the mountain. "This is really stupid," she muttered.

True. But Burnett had kept her in this job because of the very instincts that had her hustling down into the veritable den of tigers. The night before she left the base, he'd all but vowed to send her packing if she didn't find something.

Her boot slipped — rocks, pebbles, and dirt dribbled down. She froze, swallowing hard as she waited to see if the wind had carried the noise to the Taliban. Satisfied it hadn't, she hurried along. Kept herself tucked into the shadow of a cleft that gave protection against the angry wind and the probing eyes of the men down in the settlement.

She scurried along the shelf to where the mountain tiered down to the valley floor with what looked like hand-carved terraces. Once used for farming, no doubt. For her, they served as stairs and a quick path — but also an exposed one.

Squatting at the base amid a tangle of brambles and boulders, she peered over a large boulder toward the far right where a fire roared. Men laughed and talked. If she was caught, they'd kill her. After a brutal gang rape, no doubt.

She squelched the thoughts. No use going there except to remind herself to be quick and careful. No mistakes. In and out. Back to the campsite —

Stupid, stupid, stupid. If someone figured out she was missing . . .

Half-bent, Darci sprinted the fifty feet across the open and scrambled up behind the building. Back pressed against the wall, she felt it shift.

Rocks and dirt rained down on her. Dust plumed around her face.

She blinked and choked back a cough. Cautious, she peered around the corner. Laughing continued. So did she. On her feet, she crouch-ran along the wall to the far side where she'd seen through to the other side. Enough would be missing to allow her to gain entry without being noticed. True to her expectations, she found the hole. Glanced over the twelve-inch ledge — and bingo! The debris spread over the ground. Inside.

So, what was going on? Why were the men outside when they could patch this place up and take shelter for the winter and from the coming blizzard?

Darci slunk through the darkness, blinking against a gust of wind that nearly knocked the breath from her chest. Inside the home, she confirmed her suspicions. Empty. Abandoned. She moved to the wall and peered around the cloth that still hung in the window.

A dozen men now gathered around the fire.

Where are the women?

The realization hit her in the gut. No women. This wasn't a Taliban *settlement*. Her gaze pinged over the men. Laughter barreled up from one side. Two men roughed around, tangling with each other. A pagray tumbled free. The man who'd knocked it loose threw his head back and cackled, his laughter howling with the wind.

The man who'd lost his turban retrieved the length of material from the ground and straightened. Like a dance of demons, firelight flickered over his face, revealing his origins.

Darci sucked in a hard breath. *Him!*

ELEVEN

What were the Chinese doing hundreds of miles from their border and dressed like Taliban fighters? Darci jerked away from the window and pressed her spine against the cement-block wall. She slid down, her mind thundering with what she'd just seen. Panic swirled and whirled through her body, overloading it with adrenaline and heat. In particular, what was Tao doing here? And if he was here, then so was . . .

Oh man. Out now. *"He nearly killed you."* Ba's warning haunted her. She had to get out of here before they discovered her.

This was bad. No, no. This went beyond bad. This was Threat Level Red. DEFCON 1. Threat Level Critical. And any other "extreme" world system panic code.

Heart jammed into her throat, she pushed back against the cold cement and stared up through the hole-laden ceiling to the blanket of black. *Don't do anything stupid.*

Steadying her pulse was the first objective. If she couldn't get herself under control, she wouldn't be able to think. To devise a strategy and get out of here alive.

If they found her —

No. She *would* get out of here. Get back up that mountain without being seen. Get the team back to Bagram where there were lots of guns and battalions of men trained to fight.

No go. Chopper wouldn't extract till morning.

Yet . . . she felt her pulse slowing, calming. If she could sneak back into the rugged terrain without these men seeing her, then she could hoof it back to camp, night would pass, and the chopper would come. No one would be the wiser, but Burnett would have his information. The team would be safe. She would be safe.

The last time she believed that, she'd almost died.

So did he.

This can't be happening!

Chinese in Afghanistan — hiding and far away from the mines they were authorized to work. It didn't make sense. What were they doing here?

Darci slowly rose to her feet, lifted the NVGs to her face to construct more data, knowing full well she'd have to give a complete report. Were all the men Chinese? Or just some?

She slid aside the panic and adrenaline and replaced it with the uncanny ability that had gotten her recruited into military intelligence: her ability to divide her fear from her reason and carry out the mission all the same. Some might call her coldhearted, or a colorful metaphor. To her, it was just intuition. Instinct. A gift for survival.

Yes, Chinese. All fifteen. They had weapons. But they also had crates in their tents — nicely fitted tents with rugs and pallets, cooking stoves. But nothing else. Like vehicles. How had they gotten here? Which route delivered them to this Afghan province? How had they not been seen and reported?

The clothes. They dressed like Taliban.

Move it or lose it, Darci. Using every ounce of training, she shifted toward the hole she'd climbed through minutes ago. Sound took on a deafening level, as if each step shouted her presence. Halfway across, she lifted her booted foot over a crate and set it down. Then her other foot. Relaxed. Focused. Stealthy.

Rolled rugs cluttered the dirt floor. She used one to step around the others. A strange noise hissed from the carpet. She leapt aside, staring at the dark bundle. A sickening feeling tightened her stomach.

No, no time to sort it out. Just get back to the hills.

Toeing her way to the entrance, gaze locked on the sliver of space that afforded her a view of the Chinese encampment, she kept moving. Wind ripped the thin material covering the window and jerked it back.

Darci froze, afraid the men might see her dark form shift in the night.

But with the wind came a scurrying sound. She stilled and let her eyes rove the interior. Something . . . something wasn't right.

The rug she'd just stepped on, the hissing one — okay, that made her sound like a loon — it had shifted. That's not how it had been a second ago.

Another sound. This time it almost seemed like a whimper. An old stove huddled against the far wall. A shelf dangled on the wall, a pile of pottery shards on the floor. Rugs. A low-slung bed frame without a mattress. A blanket draped over it. Whites of eyes peeking back at her.

Darci shoved herself back. Gasped.

The whimper rose.

Her gaze shot to the window. The laughter

and insanity continued — stupid men thought they were impervious and invincible — so no one was the wiser to her presence. It was just her and whoever lay beneath the bed, which . . . too small a space to conceal an adult. That pushed her toward the frame.

Slowly . . . she stalked closer, her hand going to the small of her back. Darci went to a knee. Craned her neck to the side and peered under.

Tears slid from wide dark eyes, dusted by bangs and jet black hair. A small child peered back. Hand in her mouth, the girl seemed to be stifling her cries. Face screwed tight, she drew back.

"Hello," Darci whispered in perfect Pashto. "Where is your daddy?"

With slobber-coated fingers, the girl pointed to the middle of the dwelling. Darci didn't have to look to know the girl was pointing to the pile of rolled-up carpets. The very ones Darci had stepped on.

"Your mother, is she . . . here?"

The girl shook her head, freeing more tears. Dead, too, it seemed. How on earth had this little girl managed to hide? And from the Chinese men who'd slaughtered her people, who just happened to be in the wrong place — their own home!

Double snap. This complicated things. She

couldn't leave the child. But taking her into the mountains could get them both killed. Something about this little girl reminded her of the mission Darci almost didn't survive. She'd expected to be abandoned, she'd been so near death. But she fought to stay alive. Fought to find a way out. And she did.

Just like this little angel. She'd stayed alive against impossible odds. No way would Darci abandon her now. *Time's short.* "We must leave. Before the men see us."

Another frantic shake of her head.

"They are bad, yes?" she continued in the tongue of the little girl, who readily agreed. "I have friends in the mountains who can help us. We will go to the Americans."

A sniffle.

Darci held out her hand. "Please? Before they see us."

The little one reached up and pushed back the blanket. She stood. Even in the darkness, Darci could see the blood that coated the girl's clothes, making her ache. Had she witnessed her parents' murders, hidden here? The girl couldn't be more than three or four. Darci lifted the girl, who kicked free of the blanket that tangled around her feet. Her foot hit the frame.

Thud!

"Augh!"

She clamped a hand over the girl's mouth. "Shh."

"Check it out," came the terse command, followed by thumping of booted feet.

Darci pinched her lips and hurried to the opening she'd come through. Adrenaline jolted through her veins, heating her. The child was heavy, which made Darci's steps louder. But if the girl walked on her own, she'd slow them down. Darci scrambled to the safety of the low-lying wall. They were doomed.

God . . .

Why she'd even gone there, she didn't know. God hadn't helped her mom. Why would He help her? She believed in Him. She did. She just wasn't sure —

Just move!

Holding the girl tight against her chest, she peered over the wall to the men clambering into the building. Rowdy and sloppy, they pushed and taunted each other, clearly not taking the noise as a serious threat.

Good. Eyes on the mountain, Darci plotted her path. Once she got far enough away, she'd unzip her jacket and tuck the slight frame of the child into its warmth. Wind tugged at her as she darted to what looked like an abandoned well. Crouched, she checked the men.

Still oblivious.

"Just a little farther," she said to the girl, then scurried out into the open, aiming for a cluster of shrubs and brambles that lined a dry creek bed. Halfway there and still safe. Her panic began to subside. At least, the edge of that panic. She knew better than to let her guard down until she was at base.

Squatting, she set down the child and unzipped her jacket. She motioned the girl back into her arms, then instructed her to wrap her legs around Darci's waist. Once in position, she tugged the jacket, tugging hard to make it zip.

"Okay," she whispered. "Hold very tight. Do not let go."

The moon reflected off the obsidian orbs peeking from below dark bangs. The tiny arms tightened around her. "Tighter." The girl complied, but it still wasn't nearly as much as Darci preferred.

When an explosion of laughter ripped through the valley, Darci seized the chance. She shoved up and launched toward the mountain. She plunged onward, feeling as if she had a fifty-pound rucksack strapped to her front. The ground before her rose enough to make the run harder. Her breath came in snatches.

With one arm she braced the girl's bottom and pumped for speed with the other arm.

A shout rang out.

Crack!

Dirt burst up at her, peppering her face. Rifle fire!

TWELVE

Camp Eggers, Kabul, Afghanistan

Amazing. It hadn't changed in the two years since he'd left. Barren, flat, tan — it's the reason the country was named Afghanis*tan*. But then again, when he glanced down the heavily fortified and fenced road to the gorgeous Hindu Kush — formidable, daunting, stunning — nothing was barren about this place.

A gust of wind stirred up a sand demon that prowled the monochromatic scene dotted with splotches of green from occasional shrubs. Small trees reached toward the heavens with bent, gnarly hands, as if begging for water. Fear and awe wove a wicked tapestry through him as the quiet terrain erupted with ghoulish memories. Bombs. IEDs. The *tat-a-tat-tat* of M4s.

Heath jogged down the steps to the temporary bunk, Trinity's lead in one hand and his duffel in the other. His performance last night came in a distant second, considering the attack. Between the adrenaline, the performance, and predawn rise this morning, exhaustion weighted his limbs. He was out of shape. Plain and simple.

A furry head nudged beneath his hand. Without taking his eyes off the phantom plain beneath the sun's unrelenting oppression, Heath rubbed Trinity's ears. Could she sense it, too? The ominous feeling he'd felt thick and rancid after that attack? Was she remembering that horrific day that left her with a small scar and him with one bigger?

A Humvee squawked to a stop just feet in front of Heath, pulling Trinity into work mode. "Easy, girl."

Two men piled out of the vehicle. One strode toward him.

Heath held up a hand. "Approach slowly. She might not be government issue now, but she's still got razor-sharp instincts and teeth."

The specialist smiled beneath his helmet and sweat, compliments of the mountain of clothing, vests, and gear. "Daniels?"

Sack slung over his shoulder, Heath extended his hand.

"Specialist Randy Farley. I'm your tour guide back to Bagram."

Specialist. The specialist who'd driven the MRAP was dead. Would this one end up that way, too? What about Jia? Where was she? Was she safe, out of reach of the Taliban or other extremists? Man, that near-kiss . . . was something . . . like near-stupidity.

Shake it off.

"First stop — the training field."

"No rest for the weary." Heath glanced back at Hogan who trudged down the steps of the portable building they'd crashed in last night. She wore a frown the size of "who authorized you to disturb my beauty sleep?"

Stuffing a hat over her standard ponytail, she grunted. "Couldn't we do this tour after lunch, or even better — never?"

"If you want to sleep, you should've stayed home." That she'd manhandled her way into coming still bugged him. That she thought he needed babysitting downright angered him.

He had, after all, handled himself fine with that terrorist who had the rocket launcher.

Farley shot Hogan a nervous look. His face turned red.

Figures. Hogan had attitude that rivaled Cruella de Vil but the looks that went with any homecoming queen. Soldiers would fall all over themselves to talk to her. And Aspen, though reserved, with her white-blond hair and blue eyes, might be mistaken for a new Marilyn Monroe, minus the sex-symbol status. He just couldn't see Courtland prancing around in a gown, blowing kisses to the camera. Boxing a camera? Definitely.

Heath cleared his throat. That was way more imagery than he needed about Courtland. Or any female. *Except maybe Jia.*

Augh. He needed someone to smack him upside the head to dislodge the thoughts of the mysterious woman.

"Ready?" Farley climbed into the Humvee, and Heath claimed the seat behind him. "There's a few teams training nearby." He looked at Hogan. "Thought y'all might like to check them out."

"Who's training?" Zipping his jacket against the cold winds, Jibril asked from the front seat.

"We've got a regular menagerie training." Randy glanced back. "There are a half-dozen dogs out there." He grinned at Trinity, who sat on the seat beside Heath. "Oh, and SOCOM sent some guys in here late last night, so I think you might see them. But they don't talk to us grunts. They keep to their own."

I used to be part of that "own."

Jibril turned to Heath, his green eyes bor-

176

ing into him. Heath didn't want to talk about it. He shoved his attention out the window and stroked Trinity's fur. SOCOM. Special Operations Command. The source of his discharge. Trinity's classification as "excess."

They headed off base, and the ride was pretty typical as they passed embassies and schools, homes, shops, and just about everything else, making their way out of the city. Soon the Humvee lumbered over a rise, then the front end dipped and provided a perfect view of the valley below. More of the same, flat terrain for another half hour before they reached Forward Operating Base Robertson, where they'd separated from General Burnett two nights ago.

Heath sighed as they were unloaded at a gate where MPs waited. Two dogs made their circuit around the vehicle, then the MPs waved the vehicle past the checkpoint. Inside, they drove a short distance and exited the established perimeter of the FOB into a cordoned-off area with a dual-rutted path before coming to a stop at a small camo canopy.

Heath climbed out with Trinity and surveyed the land. Familiar, yet not. The same, yet different. Natural and unnatural. Watching the men in training maneuvers, the experience not a part of his life for the last eighteen months. All the same, he could remember it, taste it like the dust in the air.

On her lead, Trinity tugged against the restraint. She wanted to play. Catch the bad guys. So did he. They had a little of the action yesterday, and she seemed still a part of that game. To have purpose and meaning. To matter. At least Trinity did.

What hurt more, bothered him worse, was that he recognized the men leading the training exercise. Watters. He'd seen the fierce warrior heading out at Bagram. What were the chances he'd end up here, too? Watterboy shouted orders to the soldiers. The Green Beret had loved his moniker, despite it sounding trite and demeaning.

"Nah," Watterboy had said. "It's a role of support, encouragement, refreshment. Can't have a better mantra."

The guy always did have a unique way of seeing things. Like the way he saw the man jogging at his side — James VanAllen, aka Candyman. A guy with a long line of military ancestors, including some elusive connection to a Revolutionary War general named "Mad" Anthony Wayne. Candyman insisted Mad Anthony was misunderstood — he wasn't crazy in the head. He was crazy in the heart — for his country.

"Just like me," Candyman had said, grinning within his wiry brown beard and olive skin.

That's the reason he donated all the candy and goodies from his care packages to hand out to the Afghan children while on patrol. One candy bar went a mile in public relations. To Candyman, he was buying the hearts of the children one chocolate at a time. Behind those Oakleys rested piercing eyes that had melted far too many feminine hearts.

A greedy, icy wind swirled around them, winter clinging on for one last hurrah. Hands slick, Heath stood at the edge of the training field marked with rocks and sand-filled barrels. Anything to demarcate the perimeter. Other handlers worked with their furry partners, clearing buildings, detecting explosive materials, and taking down one heavily padded "bad guy."

Man. It'd been . . . forever since he'd hung out with these guys. It'd also been all too near since they stood over him at the hospital after the ambush. Beside him, he could feel the questioning, waiting gazes of Jibril, Aspen, and Hogan. Let them wait. He wasn't going out there till the acid in his stomach turned from a puddle of anxiety to a solid mass of courage.

Then again, at this rate, that'd be the day after never.

Trinity nosed his hand.

"Yeah, yeah. I know." He rubbed her ears. "Don't get pushy." But his girl always knew best. The scars on his hand reminded him to listen to her.

Bolstered by her anxiousness to get to work, he stalked onto the field. Steps crunched behind him, assuring him that the other A Breed Apart team members had his back. He was grateful they hadn't pressed him, urged him onward. Especially Hogan. Her emotional magazine was loaded with aggression and very little patience to temper that fight-now instinct.

As the four of them crossed the field with Trinity trotting ahead, sniffing, and tail wagging, Heath noted Watterboy hesitate as he spotted them.

With a laugh that carried the fifty feet, Watterboy clapped his hands. "Knew they couldn't keep you away for long, Ghost." When they met, Watters gave him a one-armed hug, back-pat greeting. "Sorry I couldn't stop and talk at Bagram."

Heath shook his head. "Man's got work to do."

A half-dozen feet away, attention focused on the grunts, Candyman spun. "Ghost?"

He locked gazes with him. "Speak of the devil . . ." Two long strides carried him close enough for a strong-armed hug.

Heath's chest squeezed at the welcome. "How's it going?"

The two men lowered their hands for Trinity's assessment. Her nose twitched, then she turned and scoped out the action on the field.

Both men eyed the others with Heath. "Who's your posse?" Candyman asked.

"Oh, sorry." He'd so expected a scowl-faced greeting, their acceptance rattled his cage. Heath turned to A Breed Apart's owner. "This is Jibril Khouri —"

"Yeah, sure." Watterboy shook Jibril's hand. "I remember working an op with you three years back. Helmand Province?"

"Kandahar." Jibril smiled. "I'm surprised you remember."

"Never forget a face." Watters held out his hand to Aspen. "Dean Watters."

"Aspen Courtland, and this is Timbrel Hogan." She freed her hand and motioned to Hogan. Was the heat getting to Courtland, or was she blushing?

"A pleasure, ma'am." Watterboy smiled down at her.

"What's the holdup?" Someone shouted as they drew closer.

181

Trinity lunged into a protective position, snarling.

"Trinity, out." Heath eyed the black-haired guy who wore the same patch Watterboy and Candyman sported.

Watterboy gripped the man's shoulder. "Rocket, meet one of our own — Heath Daniels."

"One of our own?" The guy appraised him, distrust stiffening his posture.

Candyman elbowed him. "Dude — it's Heath Daniels. You know, *Ghost*."

Rocket's eyes widened. "Seriously?"

Grinning, Candyman nodded. "We talk about you and that mission all the time."

"Mission?"

"The one that 'bout took us all out."

Rocket offered a hand. "Nice to meet you, sir."

Warmth not related to the sun soaked Heath. Hearing their approval, knowing they'd talked about him to newbs and that they still called him one of their own . . .

Man it was good to be back.

"So, what brings you to this godforsaken desert?" Candyman asked.

Truth or dare. He knew this time was coming, so on the plane over, he'd practiced the most casual answer he could muster. "Brass thought you grunts could use a motivational speech."

Rocket shouldered between Heath and Candyman, who held out a hand to Hogan. "Thanks for coming all this way to inspire us, Miss . . ."

Hogan's expression remained impassive. She gave no response.

Rocket slapped Candyman. "Knuckle-head. Ghost's the speaker."

"I know."

A frown tugged at Hogan's lips. "Then why'd you thank me?"

"A face like yours would inspire any man to get home alive."

Watterboy groaned. "Down boy. Back to the fight." He shoved Candyman toward the training field and chuckled. "You'll have to pardon him. He's wiry —"

Hogan crossed her arms. "More like needs his mouth wired shut."

Another shout from the field drew Candyman round. He jogged a few steps then spun, walking backward. "How long you here for?"

"A week."

Candyman nodded. "I'll try to catch you later."

"Sounds good." Heath watched, envious, and remembered the day when he'd been in charge of training, in the thick of combat-training maneuvers. He missed it. Missed being part of something bigger than himself. Missed being strong. A hero. The highs.

What he didn't miss were the lows. Hard to miss something you experienced every day. And the emptiness that gripped his throat right now at *not* being a part of that team. Of not being one of the guys running down there and barking orders.

"Want to look around?"

Heath grinned. "It'd be nice, but I won't beg."

"Never would," Watters said with a laugh. "C'mon. I'll take you around."

Parwan Province, Afghanistan
Fire lit through Darci's shoulder.

A guttural sound escaped her lips as she stumbled forward. Her fingers scraped the ground, but she pushed on. The little one clinging to her cried out.

"Shh, shh." Darci ignored the wet warmth sliding down her arm and raced into the anonymity of the mountain. Over one crest —

Rock blasted her face.

She ducked and hurried around a boulder, zigzagged upward. Slipping into a narrow crevice, she used it as a shield to protect them from more shots. But it also forced her to walk sideways, shuffling — slower. If it would just give them a barrier to get high enough that they could lose anyone following . . .

Maybe the Chinese would think she was a settlement survivor, that she wasn't worth pursuing.

Yeah, keep telling yourself that.

In the darkness, she scrambled onward. Slipped. Her foot dropped. Her weight shoved it into a gouged area — stuck! She grunted and jerked her leg, trying to free it.

Shouts below grew louder. Nearer.

"Hurry," the little one said with a sniffle.

Rock cut into her palms as Darci jerked and yanked to free her foot. Still no good. She pulled hard — flopped backward.

Out into the open.

Thwat! Thunk!

Shattered rock pelted her cheek, stinging. Darci rolled, arching her back as she went over the little one strapped inside her jacket, and pushed to her feet. She found a trail and used it to gain distance and speed. Couldn't stay on it much longer or she'd lead them to the camp. Her legs grew leaden. She stumbled but did not stop. Stopping would get them killed.

And to think — she'd thought getting out of the valley would be the hard part. Finding a safe passage with a three- or four-year-old child up through the mountain . . .

Remind me to never do this again. Heath would probably take care of that for her. The thought pried a smile out of her weary soul. Not at him calling her on it, but just . . . him.

Clattering through the darkness, she pressed on. Ten minutes later, she moved off the hard-packed path and climbed upward, over rocky ledges, and around bushes. Anything to conceal their movement and direction.

After heading north for several minutes, she eyed a ledge about four feet straight up. She'd never be able to get up there with the child. But maybe . . . With their options down to zero, Darci had to try. Kneeling to the side, she unzipped the jacket — and froze. Where was the phone?

Frantic, she scanned the area. No sight of it. Shouts and the bobbing light beam told her she didn't have time to search for it. But without the phone, how would she get out of here, warn Burnett? Save the team?

The girl's whimper pulled her sanity back together. The girl tensed, her muscles constricting around Darci.

"What is your name?" Darci asked in Pashto and a soft whisper as she helped her climb out of the warmth and onto the ground.

"Badria." Moonlight reflected off the girl's large, dark eyes. She shifted back and glanced down at her clothes. Dark spots splattered her tunic.

Darci peeled back the shoulder of her jacket and inspected her wound. "See? Not bad. Just a small scratch." Though to this little one, it probably looked like more. But now was not the time to distress her. "Badria, you've been so brave. We must climb up there. I'll help you. Ready?"

The girl shook her head.

"I know you're scared, but it's okay. I am, too." Only as the words left her lips did she realize how very true they were. A deep, heavy fear had settled over her since . . . well, since when? Since starting this mission? No. It was more recent.

She huffed a smile. Since leaving Heath.

Get over it. He's not here. There's little chance you'll see him again. It'd been why she was willing to have lunch with him. Play the game. Though, with the way he seemed to anticipate her, she half expected to see him around the next corner. Okay, not literally, but . . .

Darci lifted the girl, cringing as fire raced down her shoulder. That might be a graze but it hurt like crazy. Tightening against the slice of pain that accompanied the movement, she hoisted the girl onto the ledge. "Climb up and lie flat."

Surprise snaked through Darci when the girl did as requested. This wasn't the first time she had to hide, and that rankled Darci. No child should have to live like that.

Grateful for her love of rock climbing and the numerous adventure trips that gave her experience, Darci bent and rubbed her hands in the dirt. Not as good as chalk, but it would help. Then she wedged her toe into a gouged area and pulled up.

Pain sluiced through her again. *Gut it up and get moving.* She pushed herself up, caught hold, and dragged her legs over the ledge before rolling onto her back. With a breath of relief, she gazed at the stars. Wind tugged at her, whistling over them. They had to make it back. She had to tell Burnett about these men. Something was going on down there, and it couldn't be good if they were masquerading as Taliban.

Her gaze traced the edifice that rose another twenty feet. Only as she lay there did the tree dangling over the ledge register. It was less than fifteen minutes from the camp. But getting up there . . . climbing that height with the child and an injury . . .

Shouts came from her right. She peeked out and down toward the voices. Shadows flickered in and out of the moonlight. Beams of light danced up and over, some bobbing in a strange dance against the face of the mountain as the men hurried. Snap. Had the entire camp come after her?

Okay, choices just vanished.

They *had* to go up. If she tried to take the route she'd come, the Chinese would be on her in minutes. She had to buy time by scaling the cliff. It'd be okay. As long as Badria could hold on tight. And Darci's injury wasn't deep and poisoning her or bleeding her out.

A strobe of light struck overhead.

Darci flashed a hand to Badria. "Don't move." She turned her head toward the cliff face as the light dropped on them. Her breath kicked into the back of her throat as the beam slid over her body. At least she'd had enough sense to wear a black jacket and jeans — it'd help her blend into the shadows.

Keep moving, keep moving, she mentally urged the men.

The beam traced the rock, slipped down the path, and vanished into a tangle of trees and shrubs.

Once sure the men weren't searching this

location anymore, Darci pushed onto her knees. She removed her jacket and guided Badria onto her back. She slid the jacket back on and zipped it. "Okay, I need you to be brave and strong." She patted the girl's hands knotted around her neck. "Hold on tight — and don't look."

Darci tucked dirt into her pockets, then reached for the first hold. Keeping her movements slow and meticulous, she began their ascent. With each rise, Badria's arms tightened around Darci's shoulders and squeezed. Sweat broke out over Darci's brow. The rubbing against the wound made it raw, burn. She blinked past the pain, determination hardening her resolve to make it.

In a secure toehold, she freed one hand and dug in her pocket for dirt. They were within three feet of the upper ledge when the voices once again returned. Not right under them, but she and Badria would soon be discovered if Darci didn't hurry. As she tried to secure another foothold, she wished for the professional climbing shoes. Not the heavy boots she'd donned to withstand the bitter Afghan mountain nights.

Her foot slipped. Scraped along the rock. The slip jarred her shoulder.

Badria cried out and wrenched her legs.

At the stab of pain, Darci bit down to stop from crying out, too. Arms placed to the side as if she were a giant spider, she hung her head and let her brow rest against the rock as she regained her composure, shoved aside the burning.

Shouts below.

Her eyes snapped open. Straight down, she saw men.

They'd been discovered.

Tempted to hurry, she knew they couldn't. One wrong toe placement . . .

Then again, if the Chinese started shooting again, toes wouldn't matter.

Darci rammed her foot into a hold. Used all her remaining strength and threw herself toward the upper ledge. She caught . . . then slipped.

Rocks dribbled down.

"No," she ground out as she scrambled. Her fingers clawed dirt.

Rocks.

Sliding debris.

Gravity snatched them.

THIRTEEN

2 Klicks outside FOB Robertson

Cold poured into their Humvee without mercy. Dull and aggravating, a throb annoyed Heath as they trounced over the hard-packed roads through the training area. He should've eaten a good meal before heading out. If the headache continued to increase, he —

No. He wouldn't go there or let that happen. He freed his CamelBak straw, clamped down on the bite valve, and inhaled. The water felt good, but the throb didn't ease. Probably because the pounding wasn't from water deprivation. But from stress. From the TBI. He had to make it. Couldn't go south now with his health.

A wet nose nudged his cheek. Then a wet tongue.

"You want some, girl?" Heath aimed the valve at Trinity and squeezed. Water squirted her nose. She jerked back but then lapped

192

the liquid, half of it splashing on him at first. He chuckled as she settled next to him and seemed ready for a nap.

Heath swiped his arm over his face and mouth as he squinted out the windshield at the maneuvers. He'd seen a sniper take out a target without being spotted. He'd seen a Ranger battalion on the range, and he'd seen tanks and MRAPs practicing.

"Where are the dogs?"

"Come again?" Watters steered around an incline, then ramped up another.

"Specialist Farley said there were some working dogs out here."

"Oh. Yeah, yeah." Watterboy adjusted his weapon strap. "Command ordered them down to Helmand. Got some HPTs coming in, so they sent the dogs."

Heath nodded, remembering the mission that had been his last. "My last gig was for HPTs, remember? They're expensive."

Watters nodded. "No kidding. Cost a lot in equipment, training — and if things go bad, body count."

Heath held up his hand. "It goes bad."

"It was a close call. At least you'll never forget — and neither will I."

As he lowered his arm, Trinity nudged his hand up and licked it, pulling a laugh from him. Heath didn't need to see behind the

Oakley sunglasses to know Watters's hazel eyes studied him. He nodded to Trinity. "Think she remembers that mission?"

"I guarantee it, but she doesn't spook easily." *Wish I could say the same for me.*

The thought of a spooked dog pushed his gaze back to Aspen. Just as he turned, her curls bounced as she turned her head away. Maybe now would be a good time for a topic change. "So, you guys seeing a lot of Taliban up here?"

"You know how it was a hot spot here for a while, so we were ordered into the mountains. Then things quieted down and we were sent south." Watters shrugged as he pulled up along another Humvee. "Now the bad guys are back." A broad white smile stood in stark contrast to Watterboy's very tanned face and dark beard. "So are we."

Stepping out into the cold seemed to invite the Afghan desert to drum on his skull. Heath winced as he strapped his helmet back on. The thing felt like a ton of bricks. A little more water and he'd be okay. All he had to do was stay in the shade as much as possible. Hydrate. Avoid stress.

Right.

They rounded a bend, stepping down a narrow gorge that emptied into an open valley guarded on all sides by limestone. The shape of the terrain reminded him of an upright tunnel.

Squinting, he peered up at the unrelenting sun layering its way into the gorge. Shade. "Right." After one more sip of water and a squirt for Trin, he kneaded the back of his neck.

"You okay, Prince Charming?"

He eyed Hogan and knew she was waiting for him to fail. To prove her right. To be weak. "Peachy."

She gave a cockeyed grin and stepped past him. "Be glad Beowulf's not here. He can smell a liar."

Heath hesitated.

Hogan laughed.

And the sound plucked on the frayed ends of his nerves, pushing a scowl into his face. The knotted muscles added to the thunder rumbling through his thick skull.

Jibril touched his shoulder. "Easy. She just likes getting you worked up."

"She's good at it."

"My sister has the same talent with me." Jibril smiled, his beard fitting in with the dozen Spec Ops soldiers they trailed into a makeshift shelter.

Three MRAPs sat in the northern quadrant with a tarp stretched over them, providing the only source of shade. The immediate relief to his throbbing head almost made him wilt in gratitude. Huddled around their leader, the men talked as if lives depended on their chatter.

Heath could sense a shift in the force. Scowls. Tensed shoulders. Hands fisted. Lips set in determined lines.

"Hold up," Watters said. "Looks like something's happening. Stay here."

Suspicions confirmed, Heath lowered himself onto the bumper of one of the MRAPs and rubbed Trinity's head. She whimpered, scooting forward every few seconds. She could sense it, too. Huh. Maybe his subconscious had picked up on her antsy behavior, and that's what alerted him, since dogs had heightened senses. No doubt by the scent of fear. Maybe even aggression.

It was in the air, too. As if the spirits that roamed this country were . . . Were what? Alive? Of course they were. The Bible spoke about the spirit of a place. So why did it surprise him? "Because it's almost tangible."

"What?" Aspen looked at him.

"Nothing." He tightened his hold on Trinity's lead.

"What do you see?" Jibril lowered himself to the bumper.

"They're planning. Something on the

196

spot, need to move fast. Probably got wind of suspicious activity nearby." Otherwise, they'd be packing up and rumbling back to base camp. "Not too urgent, or they'd be yelling back and forth with SOCOM."

Watterboy and Candyman approached.

Heath stood and Trinity with him. "What's up?"

"Command got word of a potential drug lord's location about ten klicks east. We're going to check it out." Watters squinted as he looked at them, then to the ladies. "You're cleared to go along, but you stick like glue to us."

"Let's move," Hogan said.

Heath glanced at the girl, who didn't seem to understand what a threat was, that they could go into this village . . . and never come out alive. Wait a minute, wasn't this what he'd wanted three weeks ago? To get back in the action, prove he still had what it took?

Parwan Province, Afghanistan

He'd never taken kindly to traitors. Staring down the face of the cliff where Jia struggled to maintain her grip, he toyed with letting her drop.

But Peter Toque needed her. Needed to know what her mission was here. Because one thing was certain — she was a part of the geological survey team, in name only.

A yelp yanked his better judgment to the front. He hooked an arm around a tree that shot up out of the rocky terrain and swung down, catching her arm.

The sudden shift in her weight jerked them down. Wide, almond-shaped eyes came to his, the moonlight glowing off the whites. The tree cracked. Popped. Gravel dug into his belly as he strained against her weight.

She slapped her hand up and coiled her fingers around Peter's forearm. "Don't let go."

Don't tempt me. He gritted his teeth, dug his heels in, pulling himself into a hunch, then hauled her up. Shouts and clamoring voices drew closer.

She twisted and flopped onto her back, rolling away from the ledge, and thudded against a rock. A grunt hissed out.

He half expected her to lie there, but in a lightning-fast move, she hopped to her feet and sprinted away.

Peter cursed his hesitation and darted after her. He'd — once again — underestimated the Asian woman. Since they'd met in the warehouse and she'd shown more awareness of the geopolitical nature of the area than the geological makeup, he'd watched her. Back at Bagram, she'd been pulled into a meeting with a general after saying she'd filled out paperwork wrong. She returned an hour later, and all paperwork questions vanished. Good thing he didn't believe her geology student status.

Rock and dirt exploded, peppering his cheek. A piece flicked against his brow. He cursed and ducked, wanting to stay intact, and propelled himself around the next corner. Pumping his arms faster, he vowed to get the truth out of Jia — if they survived tonight.

He broke through a small cluster of trees — and rammed straight into Jia, shoving her forward. She yelped. Why wasn't she moving faster? "Move! Go! They're right behind us." Peter pushed her.

She stumbled, recovered, then ran again. But her legs seemed tangled in vines. After a few missteps, she regained her footing, and they hurried farther and farther from the gunshots.

They tumbled into the camp almost on top of each other.

Jaekus leapt from his canvas chair by a fire. "Whoa!"

Jia dropped to her knees with heaving breaths.

"We've got trouble. Get everyone up." Peter spun to Jia. "What have you done? Where did you go?"

Eyes hooded in pain, she barely acknowledged him as she fumbled with her zipper.

Only then did he notice another set of eyes peeking at him. A child — in her jacket! "Who is that?"

The little girl wiggled out of Jia's coat, dark spots sprinkled against her clothes.

"She's bleeding!"

"No," Jia said with a gulp. "She's okay." After another labored breath, Jia looked to the right and slumped back onto her legs.

Alice came from the tent. "What's happening?"

Jia nudged the little girl toward the only other female in the camp. "Alice, get her clean clothes and some food. She's been alone for a while."

The nymphlike girl rushed into action, ferrying the child into a tent just as the professor emerged from his quarters, firelight accenting the bags under his eyes and the askew salt-and-pepper hair.

Even as the others fretted over the little one, Peter knew something was wrong with Jia. She'd been a pillar of strength and defiance since their first meeting at the university. When she tried to stand just now and tripped, his suspicions were confirmed.

"It's you. That was your blood on her."

Not responding or even acknowledging him, Jia pressed a hand to her shoulder, pushed onto her feet. "Everyone pack up. We've got a truckload of trouble about to hit us." She trudged toward the tent she shared with Alice, her boots dragging heavily on the dirt. As she reached the opening, Jia paused and looked back.

Jaekus and the prof stood around, dazed.

"Move, people! They're coming to kill us, not have tea." Despite the vehemence in her words, the strain couldn't be missed. "Move! Now!" She wavered.

Peter stepped into her path as she eased into the darkened interior.

"Get off me. Pack up."

"Screw the stuff. You're hurt. Let me see it." He pointed to her cot.

She shoved him back. "Get out! Don't you get it — ?"

"Yeah, I get it. You're Lara Croft's sister and don't like her showing you up. But if that" — he pointed to her shoulder — "kills you, nobody will have to worry who's stronger."

"Nobody should be worrying — period!" She reached under the bed and grabbed her pack. When she swung it onto the cot, she jerked and held her arm. She recovered, then dug in the pack. Sweat beaded on her pale face.

Her stupidity would get everyone killed.

Not if I can help it.

Peter snatched the Glock holstered at his back.

FOURTEEN

Gun in hand, Darci spun. Staring down the barrel of a Glock, she hauled in a breath. Her gaze jumped to the owner. "Toque." His name came out like a breath. A disbelieving breath. "What are you doing with a firearm?"

He knocked his against hers. "I could ask the same." A smirk. "Thought I had you pegged right." He cocked his head and nodded toward her HK 9mm, then his weapon. "Same time?"

Yield? Was he crazy? "I'm eating your barrel and you want me to stand down?"

"Together."

"Who are you?"

"Weapon first." He motioned toward her cot with his free hand. "On the bed."

Clenching her jaw, Darci considered the showdown. She should've been alerted to him. In a way she had, with the way he stood out, annoyed her, trailed her. But she hadn't clued in, and that was a deadly mistake. When had she last made such a grievous error?

Who was he? He couldn't have known her mission, so what put him on her team in the middle of Afghanistan? This couldn't be a coincidence.

"You said we had to hurry," he said in a calm, smooth voice.

Darci flicked her wrist so the firearm pointed toward the ceiling of the tent. Eyes locked on Toque, she backstepped away from him and bent as he did the same. She set the weapon down and backed up. Mentally combing her belongings. Where had she put the Gerber?

Toque set his Glock down and straightened. Hands on his belt, he flashed that cocky smile. "So, what part of the alphabet soup are you?"

"If you had any brains, you wouldn't ask."

"Let's just say I'm short on those at the moment."

His arrogance kneaded her frustration. Cold wind flapped against the tent opening and swirled around her hands and face. "We can play Scrabble with our letters, or we can get everyone packed up and out of here — alive."

"Who's coming? You never said."

"Does it matter? The brand doesn't matter when it's a bullet through the skull." Truth or Dare. If she told him it was the Chinese, he'd never believe it. She sure wouldn't have if she hadn't seen their distinctive faces with her own eyes.

"Matters a lot to me."

"Then you can die alone." Darci dug into her pack. She'd learned long ago how to get by on little. And survive on less. She glanced at him as she tugged out the blast-proof box. Spinning it to the right combo, she tried her best to ignore the man standing over her.

"You're spooked. So I'm going to guess it wasn't Taliban. What? Has someone with a vendetta found you at last?"

She popped the lid, removed the canister of oxygen, then pressed down twice in rapid succession. *Click!* Darci dug her fingernails into the hair-thin space between the platform and the interior hull and pried up. The false bottom gave way. She pulled out the tiny satellite phone.

"*Last resort, Kintz. A call from that phone should precede your death by seconds.*" The general's warning boomed through her mind as she powered it up.

Toque cursed.

Darci recognized the move that followed

his curse and dove for her weapon.

Dead weight dropped against her arm. Pain snapped a yelp from her.

"Who?" Toque growled, his face against hers.

"Idiot!"

"Who followed you?"

"I am not authorized to divulge that information."

"American?"

Darci met his hard expression, their noses an inch apart. She knew what he was asking — since she had slanted eyes and high cheekbones — was she loyal to the Asians or Americans? And she hated the operative before her for even questioning her loyalty.

"You're the spook," she ground out. "You tell me."

He didn't budge.

"What — what's going on?"

At the startled voice of Alice Ward, Toque stood. In the second it took him to stand, Darci flipped the blanket over their weapons, folded it up, and tucked the bundle in her pack. "Nothing. We're packing up. Toque was getting fresh."

Toque spun, his gaze skimming the bed, then nailing the backpack as she slung it over her shoulders and secured the straps around her waist. "Hey!"

"Out of time." She looked past him to Alice. "How's the girl?"

"Clean." She swallowed, still disconcerted and not buying the cover Darci had thrown over their standoff. "She's asking for you."

"What about the others?" Darci stepped around the cot.

"Jaekus is packed and waiting. The professor is muttering and not doing much of anything else."

"Alice, make him! Or he'll be dead within the hour." Darci rushed toward her. "Now!"

Mouth open, eyes wide, Alice took a step back. Nodded. Then another step backward. "Right." She spun and hurried into the morning that washed with the blue specter of dawn. Odd. She'd never thought of dawn in that way, but knowing daylight could reveal them if they had to hide . . .

Fire ripped through the back of her head. Her world tilted upward.

Toque had her hair in a fist. He hauled her against him. Something pinched her throat.

A knife!

Planting one hand on the handle and one on the blade, she forced herself not to fight him. To set him off balance and seize the chance. "You won't get anything out of me like this."

"It seems there's no way to get anything out of you. But I have a feeling you'll talk if I go after that girl."

"N—" She clamped down on the panic.

He chuckled. "Thought you might reconsider. Now cough it up."

The girl wasn't just a child she'd gone soft for. Badria could possibly identify who'd murdered her family. Yielding now insured Darci could get the girl back to Bagram, back to the general and the experts.

"Who's coming, Jia?"

"Release me."

"We tried it your way."

"You're going to get us killed."

"No, you wasting time is getting us killed."

Anger tightened her chest. "Fine." As soon as she said it, the pressure on her throat eased. She pushed the knife away and straightened, moving toward the tent-pole support. If she needed to, she'd use it somehow.

"I want my Glock and the information."

Thunder rumbled through the predawn hour.

Wait! That wasn't thunder.

"Chopper," Toque said. Three large strides carried him to the entrance.

Darci was at his side. She whipped open the flap.

"Good," the professor announced. "They're just on time."

"Who? Who's coming?" Darci hurried forward, fury coloring her vision red.

"I called the Army, told them we needed to —"

"Fool!" Toque shouted.

Darci gulped the adrenaline as she lifted Badria into her arms. "You've led them straight to us."

"Of course I did," the professor said with a chortle. "Wasn't that the idea?"

"Not them, the *enemy*!"

White hair rimmed wide eyes. "What enemy?"

Toque leaned toward Darci and placed a hand on Badria's black hair, severing the dance of firelight on her face. "Who is it, Jia?"

It wouldn't matter in a few minutes. "Chinese."

His eyes rounded. He spun toward the chopper.

As if in response, a stream of hellfire dotted the dark sky as if lighting the way for the missile streaking toward the helicopter that now hovered above their camp. But Darci knew — the dots were the missiles.

"Run!" The backwash of the rotors drowned her words.

Darci crushed the girl to herself and dove away from the chopper. Two routes presented themselves: through the main tents, down the path that led to the gorge where they'd collected water and showered. Or to the right, up the rigorous terrain and deeper into the unforgiving Hindu Kush.

High ground has the advantage.

She dove to the right. Sprinted between the base-camp tent and her own. A hand on her shoulder told her she wasn't alone. No time to look back. To consider who was with her. Who was against her. Pain niggled at her, reminding her of the graze. She reached for another crag.

Night turned to day. Brilliant white. For an instant.

Darci tensed.

Booom!

An invisible hand shoved her face-first into the rock. White-hot pain flashed through her skull. Then blacker than black, night devoured her whole.

FIFTEEN

10 Klicks outside FOB Robertson

The village felt haunted. Emptied, yet he knew it wasn't. Couldn't be if Command had sent them here. Heath peered through the slats of the MRAP as it lumbered around a row of buildings. Arabic script ran down the walls on either side of doors. Some sported both English lettering and Arabic. Closed doors. Closed windows. Closed hearts. Heath had seen it time and again in Taliban strongholds. The only thing some wanted from Americans was death — of said Americans. Every now and then that distinct feeling wafted on the wind and brought with it a warning.

This was one of those times. His words from the night before about God having their backs echoed in his mind. He sure hoped he hadn't lied.

"Looks like they knew we were coming," Candyman called to Watters.

"Yep." Watters shifted and glanced down.

Heath traced his line of sight. Pride swelled as he realized Watters was assessing Trinity for signs of concern or agitation. But his partner sat at his feet, snout resting on his knee. Until he put her into action on the ground, she wasn't interested. He ruffled her head and shrugged at Watters.

Watters banged the hull. "Let's get up close and personal."

The MRAP slowed to a stop.

Two sergeants at the back climbed out, one taking point on a knee, the other flanking him. "Clear."

Heath and Aspen waited as the rest of the detachment filed out. Waiting and acting like a spectator. As he bent and stepped from the steel coffin, he realigned his mind. Civilian or military, he was in a hostile situation. Not being ready mentally could get his head blown off.

Trinity tugged on her lead, straining. She looked at him, wagged her tail as if to say, "Ready to play?" then sat down and stared at her objective.

Heath glanced at Watters, who was giving his team orders. "She's got a hit."

"You aren't — aw heck, never mind." Watters motioned to Candyman to take a team and scout north. Watters would sweep south, and they'd meet up in the middle again. With four guys behind him, he nodded to Heath. "Lead on."

Heart pumping fast, Heath released Trinity. "Trinity, seek!"

With a small lunge, she barreled onward, nosing the ground. Her head turning right, then left as she continued. Exhilarated, Heath looked to his friends, only to see Hogan's narrowed gaze behind Aspen. Something needled his conscience. But what? Trinity loved this. Heath might have a pounding headache, but Trinity was pounding the ground.

Jogging behind his canine partner, he felt the telltale thud in his skull. *Too much.* He'd done too much in too short a time. He knew it. But slowing down equaled defeat. And he wasn't going there.

Trinity stopped, sniffed, then sat back on her haunches and looked at him. Then at the closed door.

Heath signaled to the team leader.

Watters and his team edged in, weapons up. "U.S. Special Forces," he shouted to those inside. "Come out with your hands in the air." He shouted the message again, this time in Pashto. Then Arabic.

Heath clipped the lead back on Trinity and took a firm grip.

The door eased open.

Trinity lunged. Barked.

Sucking in a breath, Heath grabbed a tighter hold on the lead and pulled her back. Which was about like trying to harness a tornado. "Trinity, out!"

An Afghan man screamed, then bent away, covering his head. Cowering.

The rest of Watters's team rushed into the home. Shouts came from several directions. Down the dusty, hard-packed street, Heath saw the other team members clearing a store. Heath walked Trinity in a circle around the small crowd of Special Forces troops and the family of six or eight who stepped into the cool morning. A good hit, but that was enough. The weakness in his legs and arms told him so. The erratic heart rate told him so.

Then why couldn't he just let it go?

With a fair distance between them and the others, Heath let Watters do what he did best and took a knee next to Trinity. He wrapped an arm around her thick chest, proud that even after thirteen months off the grid, she still had what it took. "Good girl."

Trained on the others, Trinity was distracted just long enough to turn her head to him, swipe her tongue up his cheek, then refocus on the action unfolding. She missed it, the action, being useful, being part of a team.

He patted her side. "Me too, girl." He sighed. Or did he?

In his periphery he saw Jibril, Aspen, and Hogan monitoring the progress of the SF team. It hit Heath then — *I have a team, a new team.*

Trinity's ears flickered. Swiveling like satellites, they twisted to the rear. She looked over his shoulder. In a split second, she launched over Heath's shoulder.

The lead ripped out of his fingers.

Heath spun — so did his head. He shook it off as he shoved to his feet, searching for Trinity. Scanning the structures, he tried to make sense of the almost monochromatic setting. Brown roads. Brown buildings. Wait — there. To the right. Third building. Trinity once again took up an aggressive stance, snarling and snapping.

"Trinity, heel!" He glanced to Watters. Should he shout for help? When he turned back to Trinity, his heart stuttered. She was gone!

"Trinity!" He took a step forward. Crap. He wasn't cleared to engage hostiles. Then again, he wasn't leaving Trinity to end up dead. She hadn't left him — he wouldn't leave her. Again, he double-checked his six.

The villager was arguing with Watters, his team helping with small children from the home.

Too busy.

Heath rushed after Trinity. *This is real smart. You have no weapon. No backup.* He didn't care. He wasn't losing Trinity. Not now. Not here. At least he had a vest and helmet. With each plant of his boots, Heath steeled himself. His head felt like it was taking assault fire. *Boom. Boom. Boom.*

His vision blurred.

No!

He pushed it aside. It resisted. He shoved forward. Farther. "Tri . . ."

Everything went black.

Panic snapped his eyes open. Heath glanced around. How long had he — ? *On the ground. I'm on the ground.* On a knee. Heart and head still pounding. That was good then, right? Meant he'd only been out a few seconds. Right? *Please, let it be right.*

"You okay?" Hogan shouted as she ran past him. "I got her."

"Yeah . . ." The answer proved weaker than his legs. Walking through pudding would've been easier. He trudged onward.

An Afghan male stepped out of the hut.

Armed. Aiming at Hogan.

A strangled yelp whipped out of her. She skidded, trying to stop, and landed on her rear.

Heath hauled in a breath as the guy shouted, "*Allahu Akbar.*"

Heath's breath backed into his throat. A million thoughts pinged off his addled brain: Where was Trinity? Was the guy alone? Had he killed Trinity? *I don't have a weapon. I'm going to die. Hogan's going to die.*

As the telltale crack of an M4A1 split his thoughts, Heath watched the guy fall to his knees. A dark spot spread over the tan tunic he wore. He flopped into the dust.

"Yes, indeed." Candyman laughed as he trotted toward Hogan. "God *is* great. But maybe not his god." He grinned at Heath and knelt to check his pulse. " 'Cuz I'm thinking my god — whoever he is — just won."

Behind them, a team snaked into the house. Trinity tore out a few seconds later. Heath gathered her into his arms, his biorhythms off the chart. Face buried in her fur, he clung to the wriggling mass of energy. "I thought you were a goner, girl." Once he'd regained his head, he ran his hands along her amber coat for injuries.

Clean. Weird.

Boots crunched as a sergeant approached. "He shut her in a room."

"Why didn't he shoot her?" At the thought, Heath ran his hands over her body again, wondering if he'd missed something.

The sergeant shrugged. "Hey, I'm not a psychologist. And he's dead, so I can't ask."

Heath nodded. The question was dumb. One they wouldn't be able to answer. But he could thank the Lord for watching out for both of them. As he got to his feet again, he had one thought: *I don't belong here.* . . .

It wasn't the first time he'd thought that since setting down at Bagram, but this time a deadly danger hung over the words. He'd nearly gotten himself, Trinity, and Hogan killed.

Hogan came up next to him, arms folded. "You enjoyed that."

But he couldn't let on to his fears, not in front of the others. "What? Seeing you fall on your butt?" Heath grinned as he fed Trinity a treat. Had to play it cool. "One hundred percent."

"Ha. Ha." She nudged his shoulder. "I meant being back in action. You got so happy-slappy, you nearly did a face-plant."

"Nearly. But not quite." The five-second blackout . . . what if it'd happened after he made it to the building? If the terrorist pointed the gun at *his* head instead of Hogan's? A shudder rippled down his spine. The others would've had brain soup for chow.

Yeah, he needed to distance himself. Squinting, he brought his gaze back to Hogan and saw in her wheat-colored eyes, something . . . *She knows.*

Would she call it? Tell him — or worse, tell Jibril — that he was unfit for duty?

It'd happened once before with a colonel who felt Heath had become more a liability than an asset. He'd yanked Heath, tanked him, and sent him packing.

I'm not going back. Metaphorically or literally. But he had a responsibility. To Trinity. To the men and women around him.

Thunder streaked through the heavens.

Something went still in Heath. A knowing. A deep knowing. "That wasn't thunder," he muttered as he turned a circle — and stopped cold.

In the mountains, a cloud plumed, thick, black, and angry.

Parwan Province, Afghanistan
Can't breathe!

Someone had a hand on her throat. Darci jerked up — but saw nothing. She coughed.

219

Again. No, not a hand. Smoke! The blanket of darkness smothered her. Her eyes watered. On all fours, Darci scrambled along the ground.

"Alice? Ba—" Another cough choked off the little girl's name. Where was the girl? Darci had her in her arms when the explosion knocked her out.

Explosion. The geological survey team.

She squinted, trying to see past the pillar of smoke. No-go.

Okay. She had to find Badria and get to lower ground, out of the small fire eating through one of the dense green sections of the mountains. Darci ripped off a stretch of her shirt and tied it around her face. "Badria! Where are you?" she asked in the girl's language.

Scooting along the route she'd taken, she searched for the small form, praying the little one hadn't survived the slaughter of her family to end up dead.

Her fingers traipsed over the rocky edifice. Forcing herself to recall what she remembered of the shape, Darci crawled, afraid she'd plunge down a drop-off she hadn't noticed before. Though determination held her fast, her priority had to be getting out of sight. If a gust of wind cleared the air, she'd be visible. Whoever had taken down the chopper would no doubt be looking for anyone escaping.

Darci dropped down a two-foot ledge — her ankle wobbled on the uneven surface. She shifted, then realized — a leg!

She traced the body. Too big for Badria. "Alice?"

A small groan. The legs moved. Arms. "Wha . . . ?"

"Are you hurt? Is anything broken?"

Coughing, Alice shifted onto her side. "No . . . I don't think so." In the haze, Alice's face appeared close. Her thick black hair tumbled free of the binding she'd had it in before the blast.

"Where's Badria?"

With more coughing, Alice shook her head. "I don't know. She was with you."

An urgency gripped Darci she couldn't shake. "We can't leave her." She wouldn't leave the girl behind. "Help me find her — but stay low."

Wide brown eyes watered and turned red. Not from crying but from the smoke and ash eating the sky and oxygen.

Rocks and sharp shards digging into their knees and palms, they searched the surrounding area. But to no avail. Darci's heart pounded. She couldn't leave the girl. Not the way —

221

She stilled. *Not the way, what?* Her psyche warred with her past. *Not the way Ba left my brother.*

Slumping back against the mountain that rose several feet over them, Darci tried to catch her breath. This wasn't about her family. This was about a national — no, *international* crisis. If China was up to no-good here in Afghanistan, it could unseat everything.

Then, as if an invisible hand reached down, the cloud of smoke shifted to the east.

And before her, thirty or forty feet down, a hunk of twisted metal lay scattered over the remains of what used to be their camp. Small fires pocked the flat space. Gathered in a northwestern corner, about twenty shapes.

Darci pulled back. Too many fires still burned, stirring up ash and smoke, making it impossible to see who was down there. Who among their team had survived. She'd need to get closer if she had any chance —

"What's going on?" Alice whispered from behind.

"They've rounded up survivors." Darci scooched forward, her boots too loud for stealth. She slowed and made deliberate efforts to lift and place her foot with each step.

As she rounded a corner and hid behind a boulder, something in the southern corner, near a large piece of wreckage, caught her eye. A flash. Where was that coming from? She scoured the black, charred remains —

There. Again. Another flash.

She narrowed her eyes and leaned in. A shadow? No! A burst of relief shot through her. Not a shadow. It was Toque. Covered head to toe in ash and soot, he crouched next to the belly of the downed chopper. Had he rolled in the ash?

Another flash. A thought niggled at her brain. Was he sending her messages?

Pay attention, Darci.

Patting herself down, she searched for something to let him know she was listening. Wait. No. If she did that, the attackers would see her. She looked down. Against her North Face jacket, her hand would stand out. She gave the move-out signal.

The glare of whatever he was using scorched her eyes. But she forced herself to read the message. It came through:

. ‒ ...... ‒.. .‒‒. .‒.‒.‒ ‒.. ‒‒‒ ‒. .‒‒‒‒. ‒ .‒.. ‒‒‒ ‒‒‒ ‒.‒ ‒ ....‒ ‒.‒. ‒.‒ .‒.‒.‒

E-T H-E-L-P-D-O-N-T-L-O-O-K-B-A-C-K.

. . . et help. "Get!" *Get help. Don't look back.*

She relayed her understanding, but . . . she didn't understand. What did he mean, don't look back?

As if in response to her question, Toque rose and stepped around the hulk.

No! You're exposed!

Hands raised, he shouted at the enemy.

Gunfire erupted.

"No!" Darci lunged forward but just as fast threw herself back down.

Rocks exploded around her.

She'd drawn their attention. Her pulse thundered through her chest, reverberating off what she'd just seen. No. He couldn't be dead. He might've been a spook, but if anyone had a chance to help the team, it would've been Toque.

Something tickled her back. Something small, spider —

Darci whirled.

A pair of beautiful brown eyes stared out from a small hole. Badria! The little girl pushed aside some rock and rubble. On her belly, she wiggled backward, waving Darci to follow. As the girl cleared the opening, Darci saw it —

A tunnel!

Sixteen

Camp Eggers, Kabul, Afghanistan

All the demons of war must have him on their hit list. He'd made an impact here, saved thousands of lives from burning in hell. And the immortal beasts wanted him gone. His grandfather, Woundedknee Burnett, would've told him it was the spirits. But his grandmother, who'd drawn the grouchy ol' Cherokee from his reservation with her blue eyes and firm Christian faith, would've said he was right. The demons wanted to stop the Kingdom from advancing.

Right now, Lance didn't care who he was fighting as long as he won. With a four-man crew, he stalked down the long corridor that bisected the large building. Ahead stood General Early and his entourage.

Lance offered a salute. "General."

Early did the same. "Sorry about your adventure in that village."

"Comes with the territory. Had things to take care of, someone got a lucky hit in." He shrugged as he motioned to the steel door marked with a number 5. "So, we're both here now. What've you got?"

General Early nodded to one of his lieutenants, who swiped a badge down a reader. The light swam from red to green with a quiet beep before he tugged open the door and stepped aside.

"I tell you, this is the darndest thing. About zero-two-hundred, I wake up to the guard dogs going berserk, MPs shouting, and soon after Lieutenant Zeferelli here" — Early stabbed a finger at the lieutenant who'd accessed the room — "is banging down my door."

Lance smiled at the L-T who ducked, nerves jangled. "Don't you know privates have been sent to Leavenworth for less?"

The man's stiff composure softened beneath the joke. "Yes, sir. I've heard that, General, sir."

Lance laughed. "Get hold of those nerves, Zeferelli, or you'll wet yourself." He couldn't help but grin at the red spreading through the young man's face. "Go on."

Zeferelli looked to Early like a good dog. "Well." He licked his lips. "MPs rang my room, said they had a Chinese national.

Three, in fact."

"And why would this news alarm you so much that you'd interrupt the precious sleep of your base commander?"

"Because, sir, the men asked for General Early by name."

"And every Afghan and Taliban terrorist roaming this godforsaken area knows that name."

"Yes, sir. But they don't know yours."

Lance stilled, listening to the whir of the minimal heating unit battling the exterior elements to afford a minuscule degree of warmth. "Come again?" His presence here wasn't common knowledge. He'd made sure with his delicate work of protecting operations and operatives.

"He asked for you. By name, sir. Said he would not talk to anyone but you."

"I thought he asked for Early."

The L-T nodded again. "Actually, his words to the MPs were, 'Tell General Early that if he wants to stop an international incident to get General Burnett here.' "

What was he saying about those demons earlier? "You gotta be kidding me," Lance said to General Early.

Shorter, grayer, and more wrinkled, the man fooled a lot of grunts with his size and age. "You been dancing with the wrong man's daughter again?"

Lance would've laughed at the memory, but this wasn't the time. He eyed his friend as they stepped into a monitoring room. Through the one-way glass, he found their guest.

And for one second, one painful, past-hurtling-to-the-present second, his heart stopped. Then his Catholic faith rushed up his throat in a hoarse prayer, "Sweet Mother of God . . ."

"My son! My son is still there."

"We'll get him out."

"No!" The man buried his head in his hands, sobbing. Finally, he hung his head, shaking it. "You cannot — they will be watching him. Watching his every move. If they suspect, they will kill him."

"I can get him. I'll do it myself."

"No, no, you cannot." The man lowered his head, and he slumped in the hard plastic chair. He wept. "He told me —" A shudder severed his words. "He say, 'They watching me. If we all go, we die.' "

"What was that?"

General Burnett dropped into the rickety, creaking chair at the table stretched before the rectangular window. He picked up the shattered pieces of the past and cleared his throat. Put on his game face. A handful of people were privy to that mission. But nobody in this room. "What do you know about him?"

Zeferelli lifted a hand in defeat. "Name, rank — only by his uniform."

Lance nodded, his gaze skimming the PLA uniform. The rank on the shoulder. The gold aiguillette. But the one thing he couldn't tear his gaze away from was the familiar eyes.

"We've spent the last few hours digging up information while we waited for your arrival. His name is Colonel Zheng Haur," Lieutenant Zeferelli said, his dark hair rimming a young face. "According to our brief research, he is the personal aide to General Zheng, the minister of defense."

Why on earth would Zheng put Haur into enemy hands? Lance had tried to send in operatives to retrieve this young man, convince him to switch sides, but nothing — *nothing* — could draw him out. Because General Zheng had so thoroughly brainwashed and leashed him.

So what changed? Were they seeking revenge?

His breath backed into his throat — did they know Darci's location?

No. No way they could know she was in country.

Or had Zheng sent Haur to prove his allegiance once again? Unfortunately, Lance couldn't share what he knew with anyone in this room, or the next. Forbidden territory, all of it.

But . . . could he snatch this kid? Have him vanish from this very building and disappear into thin air — thin air called anonymity? Would Haur go? Or would he fight him?

Lance didn't know enough. He'd have to ply information out of Haur. Figure out where he stood. What he wanted. Man, Lance could use a Dr Pepper about now.

"Let's find out what he knows." Lance pushed out of his seat, surreptitiously wiped his palms on his slacks, then strode to the door. "Z," he said to the L-T as he swiped his card to gain access to the galley between the two rooms. "Did he say anything else?"

"No, sir." Zeferelli glanced at the general with his card poised over the reader.

Lance gave him the go-ahead. The light zipped green and a soft click echoed in the steel-reinforced chamber.

The L-T posted himself at the door as Lance moved to the table. The face before him so familiar, yet way too old for the few years that had passed.

Haur stood. "General, thank you for coming."

For cryin' out loud. The kid even sounded like his old man. Lance felt like Atlas, with the weight of the world on his shoulders. With the fate of one family he'd ripped apart twenty years ago dangling before him. But he had to play this right. Be the deputy director.

"First things first, Colonel." Lance stuffed his hands in his pockets, not wanting to put the man on the defensive. "We need your name, rank — you know the drill."

With a curt bow of his head, he assented. "Maj— Colonel Zheng Haur with the Ministry of Defense. I am here to speak with you on an urgent matter."

"If it's so urgent, why wait for me to show up? And what's wrong, can't you remember your own rank?" He tapped the table with a finger. "You know what I think? I think you're wasting my time. You didn't want to talk to me. You're buying time while your cohorts are out there plotting to destroy the base."

The man stiffened. "Of course not."

"Then what's the story? Why not talk to General Early — it's his base, for cryin' out loud. He can do anything I can."

Haur's face twitched. "No, sir. Not this time."

Little alarms buzzed at the back of Lance's head. But he told himself to play along. Play nice. No strong-arm tactics. Unless it became necessary. "And why is that?"

"You are familiar with the minister's son, yes?"

The conversation just took a giant leap toward Darci. "A hotheaded fool."

The tense brow smoothed, bringing a slight smile. "We agree."

Not the answer he expected. What he wouldn't do to plug this kid into a machine and figure out if he was playing them or what. Then again, Lance's own operatives were trained to defeat lie detectors, so he could expect no less from the Chinese officer standing before him at attention. "I'm sorry, Colonel, but I'm not here to deal with paternal issues. If the minister —"

"Colonel Wu has gone rogue."

That may be the worst news the man could've delivered to Lance. Colonel Wu, born Zheng Jianyu, had more patience, which wasn't a good thing in this case. It was a lethal thing. Jianyu knew how to play his enemy, taunt him, bring him into submission until he crushed his spirit so he'd never be the same again.

Lance had seen the man's handiwork with his own eyes.

"What in Sam Hill do you mean? Rogue?"

"His assignment was to oversee the integration and implementation of the teams working the mine in Jalrez Valley in Wardak Province. When I arrived to escort him back to China —"

"Why are you escorting him back to China?"

Haur's jaw muscle flexed, strength and anger bouncing on the nerve. "When I arrived, the mine director informed me that Colonel Wu had left the site."

Another yard closer to Darci.

"Good, he went back home." Lance said it to remind Colonel Zheng of the only acceptable answer. The way things should be.

"No." Frustration oozed out of the colonel, just as Lance intended. "He lied to the director of the mine, told them the general had recalled him. That is not true. He left with few supplies save his elite warriors."

Yanjingshe. The fiercest fighters and trackers Lance had ever witnessed. If they were out there . . .

One more baby step.

Mother, may I, please kill him?

Keep it cool. He had to keep it cool till he had cold, hard proof that Wu Jianyu knew the location of one of the Army's most prized assets. "Again, I'm not here for father-son fights. I have a region to stabil—"

"Then let me speak plainly, General." Haur let out a long sigh, fingertips pressed against the table. "You and I both know you are not here to stabilize anything."

Lance itched for a Dr Pepper with its hefty dose of sugar and caffeine.

"You are deputy director of Defense Counterintelligence and HUMINT Center. You are responsible for dispatching teams of linguists, field analysts, case officers, interrogation experts, technical specialists, and special forces. You've had personnel in countries that could systematically destroy your reputation with the UN and even your closest allies."

Haur leaned forward his chained and cuffed hands jangling against the metal table. While there was no malice in his face, a fierceness edged into his until then calm demeanor. "Would you like me to lay out, in front of all these witnesses, what covert missions you are operating in this region?"

SEVENTEEN

10 Klicks outside FOB Robertson

Smoke snaked into the sky, the snowcapped mountain marred by the black pillar stretching high over the spine. Dark and angry, it told Heath this wasn't a wood or forest fire. Black and billowing meant fuel and oil. And lots.

"Not exactly a small campfire, huh?" Aspen asked quietly. "What do you think happened?"

Green Berets huddled around the MRAP drew his attention. "Let's see if we can find out." Heath trotted that way.

Tense, quiet conversation carried between Watterboy and Candyman, hunched over a relief map. Of the mountains, if Heath guessed right. Candyman stabbed a finger at the one-dimensional topography, his expression intense. Watters held up a placating hand.

Slapping both hands against the hull of

235

the MRAP, Candyman growled, "This is bull."

With a step back, Watters leaned in as if to say something to Candyman, then noticed Heath lurking. Man, he felt like some criminal eavesdropper.

Heath cleared his throat and gave a nod to them. "What's going on?"

Candyman turned to him and rolled his eyes. "Classic bureaucratic bull." He stomped off.

Asking again would agitate the man he'd worked with, so Heath waited.

Watterboy jerked toward him, a squall of anger hovering over the storm in his eyes — but it dropped flat as he sighed. "Look, I'd like nothing more than to tell you, but I can't. It's —"

"No worries." Hand held up, Heath cocked his head. "I get it."

Into a secure phone, Watters said, "Yes, sir. Holding."

Holding? Heath chewed that nugget as he returned to his team. Was that "holding" as in holding position and not returning to base, or holding on the line? By Candyman's frustration and anger, Heath bet it meant staying here. In hostile territory. No RTB orders and no going in to help with whatever had happened in the mountains.

"What did he say?" Jibril's brow knotted in concern and consternation.

"Nothing. He won't tell me what's going on because I'm not authorized personnel. But I heard him say they were holding."

"Holding?" Aspen folded her arms. "Holding what?"

"Position, most likely." Jibril's gaze rose to the lingering smoke. "The fire is still burning."

"That wasn't a house fire," Hogan said as she adjusted the helmet that bobbled on her head. "Something bad happened up there."

"You got that right." Candyman's voice erupted behind them.

Heath glanced past Hogan to his old buddy. Hogan arched her eyebrow at Heath, and somehow he knew what she was going to do.

"So, it's bad?" She sounded like a doe-eyed woman.

Candyman hesitated as he looked down on her, their nearly twelve-inch difference exaggerated with them side by side. "Baby, don't work me up if you're going to work me over."

Hogan laughed. "I like you."

"Mutual." Candyman smiled, then looked at Heath. "Running this morning, I saw one of my former buddies hustling to a chopper. They were sent out for an emergency extraction of some stupid survey team up in the Kush."

"Survey?"

"Yeah, checking out the rocks or something. Hanged if I know, but why on this insane planet anyone would be up there in the first place if they aren't wearing an Interceptor and carrying" — Candyman hoisted his M4 — "at least one of these . . ."

An image erupted in Heath's mind. Warm almond eyes. "Wait." He gripped Candyman's vest. "Survey team. You mean the geological survey team?"

Candyman shrugged. "Yeah, maybe. Don't know."

Aspen shouldered in, her blue eyes locked like radar onto Heath. "You think she was with them?"

"Who?" Candyman glanced between the two of them.

Jia. Heath wanted to look at the smoke-streaked sky, but it'd give away his concern. *Play it cool.* She wasn't anything. . . . Except the only person who'd made him consider the future. The woman who made it easy to talk and be around someone of the opposite sex. The woman who —

Was so scared of what she felt for him,

she wasn't willing to feel it. That fake e-mail address — RockGirl — told him he wasn't worth the effort to get to know. Which he could've informed her from the beginning. But no, he'd let himself off-lead when it came to her. And been downright brazen about their mutual attraction.

She was up there. . . . His pulse hiccuped at the thought of her being near — or in — that explosion.

A wet nose nudged his hand.

Yeah, Trinity knew. She always knew when he was off-kilter. Knew when he needed space to breathe. He lifted her lead and mumbled to the others, "Excuse me, I think Trinity needs to do her duty."

"Heath." Hogan's voice trailed him, but he kept walking.

Watterboy intercepted him. "Hey, stay close." When his gaze rammed into Heath's, he must've seen the panic. "We've got unfriendlies here still. And with whatever just happened" — he motioned to the mountains — "who knows where we'll end up by nightfall."

Heath caught on. "It'd be smart to move a little closer. Get us out of here where we've got headhunters breathing down our necks. Then we'd be closer and in position. If needed, I mean."

Eyes crinkling, Watters slapped him on the back of his shoulder. "Good thoughts, Ghost." He stalked away.

Heath walked Trinity to an area where the dead grass matched the hard-packed roads. After taking care of business, Trinity trotted over to a building and flopped down in the sliver of shade provided. Pink tongue dangling, she panted, eyes squinting sheer pleasure. She thrived on this scene. Loved working.

Heath started toward her, smiling. Somehow, that seventy-pound fur ball made everything seem okay. When everything wasn't.

Just above her right ear cement erupted.

As if punched in the chest, Heath sucked in a breath. "Trinity, down!" He dropped to a knee, knowing the shooter was somewhere behind him. "Taking fire, taking fire!"

His beloved canine flattened herself against the earth.

Heath used his torso as a shield to break the line of sight between the shooter and the only girl who'd ever protected him. She fastened those amber eyes on him. He signaled with his hand. "Come," he said, quiet and hoarse.

Trinity low-crawled toward him, a stealthy thing that made his heart balloon with pride. She was incredible, her trust implicit, her loyalty thorough. Her snout puffed dust around her. When she reached him, Heath covered her. Trinity was a prized asset, but more than that, she was his best friend. Soldiers and civilians alike knew whoever killed a war dog lived well for the next decade.

They'll have to go through me first.

"Ghost!"

With Trinity huddled beneath him, dust and grit billowing into his mouth as a cold wind pulled at his clothes, Heath shot a glance to the side. Amid another plume of dust, Watters and Candyman knelt by the MRAP for cover. "Where?"

"Shooter," he gritted out, inching his way toward them. "My nine o'clock."

As soon as the words escaped his lips, the team pelted the building. Heath scooped up Trinity and sprinted. A half-dozen feet from safety, something plowed into his back. Like the mighty hand of God shoving him face-first into the dirt. He released Trinity, who skidded out in front. On the ground, he felt himself dragged to safety by two or three men.

Hauled out of the line of fire, he scrambled to see Trinity. She sat beside him on her haunches, tail thumping, as if this had been a day in the park. "Only you, girl." Chuckling, he ruffled her fur — pain snapped through the tendons and ligaments in his arm and back.

A slap on that same spot about made him come out of his skin. *Augh!*

"How's that shoulder?" Candyman asked.

That thing would leave a nice, shiny bruise. Pushing to his feet, Heath grunted. His back felt as if someone had driven a stake through it. "Much better now that you hit it." Rotating his arm to test the range of motion, Heath took up Trinity's lead with his other hand. When he turned, he met malice-hardened eyes.

Four men wrangled an Afghan to his knees a few feet away.

"Here's your dog killer."

"Or attempted killer," another sergeant said.

Gaze locked on the shooter, Heath lunged.

So did Watters. "Hey!" Caught him by the arm. Swung him around. Candyman was there in a heartbeat, too, both strong-arming Heath back a safe distance.

"He tried to kill Trinity — took shots at her. I'm not —"

"Ghost." Watters shoved him back with his shoulder, then braced him with two palms against his chest. "We've got him."

His calm, in-control gaze stilled the fury in Heath's chest. "He's not going anywhere, no more weapons."

Only as he saw the concern in his former buddy's face did Heath grab hold of his sanity. *What is wrong with me?* Nerves buzzing, he stood down. Blew out a breath as he turned a circle.

Rather than longing to be in the middle of combat, taking a bead on the enemy, suddenly Heath wanted nothing more than to jog the trail at the ABA ranch. Escape. Again, it hit him: *I don't belong here.*

Parwan Province, Afghanistan

"Push in, push in," Darci said, scooting along, palms flat against the wall of the cave, her mind hooked on Toque's sacrifice. Why? Why had he done that? The shot she'd heard as she dove into the cave and tripped . . . had that been the signal that he was dead?

Think positively.

Darci squinted to see the thin thread of light that filtered in from the opening thirty feet back. But slinking farther into this cave to hide was as bad as trying to hide in a coffin. Dark, no air . . . death.

Think. Positively!

Her shoulder ached, a sticky mess after all

the exertion and trauma. Darci gritted her teeth against the pain. She had to get Badria and Alice to safety. Back to Bagram.

"Why are we in here? Won't they find us and . . . ?" Alice's voice trailed off.

"This area is home to thousands of tunnels," Darci said, crouch-walking inch by inch. "It should lead us to a safe location."

"And if it doesn't?"

Darci sighed. "Let's keep our options open, okay?" If they didn't, they'd give up before they started. But she was determined to find a way home. She wouldn't abandon her father, no matter what he had done in the past.

"Right." For a young, naive girl from the country, Alice had a strength about her that surprised Darci.

"Trust me, we'll be fine."

"What about the others?"

Frustration coiled around Darci's mind. "Let's not talk for a while. We have no idea if they've followed us, and we don't need to be a homing beacon." Besides, she needed mental space to think and work out a plan.

"Right."

As darkness gathered them into its arms, Darci knew she had to push her mind somewhere pleasant or she'd suffocate herself. Okay, so . . . where? Home? With her father?

No . . .

On the training field. A dog barking. Warm gray eyes that led to a very deep, rich — but tortured — soul. He'd been so crushed when she tried to lower the boom that they didn't have a chance that she'd wanted to take back the words, feed him empty promises. And yet . . . yet, he'd pressed in. Yanked the truth out from behind her barriers like some thief. Some guy who thought he owned the world.

And yet . . . he didn't. What a strange dichotomy in him. Broken, but strong. Confident, yet uncertain.

She'd left their lunch date without handing out promises. That had been intentional, and his hurt lingered in her mouth like a bitter herb. But she wouldn't. She worked targets and objectives. She wouldn't work a guy she . . . liked.

Look how things ended for all of James Bond's girls — dead or gone to the dark side. No thanks. She wouldn't bear the blame for things like that.

If only the double life she led could compare to the glitz and glamour of James Bond. And yet Bond had a string of heartbroken women in the wake of his speedboat-style life. That's the reason Darci never went there.

Okay, so the mission in China had taken longer than usual. Jianyu had gotten under her skin, under her defenses. The biggest mistake of her life. She hadn't seen the real him. And when she had . . .

A shudder ripped through Darci. She blamed it on the clamminess soaking her shirt. But she knew better.

"Why'd you stop?" Alice's whispered words skidded into the darkness. "What's wrong?"

"Sorry." Darci hadn't even realized she'd stopped. "Leg cramp."

A small hand touched her knee. Darci wrapped hers around the tiny, icy fingers. This far up in the mountains, coiling their way through the innards, lowered their core body temperatures. They couldn't stay hidden from the sun much longer. Holding Badria's hand, Darci used the wall to push to her feet. Hot and cold swirled through her, the pain mind-numbing. "Just a little farther."

"You've been saying that for an hour." Exhaustion tugged at Alice's slow words that bounced off the walls.

I have? Had they really been hidden that long? What if they never made it out of here?

Don't think that!

Why hadn't Darci listened to the promptings that told her this mission would be her last? What made her think she could do this job indefinitely? She didn't want to. Weariness tugged at her the last few missions.

She'd loved this job once. With a brutal passion. It helped her feel like she gave hope to people who didn't have any. Her psych assessment before she took the job revealed she wanted this role because of what happened to her mom. The evaluation didn't make sense to her, but if she somehow honored her mom, helped others who were in danger and didn't know it, then that was a good thing.

But . . . to what extent? What did she have left? What hope did she have?

"Because of what's happening right here." Even at the memory of his husky words, Darci felt the warmth she'd experienced several nights ago in his arms.

If only it could happen. If she could walk away . . .

"How much farther?" Alice said through a yawn.

Too bad Heath wasn't here. With that gorgeous dog of his. Trinity would find her, find an escape. "It can't go on forever." She hoped.

"My thoughts exactly." Alice pulled in a breath. "But what if it does?"

"Alice."

"Right."

Around a corner, the shadows lightened. Air swirled as if . . . Trekking her fingers along the ribs of the cave, she slowly rose to —

Her head thudded against the ceiling. She grimaced but was glad she could stretch her legs. "Let's stop." As her eyes adjusted to the open area, Darci noticed light streaming through two different locations. Straight ahead and at her two o'clock.

"But that . . . that's light. It means there's an out, right?"

Yes, but where precisely would they exit? What if they'd managed to come full circle back to the camp? What if they dumped out into a Taliban stronghold? Despite her best efforts at keeping her sense of direction, Darci had only an educated — if you could call it that after so many twists and loop-backs — guess about their direction.

"Is something wrong?" Alice's voice skated along Darci's cheek.

The girl was close. Then again, in a narrow cave tunnel with darkness, everything felt close. "Just resting."

Darci knelt and tugged her pack from her

back. She fished through it for her sat phone. Normally she wouldn't take this risk, but they were out of options. Odds said the team had been killed. Toque —

Darci squeezed off the thought as she pulled out the phone. Her thumb slipped into a depression. A hole? Since when did her sat phone have a hole? She angled it toward the lone halo of light and stilled. A bullet blinked back at her, the light glinting off the surface. They'd hit her — the phone — and she'd never known. Heat speared her stomach at how close she'd come to dying. She couldn't even recall feeling the impact. Adrenaline had shoved her through the opening. Besides, after the pain from the first bullet, with another Death would come knocking.

"Ah, Death, the spectre which sate at all feasts!"

As if hearing her Poe quote, the light beam straight ahead fractured.

Darci pushed back, drawing Badria into her arms. "Quiet," she hissed to Alice, whom she expected to start peppering her with nervous questions.

Shouts slithered into the cave. They bounced off the walls as if searching for them.

Positive thoughts gone. *We are dead.*

EIGHTEEN

En Route to FOB Murphy, Afghanistan

Despite the chill, body odor and tension radiated through the steel hull of the MRAP as they lumbered out of the village and gained speed. At the village, the Green Berets requested and received clearance to move to FOB Murphy. Eighty minutes had passed since the explosion. Though no official orders had come down, the new location would put them closer to the base and the mountains.

Watters was no dummy positioning his team in a prime location. Heath could tell by the way he was moving his team and staying on top of updates. That's the way of it in the military. If you suspect your fellow American troops are getting hammered, military branch divisions and rivalries vanish. You help. You help fast.

Then later, after saving the rivals, remind them constantly who saved whom.

Chin resting across Heath's and Hogan's legs, Trinity yawned and moaned as he ran a hand along her back. Hogan smoothed her coat, too, eyes closed. No doubt she took comfort in Trinity's rhythmic breathing. He had. Did now. Even during furnace summers out here, it never felt hot or suffocating to have his furry partner stretched across him as he waited in the field. Laid prone on lookout, her side pressed to his.

At the FOB, soldiers went one way while A Breed Apart entered a three-story structure that housed a small eating area and multiple rooms with bunk beds. Grabbing rack time when possible kept soldiers alive and alert. Heath opened an MRE and dropped onto the bunk beneath Jibril. Meals-Ready-to-Eat had other infamous, derogatory names, but they supplied enough calories to keep him from caring. Across from him Aspen and Hogan occupied the other bunks.

Heath fed half his meal to Trinity and provided her a bowl of water from a cooking pot he'd reallocated to himself from the kitchen. When they geared out, it'd be returned, with the addition of some slobber. Served them right for cutting him and the team out of the mission briefing.

Munching a chocolate candy-bar stick-looking thing, Heath rose and went to the window, clouded by years of grime and dust. Blending with the landscape made a ragtag huddle of buildings that served as a checkpoint almost indiscernible. For years, locals paid what little they had to clear the checkpoint, contributing to the bloated recreational funds of corrupt officials and their perv underlings. Liberal media outlets might call this war useless, but try telling that to the average Muslim trying to make his or her way across a land polluted with corruption and greed. Now they could traverse it without selling their souls.

Jia.

As the name lodged into his still-pounding skull, he looked to the mountains, but his mind looked to that heart-shaped face. The kiss he'd almost stolen, wanted bad. Though his TBI had been an excuse to pull back from the world, Jia made him want to reenter it. Be there with her, for her, beside her. . . .

Was she up there? The explosion — did she die?

He kneaded the ache in his temple, thinking through how he'd find out if she'd been on the casualty list — if there was one. That was the thing of it. Nobody knew what happened.

Correction: They knew. He didn't.

In fact, he had little doubt they were getting briefed on it as he stood here.

"You weren't ready."

Heath felt the words as much as heard them. Coarse, tight, controlled, but vitriolic all the same. He looked over his shoulder.

Hogan hovered less than a foot behind and to the side. She glanced back, and that's when he noticed the others had cleared out. "Where'd they go?"

"Don't ignore what I said."

The challenge pulled him around. "I'm not." He stared her down. Though she couldn't be more than five five, the woman made up for it in attitude. "But what I do and when I do it — that's not your concern."

"It is when you black out in the middle of a gig." On her toes, she leaned in. "When you put my life, and Trinity's, on the line."

Heath cocked his head. She'd just accused him of putting his dog's life in jeopardy. "Step off."

"No."

Heath drew himself straight. "Hogan —"

"Look, I get it."

"I don't think you —"

"You wanted this." Intensity flamed through her irises. "But that scar you got wrecked everything. So you get this chance to be back here and you grab it." Her expression softened. "But you weren't ready . . . yet."

Amazing that a three-letter word could stand him down when a 120-pound woman couldn't.

Her brown eyes searched his. "Heath, I saw you black out."

Could she hear the shelling of his heart? She had said nothing to the others. When he didn't respond, she plowed on as Hogan always did. "I have a feeling it wasn't the first time since the plane touched down. And you've had a headache the whole time, haven't you?"

Heath swallowed. The last time he felt dressed down by a woman, Auntie Margaret had chewed him out for skipping football practice his senior year. That was two summers before she died. He'd joined the Army a month later.

"And then that Asian chick. You freaked out, thinking she was in that explosion, right?"

"I —"

She thrust a finger in his face. "Don't bury feelings. She may be the only piece of heaven on earth to keep you sane. I'm not saying you have to get all gooey over her —

God knows I don't need to see that — but feel what you feel." Sincerity pinched her eyebrows as she bobbed her head at him. "Don't bury it. You're stressed out of your mind, and that's what's making the headaches worse."

He blinked. She was right. He knew she was. But owning up to it . . .

"Despite my objections about you coming, I think there's a reason you're here."

Heath stared at the fiery wonder. For an annoying, mouthy woman, she was all right. *Little sister* came to mind. "You covered me." It was hard to read her expression thanks to the bangs that fell into her eyes. "Out there, in the village when I went down."

She gave a curt nod.

As voices floated down the hall, Heath glanced toward the closed door, then to her. "Why?"

"You get whacked out and A Breed Apart is shot." She backed away and climbed onto the top bunk. "You think you're the hot snot now, but wait till I get Beo under the spotlights."

"His drool alone would wipe out the audience."

Grinning, she flung a wad of MRE trash at him.

He caught it, his mind weighted by the profound conversation. One he'd never expected from Hogan. He'd underestimated her. And on every count, she was right.

Talk about cutting a man down to size. Big chunk of humble pie, hand-fed by a woman he'd detested a week ago.

Heath glanced at her. Looked down, ashamed. "Thanks."

"Don't thank me." Arms stretched behind her head, she closed her eyes. "I'm trying to convince you to get out. I want your job."

Parwan Province, Afghanistan

"Back." Darci caught the edge of Badria's shirt and tugged her backward. "Farther." She bumped against Alice, who scrambled back into the gaping maw of darkness.

Darci's world spun, a feeling of lightness and swimming all at once. She shook her head, strained to see. If her head felt so light, why did her legs feel like lead weights?

Stumbling, she gripped Badria tighter, tumbled into the cave wall. Fire lit down her arm again. Darci steeled herself against the wave of nausea and light-headedness that wrapped her in a tight cocoon. When was the last time she ate? Or had anything to drink? At this rate, she'd never get Alice and Badria to safety. Propped against the wall, her arms still around the precious girl, Darci swallowed and let out exhausted breaths.

"What — ?"

"Quiet!" That whisper had razor-sharp precision, severing Alice's question. Though guilt bit at Darci, desperation and pain chomped into that guilt. She rolled her head to the side, to the other route of darkness, knowing that a dozen feet that way were two more tunnels. Two avenues of escape. They couldn't see the light beams, so they didn't know if they were being searched. And in the cave, noise echoed and popped off every surface with maddening clarity, making it impossible to know from which direction the noise originated. To the right, the way back to camp. More than an hour's journey. They couldn't do that. She couldn't do it.

Banging her head against the wall did nothing to shake off the haze. Panic fisted itself around her heart — if she was blacking out, she wouldn't know till . . .

Well, she may never know if they killed her.

Okay, genius. Do something.

To her left lay the dual tunnels. There people were searching. No doubt the Chinese. Nobody else would be looking for them, at least not on foot. Not this fast.

So, if she led them out the wrong tunnel . . .

Searing, an image of Badria soaked in blood popped before her.

Darci squeezed her eyes tight. Okay, no good. Why did it feel like a brick sat on her chest?

Shake it off, Darci. Get them out of here — alive.

"Okay," Darci said in a whisper to her right, to where she imagined Alice hunkered. "We have to split up and —"

"No!"

"Listen!" Darci took a breath. "I'll distract them, then backtrack."

Only heavy breathing met her words.

Arms trembling, she guided Badria over her legs and toward Alice. Cold fingers latched on to Darci's, the tiny fingers digging into her flesh as the little one yelped.

"Shh, shhhh." In Pashto, she explained to Badria that she needed to go with Alice to save the others, that they'd meet up at the foot of the mountain. "It'll be okay," Darci said with little confidence. "Alice, take her. Get down the mountain. Get to Bagram, ask for General Burnett. Don't stop for anyone and don't talk to anyone else. Burnett. Nobody else. Got it?"

"What about you?"

"What was his name? Tell me who you're going to talk to."

"Only General Burkett."

"Burnett. *Nett*, Alice."

"Right. Burnett." She huffed. "What about you?"

"I'll be right behind you. Even if you can't see me, just keep going. I'll find you at the base." There was a greater chance of not being able to evade the Chinese, of getting drilled full of holes. "Okay?"

"I . . . yeah."

Mouth drier than the land around them, Darci gulped. She didn't have much time. And she had to *buy* them time. "Then let's do this."

"Darci, wait." Alice's fingers swiped over Darci's side, then caught her arm. "Are you . . . what are . . . ?" A weighted breath. "Please don't do anything . . . heroic."

"Who?" She winced at the knife that sliced through her courage again. "Me?" Slinking back into the somber glow, Darci looked for movement.

"I hear something!" a voice shouted.

Darci pointed to the other tunnel. "Go!" She nudged Alice to prevent her from arguing.

Wobbling into a crouch, Darci fell back

against the tunnel wall. A gasp behind her told her Alice was hesitating. "Go," she ground out and pushed herself off the rocks and toward the opening.

Her feet felt like writhing snakes, tangling and thick. She had a mission. She had to get this done. Had to protect the others. The river of light drew closer, spilling over the rocks and glinting in her eyes. No, not just glinting. Glaring.

Hand just inside the lip of the cave, Darci paused. She closed her eyes, shutting out visual cues that would deceive her and trained her mind on the sounds outside. Wind. Cold, bitter wind. The temperature had dropped since they'd entered. Would Alice and Badria be okay? Would the storm hit before they made it to the base?

A bird squawked in the distance, but she could sift no other sound from the surroundings. They must've —

Rocks dribbled against each other.

A grunt.

Darci smiled. *Ready or not, here I come . . .*

She drew in a breath for courage and blew it out. *God, help me do this. Help me to not get killed, so I can go home and have tea once more with Ba.*

A rumble of noise and shouts froze her.

But only for a second — they'd spotted Alice!

Darci stumbled into the open. A three-foot ledge provided minimal protection against a fifty-foot drop. Her stomach squirmed as adrenaline exploded through her veins.

She straightened and turned toward the noise. "No!"

Her panicked shout stopped several men.

She widened her eyes in a pretense of fear.

Though she pretended to scramble away, Darci glanced back. To her pursuers, she'd look like a terrified woman. But for her, it was her reassurance that Alice and Badria would get away.

"There! It's her — Meixiang! Grab her!"

Yes, come and get me.

She went down. Glanced back and threw her arms up to protect herself against their blows.

Two men still followed the girls.

"Please," Darci said loudly. "Don't take me to Colonel Zheng!"

In her periphery, the other two hesitated.

"Please," she said in a begging tone. "Jianyu will kill me." Okay, there was too much truth to that for her to fake. They saw it, too.

With one last glance to Alice and the little

one, Darci surrendered to her fate. The major towering over her leered, then raised the butt of his weapon and slammed it into her temple.

NINETEEN

FOB Murphy, Afghanistan

Stretched out on his back, Heath stared at the slats of the bunk above where Jibril slept, a snore filtering the awkward quiet. *Scritch. Scritch. Scritch-scritch.* Heath lolled his head to the side where Trinity lay pressed against him, her legs racing to an unseen dream destination. Maybe she was making the same route he was — straight to Jia.

Three feet away, Timbrel lay on her side curled into the fetal position. Vulnerability cloaked her in a somber embrace. But he knew better than to think that girl was vulnerable. Then again . . . maybe she was. That tough-mama persona, the GI Jane attitude, probably concealed wounds beneath that stone mask. He'd never tried to find out.

Good thing he hadn't made it into the chaplaincy program — he hadn't been able to look past big attitudes and loud mouths to see a person's wounds.

Because, in truth, explosive anger and powerful defensive mechanisms served one purpose: to conceal and protect what lay beneath the surface of that superficial display of strength.

So, what's eating at you, Hogan?

A swish of material drew his attention to the top bunk where Aspen dropped back against the gray mattress. She stared up. Her chest rose and fell unevenly. She lifted a hand to her face. Wiped something . . .

Concern pulled Heath up, his elbow under him for support.

Aspen glanced over — then jerked her gaze away.

In that split second, her watery eyes cried out to him. No way he could let that go. God had put him here. Didn't Hogan say something to that effect — that he had a purpose for being here? Heath climbed off the mattress. As he slipped over to the bunk, he heard Trinity sit up and start panting. He touched Aspen's arm.

A tear rolled down her face, and as she brought her gaze to his, the tear splatted on the mattress.

Soundless, he mouthed, "C'mon." Heath lifted Trinity's lead from the table and motioned for the door. Behind him came the sounds of Trinity's nails clicking on the cement and the gentle groan from Aspen's body scooting across the mattress. Then the soft thump of her landing on the floor coupled with a sniffle.

"Hey," said a drowsy Hogan. "Where you . . . going?"

"Nowhere. Rest," Aspen whispered as she eased out and pulled the door closed.

Sunlight streamed into the building through a narrow slice between the door and the foundation. Strange to think it was midday since they'd put a blackout blanket over the window so they could sleep.

Heath walked to a bin with water bottles and withdrew two. He handed one to Aspen. "Drink it slow."

Red rimmed her eyes, but they weren't puffy and swollen. Either she hadn't cried long, or it wasn't a hard cry. "Thanks." Blond curls akimbo, she brushed them back and took a mouthful, swished it, then swallowed. "I need to let off some frustration. I need a speed bag."

Arching a brow, Heath considered her. "Speed bag?"

Amused blue eyes sparkled in the sunlight. "I did ten months in Iraq when I was enlisted, but I got stuck in a building doing paperwork all the time." A breeze swept along the alley formed by the buildings and tousled her hair. "Drove. Me. Nuts." She flashed him a smile, and it was a good thing he didn't feel attracted to her because her beauty had killer written all over it. "Austin taught me to box to work off the mind-numbing boredom, but he also wanted me to be able to defend myself against predators."

"And Austin is . . ."

"My brother." She looked down the road, but he guessed what she saw wasn't down that empty road to the mountains but the road to the past.

Heath started walking, Trinity trotting ahead a half-dozen feet, nose to the ground, tail wagging. "He the one you're crying over?"

"Yeah." She took a sip of the water. "He vanished on a mission."

Heath was tracking. "Talon's handler, right?"

Another nod. "He and his team were ambushed. They didn't tell me much, only that in an explosion, Talon was thrown away from Austin and found twenty feet away. Broken leg, but that was it as far as visible wounds."

As they rounded a corner, an armored

personnel carrier rumbled out the gates and into the open terrain. Boots crunched. Trinity zigzagged the way she was trained.

"Yeah, it's those *in*visible wounds that get tricky." Heath considered Trinity, who sauntered through combat like a walk through the hills of A Breed Apart. "So that's why he has doggie PTSD."

Aspen sniffed a laugh but nodded. "Yeah, and that's the only reason they let me have him. He had too much baggage for them." She shifted toward him, thoughtful.

"What?"

"Ever heard of someone declared MIA, presumed dead, that came home?"

This was delicate ground. "No, but since we're taught to never leave a man behind . . ." He tread carefully. "You think he's still alive?"

Shoulders drawn up, she stuffed a hand into her jacket pocket. "Don't know." She shoved her fingers into her ringlets, holding them from her face. "Look." She pivoted toward him. "I appreciate what you're doing here, getting me to talk things out." Aspen wrinkled her nose and shook her head. "But I'm not interested in dialogue."

"Only a speed bag." Bottle in hand, he motioned to a tented area. "Will that work?"

Relief swelled, pulling her straight, then it

whooshed out. "Perfect." Aspen smiled. "Thanks for understanding."

"No worries." He backed up and waved. "Trinity and I are going to take the grand tour."

"Okay, catch you later."

Jogging wouldn't alleviate his headache but he'd feel better. Heath whistled to Trinity nosing through a couple of crates outside a building. She loped into a run and caught up with him. This team thing with the people of A Breed Apart might just work after all. And to think he'd joined to find purpose again, to feel useful. To get back out here, in the action. Okay, so he never expected to actually fulfill that dream, but it'd happened.

Heath slowed, hands on his sides as he walked the fence to snuff out the burn in his chest and muscles. He'd gotten his dreams back — well, somewhat. But if he could book some more gigs through ABA, then who knew what opportunities would arise.

A niggling wormed into his thick, pounding skull.

Hand a few inches from the fence, Heath hesitated, listened for the familiar hum of electricity. Convinced it wasn't hot, he gripped it and arched his back, stretching muscles wound tighter than a primed trigger.

He dropped back against the links and held his knees. What was bothering him? Why couldn't he ferret out the truth the way he'd ferreted out terrorists in the desert?

Heath mentally reached for the tenuous threads of that niggling. What was it? What was hanging there like a phantom? Present but intangible. He felt it — not with his hands. It was stronger than that. Bigger.

God, I'm missing something here. That probably wasn't anything new to Him. *Just . . . help a guy out, okay?* God had shut down his career. Removed the chaplaincy option. Now . . . what? What was he doing here, in a place where it couldn't be clearer that he didn't belong anymore?

What do You want with me?

Trinity lunged, rattling the chain links as she pounced against the fence. She barked.

Heath flattened himself against the ground and rolled, expecting to see someone there with a weapon. Wouldn't be the first time. But only as his gaze streaked the horizon did it register.

Her bark. Not aggressive. It was . . .

Trinity whimpered, stalked back and forth. Attacked the chain link. Pawed at it.

Another whimper.

Heath pulled himself off the ground, squinting as he searched the road and field of brown, tan, and pocks of green. Heat plumes wavered —

Wait. It wasn't hot enough for heat plumes.

That was someone . . . coming, wavering, staggering like a drunk.

Or one seriously dehydrated. Or wounded.

Heath spun around and sprinted to the tower guard. "Nocs, where are your binoculars?"

Wide-eyed, weapon resting against his chest, the specialist handed him a pair. "What's wrong, man? D'you see something?"

"Get your boss out here. Now!" Heath darted back in the direction he'd come, vaulted up on an MRAP to see better.

"Hey!" someone below objected.

Trinity raced around the vehicle, then sprinted back to the fence, barking.

"Good, girl." Heath knelt awkwardly on the steel trap and aimed the binoculars toward the figure.

Commotion ensued around him. Several asking what was up, others jogging to the fence to figure out what he saw.

Seconds after a door banged against a wall

came Candyman's shout, "Whaddya got, Ghost?" His voice and pounding boots drew closer.

"A woman — she's . . ." He strained to focus the lenses. "American!"

Curses and orders flew through the cool wind. A vehicle revved to life.

Heath craned his neck, as if the few inches would make that much difference. Whatever she held in her arms made her steps uneven. Clumsy. Something near her shoulder moved. His heart catapulted over what tunneled through the lenses to his brain.

"She's got a kid with her." Just as the words left his lips, the woman collapsed.

"Move, move, move!"

Camp Eggers, Kabul, Afghanistan

"I don't like it."

The words grated on Lance's conscience, and he glared at Zeferelli. "That's a lame line from a bad book."

"Yeah, but he's right," Early grumbled.

"I don't care if he's right." Lance pushed to his feet and paced in front of the one-way glass. "Nobody likes this. Besides, every time someone says that, something bad happens. And I don't know about you, but I think we've got enough bad without adding to it."

Zeferelli and Early exchanged a look.

Fingers pressed to the cold table, Lance leaned over the surface. "What?" The growl in his voice seemed to prowl the walls.

Zeferelli touched his nose, then spoke. "There's a blizzard whipping up, pretty mean, over the Kush. It'll hit here in a day, two at most."

He needed an exorcist to get rid of those demons. What else could go wrong? Head tilted back, Lance held then let out a long breath. They didn't know about Darci, so he needed to tread the fine line. They also didn't know about her mission because of its extreme sensitivity. And if Early figured out Lance had placed an operative in his territory, he'd go off like a scud.

He traversed a very slippery rope. With Darci out there, Wu Jianyu skulking through the country, and Zheng in here . . .

Maybe two exorcists. "How bad's the storm?"

"Bad. We're prepping supplies for the troops and SOCOM guys in remote locations. Command suggested pulling our guys back from FOBs till this blows over."

"Oh, and Burnett," Early said. "I think you best haul those geology freaks back before that storm hits. Lord knows I don't want the deaths of civilians on my head, too. The media would scream holy terror." Early leaned back in his chair, stretching.

Lance couldn't yank Darci now. She'd been convinced something was there. He'd seen the light in her eyes, and before they had another string of attacks against the men, they needed to know what sort of numbers they were dealing with.

He wanted to curse. "You know what kind of money we put into that team? If we don't let them get this done, that grant money is down the tubes. That's going to look real bad when I go up against the Hill trying to justify our funding and programs."

"Imagine how bad it'd be trying to justify leaving them there and dragging home frozen corpses."

"It just can't get any worse."

"Unless someone comes through that door with bad news." Early chuckled.

Lance glared at Early. Yet at the same time, a squall of warmth washed down his spine and pushed him into a chair. "If someone does come through that door, I'm pinning it on your head, Early."

Laughing, Early and Zeferelli shot nervous looks to the steel barrier that kept them safe from the surrounding chaos.

Mischief-laden eyes locked on Lance as the general thumbed toward the door.

"Frank, take a load off the general's mind, please, and lock that."

With a rumble of laughter, Frank came out of his chair. "Yes, sir."

Lance again shot another glare at Early for taunting him. "Sit down, Lieu—"

Bang! The distant, hollow thud of a door hitting a wall reverberated through the building. Shouts climbed the cement hull and snaked along the floors, stretching closer . . . closer. "General. General!"

The weight of the next few seconds anchoring him to the chair, Lance cursed. God forgive him, he didn't mean to, but he did. He waited with the foreboding that had been inescapable since he rolled out of the rack this morning.

"Where's General Burnett?"

At the sound of Major Otte's shout, Lance shoved to his feet. He pivoted and strode for the very door they'd almost locked. He yanked it open and stepped into the coffin of a hall. "Otte."

The lanky officer turned, eyes bulging. "General." The rush of relief flooded his words. He pulled himself back in line. "Sir." He saluted. "Sir, I have news." His gaze drifted over Lance's shoulder to where he could sense Zeferelli and Early hovering.

Another flurry of noise filled the narrow

space behind, and Lance knew the void where the ominous news lingered would soon be filled with anger, revelation, missions . . . "If you'll excuse us, gentlemen." He took his aide by the shoulder and guided him into the room. As he closed the door, he essentially closed out the other two.

He flipped the lock. Sucked from the dregs of his courage and faced the man.

"Sir. We've lost communication with the geology team."

Lance felt prepared for just about anything at this point. "Sat imaging?"

A nod. A breath. "Not good, sir." Panting. "It's a mess. From what we can tell, they were attacked. Fire. Everything's destroyed."

"Who's responsible?"

"Uncertain, sir. Nobody's claiming it yet. And if SOCOM hadn't gotten a call this morning from Dr. Colsen, we probably wouldn't know about any of this."

"The professor?" A scowl crowded Lance's face. "Was he calling to report the attack?"

Sweat slicked the tips of Otte's dark hair as he shook his head. "I don't believe so, sir. He told Command they had to get out of there, that Jia awakened the camp, saying someone was coming after them."

His pulse stumbled at the mention of Darci's alias. "What time did his call come?"

"Zero three hundred, sir."

"That's almost five hours ago."

"Yes, sir, it's taken me that long to authenticate the reports."

The words faded as one name grew loud in Lance's mind: Jianyu.

". . . explosion. It's all we know, sir."

"Explosion?"

Otte nodded.

"From what?"

"The Black Hawk, sir. SOCOM went to rescue the team." Otte said it as if he'd already mentioned it. Maybe he had.

But Lance's mind couldn't surrender the thought of Darci up there in the middle of an attack. What was the probability that Jianyu had found her? "What happened?"

"They were shot down."

He'd need to get an assessment team up there to find out who . . . "The geology team." He looked at Otte. "Are they alive?"

"Unknown." His aide paled.

Lance knew what was on the line, *who* was on the line with that team. His heart tangled over the news and twisted into a hard knot. Otte wouldn't be here as if he'd lost his first pet if the team was alive and in communication with the base.

Otte continued. "At this time, we are officially listing them as MIA."

In other words, presumed dead.

Parwan Province, Afghanistan
Free-falling snapped Darci awake. Her arms shot out and she yelped. Rocks scored her palms as she slid along the ledge. Her face smeared the ground. Head spinning, wet, warm stickiness sliding down her neck and chest, she groped for her bearings. Something fluttered down around her. White . . . light . . . Snow?

"She came at us from out of a tunnel like the snake that she is."

Inwardly, Darci cringed. She knew that voice. Knew that meant she was in a very bad position.

"Did you think you could escape with our secrets and not face the consequences?"

"Jia," a hushed whisper sailed amid the Chinese flowing like the fat white flakes around them. Cold bit into her fingers still planted on the ground, thanks to the boot pressing against her back. She blinked and rolled her gaze around, trying to find the source of English.

She spotted Toque, pinned between two guards.

"Get her up."

The world swirled in a mural of white and olive green as the uniform gave way to the hauntingly familiar face of Wu Jianyu. Hair grown out and pulled into a ponytail, he leered at her. "Why are you in these mountains?"

"Enjoying the view," she spit out in Mandarin.

His jaw muscle popped as he walked to the side, pulling her gaze with him. He stood next to Toque. Walked behind him.

No. No, don't do it.

He was testing her reaction. If she showed one, he'd kill Toque. But she would not give him one. Instead, Darci locked her attention on him as he paced behind the survey team. The professor and Toque had been roughed up a bit, scratches clawed into their lips and cheeks. No doubt they'd provided a little resistance.

In Chinese, he said, "You cost me everything."

"The only thing I cost you," she replied back in Mandarin, "was pride. Everything else was your own doing, Jianyu."

Fury exploded through his expression. He shoved between Jaekus and the professor. "No! *You!* You cost me everything."

"If you had been half the soldier you claimed to be, I never would have gotten as far as I did." The words were cruel, and she should've reined them in.

As if a stone mask slid over his face, the anger fell away. "Let me show you the cost of your actions."

He turned, exposing his firearm. Jianyu raised it and aimed at the professor.

"No!" Darci lunged, but two of his elite Yanjingshe fighters secured her, yanking her backward — hard.

The report of the weapon ricocheted through the canyon and through her heart as Professor Colsen slumped to his knees, shock frozen on his face.

With a kick, Jianyu shoved him over the cliff.

TWENTY

FOB Murphy, Afghanistan

Trinity at his side, Heath waited with a medic as the retrieval team barreled through the secured gate. Amid a plume of dust, the MRAP skidded to a stop, spitting dirt and rocks at Heath. He didn't care. The woman — he was sure he'd seen her with the geology team.

The back door flew open, and Watterboy stepped out with a girl in his arms. Their gazes collided for a second. "Dehydrated and scared out of her little mind. Get us a stretcher."

The medic took the child and vanished into a building

"What about the woman? What's wrong with her? Why does she need a stretcher?"

"Ankle's messed up pretty bad, but no other visible injuries. And she keeps asking for Burnett."

Heath peered into the vehicle where Candyman crouched next to a woman. An IV snaked into her arm and disappeared beneath her skin. "Who's Burnett?"

"The boss's boss."

As Candyman stretched to the side to adjust her fluid bag, Heath saw the young woman's face up close. "She was with the geology team."

Watters glanced at Heath with an undecipherable expression.

"Did she say anything about" — Heath swallowed the words that would've exposed his true interest — "the others? Why is she wandering around the desert? Why isn't she with her team?"

"If she'd talk, I imagine she might answer them. Said she'd only talk to Burnett."

Two more medics emerged with a stretcher. "Coming through."

Heath and Watters shifted aside, but no way would Heath let that woman out of his sight. She knew about Jia. Knew what happened to the team. Knew if that explosion they'd seen was connected to the geology team.

Mind buzzing, Heath ignored the hammering against his temples. He grabbed the bite straw of his CamelBak and squirted some water into his mouth along with three ibuprofen. As the medics disappeared with the woman, it took everything in Heath not to follow. Instead, he locked his gaze on the mountains. On the spot where he'd seen the smoke billowing hours earlier.

There was one reason that young woman would be wandering the desert just before a storm, alone, and with an Afghan girl. Something had gone wrong. Terribly wrong.

"Should get a team up there."

Watters clapped him on the shoulder. "You can take the soldier out of the war, but never the war out of the soldier."

Heat infused Heath's face. He lowered his head. "Sorry."

"No way, man. You know the drill, you know what needs to be done." But that expression flickered through Watters's face again.

"What is that?"

His friend shifted. "What's what?"

"That look on your face." Ibuprofen hadn't kicked in yet. And the telltale pressure in his chest told him the anger rising through him wouldn't help. Besides, why was he letting things get to him?

Because he was assuming the worst, that Watters didn't think he should be here. That he didn't have a right to be here.

But Watters had never been anything but supportive and encouraging.

In Heath's periphery, a shape slid into view. Timbrel. Then a cold, wet nose nudged his hand. All signs and warnings that said, *Get a grip, man.*

Mentally, Heath took a step back. He wouldn't face off with one of his only allies here. "Forget it."

"Ghost . . ."

He didn't need to be placated by a warrior brother. "I get it, man." It was a bitter pill to swallow, like pieces of charcoal going down. "Just . . . keep me posted about the geology team. 'Kay?"

Watters looked down, then nodded. "Sure." He spun and entered the building where they'd taken the woman.

Heath pivoted on his heel, and the world spun. He stiffened and waited for the feeling to pass. As his vision and focus realigned, he found the team staring at him.

Aspen stepped forward, chin and shoulders up. "I'm sure she's fine, Heath."

"No." He didn't want to live on false hopes. "Nobody knows that." Curse himself! He'd just indicated his interest in Jia with his roiling emotions. "It doesn't make sense that she'd be out there, wandering the desert alone with that little girl. Something happened."

"Do you think they're still alive?" Leave it

to Hogan to be straightforward.

Like a bad action movie, the explosion played over and over in his mind. What he couldn't get around was that it'd take something large and mechanical to create an explosion like that. A chopper. And if she'd been on that chopper, she wouldn't have a prayer.

"Hey." The quiet, firm voice of Hogan snapped — once again — through the self-beatings of his attitude. "Got a sec?"

"No." Heath extracted himself from the familiar and took a jog with Trinity. Alone with the one girl who'd never expected anything from him, except to be there. The only thing God asked of Heath was obedience.

And what had he thrown back at Him? Rebellion in the form of control and anger, borne out of hurt and/or fear. Why had God allowed him to get so messed up? Why had God stolen his career from his fingers?

He wasn't angry, but it rankled.

Well, maybe that wasn't the complete truth. Because if he wasn't angry, things like this wouldn't bug him. He'd deal with them, release them to God's all-powerful hands, and take the next leap of faith.

The thought of something happening that would require him to leap with faith . . .

God . . . please . . . don't. Give a guy a break, okay?

Heath groaned. Already, he could feel it coming. It would hit him head-on. And he'd crumble because he no longer had faith or strength. He'd come out here, insisting this was what he wanted, to be back in the action. He'd never been more wrong in his life.

Camp Eggers, Kabul, Afghanistan
"Think this is connected to the Chinese?"

"Think? Yes." Lance paced the small room, itching for an IV line to a Dr Pepper keg. "Prove? Not at all."

"You going to make Colonel Zheng talk?" Otte asked.

"How? Beat it out of him? And what does that do but tip our hand?" They were trapped right now. Just enough poison to smell and know someone would die. Not enough to know who was contaminated and would fall victim. Besides, Lance would be hanged if he'd let that man out of his sight without figuring out what he knew.

He gulped the last of the syrupy sweetness and tossed the can in the trash. "Get a chopper lined up to take us back to CJSOTF-A. And find out what teams are there."

285

"Sir." Otte left the room.

Slumped in a chair, Lance steepled his fingers. What Zheng told them and what Zheng knew were two very different things. Lance could feel it. In the deep marrow of his bones. But if he pushed, Zheng would know something had happened. Would know that there was a high probability that Jianyu had struck.

If it was Wu Jianyu who hit the survey team, how in the name of all that was holy did he know Darci — or Meixiang as Jianyu knew her — was here? Her insertion into that team was a veritable locked vault. He could count on one hand the number of people who knew she was DIA.

Coincidence?

That'd be a mighty amazing coincidence.

But stranger things had happened. Like the young colonel sitting in this compound with him.

Lance had to play it slow and careful. But if things were going as expected, he also didn't have time to lose. If Jianyu had Darci — Lance would have to send all the dogs of war after him.

Dogs . . .

That punk former Green Beret who'd been smitten with Darci . . . an MWD handler . . . An idea slowly coalesced —

Boots squeaked and crunched behind him.

"Lance, ODA452 at FOB Murphy just radioed in." Early stood in the doorway. "They've picked up a little Afghan girl and a young woman."

Great. More poor citizens looking for food and shelter. With this storm, he understood the concern. At the base of the mountain, that area would get hit hard by the blizzard.

"She says she was with the geology team you set up."

Lance hesitated as he glanced at Early. "We didn't have Afghans on that team."

"No, the woman was American."

Was it too much to hope? One hundred percent of his attention landed on his old friend. "What's her name?"

"Didn't say. Won't talk to anyone but you."

Thunder rumbled through his chest. It had to be Kintz. FOB Murphy was about five klicks south of the Kush.

General Early bore a grave expression. "Want me to have them bring her in?"

"No." Considering the totality of the situation and the way it seemed to be complicating matters exponentially, this was a good time to get back to where he had more assets and control. "Send a chopper. Get them to Bagram. I want them there when I touch down."

"Anything else?"

"Yeah." He knew Early meant it sarcastically, but his mind raced. "Wasn't that dog handler speaking to the troops with that team?"

"Yes, sir," Zeferelli said from behind Early. "The team was there. Caught in a confrontation earlier. A Taliban terrorist tried to make soup out of that war dog."

He couldn't lose that dog. That dog was key. "Get everyone up there. Now." He stalked to the door. "I need that dog."

"General Burnett."

The loud, firm call of his name stopped Lance before he hit the hall.

"I've known you a long time, and we've worked a lot of years together." Shorter by a head and whiter haired, Early held fast. "Long enough for me to know something is off."

"Then you also know when not to ask."

"What am I not asking?"

"Questions." Period. Early knew better. Particularly in an unsecure location like this. "As soon as I can, you'll know, but . . ."

Early waited.

"You may not like me when all is said and done."

"Who says I like you now?"

288

Stretched out against some sandbags, Trinity curled up beside him, Heath smoothed a hand over her fur. Neither Watterboy nor Candyman had given him an update in the last eighty minutes. That meant one of two things: either they didn't have anything to update, or the update was bad news/confidential.

And because Heath Daniels no longer held rank with the military, his nose was kept out of the mess.

Except, he felt waist deep in this one.

Jia had been one of the most real people he'd met. Crazy to think that, having spent only a few hours with her. She'd been undaunted by his scars and his status as a noncom.

But she'd also been lightning fast to sever the ties.

It'd rankled him at first, but maybe that was just her way of coping. Maybe . . .

Maybe you just need to let this go.

Even if she was alive, even if the U.S. launched a mission to find her — the thought dragged his gaze to the rugged Hindu Kush with its winter storm clouds that stood over them like an angry god — Heath the noncom would be sent home. Forbidden from helping.

She was right. They'd never see each other again.

Heath sat up, nudging Trinity off his chest. She huffed her objection, then stretched, which drew out a groan. "You and me both, girl." He rubbed her ears. Why did it bother him, the thought of not seeing Jia? It wasn't like he was top candidate material for dating. Imagine passing out on a date when he got stressed over things not going right. But things had gotten significantly worse since arriving here. It was almost like he was allergic to the place.

A wet tongue slurped his face.

Instinct wrapped his arm around Trinity's broad chest, and he tightened her in his hold. "It's okay, girl."

"Ghost."

Heath shot to his feet at the sound of Watterboy's voice. "Hey." He dusted off his backside. "What's the word?"

"Oh." Watters glanced back to the doors. "Nothing. She's not talking. But we got RTB orders."

"Bagram?"

Watterboy nodded. "Grab your gear. Chopper's en route." For a moment, he stood there, as if wanting to say something.

"Everything all right?"

With a sigh, Watters waved. "Yeah. Fine.

Tired, I guess." He started to cross to the bunk building, then gave another wave. "Catch you later."

"Right."

A strange ache wove into Heath's chest. He'd been good friends with that man once. They'd shared command and secrets. Laughs about newbs and girlfriends. Now the guy was stiffer than the hull of an MRAP.

"Hey, Hot Snot."

Irritation skidded into his mood as Hogan stepped out of the main building. "I don't need —"

"Ghost, chill." Her brown eyes held not condemnation or even a lecture but a twinkle of something. She bobbed her head to the side. "C'mere." She stalked away and went through a side door.

Trinity looked up at him, beautiful amber eyes sparkling with a "why not" expression. He sighed. "All right. But if this goes bad, I'm blaming you."

Trinity barked, then trotted after Hogan.

Inside, Heath paused to gain his bearings. This looked like —

"Hey." She leaned backward, her torso peeking out from a door to his right.

Heath entered the room. An examination table hogged the room. "What's this about?"

A man moved in the corner. Dark eyes. Dark skin.

Timbrel bounced over to the guy in an Afghan national uniform. The insignia on his chest identified him as an officer. "This is Mahmoud. He's a doctor." Whoa, the smile she shot that guy could blind the unsuspecting.

Ah. He knew what was happening here. Heath held up a hand. "Look, I've got an arsenal of docs back at BAMC —"

Hogan laughed. "He's a chiropractor." She patted the table. "Face down."

"That's handy" — how many chiropractors were there in this area? — "but no way."

Steel slammed into her expression. She stalked around him, around Trinity, and closed the door. "Listen, you do this or I'm going to Jibril."

"Nothing like taking hostages."

She sidled up next to him, her gaze imploring. "Heath, I talked to Mahmoud here, and we both think that maybe . . . just maybe . . . something might be out of line."

"Yeah." He huffed. "You."

Hogan rolled her eyes. "Just . . . give it a try, will you?"

Heath sized up Mahmoud. The Afghan pumped antibacterial cleanser into his palms, then rubbed them and the tops of his hands with enough friction to create a fire. "You have headache now?"

Heath gave a curt nod.

"Please. Remove your shirt."

"Look, I appreciate —"

"What can hurt?"

Heath sighed. Unbuttoned his shirt. Glared at her. "If this doesn't work . . ."

"Then I still win. You'll have headaches, and I can report you to Jibril."

Somehow in that expression he saw a stunning truth. Hogan had his back. Despite her threats, she was looking out for him.

After a brief exam with Mahmoud tracing his spine, kneading his shoulders — which about made a grown man cry — Heath face-planted himself on the table.

Cold hands, a cold table, a cold chill in the marrow of his bones made for a chilling experience. After Mahmoud had him roll onto his back, he took Heath's hands and held them perpendicular to his body, straight up.

"See? Your fingers not even."

Heath did see — that his right hand rested about a half-inch shorter.

He guided Heath's left arm down and placed it along the side of the table, then took his right, lifted it straight up, then braced the shoulder and rotated the arm across Heath's chest and —

Pop!

Pain shot through his back. And with it an immediate . . . What was it? He couldn't quite discern. And while he was thinking, the doctor held his neck with both hands.

Okay, not liking this.

Holding a man's neck like this . . . *So easy to snap my neck. Kill me. He's Afghan. But what reason would he have to kill me?*

I'm a dog handler.

Heath tensed.

The man applied pressure to the lower portion of his neck where it curved, then whipped Heath's head to the left.

Crack! Pop! Snap!

White-hot fire speared Heath.

"Augh!" His arms came up, defensive and ready to fight.

Trinity snarled and lunged.

In the split second that he realized Trinity was defending him, Heath also realized that a cool wash of freedom swam through his neck and shoulders. His heart rapid-fired, thinking of Trinity, his ever-faithful girl, attacking this doctor.

"Trinity, out." Heath swung around to find Hogan held the lead, restraining his seventy-pound dog. Trinity whimpered as her gaze hit his, then she wagged her tail.

"You okay?" Hogan's question held both expectation and concern.

"I sounded like a cereal commercial." He rubbed the back of his neck, amazed. And searching for the pain that had hounded him over the last week.

"How's your headache?"

He rolled his shoulder. "Gone." Wait. That couldn't be right.

Hogan propped her hip against the table grinning like a petulant brat sister. "It was my theory that when you took that hard hit in training, it might have knocked some things out of whack, besides your good sense."

Ya know, for a kid-sister-type, she wasn't bad. "That was some theory."

"But you feel better, right?"

"If you discount the second where I felt like someone drove metal through my skull again . . ."

"You feel. Better. Right?"

Heath grinned at her terse words. It was so easy to annoy her. "Yeah."

5 Miles from Geology Camp,
Parwan Province, Afghanistan
His body fell from the ledge.

Inside Darci lay a box. One in which she kept all her precious thoughts and feelings.

295

One where she hid what could be used against her by someone like Jianyu. It was there she tucked away the brutal reality that she had caused the death of yet another friend. Jaekus. The poor, gentle soul. A kind and generous person.

Hands cuffed behind her, she stood a few feet from where he had fallen. The bitter wind whipped and tore at her thin jacket and pants, biting into her — but it was nothing compared to the immense sense of failure that chomped into her heart at not protecting an innocent. Would God hold her accountable for that? She certainly did.

Her hair, once wet with snow, now hung stiffly and needled her face.

"See, Meixiang, what you cost those around you?"

Wooden and cold-chapped, her legs at least held her upright. Jianyu had pushed them up the pass and higher into the mountain, higher into the gaping maw of a pending blizzard. "Your idiocy is again showing," she said in Mandarin. "Taking us into the blizzard — we should be moving away. Nobody is dressed for this, not you, not your men. You're a fool!"

"Jia," Toque hissed from the side.

Jianyu's gaze flicked to the last remaining member of her team.

One pawn left.

And if he didn't shut up . . .

Darci whirled and shoved her booted heel into Toque's face. The impact sent him flying backward. The momentum tilted her world. Her legs tangled over each other. She stumbled. Landed on her knees. To the side though, she saw Toque. He'd landed strangely quiet in a bed of freshly fallen snow with a soft thump. Unconscious.

Maybe they'd leave him there. Then Toque would rouse — hopefully before his body had frozen through — and get to safety.

Two Yanjingshe fighters hauled her upright. She shuffled to a stable footing.

"Pick him up." Jianyu stalked to her. His eyes, which she once thought held power and beauty, darted over her face.

She had never feared him. Not for her own safety. But today . . .

He shoved a hand forward — right into her side.

"Augh!" Darci swooned and flopped into the elite guard. Tears squeezed past the agony and escaped her resolution not to be weak. Head hanging, cold, wet hair in her face, she gathered the shattered pieces of her courage. He'd always taken pride in his skills as a fighter. He'd never used them on her though. Times had changed.

"Shoot him."

She jerked her head up before she realized the mistake.

"Wait."

Darci closed her eyes.

"He means something to her. Bring him. He may be useful."

She snorted. "The only thing he's useful for is annoying me."

Jianyu's breath plumed in her face. "Then it appears we have something in common." He inched forward, then grabbed the back of her neck and jerked her closer. "But I told you once I do not share what is mine."

TWENTY-ONE

"Sir, she is injured and slowing us down. We should leave her."

Jianyu turned and raised his weapon, aiming at Lieutenant Colonel Tao. "You would question my authority?"

The man's chin drew up as he swallowed his objections. "Of course not, Colonel."

Lowering the weapon, Jianyu looked at Meixiang. So beautiful. Her skin like the pale blossom of a lotus flower. Her lips not the rouge color he'd tasted more than once, but blue. And trembling. She would die unless they could find shelter.

She had destroyed his plans by showing up.

Yet created the perfect storm by showing up. He'd need to make a marginal change to his plans, but through her, he could show his father what true power looked like. Not just to his father, but many more. Thousands. Hundreds of thousands. Millions.

"She will die, Colonel. It's hypothermia."

Jianyu jerked to the side. "Huang."

The captain snapped to the front and stood stiff as a reed with a salute.

"We need shelter. And a doctor."

After a curt bow, the man trotted down the path that wound up the mountain.

"We cannot go farther up. The meeting —"

"Will wait."

The lieutenant colonel's disapproval shone through. If he could not master his feelings, Tao would prove not to be as useful as Jianyu hoped.

"The storm is our delay," Jianyu muttered, so his men would cease their grumblings and accusations, the very ones they thought he could not hear, the ones they whispered when they thought the wind would swallow them.

But they would see . . . they would all see soon enough.

Bagram AFB, Afghanistan

"We leave first thing in the morning."

Heath rose from the chair. "What — how?" Did Jibril really expect him to leave at a time like this? When Jia was out there, maybe bleeding out, dying?

Calm and confident, Jibril lifted a shoulder. "It is time."

"We had one more week here."

"And now we do not. With the storm and the conditions here," Jibril said as if talking about cookies someone had eaten. "Ghost, it is time for us to go home."

"No!" Everything in Heath writhed. Coiled. Poised, ready to strike. He turned a circle, looking . . . for what, he didn't know. Something to hit? Someone to yell at? Something to change this outcome!

When he looked up, Jibril had closed the distance. "There is a great torment in you, my friend." Somber green eyes held his. "I am concerned."

Heath swallowed. "I know." Shook his head and rolled his eyes. "I know. Since I came back here, I've been . . . rigged." Ready to blow. He dropped into the chair hard. "I was so sure that coming back would solve everything. I mean, I was scared, sure, but a part of me was convinced I'd find what I'd lost here, or that they'd somehow realize how wrong they were in putting me out."

Jibril eased into the seat beside him. "And now?"

Heath straightened, elbows on the arms of the chair as he stared at his feet, at Trinity's snout that stretched over his boot. "Just more questions. More confusion. More doubt. More —" He bit off the word, but it hovered and careened against his yearning for wholeness: failure.

"So, you would say that this trip has been a waste, a failure?"

"No." *I'm the failure.* "I've enjoyed this, enjoyed the times I got to share my story, encourage those who are still here fighting, feeling forgotten, alone." Heath shoved a hand through his hair as the extra time spent with Jia sped through his mind like a F-16. "I've met some great people."

"The girl . . ."

Heath looked into a knowing gaze. He smirked, never able to keep a secret from him. "Jia."

Jibril nodded, his longer-than-normal hair dipping into his eyes. "Chinese."

"Yeah." He reclined and stretched out a leg. "But . . ."

"But?"

With a shrug, Heath sighed. "She was into me, I could tell, but she wasn't willing to go the mile." He sat up. "We had lunch, hung out, but there was still a huge emotional mile stretching between us. And now she's up there in the moun . . . tains." Was she even alive?

She needs me.

Which was the stupidest thought he'd ever had, because he couldn't even hold it together during one intense situation. "I guess . . . I just need to know she's okay." He stood and paced to the other wall five feet away. They'd been detained per orders of the base commander as soon as they'd stepped onto the base. "It's stupid."

Jibril smirked. "Why?"

Heath shoved his hands in his pockets and shrugged. "I don't even know her." Scratching the scar on the back of his head, he tried to make sense of it. "I mean, we spent like two days together. That's it." He grunted and returned to his seat. He probably looked like a loon, pacing. "Besides, she told me it wouldn't work. Gave me a fake e-mail address."

"I think," Jibril said as he folded his arms over his chest, "she did not want you pining over her when there was no realistic reason you would ever see each other again."

Heath laughed. Hard and short. "Thanks. With friends like you . . ."

"But you are a warrior, Heath."

Slouched down till his head rested against the back of the chair, he eyeballed his friend.

"You have been trained, and it has been ingrained in you to fight for what you believe is right." Jibril smiled. "Every soldier is taught to hold his ground."

What was he saying? The trap was set, Heath could feel it. And he wasn't about to step into it.

Trinity sat up and glanced at Heath, her eyebrows bobbing. As if saying, "Ask him what he means. I want to know. This sounds good."

"Traitor." Her ears were soft and soothing between his fingers. "Well, go on." He looked to Jibril. "Spit it out before you bust a gut laughing at me."

Laughter spilled through the room. "When was the last time you took interest — like this — in a woman?"

"Jibril, didn't you hear? She cut the tether."

"I think, like you, she is afraid of what could be."

Morose — no, morbid thoughts trapped Heath's mind. "We aren't even sure . . . she might be dead."

"Then why is your heart still fighting?"

A door squeaked open, and a guard thrust Hogan into the room.

"Hey!" She scowled and drew her arms back.

Trinity and Heath lunged — Heath to Hogan, to catch her before she did something stupid. And Trinity to protect him.

"Got it," Heath said to the specialist who'd manhandled her.

The guy's face flushed. "Sorry, sir. We asked her . . . she wouldn't —"

"Understood." Heath nodded. "We'll keep her safe here." When the door closed, Heath turned. "You said a bio break! What was *that* about?"

"Fact finding."

"You mean snooping."

"You spell it your way, I'll spell it my way." Unrepentant and rebellious, she sauntered to a soda machine. Kicked it. She spun toward them. "I was this" — she pinched her fingers till they were millimeters apart — "close to finding out what was going on."

All pretense of civility drained from Jibril. "Timbrel, you must stop this." He went to her. "This organization cannot gain a bad name because you won't cooperate."

She held up her hands and looked the most repentant Heath had ever seen her. "I know. I know. I'm sorry. It's just . . ." She hunched her shoulders. "Something is going on out there. There's more brass here than on the knuckles in LA — and trust me, I know. I've lived there."

Heath couldn't help but grin. "I bet Christmas presents under the tree killed you."

305

She blew her bangs out of her face. "Why? I already knew what they were."

Heath groaned. "You're hopeless."

"Shut up." The snarl in her words yanked the humor from the conversation.

"Never mind," Jibril said. "We want to be welcome to come back, so we must all" — he even looked at Heath — "be our best."

"Yeah, Ghost." Hogan's eyes flamed.

He'd said something that shifted their worlds. Whatever it was, he regretted it. Heath closed the instance. "Hey," he said in a low voice so the others couldn't hear. "What just happened?"

"Nothing."

He placed a light touch to her shoulder. "You put my nose to the fire earlier over my headaches. I'm putting yours to the fire now."

"Just . . ." Her narrowed eyes snapped to his. "Don't call me hopeless." She shrugged away and circled the room. "Where's Aspen?"

"We don't know. Two MPs came and asked her to go with them."

"This is stupid!" Hogan sat cross-legged on the floor, petting Trinity. "It's like lining up to see the principal. What'd we do?"

"Nothing, as far as we know. Unless your little bathroom diversion created trouble."

"It gave me information."

"Like what?"

"Like all the brass I saw —"

"Hey, genius. This is a military base. What'd you expect?"

"Two four-star generals, a few three-stars, and you're going to tell me that's normal at a place like this where supposedly all's well?" Her expression seethed. "Then what about the Chinese man in handcuffs, ferried into a building the brass just entered?"

"Chinese?" Heath asked.

"I overhead an MP say the Chinese guy is the personal aide to China's minister of defense."

"You've got to be kidding."

"And the little girl that the Alice chick had with her? She went into absolute hysterics when she saw the Chinese dude." Vehemence tightened her lips. "So, Hot Snot — am I useless and hopeless?"

"I didn't call you useless."

She waved and turned. "Whatever."

Along with Hogan's attitude, they had a wad of trouble on the base. Though he hadn't seen anything that set it off, Heath had sensed an electric hum in the air for a while. Something really big was about to blow wide open.

TWENTY-TWO

Sitting in a comfortable chair with a Dr Pepper in hand, Alice Ward looked like any high school sweetheart one of the thousands of specialists at Bagram had left at home. But this girl knew something.

"Miss Ward?"

Licking her lips, she straightened. "I need to speak to General Burnett."

With a soft snort, he lowered himself to the edge of the table in front of her. He tugged on his name patch. "Right here, Miss Ward."

She deflated. "Finally." Tears welled in her eyes. "I . . ." She tucked her chin and sniffled. "I . . . was so scared . . . but she . . ." Alice shook her head. "I can't . . ."

"It's okay. Just take your time." He slurped his Dr Pepper, determined not to be undone by tears. Give him a tough nut like Darci any day of the week.

Scooting up, she seemed to draw on the

last of her courage. "I don't know how she knew, but she knew. And she was so good and fast." Her eyes widened as her gaze met his. "Holy cow, that girl was so fast — like she had *skills*."

He wanted to laugh. "Who?"

"Jia. Jia Kintz." Animated, Alice related the story of Jia rushing into the camp. "She had this little girl with her, and I was stunned. We all were, in fact. Okay, maybe not the professor. He seemed annoyed, but then again, he was always annoyed. Anyway, she was bleeding —"

"Who was bleeding?"

"Jia. But she wouldn't slow down to let anyone look at it." Alice brushed the hair from her face. "She told us all to get packed up. She gave me the girl, and I got her cleaned up and put a warm jacket on her — that's when I saw all the blood. I realized it was from Jia, so I went to our tent — and there they were. Locked in a gun battle."

Alarms shrieked through his mind. "Who?"

"Jia and Toque. They both had guns — I have no idea where they got guns. It made no sense."

"Did he shoot her?" Lance tried to re-member what the dossier said about Peter Toque, but it was like trying to find a pea in the dark.

"No. I . . . I don't think so." She covered her mouth. "Wow, I hope not. I mean, he could've, I guess. He was up with her. They'd come back to camp together."

"Where had they been?"

Alice shrugged. "Don't know. Jia was always going off on her own. She said it helped her clear her mind."

More like clear an area. She'd been working. As always.

"That's when the chopper showed up. Everything went crazy from there. Jia sprinted between two tents, and I was so scared I followed her. We went into the tunnels." She explained how they'd stayed there overnight, trekking and stopping for rests only when necessary, and how Jia had this shoulder wound . . .

"How did you escape and get down that mountain to the base?"

Once again, tears pooled in her eyes. "Jia." One loosened itself and streaked down her face. "She said she would distract them, then join us, but . . ." Hands to her face, she collapsed into tears.

Lance pushed to his feet. He didn't need the young woman to tell him what happened. Experience, integrity spoke for itself.

Darci sacrificed herself.

He almost couldn't bring himself to ask the final question. "Do you know if she was alive?"

Face still buried, she shook her head. "I don't know." She lifted her tear-streaked face. "I don't know . . . I heard shouts and gunshots and screams . . . and I ran. Ran as fast as I could with the girl." She shuddered. "I should've stayed. Should've made sure she was safe, right? I mean, what kind of person does that? Leaves another —"

Lance nodded to Otte who sat beside the woman, a hand on her twittering hands, and reassured her that she'd done the right thing. That it was a smart move.

Stepping into the hall, Lance left behind the somber, smooth voice of Otte trying to coax the woman out of her sodden grief.

One thing was clear: Jia had found something up there. And someone didn't want her to tell the tale. If she'd had time to alert the team to pack up and get to safety — wait.

The child.

Lance stalked to the preview room where he thrust into it. "Zeferelli."

The man snapped to attention and saluted.

"Where's the girl?"

"In interview room —"

"No, the little girl. The Afghan. Get her for me."

Fifteen minutes later, the lieutenant lumbered back in with the girl and an older Afghan woman. A few minutes of discussion with the older woman and child armed Lance with a nugget of gold. Together, the four of them walked down the hall, the girl clinging to Lance's hand. Reminded him of his granddaughter back home, a few years younger, and Carrie had blond hair.

They stepped into interview room six.

Badria was a half step behind him. When she swung around to the front, she saw the man hunched at the table and threw herself back. Terror's greedy claws stabbed her innocent face. She screamed.

Lance nodded to the lieutenant.

Zeferelli lifted the shrieking, crying child and carried her out of the room.

"Explain that to me." Lance sat back in a folding chair, metal digging into his back. He lifted his ankle and placed it on his knee. Casual and looking comfortable.

Colonel Zheng's face remained impassive. Implacable.

"Imagine that." Lance straightened and folded his hands on the table. "A little girl, found in an Afghan village, goes into terror fits when she sees you." He slid a piece of sugar-free gum into his mouth. "Wonder what that means."

"That she is a little girl who should not be used as a pawn in games of war."

"A pawn?" Lance pursed his lips. "I'm not the one who made her a pawn. Someone who murdered everyone in her village made her a pawn."

Quick as a bolt of lightning, an expression zapped through Haur's face.

"Now, I wonder —"

Two knocks on the metal door.

The signal. Lance went to the door and opened it.

"Sir," Otte said. "She's awake."

"Ah. Good." He looked to Zheng, hoping to make the man sweat. "I'll be right back."

Door secured, he strode down the hall.

"When you mentioned that village, Zheng's thermals went through the roof."

He didn't need thermals to tell him that story worried Zheng. They both had full knowledge that Wu Jianyu was the devil himself.

And knowing that man was in this area . . .

Knowing he had a bloodthirsty vengeance against a young woman named Meixiang . . .

Who was Darci Kintz . . .

The connections and secrets were as vast as the mountains containing the greatest drama of his life.

It was time for some cooperative effort.

On his knees, eyes closed, Haur trained his mind to quiet.

Two decades.

Thousands of compromises.

Millions of words.

Quiet.

There on the precipice before him, he sensed the winds shift. Change. The course would be altered. This journey, this determination to be relentless, would bring him something far greater than he could imagine.

Would he be free? Finally?

It was a vain and selfish hope. He chided himself for the thought. There were things far greater . . .

Palms up, on his knees, he surrendered those dreams.

"What's he doing?"

Zeferelli snorted. "Meditating."

"Well, let's wake him up." Early looked to Lance. "You ready?"

Lance nodded. Together, they entered the room, and as if he rose from the air itself, Haur sprang to his feet.

Zeferelli jumped, reaching for his weapon.

Lance chuckled. "At ease, Lieutenant." He motioned to the table. "Colonel."

With a nod, Haur placed himself in a chair. Unnerving as all get-out was the absolute calm on the man's face.

Ironically, Early's storm overshadowed what was right in front of him. "You've played your cards," Early said, hands folded on the table. "Now I'll play mine."

Eyebrows pinched, Haur leaned in as if confused. "Do you not understand — ?"

"No." Early's commanding tone severed the Asian's argument.

"We do not have time —"

"Then shut it and listen." Early had a mean streak the size of the Mississippi, but it only came out when necessary. Absolutely necessary. "This is my base — American base. You don't come in here giving orders."

Plowing his hands through his short dark hair, chains dangling, Zheng pinched his lips into a tight line. He shoved back. Raised his hands in surrender. "Play your diplomatic and political games. But I will not be responsible for what happens by your waste of time."

"And what is that?"

"The general's son," Haur said, his breathing haggard, bloated with frustration. "Wu Jianyu is loose in this country. He is without the approval of our government. There is no telling what he will do."

Lance wasn't flustered. "You have an idea of what that is though, don't you?"

Tension bled through the Asian's body. "Revenge."

Early laughed and slapped the table. "Chinese getting revenge on Americans. Ya'd think he'd be more original."

"Revenge against his father." Haur craned his neck toward Early. "He will do whatever it takes to make General Zheng bleed humiliation for the entire world to see."

"Now why would he do that?" Lance asked but he already knew the story. Too well.

"Jianyu dishonored his father's name, so General Zheng disowned him. It is why Jianyu took a new surname, his mother's. He feels the punishment is not his to bear, that he was betrayed by his own people, so he wants to make his father bleed publicly, just as his father made him." Haur cocked his head to Lance. "He will kill till the blood awakens the sleeping giant. By the thousands, if he is allowed to move unchecked for much longer. He would like nothing more than to pit the Chinese against the Americans."

"That's a tall order for one Chinese soldier."

"Tell me," Haur asked. "What would your government do if they learned the son of the minister of defense antagonized and was personally responsible for the death of thousands of American soldiers?"

Foreboding truth hung like a noose in the room. "They'd dismantle that ministry brick by brick."

"Yes." Haur heaved a breath. "Do you not see? The one man in China who most wants to keep peace is the very man being set up."

"By that you mean, General Zheng."

Haur gave a slow nod.

"Easy words coming from the adopted son of said man."

"The adoption was never formalized. It is —"

"A matter of honor."

Haur inclined his head. "The very honor Jianyu seeks to destroy."

"Says you," Early said with a growl. "See, here's what I'm not understanding, Colonel. If this minister of defense is so committed to seeing this through, why doesn't he stop his own son? Why doesn't he come here himself?"

"To be here would jeopardize a great many things. And —"

Time to throw a pound of steak to the lion. Lance eased forward. "We have located your brother."

The man went stone still.

"Team of civilian geologists up in the mountains were attacked, some taken hostage —"

"Civilians?" Confusion smeared over the Asian's face. "That makes no sense. Jianyu would not do such a thing unless there was great gain."

He was beginning to know these demons by name.

Lance was on his feet. "If you gentlemen will excuse me." He'd seen enough. Had enough.

Haur shot up. "General Burnett, it was you General Zheng told me to seek out. He said you would understand . . ."

The words trailed Lance down the hall. Into the icy night. He stopped under a streetlight and drew in a hard breath. All the forces of darkness, all of his sins, were coming to bear. Oh, he understood all right. Twenty years ago, he should've gone back. Tied up some loose ends. Paid better attention and not allowed Li's wife to be snatched — though even he had to admit the Chinese went to great lengths to stage that event, taking her while Li was out of the country, the kids at school.

And now . . . Wu Jianyu, to restore his honor, may have extracted a blood price from one of the best operatives the U.S. had ever trained.

He had no more time to waste. He wouldn't wait this time. He'd waited, yielded his doubt to the benefit . . .

But now, the answers had come. The brutal, scalding truth that Jianyu knew *who* was up in those mountains, knew who he'd captured.

Lance prayed for the great blessing of being able to kill the man responsible for all this. At the very least, make him pay in a very painful, excruciating way. Snuff out some of these demons. It wasn't a Christian thought. But that's why they say, war is hell.

TWENTY-THREE

Camp Loren, CJSOTF-A, Sub-Base
Bagram AFB, Afghanistan

"Here, have a seat."

Heath lowered himself to the floor, where he stretched out, crossed his legs, and tucked an arm behind his head for a pillow. Since they wouldn't allow the team to leave the room — Hogan had to be right, something was going on — he'd make the most of it and grab a few z's. Eyes closed, he tried to settle his mind, bar it from thinking of a pretty Asian.

The soft click of nails on the floor made him smile. Soon, a soft, furry body pressed against his. With an exaggerated sigh, Trinity slumped onto his chest. Had she sensed his distraction over Jia and gotten jealous?

A cold, wet nose nudged his chin.

I'll take that as a yes. He roughed her fur, then settled into a smooth stroke along her ribs.

As he lay with his girl in his arms, Heath focused on his slowing heart rate. It amazed him that after all these years, Trin still had the ability to bring him to a point of near-stasis. She was more than a military war dog, more than the dog he handled, more than his partner. There weren't many people he'd try to explain that to, because they'd get weirded out. Few understood the incredible bond.

Trinity's head snapped up.

Heath opened his eyes, hand going to the weapon he didn't have, mere seconds before the door opened.

A tall, lanky major stood in the doorway, and Heath noted the name patch: Otte. His gaze swept the room till it landed on Heath. "Daniels, General Burnett wants you."

Heath pulled himself upright. Glanced at the others. Had he done something wrong? Maybe the whole stint with the villager taking a bead on Trin. He climbed to his feet and reached for her lead.

"Just you. Not the dog."

Heath paused. "Not happening." Too many factors went into his resolve that he wouldn't be separated from her again on this trip, and right at the front of the line was the villager who'd tried to shoot her. Though he knew Hogan and Aspen were dedicated to their canines, nobody would put their rump on the line for Trinity like he would.

"We can make you —"

Heath moved a foot back and lifted his arms, ready to take him on. "Bring it."

The major grinned. "He thought you'd say that." He tossed a nod toward the door. "C'mon. Time's short."

Heath hesitated. Who thought . . . ? What . . . ? What was happening here? He coiled the lead around his hand, shot a look to the others who shrugged. Out the door, down the hall, across Route Disney, and into HQ.

Otte pointed to a chair. "Wait here." He stepped into the room — and in the brief second before the door swung shut, Heath peeked. Packed with all the brass Hogan had mentioned, a table consumed the room. Around it stood a dozen or so men — Watters and his team.

The visual connection severed with the wood barrier. Okay, that looked a heckuva lot like a mission briefing. Or had the airings of one. He wasn't included but instead dragged to the wings. Were they trying to taunt him? Point out that he wasn't good enough?

Head in his hands, Heath closed his eyes.

Lord, what's happening? I —

"Daniels."

Heath jerked to his feet.

The major stood at the door and motioned him inside.

Sweaty and smelly, the room bore the stench of the twenty-plus bodies crowding it. And that was the word — crowd. Only three paces into the den and there was nowhere for Heath to stand, let alone sit.

"Make a hole," a deep voice boomed.

Like the Red Sea parting, bodies drifted aside, enabling him to reach the table.

General Burnett, who'd chewed Jia out that night, sat at the head to his left.

"Heath Daniels. You asked for me, sir . . . s?" He glanced around the ranks on the ACUs, and Hogan had been right. More brass —

"Daniels, you saved my life and every man on the team escorting me to Eggers." Burnett paused. "Is that right?"

"No, sir."

Burnett eyed him. "Do tell."

"I saw a hostile and engaged with my working dog, sir. If there hadn't been boots on ground, we would've been slaughtered."

Chuckling, Burnett looked around. "What'd I tell you? Team player." He rifled through some papers. "Daniels, you met a young woman while at Bagram. Made friends with her, right?"

Electricity hummed through his veins. Was this a write-up? "I met a lot of people at Bagram, sir."

Burnett leaned forward, his fingers threaded on the table. "But there was only one young woman you spent several hours with on the training field well past training hours after your speaking gig. Only one lady you had lunch with at the Thai restaurant. Is that right, son?"

Despite the heat churning through his gut and face, the snickers behind him, Heath placed his hands behind his back, at ease. "Yes, sir."

"In fact, this young woman mentioned you."

Heath's gaze betrayed him and skidded to the general, who chuckled.

"And I chewed her out, told her to get her head back in the game."

Is that what was happening that night, a chewing out? Something happened up in the mountains where she'd been . . . and he hadn't seen her since. She wasn't here. Had she died? Was Heath being blamed for Jia's death?

"With all due respect, sir," Heath said, his heart pounding, "I think you might've underestimated her. A woman who can tell a guy to take a long walk off a short pier has her head in one place — the game."

"Is that so?" Burnett sat back with a look of disgust. "Then maybe you can explain how she didn't see the attack that was coming."

"Sir, again, with all due respect, she wasn't a soldier. She couldn't have known —"

"That's where you are wrong." Burnett motioned to a man to his left.

"Daniels, have a seat." As the words left General Early's lips, a three-star rose and vacated his spot.

"This is a mission briefing with two purposes: discovery and recovery." Early slid reading glasses on the tip of his broad nose. "Daniels, you will be riding with ODA452. They're going up there to discover what happened. Who attacked, are there bodies, if so, how many. If all members of the geological survey team minus the girl who escaped are not accounted for, we need to know who's missing. If anyone is missing, the team will report back here and then launch the second phase: recovery — recover bodies, then search and locate any missing."

Standard fare. With one exception: Heath. Why was he going? The Special Forces team didn't need a broken soldier and his dog.

But the thought of helping find Jia . . .

It still didn't make sense.

Heath turned to Burnett. "Permission to speak, sir?"

"Not now, Daniels," Burnett said.

"We have sat imaging and the report of one Alice Ward, who was on scene when the attack took place." Early nodded to the lanky major who cut the lights. A projector threw images up on the wall, forcing Watters and his team to shift to view the pictures.

An aerial shot of the mountain stretched over the wall. "This was taken about an hour ago. No heat signatures anymore, thanks to the storm rolling in."

Watters's team shook their heads. This was going to be fun in reverse, but they were soldiers. And soldiers didn't complain when things got a little tough. Or in this case, a little cold.

"Now, we have this thermal image from last night."

Candyman pointed to several spots. "Fires." His finger wavered beneath the imprint of the image. "This . . ." He tapped a green spot and glanced at Watters. The grim expression spoke for both of them. Bodies . . . dying.

"You should know there are reports of Chinese military in the area."

Watters pivoted, his brow knotted. "Sir?"

"You heard me." Early tugged off the reading glasses. "Chinese. We don't know why they're there or what they're after, but if you encounter them, your orders are STK."

Shoot to kill? What was that about?

Burnett motioned to the major, who hustled to his side and bent low. The general spoke into his ear, then Otte hurried out of the room.

"Daniels, you'll stay with ODA452, use that dog of yours to see if you can find anything useful."

Again, this was all exciting and thrilling — in fact, it was what he'd wanted — but these men could do the work in half the time, grab a dog team from another unit, and they were good to go. To be honest, he didn't want to put Watterboy or Candyman in harm's way, and that's exactly what he felt would happen.

Heath pushed his attention to the grumpy general. Bulldog. Throw the dog a bone.

"Not now, Daniels," Burnett growled.

Heath let out a huff.

"Sir." Watters's tone was gruff. "Permission to speak freely?"

Early glowered. "Go on."

"Sirs, with all due respect to you and to Ghost — Daniels," Watters said, his face grim and red, "I must lodge a protest against his inclusion on this mission. Sir."

A stake through the heart would not have hurt as much. Heath lowered his head. He never expected that, for a man he trained to turn against him. Even though it made sense. If their roles were reversed, he'd do the same thing, but still . . .

"Explain yourself," Burnett said.

"Sir, I have the utmost respect for Daniels. I worked under him, then with him. He's a good man."

"So, what's the problem?"

"I've seen him in action since his return. He's still there, engaged — until his body shuts down." Material shuffled, as if Watters shifted his feet. "I witnessed him in a four-second blackout. He went down, lost sight of his dog and his team. When he came to, he was disoriented." Watters had gotten quieter with each word. "Sir, out there, in the field, that's the difference between life and death. In all good conscience, I can't put my men at risk like that."

"Understood." Burnett's gaze bored into Heath, who lowered his head once again. "ODA452, grab your gear. Head to the choppers. Dismissed."

Ghost looked haunted. Lance had seen it before. In fact, he'd been there once, back in Somalia. All his dad's shaman talk and his mom's Christianese didn't do much against those demons that plagued the mind. A counselor and years took the edge off that.

The look on Ghost told him there was more truth to Watterboy's words than Daniels would ever admit.

As if a boulder of guilt sat on his shoulders, Ghost rose.

"Daniels," Lance barked. "Sit."

Surprise clawed into the young man's face as he dropped back against the chair. The dog beside him raised her head. "Sir?"

Lance blew a hard breath against his fisted hand as he considered the young man. Darci hadn't ever been willing to stand up to him when it came to a dating interest. But she had with this former Green Beret. And Darci had been the cream of the crop in assessing people. Even though she said she'd lost that gift with Jianyu, Lance tried to get her to see that Jianyu was a different type of man. One of the most dangerous with his uncanny ability to wait out his enemy.

Back to Daniels. So this man had some good mettle, or the young woman he thought of as a daughter wouldn't go to bat for him.

The room had cleared minutes ago. They were alone. With Ghost's ghouls and Lance's demons. "Is it true? Does that scar on the back of your head go deeper than your thick skull?"

Jaw muscles flexing, Daniels nodded. "I blacked out — yes, sir."

"Do you think you put others in jeopardy?"

His mouth opened but said nothing, an automatic rejection seemingly lodged at the back of his throat. Misery smothered his hope. "Yes, sir. I guess it does . . ."

"I'm hoping you got a mighty big 'but' coming."

The man studied him, and Lance saw the burden, the passion, the warrior hiding behind the mask of failures and wounds.

Daniels shook his head. "No, sir."

Somehow, Lance wanted to reach in and haul that warrior back to the present. "No, let's hear it. Put it all on the table."

He straightened, and the highly decorated Green Beret surfaced again. "I got banged up in a training incident when we arrived. Nothing serious, but it pinched a nerve in my neck. An Afghan doctor at FOB Murphy gave me an adjustment." Heath met his gaze. "I haven't had a headache since."

"So you think it cured you?"

"No, sir." Swift and sure, the answer was the right one. But did the young man realize it? "I wish it were that easy, for me and countless others, but unless a miracle occurs and the scar tissue in my brain vanishes, I'll have problems with headaches and seconds-long blackouts. But before arriving here, I hadn't blacked out for months." He stared at his hands, then his dog. "I want to do this. I want to be there . . . for Jia."

Lance didn't know whether to punch him or thank him. "Well, I hope you're right because I need you out there."

Heath frowned. "Why? You have handlers without my issues. Just assign one —"

"You're the only one who spent time with her."

Daniels quieted.

"Son, what I'm about to tell you is to go no further than where you're sitting." Lance stared at him hard as he pushed out of his seat, came around the table, and hiked up a leg and leaned against the surface. "Am I making myself clear? Because if you so much as sneeze in the wrong direction, I will make sure you can't dig yourself out of the hole I bury you in. You tracking?"

"Sir. Yes, sir." Steady. Solid. The guy had a stellar combat record. Numerous medals. But it was the confidence without cockiness that resonated with Lance. Probably the same reason Darci had been drawn to him.

"That young woman you met is a military intelligence officer."

Gray eyes met his with little emotion.

"You aren't surprised?"

"It explains a few things."

"Like?"

"Like why she would show interest in me, then sever any chance of talking in the future."

"That was my fault. She mentioned you one too many times, and I bit her head off for it." And Darci had never been the kind to get distracted by big muscles or big talk, so there was something to the kid before him. He'd have to trust her instinct. In fact, he *was* trusting Darci by sending this former Green Beret out after her. "I think you saw that confrontation."

Daniels gave a slow nod.

"She's one of our most important assets." He reached back, picked up a folder, rifled through it, and plucked a photo from it. "This man is Wu Jianyu. A week ago, we thought he was the loyal son of General

Zheng Xin."

"Minister of defense."

"Exactly." Lance stood and stuffed his hands in his pockets, noting Daniels wasn't surprised yet again. "For years we have seen Wu Jianyu climbing the ranks, to take his father's seat when Zheng retired, we assumed."

"And now?"

"Now, he's a rogue son, bent on sabotaging his father's name, bent on igniting some long-repressed fears of a war between China and the U.S."

Daniels's gaze darted over the image. "He's the one in the mountains?"

"That's our belief. We also have reason to believe he is after Jia."

"Is that her real name?"

"It's the only name you need to know." Lance smiled, weighing what he would say next. "I need you and that dog up there. Jia might be dead, but I doubt it. She's a resourceful operative." He returned to the head of the table. "Get up there, find her, bring her back. Am I clear, Daniels?"

"Crystal, sir, but . . ."

"That sounds like a mighty big 'but,' son."

"Yes, sir." The kid gave a miserable sigh and shook his head, muttering. "This is crazy. I wanted this . . . with every breath, every beat of my Green Beret heart . . ."

"Wanted what?"

"To be back here, fighting, doing what I was trained to do."

"Good. You're back. Bring Jia home."

"No, sir."

The response knocked Lance back a mental step. "Excuse me?" Had this punk kid just told him no? "Want to try that again?"

"I mean . . ." Daniels huffed. "With all due respect, sir . . ." He glanced down at Trinity, and Lance could see the emotions rolling off the kid like heat plumes. Failure. Fear. Inadequacy. "I think Watters is right, sir. I don't belong out there anymore. My head . . . my body — they're too weak."

Lance could take this rejection and let the guy walk. But that would mean Darci might not come back. That wasn't acceptable. In Basic, the newbs were pushed until they redefined the "can't" to "yes, sir." As a former soldier, Daniels knew better than to sling whines and excuses.

Which meant Lance had one recourse. Though he hated pushing this kid, he had no choice. He kicked a chair. "Well, too bad."

Daniels blinked. "Sir?"

"I said too bloody bad." He stabbed a

334

finger at him. "You're going. I need you in there. I need that dog —"

"But —"

"No buts. You were military issue once, and I can dang well make it legit again. And I know you don't want that since you know what it'd mean to your dog." He let the threat hang rank and ominous in the chilled room. "So just get your sorry butt out there and do it, Daniels."

The man's chest heaved. "I can't. I pass out, I —"

"Well . . . don't. You know her. That dog knows her scent. That's what I need. Not some whiny, complaining grunt." Lance stomped to his feet. "You liked her, didn't you, Daniels — Jia?"

Daniels swallowed, and Lance wanted to yank his Adam's apple till the kid squawked into submission. Why couldn't the punk see he had the one thing Darci needed — someone going after her who cared. Someone who *wanted* her safe.

"Her life is in your hands."

Mouth open, Heath stared back at him.

"One more thing." He indicated to Otte, who stood by the door in complete silence during this tête-à-tête, then slipped out without a word. "I'm partnering you with Zheng Haur and his first officer."

This might be a mistake, but there were two lines of thinking here. One: Haur could be an asset. He had a vested interest in stopping Jianyu from sabotaging forward international progress between China and other countries, something for which General Zheng had been a vocal advocate.

Or two: He could be blowing a lot of smoke up their proverbial skirts. In which case, Lance wanted someone out there to protect Darci. Someone with a vested interest in Darci. Unfortunately, she cared about Daniels, too. What he hoped was that the two didn't combine those feelings and come out wanting something more. Lance couldn't lose an asset like Darci.

Heath glanced back, and when he didn't show any surprise at the arrival of Colonel Zheng, the decision was cemented. He'd picked the right man for this mission.

"Daniels, meet your new partner, Zheng Haur, the informally adopted son of General Zheng."

Daniels pulled to his feet.

"We have no reason not to trust him," Lance said. "Except that he's Chinese."

The remark had its desired effect. Outrage rippled through Zheng's expression but then faded to resignation.

Lance clapped a hand on Daniels's shoulder. "Keep a close eye on him, son." He squeezed the muscle. "If you can do this, I might be able to find a way to give you your career back."

Heath went stiff. "Sir. I —"

"Just bring her home, Daniels."

TWENTY-FOUR

So close. So very close. Yet years and miles away. Being in Afghanistan, without the eyes of General Zheng peering over his shoulder, Haur's fantasy swirled through his mind and took root.

No. It would be too risky. He could not.

They had separated him from his men save Captain Bai. Tactically, it was smart. But it also left a curtain in Haur's hidden vault vulnerable. Behind it . . . He wasn't even sure the door behind that curtain existed anymore.

It'd been so long. So very long.

"Promise me!"

The hissed, frantic words seared his memory.

With a thud and a gust of wind, a large pack dropped on the concrete in front of him. "Your gear. Courtesy of the U.S. Special Forces."

Haur rose slowly, not wanting to appear

confrontational. "Thank you."

The man thrust a hand forward, the other resting on the stock of his M4A1. "You can call me Watterboy." He twisted his upper body and pointed to the others. "That's Candyman." A man with a brown beard and sunglasses perched on his head touched two fingers to his forehead in a salute but kept working. "The others you'll get to know. The guy with the dog, your partner, we call Ghost."

"My captain, Bai, and I am Haur."

"Did he say whore?"

"Hey!" The man in front of him scowled. "Keep it clean." He smirked. "Think maybe we'll just call you 'Colonel,' but don't think for a second we're under your authority."

"We want the same thing, *Watterboy*." They did not trust him with their names. He understood. Breaking down the barriers, discovering if these men could be of help to him . . .

Smiling, Watterboy backstepped. "Not so sure about that."

"I want Jianyu returned to China." Haur glanced around. "I know him best and can assure you that is, without a doubt, what you want."

Watterboy spun, and as he did, he slowed as he passed the dog handler. The two exchanged a glance that spoke of bad blood. Perhaps it would be useful should Haur need to create division among this team.

A blue glow drew his gaze to the side.

Candyman pecked on a military-grade laptop with its virtually indestructible case. A curiosity itched at the tips of Haur's fingers. If he could just use that for two minutes . . . maybe four. It was all he needed. He could universally shift the course —

"Storm's coming," someone said as he dropped more gear. "A mean, nasty one with a butt load of snow and freezing temperatures."

A rumble of groans reverberated through the room.

His brother might just die before Haur gave General Zheng the pleasure of unleashing his vengeance on his son. To Bai, he said in Chinese, "He will not have prepared for that."

"Perhaps, but little stops his iron will," Bai spoke softly in their native tongue, his face not masking the disgust as he assessed the team. "They are weak. Jianyu will outsmart them."

Haur glanced toward the taller leader and the dog handler. "I would not underestimate them, Bai."

"Ghost."

Haur looked as Watterboy handed off a pack. "Got these from the kennel. Thought you could use it for Trinity."

Ghost hesitated, then took the packages. He unwrapped the smaller. "Doggles, sweet." He smiled, then opened the larger item. "Whoa. No way!" He held up what appeared to be a vest. "Tell me . . . this isn't . . . an *Intruder*?"

Watterboy grinned. "Yeah, don't mention it."

"I can't believe they let you have a Storm Intruder vest. This thing has everything — camera, special harness, life vest, four-channel receiver — dude!"

Watterboy and another man laughed. "Seriously. *Don't* mention it. Not to anyone. Just go with it." The meaning was not to be missed. They'd absconded with one for the man and his team, which made Haur wonder why it was not just issued to the soldier.

Ghost's smile slipped, but he nodded.

"I'm counting on you and Trinity to keep us alive."

Grating and grinding, the large steel door rolled up into the ceiling. General Burnett stood, flanked by a half-dozen men, most in suits. Which meant, not military. "Okay, ladies. Gather up."

341

Haur started forward, but Burnett held up a hand. "Sorry, Colonel. I'll need you to stay out of this one."

Haur stood mute, frozen. Overwhelmed, once again, by the certainty that he would not come off that mountain alive.

Heath tested the vest once more for a snug, solid fit. He tugged on the front around her shoulders to make sure it wasn't going anywhere. His mind zigzagged over the cost, over the question of whether he'd have to return it — of course he would, it was a forty-grand loan — and how much he wished he could keep it.

Hooking his hand through the lead, he smiled as Trinity looked up at him. She had that "I'm gorgeous and you know it" look going on.

"Daniels! Front and center."

Heath tugged Trinity forward as the team huddled with the general and suits in a corner. "Sir."

"Okay, listen up. This is Agent Bright with the SIS."

"Spooks." Candyman spat.

"That's right," the general said in a tone that explained how happy he was with this whole predicament. "So just shut it and listen up."

Agent Bright stepped forward. "Thank you, General." Chiseled jaw with a scar over his left temple, the British agent slipped into his role with ease. "What I'm about to tell you is confidential."

"And if you tell anyone, you'll have to kill us, right?" Candyman shot off.

Bright seemed to chew down the stub on his frustration. "About five hours ago, one of our operatives activated his emergency code."

"That sounds real 007ish." Man, Candyman was in his element antagonizing the spook.

"Then you'll know that Bond always gets his guy." Bright rolled with it. "And so will we. The transponder emits a signal once every hour."

"What good is that?"

"It keeps my man alive."

Candyman nodded. "Understood."

Spreading a map over his knee, Bright pointed to some marks. "His signal first emitted here."

"Geologist's base camp."

Bright nodded. "Then here, here, and here."

"That's only four," Watters said. "Thought you said he went missing five hours ago?"

"Next activation is in roughly fifteen minutes."

"And this means what to us?"

"My agent was on that survey team."

"Why?"

Bright smirked. "Even Bond never told all his secrets."

Candyman eyed the guy. "Which means you'd have to kill me — or at least die trying — if you told me."

"You're almost smart enough to be a spook, Candyman."

"How d'you know my name?" The man's face fell as he looked around, the others laughing. "How'd he know my name?"

"Listen up, ladies," General Burnett said in his booming, grouchy voice. "You know what we're after. Head up to the camp. Send me the feeds. But then, I want you with the spook at the last-known location."

Watterboy hesitated, scratching his dark beard. "*With* the spook?"

"My guy is missing, too, so I'm going," Bright said.

Several around them cursed, but the extra body could work in their favor. Heath understood the territorial nature and the belief that the more "new" you added to the mix, the more volatile that mixture became for the team. But the spook clearly had access to stuff the military didn't. And for Heath, that increased his chance of surviving this, and if the spook was still alive and sending a signal, then it was possible Jia was, too.

The building rattled as the wake of rotors rumbled in, around, and above the building.

"Your ride's here. Make it quick and clean. In and out. Let's hope for the best, plan for the worst."

"Hooah!"

Deep in the Hindu Kush
20 Klicks from Chinese Border
Hands plunged into the snow, Darci grunted. The icy accumulation bit into her hands, into her strength. She slumped back on her legs and tilted her head up. The gray sky mocked her. Not even a drop of sun to warm her face, beg off the stinging pain of freezing through.

"*Qǐlái*. Get up!"

Jianyu stood over her, leering. The muffled sounds of boots to her left warned her. "*Qǐlái!*" the elite fighter shouted as she locked gazes once more with Jianyu. In her periphery, she saw the man thrust his weapon at her.

Fire and pain exploded through her side,

the momentum of his strike shoving her sideways into the snow. She slumped and breathed hard, wishing the iciness could numb the pain. It hurt to breathe. If he hadn't broken her ribs, he'd at least cracked one or two.

"*Líkāi wǔ bèihòu,*" Darci muttered, knowing very well they would not leave her behind. She saw the gleam in Jianyu's eye. Saw the delirious hunger in him to drag her back to his father, throw her at his feet, and regain his honor.

Hands gripped her shoulders.

World spinning, she looked into the eyes of Peter Toque. "Get up, Jia. No time like the present to live." He dragged her onto her feet. His mouth brushed her ear, and out came a rush of warm words. "I have a tracking device."

A crack thundered through the sky.

No — not the sky.

She felt herself falling again.

Peter slumped over her.

"What, have you gained a new lover now that you have left my bed?" Jianyu sneered as he shoved Peter sideways with a boot. "How many have you had, Meixiang? Or should I call you Jia? Perhaps I should kill him the way you killed me in the eyes of my father."

"*Yŏu méiyŏu qítā rén.* Would he believe that there had been no others? She hoped so, because she would never sacrifice another's life to save her own. Cradling her side, she braced herself against the mountain as she tried to pull herself up, but the pain shoved her down.

Jianyu squatted, his left eye twitching as he stared into her eyes, their noses all but touching. There had been a time she'd found him intoxicating. His strong features, his charismatic manners. It'd been her job to break him.

Instead, he'd broken her.

And even now, she did not trust herself. Yes, a primal attraction existed between them. But so did his mean, calloused heart, his thirst for power and wealth. It hurt to love a man like him.

He caught her face in his hand and forced her to look at him, nostrils flaring and war raging in his eyes. "What of our child?"

TWENTY-FIVE

Rage colored the white landscape in a blanket of red.

"There was no child." Meixiang squeezed her eyes closed, cutting off his only avenue to probe her soul. See for himself if her words were true.

It was a trap. She wanted him to believe the baby did not exist. He dug his fingers into her cheeks. "Lying whore!" He rammed her head back against the rocks. A solid crack snapped a yelp from her lungs. She reached for her head, but he saw that steel strength he'd been drawn to when he first saw her in Taipei City.

"Sir — we need her alive."

Jianyu shuffled back, sliced his hand through the air, and nailed his officer in the throat. The man dropped, gasping for air. Quick as lightning, Jianyu pushed his foot against Meixiang's throat.

"I am not lying. There was no baby." She

gritted her teeth, her face reddening as she lay stretched against the path and the spine of the mountain.

How did it feel, he wanted to ask, to have the very breath cut from you by one you trusted, loved? And now, she wanted to do it again? "You think I am a fool?" He shifted and grabbed her face again. "I saw the sonogram. I was there, do you forget?"

Face pale as the snow behind her, Mei-xiang shook her head. Fingers reddened by the bitter bite of winter, she fought for her life. Tears slid free as she kept her teeth clamped tight, her tears a mixture of determination and fear.

Yes, fear. He would have that fear multiplied so she trembled. So she realized the error in leaving him, in betraying him. But he would not — *would not!* — believe her lies ever again.

Grabbing her by the neck, he hauled her to her feet. "What did you do with my son?"

"It was fake!" Her legs wobbled, and she threatened to collapse again, but he pushed her against the rocks. Pawing at his hands with her own cuffed hands, she sagged and straightened. Sagged again. "The technician was paid off to go along with it."

It wasn't true. He'd seen his son with his own eyes. "I saw it! I saw him move!" A path to redemption, to regaining his father's favor was a son.

Her brow knitted into an inverted V. "It was a video." The tears left streaks on her dirty, frozen cheeks and mingled with the heavy-falling snow. "It wasn't real."

Jianyu pushed his body against hers, pinning Meixiang between the mountain and his rage. "You lie!"

"It was the only way to keep you on my side, to stop you from betraying me."

Squeezing her face hard again, he crushed her beneath himself. "You mean, it was the only way to betray *me*." With the fury roiling through his body, he shoved his hand, flattened, into her side, fingers first. The blow would devastate the injury Tao had inflicted earlier.

Eyes popped open, mouth agape, Meixiang sucked in a breath. Her eyes rolled into the back of her head. Limp as a noodle, she slid from his grip. And he let her.

He did not believe her. Would not believe that the totality of that situation had been something she'd conjured up. There were too many facts that said otherwise. Including the photograph of his newborn son.

And now . . . now that he had her back, he would throw her at his father's feet and demand justice. Demand his honor back.

Demand his right as a son to rule.

And if his father did not relent, Jianyu would take it from his cold, frozen heart.

Of course, after he killed the old man.

Parwan Province, Afghanistan

Spotted like a dalmatian. Charred spots against the snow gave it the mottled appearance. It's all Heath could think as the Black Hawk circled the campsite-turned-crash site. Uneven, a blanket of snow had spread itself over the scene, concealing whatever lay beneath. He'd worked recovery on a building in Kandahar, and it wasn't pretty. The smell, the shock that hammers into your skull the first time you spot a limb. The revulsion that hits home when you realize the limb isn't attached to anything.

With a shudder, Heath prayed that's not what they'd find here. Hogan had said she thought he was here for a reason, and now he saw the earmarks of Providence written all over this like the charred rubble in the snow.

Or was that just him grasping for meaning and hope? Nah, he'd had too strong a connection to Jia to chalk it up to nothing.

Between his feet, Trinity shifted and leaned toward the opening. The wind battered its fingers through her thick fur. She

351

pulled her tongue in and stretched her neck even farther. The Doggles made it easy for her to look out the chopper.

With the swirling snow compliments of the rotor backwash, the storm looked fiercer than it was. Yet. He'd seen the Doppler for the next several days. If they had to hike through this rugged terrain for long, it wouldn't be pretty. He'd have to monitor Trinity, don the special insulated paw protectors.

The helo swung around, its nose pulling up and to the right, shoving Trinity in the direction she'd leaned. She jerked and back-pedaled. Heath couldn't help but smile. The bird leveled, and he felt the lift as it lowered to the lip of the plain.

Trinity leapt from the helo and onto the soft blanket of snow. Heath hopped out behind her and led her to the side, taking a knee until everyone had disembarked. As he did, he petted her, reassuring her — and himself — that everything would be fine. Under the control of the rotor wash, a torn piece of tent flapped as if telling them to hurry into its protection.

As the bird pulled away, the tent flap seemed to grow frantic in its welcome.

You're losing it, man.

Forcing himself to take a look around,

Heath braced himself for the worst. Charred bodies to account for each member of the team. Including Jia. The general might believe she was resourceful, and Heath wanted to find her alive, but he'd seen elite warriors go down in flames enough times to struggle with the sovereignty of God yet yield to it.

Heath couldn't explain the connection to Jia and the subsequent ache to see her alive. There wasn't even something special she did, like taunt or flirt with him. *That's because* she *is special — period.*

Yeah, okay, that sounded logical.

The truly logical thought would be that if she'd somehow survived, it meant she was in a heap of trouble. And trouble was a lot easier to work with than death. Heath didn't want to haul her body out of the rubble.

Watch over her, God.

Watters gave the advance signal as he swept the area with his weapon. He pointed to the two Chinese officers and told them to stay, then ordered a sergeant to keep their guests company.

Heath led in a wide perimeter. Flaps of white had been chewed up by the flames and left black and looked moth-eaten. The hulk that had landed almost in the middle of the camp and had been the source of the explosion he'd seen from the FOB was indeed a Black Hawk.

Weapons up, the team snaked in, out, and around the scene. Heath held fast to Trinity's new lead on the Intruder and walked her through the site. Nose down, she trekked through the debris. Her head popped up, she wagged her tail, then sat quietly.

"She's got a hit," Heath said.

Two of the twelve-man team jogged over and started digging. One stood back and cursed. "One of ours."

As they cleared the dirt and chunks of metal, Heath could barely discern the flak vest with most of the material burned off.

Heath tightened his lips and kept moving. *Don't think about it. Don't think about it.*

Trinity barked again, tying Heath's stomach in a knot. Another helo loomed over them, whipping the ash and dust into a frenzy. It deposited a cleanup crew, alleviating Heath's fears that he'd have to locate more bodies. At the back, Watters and Candyman worked to prop up the tent that had tumbled forward, the post snapped as if a man with only one leg.

Jibril. Heath had seen the worry in the man's gaze as he left the hangar and boarded the helicopter.

"Hey."

Heath looked up from where Trinity nudged aside some clothes waffling in the wind.

"It wasn't personal." Watters shifted, his gaze darting around the campsite. "I had to speak up."

"I get it." And he did. But it didn't make the matter any less painful. "You did what you had to. I don't belong here." As the words slipped past his lips, Heath realized those words had taken on a different meaning. He just didn't know what. "But I'm here. And I'm going to do everything I can."

"Hey, look." Candyman knelt beside a locker near a crushed cot. He spread a handful of gadgets over the rubble-strewn ground. An electric razor, a small radio, shaving cream, and a brick phone.

"She was working with the general." Heath tried to keep his explanation vague.

M4 propped over his chest and resting against his knee, Candyman stared at him, then frowned. "That's great, but this wasn't her locker." He pointed to another one that lay split in two, contents — clothes, a hand-held radio, and a pair of boots — spilled out. "That's hers."

Watterboy lifted the radio from the pile Candyman studied. "Why would an equipment supplier need a military-grade satellite radio?"

"Or more to the point," came a heavy Asian accent. "Why would he need an electric razor *and* shaving cream?"

Watterboy looked toward the opening where Zheng stood with his officer and a Green Beret. He tossed down the radio and picked up the shaving cream, assessed it, then cranked on the bottom. *Pop! Hisssss.* Watters upended the can into his hand. "HFIDs."

Why did the equipment guy have high-frequency identification discs?

Watterboy cursed into the strong wind. "They're used as short-range tracking devices."

The spook joined them. "The equipment supplier was my man." He retrieved the HFIDs. "Thank you."

Climbing to his feet, Candyman squinted out over the blanket of white against the gray sky. "Who the heck were you tracking?"

"Anyone he felt necessary."

"Is it possible your man placed one on the others?" Zheng Haur asked.

"Sure."

Watterboy nodded to Candyman. "Can you have your people run them and see if there are any hits?"

"Even if there are," the spook said, "the weather and distance will interfere. And they don't last long."

"We can try. Better have Burnett do some deep digging while we're hunting down the missing."

Heath's heart skipped a beat. "So, there *are* missing?"

"Far as I can tell, with the woman back at camp —"

"Alice." Rocket nodded.

Watters hesitated and frowned at his friend.

"What?" Rocket shrugged. "We talked. She's cute."

"She's off-limits."

Rocket snorted. "Sorry, Charlie. She's civilian and of age."

"She's the only witness we have into the deaths of six SEALs." Watterboy tapped his friend's vest. "Until Command clears her, step off."

Heath wanted to choke them both. "So! How many are missing?"

"Three."

"Found a body!"

"Make that two." Candyman slapped Watters on the shoulder and started out of the misshapen tent. "I'll check it." He jogged to where three men stood looking over a ledge.

Heath watched the team moving around the camp with methodical, meticulous precision. He tucked aside the feeling of isolation within a crowd. What happened here was pretty extreme and thorough. Who had come into this territory and wiped out a team surveying rocks? And the bigger question — why?

Watterboy started for the opening. "Let's figure out who's missing first, and we can extrapolate later, hopefully get us out of this winter mess before it sneezes rain and ice all over us." He stepped out from beneath the tarp and joined the rest of his team, counting bodies and IDing them.

Protected from the heavy snowfall by the tarp, Heath loosened his straw and stuffed the valve into his mouth and took a long drag on the water. Trinity looked up at him expectantly. "You too, huh?" He tugged the straw looser and aimed it at her.

She lifted her head, and he squirted water at her. As the water splashed over the contents of Jia's box, he cocked his head to look at a picture. A smile pushed through the depressive mood that had steeled over him. It was an image of him with Trinity. When had that been taken? He didn't recognize it. He bent and retrieved it. When he did, something slid out and landed with a soft thud on the dirt. Heath retrieved it but hesitated as the red and gold ribbon registered. Prying them apart, Heath angled the picture of himself and stilled. Scanned the information. This was . . . pre-DD214. When he was an Army handler. Still in the Green Berets. How did she get it?

"Why would someone have your picture?"

Heath met the steady gaze of his new "partner." A kindness wreathed Haur's face, in contrast to the infuriated, arrogant gleam in Bai's. "I have no idea." Though he hoped he did — he hoped she had the same healthy curiosity about him that he had for her.

Something stuck to the back of the printout.

He slid his fingers between the two.

Hurried footsteps drew his gaze to the lopsided opening. Watters leaned in. "We got a lead on the two missing."

"Yeah?"

"It's the girl Burnett wants and" — he angled a dossier page toward him — "this guy. Peter Toque. Equipment supplier out of Ohio."

"My man," the spook reminded them.

Relief sped through Heath's veins so swift and thick, he wanted to laugh. She was alive.

Watters tugged a phone from his pack and dialed.

While the sergeant radioed in, Heath glanced down to the papers in hand. What he saw made him stop. "What . . . ?" Weird. What was Jia doing with a picture of him at Landstuhl?

TWENTY-SIX

Deep in the Hindu Kush
20 Klicks from Chinese Border

Between the overzealous colonel and the dropping temperatures, they had one hope to stay alive: he must become allies with Zheng. But that would take some convincing, and the only way to do that was to provide real information. Scattered around the circumference of the small site, Zheng's men were alert and jovial. How they could be with the ragged claws of the icy winds and snow billowing around them, he could not fathom.

"I can help," Peter braved, breaking his silence as Jianyu continued staring at the still-unconscious Jia. "I have information about her that would prove useful."

"How can any information you have be useful to me?" The sneer seeped past Jianyu's lips and infected his words.

"I know her real name."

361

Snickers swirled through the snow.

"You know nothing!" Jianyu punched to his feet. "Do not attempt to become my ally. I have little use for you, American."

"I'm not American," Peter said, allowing the accent he'd hidden these long months.

Appraising eyes narrowed. "British. Spying on your own allies?" He seemed amused.

"Her involvement in the survey team had a smell to it."

Wind whipping at them, snow drifting around their heads like angry halos, neither moved. Or spoke.

Then, without a word, the colonel turned toward Jia, squatted, and traced a finger down her face, tucking her thick, black hair away from her face. "What do you know of her?"

The man had a strange sort of obsession with the woman lying at his feet. Was it possible this madman — and yes, Peter knew exactly who this rogue before him was — loved her? What was their history? That was the lone hole in his knowledge.

"Her name is Darci Kintz."

Jianyu stilled. Stood, his gaze still locked on her.

Feeding off the man's apparent interest in the information, Peter pushed on. He *must* get this man in his pocket or he would be as good as dead. "She lives in New York."

Someone coughed. A nervous one, that drew Peter's gaze to the side, but he could not tell who had made the sound or why. When he looked back —

A boot sailed into his face.

The afternoon darkened and swirled to black.

Deep in the Hindu Kush
18 Klicks from Chinese Border

Fire and ice. Pain and peace. Tumbling and turning, writhing through her mind amid screams and haunting silence. Running toward people only to see them slip away. Out of sight. Out of existence.

Dr. Colsen. Looking at her, talking and taunting. Then his head exploding.

Jaekus dropping from a ledge with a ravenous scream.

Darci jolted.

White-hot pain speared her side. She drew up a leg, covered her side, and froze. Her yelp strangled by her tears.

"Easy, easy."

Blinking, she found no difference between eyes open and eyes closed. Was she blind? Or was it dark? Wait — no, there. She could see a differentiation in the shades. She wasn't blind. So, where was she? Pulling herself up, fire lit through her abdomen again.

"Stop moving."

Even as he spoke, the memories stumbled through her mind, one on top of another. The campsite. The professor, Jaekus, then getting knocked out — she sucked in a breath. "Toque?"

"Tell me you didn't forget me."

She couldn't laugh. It hurt too much.

"But if one more Chinese person plants his boot in my face . . ."

She snorted, and a sensation like a live cat trying to claw its way out of her stomach shredded her smile. "Where . . . ?"

"An abandoned shack. Not sure how far, but I'm guessing twenty or thirty miles from the Chinese border. He seems to be heading in a very particular direction. I heard him insisting they stick to the schedule."

So, Jianyu was meeting someone.

"Look, Darci, I should tell you, I think he's got some wicked bad allies. I'd wager he's trying to attack the bases, but that's a wild guess."

Pressing her arm to her side, she pried herself up. She ground her teeth, ignoring the throb. Sweat dripped down her face and back. She let out a heavy breath as she pushed herself upright.

"And I think he has plans for you."

"Why would you . . . think that?" Bile rose in her throat at the pain.

"He knows you. Knows everything about you. More than you could possibly imagine."

"Of course he does. His father is Chinese intelligence."

"No, Darci. It's worse. He knows *everything*!"

As if her mind backfired, a crack in their conversation revealed itself. How did he know her name? "Who are you?"

"Are you that far gone? Peter Toque —"

"Equipment supplier. Who isn't an equipment supplier." She steeled herself against the fire in her ribs and for the truth. "Now. Who are you, really?"

Quiet swirled around the small hut. "British intelligence."

He'd told her. Shoot! Opening their secret IDs and placing them on the table meant the situation was much worse than she could have imagined. "I knew something about you wasn't right."

"What," he said from across the hut, where she guessed he'd been tied up. "Didn't I do the Ohio country boy well?"

She eased back against the wall, feeling the bamboo poles digging into her back.

"What were you doing" — she breathed hard and swallowed — "with the team? Why were you there?"

"When your name showed up on that manifest, I knew something was up. So did my bosses. They wanted to know what you Americans were after, so being the good spy analysts we are, I embedded to steal all your secrets."

Darci groaned. Ninety percent of intelligence came from assets embedded in innocuous positions, just to monitor goings-on.

The throaty rumble of a vehicle drowned her words as slivers of light streaked through the not-so-weather-proofed walls. Darci squinted against the brightness.

Diesel and loud.

"Sounds big."

"Really big for this mountain pass."

Considering she wasn't up-to-date on their location, she couldn't gauge that. But his notice helped. "Did Jianyu give any indication of what he's doing?"

"If he had, I would've told you."

"And I'm just supposed to trust you?"

"We're captives to the Chinese military. What choice do we have?"

"To keep my trap shut and stay alive."

He snorted. "We have to get out of here."

"You're brilliant, Sherlock."

"Thanks."

Crunching pushed her eyes open, and her pulse thrummed to find his shadowy form standing over her. Wait . . . something . . . something wasn't sitting right. Now he wanted them to work together? "I thought you were tied up."

"No, I just couldn't see you till the trucks rolled in."

Right. He really must think she was the dimmest bulb in the pack. Though her weakened state pushed her to trust him, to *not* have to work so hard, her instincts objected. Pain poked her, and she used it for an excuse not to reply.

"He had one of his men check your ribs."

She snorted again. "That explains the ungodly pain — they're butchers."

"They saw a scar . . ."

Darci stared out of the corner of her eye. Night blindness made it impossible to read his expression, but that sounded like a very leading comment. The rickety cot creaked, and the air whirled as he eased beside her on the bed.

Alarms blazing, Darci felt the first tendril of panic as she realized she would be in no shape to incapacitate him again or fight him off if he wanted to incapacitate her.

"Is it true?"

At least he had the brains to soften his voice. She was right! Indignation wormed through her all the same. He was digging for information. Most likely working for Jianyu. If that was true, then what was Jianyu holding over Toque's head to make him do his dirty work?

She'd play along. Let him dig a wide circle around the truth. He'd never know the truth if it hit him in the face, so she had time on her side. "Is what true?"

"I heard him — on the pass. He asked about a baby."

"Then you also heard my answer."

"But the scar . . ."

It made sense now, putting him in here with her. To bleed her courage. Typically, prisoners were kept apart so there was less chance for collaboration, less chance of encouraging each other, more opportunity to break them.

"Appendix," she said.

A door flung open. Light and soldiers flooded the room, and for the first time, Darci saw that they had not been alone. Jianyu stood in a corner, his eyes narrowed. His expression reeking of fury. Hands behind his back, he stalked toward them.

Toque, who sat beside her, started to rise.

Jianyu shoved him down and did not remove his grasp. "What does he mean to you, *Darci*."

A new heat swirled through her, sparking adrenaline. She looked to Toque, who hung his head. Traitor. She bet he'd tried to barter his way into Jianyu's life with a slip of information. But he had no idea the damage he'd done.

Ba.

Jianyu grabbed Toque by the neck and shoved him onto his knees in front of her, then jammed a weapon to his temple. "What does he mean to you?"

She glared at Jianyu. "What, are you going to kill everyone? What will you do after he's dead? Kill me?" She tried to stand but flopped back down. Pain drove through her side and back like an iron bar. "This is stu—"

Crack!

Warmth splattered her face.

TWENTY-SEVEN

Parwan Province, Afghanistan

"*Trust is not easily gained.*" Though Haur understood this, had been beaten with this over the last twenty years, he struggled in his present situation to accept that the men around him, seasoned in warfare just as he was, viewed him as an enemy and not an ally. It worked against his purpose, against his mission.

That must change.

And he knew just how to do it. Haur placed himself near the dog handler.

Strongly built with intelligent eyes, the man said nothing.

Haur bent to pet the dog.

"Don't." Heath Daniels stepped into his path. "She's not a pet. She's working."

Haur inclined his head. "Sorry. I did not know." It did not escape his notice that Daniels tucked the photos into his leg pocket. They'd provided him virtually no

370

information on the survey team, which was why he'd gone digging for some. He tugged the heavy, oversized jacket they'd given him closer and started out over the swirl of snow dancing over the scene. "It will be a hard storm."

"Always is," Daniels muttered as he gripped his dog's lead and moved toward the others.

He, too, was an outsider. Though he had more intel and knowledge on this mission than Haur, they had kept him out of the loop. He eased next to the man again.

Daniels shifted a step to the side.

"They are not the most trusting."

"Trust is earned."

Haur looked at the sandy-haired guy. "Have you not earned their trust?"

Daniels kept his gaze on the men. The longing, the ache to be included ran through that flexing jaw muscle. "Not this time."

"As it is with me, both here and at home."

This time, the man met his gaze. "What does that mean?"

"I see that no one here trusts me." Haur sighed. "Sent on a mission to retrieve Jianyu, I discover his betrayal and attempt to capture him with American help, yet no one here trusts me past the end of my nose. And because of my father's treason against

China, most of my own people do not trust me."

"Do you mean your biological father or the minister of defense?"

Haur gave a slow nod. So Daniels knew more about him than he'd thought. "You go to a park to skate on the frozen lake. You see the ice, you know it's ice, but you do not know how thick it is, how deep its hard facets go."

Daniels watched him.

Haur said no more.

"Daniels, Zheng."

They both looked to the leader, Watterboy, who held up a finger and circled it in the air.

Without a second glance, Daniels moved into the group with his dog, who hadn't given Haur a second glance. That was a good sign, right? The dog didn't see him as a threat.

He moved into position.

"SOCOM is running a UAV over the area to see if we can pin down the location of the missing and their captors. There's been too much snowfall to know which direction they're headed." Watterboy folded a piece of paper and slid it into his slanted chest pocket. "Daniels, once we get that lead, we'll want you to take point. You cool with that?"

The man's eyes glinted with appreciation. "Yes, sir."

Smart guy, giving recognition to the authority. Haur had this lingering feeling that Daniels had at one time been an equal if not superior to the men here.

"Zheng, we'll need you to talk to us, let us know if you expect something, if a situation would make sense." Watterboy's eyes stabbed with accusation. "You came to us, so if you want to find your man, you gotta talk to us. Clear?"

"I am not your enemy."

A shorter man with a vest strapped over a very wide chest snorted. "Yeah, that's what my last dead enemy combatant said."

Heat churned through Haur's stomach, but he squelched the fury. He expected this. Still, he must not be a doormat yet not be a rabid dog at the gate.

"Do you understand?" Watterboy asked, his lips tight. His eyes hidden behind the dark sunglasses. "I don't need trouble from you, and I don't have to drag you on this mission."

"Your message is clear."

Whatever Zheng was up to, Heath wasn't

going to be a part. Or a pawn. The guy wanted an ally. Heath could understand. But it wasn't going to be him. He would not be used to hurt his country or those he had vowed to protect fifteen years ago when sworn into the Army. It angered him to think this dude might try to play him.

"Coming online." Candyman angled a handheld device to avoid glare from the low-slung sunlight and the blanket of white.

The mention of the UAV's activation drew Heath's gaze skyward. Though he saw nothing against the swirling snow and sun, Heath knew the UAV had or soon would make its first pass.

"Getting a dual feed," Candyman said.

The Green Berets hovered over the hand-held device, blocking his view. No, not just his view — him. They didn't believe in him. Not like they used to when they'd follow him into the blackest of nights.

Maybe they're right. Though the chiropractor adjusted his spine, it wasn't a miracle cure for the brain damage that occurred two years ago.

"*Too bad, I need you on that team.*"

Wind howled and tore at his clothes, the sky darkening. While they were waiting for the UAV information, he could get a leg up on this mission. Heath jogged back to the tent where the survey team had slept. He pointed to the blanket and bedding. "Trinity."

She lowered her head and sniffed the material.

On a knee, Heath rifled through the broken box. Lifted a sweatshirt and held it up to Trinity. Again, she pressed her snout to the fabric, nudged her nose further in, then sat and looked up at him as if to say, "What now?"

She wasn't a combat tracking dog — and what he wouldn't do for that specialty like Aspen's dog, Talon, had training in — but Trinity was a Spec Forces dog. She'd been trained and handled in the higher altitudes, the rocky, uneven terrain, the brutal weather. She could catch a scent and read body language. And take down the worst of the worst.

Though he was asking a lot of Trinity, he couldn't help but question what this would take out of him. If he could even fulfill this mission. Though a migraine hadn't exploded through his head, the ever-present thump was there. But Heath knew he was asking a lot of Trin this time — to find a woman she'd only met for a few hours, on a ground now covered with snow, which would eventually freeze her sensitive snout.

Purpose and meaning spiraled through his veins. He might have sucked down there at the base, working the speaking gig, but up here, his determination renewed that he'd been brought here for a purpose. As he looked up to the sky, the view crisscrossed with mountain peaks and spines, Heath knew meeting her at the base was no coincidence.

You brought me here for Jia, didn't You, God? Maybe that was why he couldn't stop thinking about her, couldn't shake that beguiling smile and no-nonsense charm from his memory banks.

Heath stood, scanned Trin's new outfit, and couldn't help the smile. Sleek and sophisticated, the new vest made her appear top of the line. "You look sexy, girl." Smoothing a hand over her head, he whispered, "Do me proud like always." He released her lead and once again showed his girl the sweatshirt. "Trinity, seek."

She spun around, tail wagging, and headed out of the tent. Now, here was a classic example of trust. Trinity had never let him down. Even when he'd been flat on his back, unconscious.

He stayed within a half-dozen feet, monitoring her, the surroundings, and waiting . . . anticipating that second when she'd get a —

Her bark lanced his anticipation. She sat and stared again.

Good girl. "She's got a hit." Heath jogged toward her.

Trinity's powerful front legs hauled her over an incline, her back legs scrambling for purchase. Rocks and debris dribbled down, dusting Heath's face as he hurried to maintain a visual.

"Daniels, hold up!"

"No, go, go," Candyman shouted. "UAV shows movement in that area."

Exhilaration of the hunt propelled Heath onward. He searched for headache pangs, dizziness . . . Nothing.

Zigzagging, Trinity darted along a snow-covered path, her silky amber-and-black coat a stark contrast to the bed of white lying deeper with each hour. Grateful for the boots protecting his feet, Heath would need to monitor her condition. Trinity would keep working till her last breath if it meant completing the task he'd given her.

It amazed him, really. For him, it was a mission to honor his country, to do his best. For her, it was also a mission to do her best, but she lived for one goal: to please him. Loyal, brave . . .

No different than the men hauling butt behind him. To his left, he noticed a man consistently at his side. Zheng Haur.

Around a bend, Trinity slowed. Sniffed. Circled back.

"What's wrong?" Watters asked.

Heath shook his head. She'd find the trail soon. "Just give her room to work." As they waited, wind and heavy breathing from the team swirled together. Heath tugged up his collar and tucked his chin, seeking warmth against the dropping temperatures.

"Snow's probably covering up the trail." Watters hunched his shoulders as his breath came out in steamy puffs.

Heath nodded. True, but if the trail was there, Trinity would find it.

She trotted back to him, circled, then returned to a cleft. Heath walked behind her but noted the others slumping against rocks and crouching. Taking five. Anxiety crept around his shoulders and tightened. *Come on, girl. You can do it.*

A lone bark strapped through the afternoon.

Heath hurried to where she sat. "What is it, girl?"

She scooted forward on her haunches. Nose to the rocks.

"What's she got, Daniels?"

"Not sure." Kneeling, he studied where snow had piled up against the rocks. He brushed aside the loose powder.

Trinity nudged in beside him, her snout acting as an arrow.

And he saw. The snow he'd brushed aside was stained red. "Blood." He cleared away a larger area and the circle grew.

"Human? Animal?"

Heath shook his head as Watters crouched beside him. "No way to know. But with the location, and since Trinity hit on it and had Jia's scent . . ."

"We know Jia was injured — the girl said she was shot. Might be her blood."

Nodding, Heath stood. "Maybe they took a break here."

"Or she fell."

"Possible. Maybe both." Heath turned and surveyed the path. "So, if they came this way . . ." The path wasn't wide and didn't branch off, so there would only be one course of action. "Why can't Trin catch her scent?"

"Perhaps she was unconscious." The thickly accented voice came from behind.

Heath and Watters turned toward Zheng Haur.

Zheng shrugged. "They would have to carry her, which would mean her scent would not be as strong. Yes?"

"No. There are different types of tracking — air-scent dogs and tracking dogs. Trinity is trained mostly for air scent, but she does have tracking, or trailing, training." Heath looked around the scene. "Which makes her losing the scent a mystery." Vertical collided with horizontal. The path disappeared around a bend. What options were there that might preclude Trinity from maintaining course? Hidden trails? The escapees getting choppered out? Nah, the peaks were too jagged and close together to allow that. So . . .

Hand along the cliff face, Heath wondered . . .

Watters leaned in. "What are you thinking?"

"The woman who brought the Afghan child to the FOB said they hid in a cave-like tunnel."

Watterboy spun toward the rest of the team. "Search for a tunnel."

Heath stepped back and peered up at the overhang that partially covered this section of the path. He visually traced it as he moved until a jagged crescent blinked at him. "See that?"

"A ledge broke off — small avalanche."

Heath jabbed his hand into the mound

380

and hauled back a section of snow. The others moved in without a word to help clear it away.

"Got it!" Candyman announced. "There's a tunnel."

Manpower tripled on the site to clear the debris away. Once a hole was made, Watters waved everyone back. "Give Ghost and Trinity room to work."

Nodding his appreciation to Watterboy, Heath motioned Trinity into the opening that yawned in the face of the mountain. The rubble inside shifted as Heath maneuvered into the darkness. Weapon up, Sure-Fire button pressed, he sidestepped into the black hole. Trinity's claws clicked as she moved beneath the beam of light. She barked and kept moving.

"She's got it." Heath twisted and turned back.

When he did, a loud *whoosh* breathed through the tunnel.

Darkness collapsed on him.

TWENTY-EIGHT

Deep in the Hindu Kush
18 Klicks from Chinese Border

"Move!"

A weight plowed into her back. Darci pitched forward. Her palms poofed the new fallen snow. Though they'd stuffed her in a heavy jacket, it was several sizes too big and made movement awkward at best.

Gentle hands helped her up.

Though inclined to accept the help, she shoved away. Surprise rippled through her — she'd thought Jianyu had shot him. Thought it was over.

"Hey," Toque said. "I'm just trying to help."

"Help by staying out of my way and mind."

"What in blazes does that mean?"

Shouts collided with their argument. Two of Jianyu's men pried Toque away from Darci. As they supported her, she eyed

Toque. Though not an enemy, the Brits had been notoriously antagonistic and arrogant in their presumptions about Americans. She had no reason to trust him. Considering he'd hidden his identity from her, infiltrated her mission, she had all the facts to hold him in contempt and as an enemy.

Spies didn't trust other spies. When one lives a life of constant vigilance, it does not lend itself well to relationships. But oh, she'd like to change that. This mission — she didn't think she'd make it back alive. Not this time. Escaping Jianyu last time had been a miracle. She spent a lot of time in church, thanking God. But she wanted to make it back this time. She had something she wanted to explore. Heath. A relationship. Jianyu sauntered toward her. Though he had the looks, behind his eyes lay malice. Why hadn't she seen it before . . . before it was too late? How had she ever seen anything desirable in him? Stark and startling, the differences between Heath and Jianyu were like winter and spring. One icy cold and brutal. The other warm and inviting.

"Can you walk, or must I shoot you like an injured cow?"

Indignation flared across her chest, but she batted it aside. "Please." She tightened her mouth. "Do me the favor."

With a flourish, he whipped out a Type 92 heavy machine gun and aimed it at her.

Darci quaked inside but could not show that he held any power over her. "If you shoot me, you can't drag me back to throw at your father's feet."

A small twitch flickered through his lips.

"That is what you're doing, isn't it? Right after you make this rendezvous?"

Raising his chin, he stuffed the weapon in its holster. "Do not try to bleed me for information, Meixiang. I have none after what you did to me in Taipei City."

"You would do no less in the name of China."

"I would not have condemned the one I loved to humiliation and dishonor!"

"Don't be a fool. Of course you would have — you do it *now*!"

His hand flew, the slap stinging against her cheek.

Darci stumbled back into a steady hold. A face appeared over her shoulder. Toque. Again. She shrugged out of his grip. "Don't touch me."

"See?" Jianyu gloated. "She treats even allies as enemies." He swung his arm toward the front. "March."

"We don't have the supplies to make it over the pass." She needled his confidence, at least she hoped she did. Darci thrust her chin toward the slope of the mountain. "That's where we're going, right? Over the pass into China?"

"Move, or I will drag you."

Darci plodded onward, using the steep incline on her right for support. The cold pouring out of the rock seeped into her fingers. Traveled up her wrist and all the way into her heart. As the sun lay to rest in the embrace of the Hindu Kush, she lost all feeling in her hands. Her toes. Her heart.

"You're being idiotic," Toque muttered as they slowed.

"I don't care what you think."

"I'm your ally, Darci. Let me help?"

"An ally in what? Death?" She pushed away from him, shoved her hands in the deep pockets of the coat, and burrowed into herself. Focused on staying alive. Getting better wasn't an option right now. They'd wrapped a stiff bandage around her waist, but she could feel something deeper sinking into her. Maybe it wasn't the broken ribs that bothered her, but the wound in her soul.

Darci planted one foot in front of the other. That was her only goal. But with each step, her legs grew heavier. Her mind slower. Her heart emptier. Somehow, without her permission, her thoughts drifted to a handsome handler and his energetic war dog. He had strength in a way few men did, but something had buried it beneath layers of self-doubt. Still, she could tell he'd once been a no-holds-barred warrior. The way he'd called her out, been unafraid to challenge her halfhearted attempt to shove him out of her life.

Oh, she'd wanted anything but that. In a whirlwind life of betrayals, deception, distance, and loneliness, a warm inviting wind blew during her time with Heath Daniels. He'd noted her throwing arm, a skill she'd honed and few cared about. It was silly, but he seemed to approve.

"*Thought so.*" Those gray eyes of his had caressed her face as he stared down at her after she'd . . . chased after him. Chased? Since when did Darci Kintz, military intelligence officer, *chase* after anyone except a mark?

Darci, you've lost it.

No, no she hadn't. There'd just been something about him walking away, thinking she wasn't interested.

Not that she could pursue a relationship.

Why not? Being human gave her that right. And she was free.

You're an operative. United States Govern-

ment Issue. Property. Owned.

Did that mean she couldn't have a life?

Hesitation caught her by surprise. Until now, she would've said yes because her moral obligation was to her country.

Darci shook her head. Insanity. Here she sat, thinking about the possibility of a romantic relationship with a man who probably just wanted a casual date. Who said he was looking for more?

Besides, none of that mattered right now, considering Jianyu held the reins on her life and intended to drive her straight into Taipei City.

What if Heath came after her? Came to rescue her?

What? Now you're a damsel in distress?

"Might want to drag your head out of those clouds and pay attention."

Darci scowled at Toque.

"Something's happening."

Elbowing past him, she regained her bearings. Unfortunately, he had a point. They'd slowed, and Jianyu now stood with another man at the crest of a hill, radio held near his ear.

Radio? Up here?

Dread swiped through her.

A radio meant two things: He had contact with someone in the area.

And that meant his allies were within range.

A chorus of cheers shot up from the others.

"What is it?" Toque asked.

Darci urged herself forward, and when she reached the edge, a wide valley swept out below them. Several small, dark plumes snaked up across the bed of white. A village. Small but inhabited.

What haunted her was not the half dozen huts huddled against the storm. Nor the smoke rising from offset roofs, but the disturbed snow leading into the village. Tire tracks. Large, wide tire tracks that rushed right up to a gathering of trucks.

Russian military.

TWENTY-NINE

Deep in the Hindu Kush
25 Klicks from Chinese Border

Heath froze as he stared at the blackened rubble that two seconds ago had been an opening. Indecision gripped him tight. Should he dig his way through or . . . ?

He looked to his left and killed his torch. Was that . . . ? He squinted and waited for his eyes to adjust. Was he seeing things? Pulling himself off the wall, he heard shouts muffled by the avalanche of rock and debris from behind. Ahead the darkness seemed to surrender its power to a light source.

Heath bathed the tunnel in light. Two eyes glowed back at him. "Trinity, seek." The eyes vanished, and he knew she'd looked down the far length of the tunnel. Her claws scritched over the rocks. Heath moved fast and with as much stealth as he could muster, deeper into the belly of the mountain. He'd heard about these tunnels, as vast as the blades of grass and rock that peppered the terrain. Taliban had hidden themselves, hidden high-value targets effectively. Too effectively.

Ahead, darkness lost its power. Heath turned off the lamp as he rounded another corner. Light stretched into the tunnel and embraced him. His pulse thrummed at the sight of the opening. Silhouetted by the light, Trinity stood at the mouth.

"Trinity, heel," Heath whispered.

With a flick of her ears, she turned and trotted back to him.

Inching closer, he drew up his weapon. Pressed himself against one side, unwilling to become a block of swiss cheese, compliments of the Taliban. Or any other well-armed, terrorist-minded Afghan.

Heath peered out, breathing a little easier when only a strong wind and a stomped path met him. Easing out, he scanned left, then right down the scope. Footprints matched his theory that this path had been traveled recently. Dark spots pulled him to a knee. Blood.

"Daniels," came an echo-laden call.

Heath shifted and glanced back to the tunnel. "Here. Just around the corner. It's clear." Once more, he scanned the area. No more than four feet wide, the path disappeared in a northeasterly direction, and if he missed that path, the valley floor would be a jagged, painful hundred-foot drop to another swirl of paths ringing a lower, rocky peak.

With the pressure building in his head and his chest, Heath knew they were pushing into higher altitudes. This is where the Kush divided the men from the boys.

"We thought we'd lost you." Watterboy emerged from the tunnel with a shudder. "Man, I hate those things."

"Claustrophobic?" Bai sneered as he and Haur joined them.

"No." Gaze dark, Watters scowled. "I saw a team get ambushed in a tunnel."

"The path is trampled, and you can see blood spots." Heath pointed them out.

"Seems our guys knew where they were going." Watters made way for Candyman and formed a huddle.

Trinity nudged her way past Heath's legs and sat in the middle, panting as she smiled up at him. He rubbed her ears, rewarding her discipline and good trekking.

"Can't say it's a convenient accidental detour." Candyman winked. "Taking one of those tunnels, you could end up in South Africa. It'd be a mighty lucky guess."

"Or perhaps the weather drove them into

the tunnel, and they merely happened upon a shortcut." Haur scooted aside so more of the Green Beret team could fill the path.

"Right." Watterboy nodded to Heath. "Let's get moving. We're losing daylight fast, and I don't want to take a wrong turn and fly to my death."

"Agreed." Heath reached for Trinity, and she moved into position beside him.

Dirt and rock spat at him. In the seconds it took to register, Heath heard shouts from behind.

"Taking fire, taking fire!"

Heath pressed himself to the ground, doing his best to shield Trinity.

"Where are they?"

"Anyone got eyes on the shooters?"

Heath urged Trinity closer to the rocks, and his girl low-crawled, ears flat and belly against the rocks, to the solid wall. Twisting on his side, Heath brought up his weapon and scanned the outlying area.

Seconds lengthened to minutes as they searched for the shooters.

"Think they left?" Candyman asked.

"Put your head up and find out," Watters said, his face void of the sarcasm his words implied.

A soft pop and dribbling rocks sounded to Heath's left. Then a hard breath.

"Who was stupid enough to lift his head?" Watterboy asked.

"What are they waiting for? They could wipe us off the map."

"Exactly," Heath muttered. "They have us trapped. They live to kill Americans, and they've been waiting for this. No way they'd give it up."

"Agreed." Watterboy's gruff voice rattled the air.

"Then why aren't they shooting?"

Haur's question was a good one. Heath had been wondering about that same thing.

Tsing!

A whiff of gunpowder stung his nose a second before more debris peppered the back of his head. "Down." Heath swept his reticle along the ridge. "They're below us." Which explained why they hadn't been shooting — they couldn't see the team flattened on the path.

With care, Heath scanned the striations on the opposing ridge.

A glint flashed at him. As bad as flashing their backside. He wanted to laugh. The sun had been in the favor of his team, glinting off the reticle of a weapon. Heath used the mental snapshot of where that glint appeared and homed in on the spot. Though he saw nothing that would mark a sniper, he fired.

"What're you shooting at?"

A shape shifted in the reticle.

"Gotcha." Heath waited and saw more forms lined up. His heart pounded. "Lower left ridge, two mil right."

As soon as the words left his mouth, a barrage of weapons fire assaulted the position.

"Ghost, move!"

Heath grabbed Trinity's lead and hauled it up the path and around the bend. Out of sight, he hoped, of the shooters. Using the bend for cover, he aimed in the direction of the ledge and provided suppressive fire as Watters and the rest hustled into the safety and protection of the bend. Once clear, Heath eased out of sight and slunk back to the team, who'd huddled.

"Keep moving, people. Don't give them an excuse to find us." Watters's direction was met with groans but also compliance. They all knew he was right. They had to keep moving, not just to avoid getting shredded by bullets but because of Jia. She was out there, somewhere. Injured, if their guess was right.

Heath drifted closer to Haur — and noticed Bai clutching his arm. "You got hit."

Bai shrugged. "A graze."

"Hold up," Heath called to the front

where Watterboy and Candyman led the pack. He tugged Bai's hand away and nodded. Seared by the bullet trail, the flesh hovered red and angry around a hole. "You bit one."

Bai pried away Heath's arm. "I will survive."

"No, you need to have that looked at."

"It is nothing."

"Yeah." Watterboy motioned a sergeant toward him. "Well, my guy will make sure."

Heath tugged Haur aside, away from the captain. "Hey, Jianyu — would he be the type to seek help for his man if he got shot?"

Haur looked at Bai. "Most likely, he would shoot him and finish him off."

Yeah. Exactly. "That's what I thought."

"Why?" Watterboy's voice was close and drew Heath around.

"Jianyu's behavior indicates he has one goal in mind. We don't know what that is, but I don't think he's going to let anything get in his way, especially not a wounded soldier. It'd slow him down, cost him time and resources."

Watterboy tilted his head to the side. "So if the wounded was a soldier, he'd kill to get him out of the way."

Heath nodded. "That was my thinking."

"Or it is Jianyu," Haur said.

Heath considered Haur, the reason behind the suggestion. Was he trying to wear down their defenses, or was he legitimately trying to help them process this situation? "True, but they're moving too fast for their leader to be down."

"Agreed." Watterboy smiled at Heath.

"What?"

Head down, barely concealing a smile, Watterboy shook his head. "Nothing."

Only it wasn't nothing. It was a grin of approval. Finally! He'd done something that merited the proverbial thumbs-up from the men he once considered to be like brothers.

"Incoming from Command," Candyman shouted.

Watterboy clapped Heath on the back and stalked away. "Fire it up."

Still soaking in the pleasure of gaining Watterboy's approval, Heath stared down at Trinity. Yeah, it'd given him pleasure, but not as much as he thought it would've. Tides were shifting.

"My brother will stop at nothing once his mind is made up."

To his left and behind a bit, Haur's voice drifted around Heath in the swirling elements. Heath waited, surprised the man had opened up. But he also seemed to be telling him something, or trying to imply something. "And what is his mind made up about?"

Snow crunched as Haur came forward and his gaze slid to Heath's.

Speaking of tides, Heath felt the tidal shift of two countries. An ominous element shrouded this night.

"Ghost!"

He pried his gaze from Haur's to Watterboy.

"UAV has movement ten klicks north. Team of twelve, holing up in a village." Watters ordered the men to eat and rest up before they headed out to engage or capture their targets.

"General Zheng drove Jianyu from his arms, but my brother bore a wound more grievous. One that drove him mad, changed him."

This wasn't just information for information's sake. The man had thrown down the die. "I'll play your game," Heath said as he tugged his bite straw loose. "What was that wound?"

"A spy, one who infiltrated the highest levels of our government, dug beneath the impenetrable barriers of one of the nation's most ardent loyalists — my brother." Haur lowered his head. "General Zheng discovered the spy's activities before my brother, but he did not tell him. They fed the operative false information, trapping the spy. And my brother. I think it angered the general that his own son could not see what was happening, even though all had been deceived." Haur toyed with the tattered edges of his gloves. "They disgraced Jianyu for failing to detect and stop her."

"Her?" Heath choked on a draught of water. "The spy was a woman?"

Haur gave a slow nod. "Known as Meixiang, she destroyed my brother's life."

Heath's heart chugged through the swampy story the man had just churned.

"It is ironic, is it not, that one of the two Americans missing is a woman." He dragged his attention to Heath. "And the only vengeance my brother has ever sought was to throw an American woman at the mercy of the Chinese government."

"Are you telling me you think the woman we're searching for . . ."

"I do not know who we are searching for, only that it is one American woman and one male." Haur's smile did not reach his eyes. "But the irony does not escape me."

"No kidding." Was it . . . could it be . . . ? What if Jia was this spy? Oh man, that made so much sense. Didn't it? Or did it? In a blink, everything seemed tenuous. Innocuous. Veiled.

"If my brother found this woman" — serene, thoughtful eyes drifted to the darkening horizon — "I would fear for her life."

Camp Loren, CJSOTF-A, Sub-Base
Bagram AFB, Afghanistan
"Enter."

The door creaked and musty air snuck into his office as he glanced once more at the UAV images.

"General Burnett, you have a, uh, visitor." Otte slunk into the office.

"You know I don't have time for this. Tell him to come back." Was this really a Russian tanker sitting in the middle of the Hindu Kush? What were the Chinese and Russians planning? Could he head them off in time?

"Uh, sir —"

"Are you still here?" Lance threw down a pen and groaned. "Didn't I tell you I was too busy?"

"Yes, sir." The man shifted, nervous. "But . . . but I think you'll want to see this . . . visitor."

"And why would you think that?" Lance snatched some printed images from the shelf behind him. Compared the two. Flipped to the enhanced images. Confirmed twelve men and a woman.

"Because, sir, it's General Zheng."

His mind staggered over that name as he continued studying the images, thinking, plotting. As he did, the title of *Colonel* fell away from his expectation and skipped to what had just been said. "Wait. Did you just say *General* Zheng? As in Zheng Xin?"

Otte shifted on his long, lanky legs. "Yes, sir."

"Why on God's green earth didn't you say so in the first place?" He punched to his feet. "Where is he?"

"General Early won't let him —"

"Good for him," Lance said with a laugh. Anything to annoy the crud out of that arrogant Asian. "Keep the Chinese on their toes." He shoved around the side of his desk.

Lance stormed down the hall to the secure conference room, which — to his dismay — was right next door to the command center overseeing the mission to track down the man's son and Darci.

Voices, raised but controlled, sifted out of the room and drew Lance inside. Early sat at the head of the table, leaning forward and pointing a finger at Zheng. "I don't care what your reason is. This will not fly."

"And what would that be?" Lance asked.

Early pushed back, eyes ablaze. "You were right."

"Yeah?"

Nostrils flared, Early flung daggers at Lance. "I don't like you much right now."

"Ah." So he'd found out about Darci. Ignoring the revelation, Lance shook hands with Zheng. "General, a surprise to find you here. You Chinese are getting mighty slippery, getting past our security forces."

"General Burnett," Early said with a huff. "I think you'll find his story amusing."

Lance stayed on his feet, opting to maintain a sense of control, of which he clearly had none if two high-ranking Chinese officers could slip into this sub-base without his awareness. "That so?"

Face red, Early leaned forward. "Go ahead, Zheng. *Regale* him. Tell him the tale you told me."

Placid and unaffected by the hatred roiling off Early, Zheng took a long, measured breath. Then delivered the death knell. "My son is here on an unauthorized mission."

With a hearty laugh, Lance leaned back and shook his head. "Hate to disappoint you, General, but we already know about Colonel Wu's activities."

The face remained unmoved save a twitch of the man's right eyebrow. "I do not speak of Jianyu."

Lance frowned, his heart powering down.

"I come to you to find and stop the boy I attempted to raise as my own, the boy I tried to influence and provide with a solid, exemplary upbringing." He looked stricken. Ashamed. "It is true, as they say, 'distance tests the endurance of a horse; time reveals a man's character.' " Chest drawn up, he let out a weighted breath. "The one who must be stopped at all costs is Haur."

THIRTY

Deep in the Hindu Kush
15 Klicks from Chinese Border

Taking risks had a certain amount of stupidity to it. Most times, a person risked that vulnerable part in the belief that things would work to the benefit. And for the most part, Peter Toque had gambled and won, came out on top, ahead of the game, ahead of the target.

Maybe his luck had run out. After all, a man could get so far on raw luck and experience, right?

He fisted his hands as the Yanjingshe, handpicked by Jianyu, huddled around the fire pit in the middle of the hut. Snow twinkled down into the fire, melting before even being kissed by a spark. Blazing, the fire roared, spreading its heat throughout the twenty-by-twenty space. An Afghan village gathering hut overtaken by Chinese warriors.

Once they'd entered the village, the men swept through, ruthlessly overpowering the villagers, who were even now holed up in their homes. Two had been shot and killed in their attempt to defend their village. A village that had put them in a daunting proximity to the Afghan-Chinese border.

In fact, Peter grew more convinced with each passing minute that his gamble on fronting Darci Kintz — a maneuver designed to ingratiate himself with Wu Jianyu and ultimately control the man — had failed. It wasn't because of bad intel that he'd misjudged this man. He'd studied the Zheng dynasty, knew of the bad blood between the young colonel and his father, knew of the former's expulsion from grace and power. A shift had occurred in Wu Jianyu, one that made predicting his actions next to impossible.

Which explained how he'd ended up here without anyone in the "spyverse" knowing. No word had filtered through the back channels about the man's location, so to find him slinking around the mountains of Afghanistan, where he just so happened to find Darci . . .

What were the odds? Had someone tipped Jianyu off that she was in the area? Or was it just dumb luck on the part of the fierce, revenge-driven soldier?

Peter's superiors had monitored Darci's movements since her narrow escape from the clutches of the Chinese. When she'd started the gig for the geology team, they knew something was going down. Forty-eight hours later, he had a new identity — Peter Toque — and an entire new history to corroborate even the most thorough of checks.

Why? Because while Darci Kintz didn't hold the record as the best operative — that title usually went to the more flamboyant, kick-butt operatives — his brief encounter with her a decade ago told him she was someone to watch. His instincts proved correct. She'd gotten into the heart of Chinese intelligence, slept with the enemy as it were, and gotten out alive — she was ahead of the game and a master at her job. He'd been told to try to pull her into working with them, doubling of sorts. But he'd told his people that the loyalty pumping through her veins was too thick to allow her to break that morality code. Peter liked her. Admired her. Held her in the highest esteem.

And you just fed the lamb to the wolf.

And the lamb's father was in danger now, too. Dumb, dumb move. He'd need to send a relay as soon as they got out of here, to alert his people to monitor Kintz's father. Even though he'd given Jianyu the wrong state, the man would no doubt feed Li Yung-fa to the beast of China — his father.

Two for one.

Peter cursed himself.

The door burst in and with it Darci Kintz. Yanked in, she tumbled and landed with a thud against the wood floor. A deathly silence dropped on the room, backlit only by the fire and its thundering cracks and pops. At least they seemed to thunder over the hollow quiet.

Nostrils flared, Jianyu sneered around the room as Lieutenant Colonel Tao eased in behind him and closed the door. If there was ever a doubt about the fear this man instilled in his men, it flickered away like a wisp of smoke.

"Secure her." Jianyu waved a hand toward Darci and smoothed back his hair with the other.

The men were swift as they hauled Darci up and held out her arms. Firelight glistened over her hip. Peter frowned. A fresh circle of blood spread out on the new shirt they'd stuffed her in. A sheen covered her face, which seemed paler than normal.

Lip curling, Jianyu turned to Peter. "You." His head bobbed. "You say you are on my side." He held out a Tokarev. Why use a Russian handgun? So he could blame his new bedmates? "Prove it. Shoot her. Get rid of this woman."

Peter might've been wrong in handing Darci to them, but he knew what road to take now. "I am not on your side. And if you'd wanted her dead, you would've done it yourself hours ago rather than have your surgeon tend her. And I see now you have injured her further."

Uncertainty trickled through the man's face, and he looked at Darci, then glowered at Peter. "You admit you are not aligned with me and expect to live?"

"I admit that I do not take sides. What has passed between you and this American woman has nothing to do with me, save that we're all breathing the same air." *Easy, now.* Jianyu had his heart planted in the middle of this fiasco. And his attachment to Darci was palpable. If he felt Peter was willing to get rid of her . . . wait . . . it was a test. "Personally, I like her. She's smart. Attractive —"

As soon as the man shifted and dropped his shoulder, Peter knew what was coming. Since he wasn't about to eat another boot, he ducked. The strike sailed just millimeters past his head. He stepped back —

Thud!

The hit from behind stung. Peter stumbled forward, pain spiraling through his neck and shoulders. Another blow sent him to his knees. Fingertips on the dirty floor, he coughed, trying to recapture the breath they'd knocked out of him.

Laughter filtered through the room. Peter didn't care — he saw Jianyu's boots moving away. And that meant for now, he was alive.

Easing back to his feet, Peter froze mid-move.

Jianyu's men had anchored Darci's arms out, tethering them to the wall. She had a sweet, innocent face, one that — were her features a bit more Chinese and less European thanks to her mother — belonged on a geisha. Fair skin blotched from a blow or two but appealing against her jet-black hair. Even in a dirty brown tunic, tactical pants, and hiking boots, she seemed delicate.

But he knew better. He still had an imprint, at least mentally, of her boot on his face.

Wariness crowded the soft features of her face as she wobbled but braced herself. She swallowed and looked at Peter.

No regret. No anger.

Pure determination — to survive.

"I want to know," Jianyu stood behind

Darci, "who worked with you in Taipei City."

"Nobody worked with me," Darci gritted out.

Standard answer. Peter expected no less. But even that single question ramped up his pulse. Darci was in no shape to endure hours of torture. She'd hold on for a while, but if she wasn't rescued soon . . . He gave a slow, almost imperceptible nod, encouraging her to hang in there. Help was coming. At least he hoped it was.

"That is not the truth." Hands behind his back, Jianyu circled her until he severed Peter's visual connection with her. "We have surveillance of you in the Crypt. You're hidden in the shadows, but there is a man with you."

"There was no man," Darci said.

Jianyu's shoulders drew up.

"Except your Colonel Tao."

Rage flung through the colonel's face. He shifted toward her, jabbed a flat-handed thrust into her side.

"No!" Peter's shout mingled with Jianyu's.

A strangled, blood-curdling scream shot from Darci.

She dropped to her knees, limp.

Hunched against the brutal, driving elements, Heath knelt and shielded Trinity from the bitter wind as the team paused to strategize. He tugged his zipper up, wishing he had a thermal suit. Anything to ward off the cold that snuck past the gaps, that whipped into his nostrils each time he breathed.

"Storm's getting bad," Watterboy shouted to the team huddled close together. "Last report said we were going to get buried. We're two klicks from the village."

"Get in there," Candyman hollered. "Get it done. Get out. Get home."

Sergeant Putman looked up from the comsbox. "Lost communication."

Watterboy scowled.

"Storm's pulling major interference," Putman said.

"We're losing warmth faster than daylight." Watterboy looked at Trinity. "Ghost, how's she holding up?"

Ears perked and swiveling like equilateral radar dishes, Trinity seemed at home with the elements and the situation. "She's good." Heath coiled an arm around her and rubbed her chest, trying to infuse some warmth and reassurance — for him, not her.

She wasn't easily rattled. He was another story. Especially with all that was happening. Wind, snow, stress. Thinking of Jia, wondering why Haur had picked him to buddy up to, fear of failing . . .

With his track record, he should pass out any minute now.

Please, God. Help me.

"God is our refuge and strength, an ever-present help in trouble." The first verse of Psalm 46. He knew it, quoted it. But did he believe it?

Of course, it wasn't God who'd tanked on keeping His end of the bargain. Heath had given talks about God having their backs, about not walking away from faith and belief, and hadn't Heath done that very thing?

What Heath believed in and what he did — they'd become two very different things. Saying those words, spouting scriptures was easy. Almost second nature.

A habit.

His heart dropped against that revelation and landed cockeyed in his chest.

It is not good to have zeal without knowledge, nor to be hasty and miss the way.

Heath stilled at the admonishment. Wished he'd worn his spiritual steel-toed boots for that verse. Was he being — ?

Yes. No need to even finish that thought. Hasty was the precise word he'd use to describe his personal mission — or was it a vendetta? — to prove he still had what it took. With all vigor to get back in the game. To feel useful, needed, and important again.

"Hey!"

Jarred from his internal diatribe, Heath blinked through the snow and wind to Watterboy.

"Use Trin's NVG camera to lead the way."

Heath flicked up the camera, which stood perpendicular to the spine of the vest, and retrieved the monitor from his pack. He turned it on, the screen smearing an ominous green glow across the darkness. "It's up and working."

"Good, let's move. I want to get home and thaw out before this storm goes blizzard on us."

"Ain't this a little late for a winter storm?" Candyman said with a growl. "Winter is over in three weeks."

"Wasn't too long ago," Heath put in, "Afghanistan had their worst storm in fifty years. Maybe they're trying to top it again."

"Well, they can stop."

"Okay, move out, people!" Watterboy said.

Trudging forward, his gloved hand gripping the readout, Heath realigned his

412

thoughts with the mission. But there in the chaos of his swirling thoughts and the snow, he wondered what propelled him. What drove him to risk another blackout, to risk his life — and considering these elements, Trinity — to save a woman named Jia? A military operative who had hoodwinked one of the most powerful men in China.

Okay, that was a big leap, but considering what Haur mentioned, Heath couldn't help but entertain the thought. What if she was that operative? Burnett hadn't mentioned her occupation, just that she was military intelligence and needed to be found. But military intelligence could be anything. It didn't mean she was the spy, right?

Even he knew he was reaching with that one.

"That's the only name you need to know."

The general's words whispered on the wind of doubt. It implied she had other names. Who had other names besides operatives? Fugitives. Entertainers seeking to protect their privacy. Since she wasn't in the latter group, and he couldn't think of another category, Heath was left with the option of buying into the fact that Jia was a spy.

Clandestine, then, was her middle name.

Jolts of fire thrust Darci from the greedy claws of sleep. A scream echoed in her thoughts as she came fully awake. She blinked in the semidarkness, searching for the source of the cry. But as the resonance settled, she came to the gaping conclusion that the scream had been her own.

A shape shifted nearby, drawing her focus to that spot. The blurs morphed into the form of a man. With the light behind him, he stood as a perfect silhouette. Jianyu? He seemed to have the same build, but the angle made it impossible to know for certain. What she did know for certain was the glint and clang of metal told her what was on the menu. Her brain.

So, torture.

Fear wiggled through her gut. Weakened from the broken ribs, beatings, and no food, she wasn't sure how long she'd last. Darci slumped back, fingers trailing what she lay on. A table? It wasn't metal. Wood . . . thick enough to hold her but not too solid she couldn't break it. If she could just move her feet — no go. Restraints pulled against her ankles.

God . . . I'm not even sure what to ask. . . . Just let me know You're here.

"Names, Meixiang," came Jianyu's voice from behind.

Eyes shuttering closed, Darci braced herself.

"I want the names of those who helped you gain access to the highest levels of security."

"I worked alone."

"No! That is impossible!" His warm breath crawled along her ear and down her neck. "What you accessed required security protocols only someone in the highest levels could provide."

"Maybe you provided it," she said, feeling out of breath. Fire again wormed through her side, the spot where the soldier had cracked more ribs. "Maybe you talk in your sleep."

A snicker made Darci still. Who else was here?

"You would like me to think that, but I do not sleep that hard."

"That's true," Darci said. "You're so haunted by your failings and insecurities you can't sleep at night."

Something touched her arm.

White-hot fury bolted through her body, thrashing her secured limbs. Darci clenched her eyes as the smell of burning flesh — her flesh — filled the frigid air. "You coward!

Using electrical torture!" She arched her back as the electricity zipped through her body, using the water to conduct its fiery path.

Silence gaped as the current died, and Darci slumped back against the table. Panting and grunting against the agony, she willed herself to hold on.

Hold on for what?

A rescue? In all her years as a military intelligence officer, she hadn't been rescued. No supernatural intervention. But she'd had a lot of situations that worked in her favor that convinced her God was watching out for her. She clung to the faith her mother had died for.

But that was just it: Her mother *had* died. Believing God.

Was that Darci's lot in life, too? To die?

God, I don't want to die. She didn't feel like her life was over. That her usefulness had dried up. Maybe her desire to continue this occupation had dried up, but her will to live, her curiosity over a certain guy . . .

Trinity.

Was it a foolish hope that his dog would help him find Darci?

Right. Twenty-four thousand feet above sea level, in a snowstorm?

Might as well expect angels to float down

and cut her restraints right now.

Darci held her next breath, her mind trained on the bindings on her wrists and ankles. Waiting for them to be loosed.

She wriggled her hands. They didn't budge.

Didn't think so.

"Names. I want names, Meixiang."

Humor. She had to keep her humor, keep him operating out of anger so he didn't have time to put thought into what he was doing. "Pinocchio, Cinderella, Aurora — she always was my favorite."

Volts snapped through her body. Her teeth chattered. Bit into her tongue. Sweet warmth squirted through her mouth. It lasted longer, stronger than the previous time. He was escalating. Another indication he wasn't here for the long haul. He had to get answers fast and move on.

That both pleased and worried her. Pleased that she wouldn't have prolonged torture. Worried because he could pull out some big guns of torture. And while she thought she could survive it, Darci would prefer to keep her body parts intact.

Slumped against the wood again, she tried to swallow but found her mouth parched. She stroked the salivary gland beneath her tongue, trying to wet her mouth. As she sucked in heavy breaths, she heard a creaking.

Footsteps.

Quiet.

Lifting her head, she looked around. The light still glared at her. But shadows sulked in the corners. Alone? She dropped back and let out a grunt-whimper. *Get it together, Darci. You can do this. You* have *to do this.*

Soft rustling to her right drew her head around, then a clanging.

She stilled.

"Darci."

·She let out the breath she'd held. "I thought he shot and killed you."

"Just my leg." He angled it toward her.

Sympathy wound. Still working her. She groaned. "What do you want, Toque?"

"Hold on, Darci. You're doing great."

Twisting her neck to see him didn't help much. She couldn't see all of him. "If I'm doing so great, why don't you switch" — pain stabbed her side, and she jerked with another grunt — "with me?"

"He's still soft on you."

"I'd hate to see your definition of hard."

"He killed the guy who hit your side. Shot him on the spot."

Darci hesitated. He'd killed one of his elite?

"And just now, you couldn't see his face, but I could. I've never seen the guy look so tortured. It was killing him."

Darci laughed at his choice of words. "I think he's killing *me*."

"Listen, I have people on the way. Just hang in there."

"Yeah?" She hissed as her still-tingling extremities ached and her head pounded. "Well, forgive me if I don't buy that."

More clanging, and this time he shifted into view. "I think we can use his sympathy for you. Milk it, get him to stop torturing you. Buy time till my people arrive."

"Your people?" She snorted as the room began to darken. She was fading. "Who? How do . . . know?"

"I have a tracking device. I activated it when the Black Hawk went down. They use it to home in on my location." His voice grew animated. "They'll be here."

"And what if I kill you?" came Jianyu's voice.

Darci snapped her eyes open and looked in the direction of the new voice.

Shadows. All she saw were shadows.

"Jianyu, no."

Bright muzzle flash blinded her.

THIRTY-ONE

Deep in the Hindu Kush
15 Klicks from Chinese Border

Tucked into a tiny cleft and shielded from the raging elements, Heath tugged Trinity onto his lap to get her paws off the bitter, freezing terrain. From his pack, he tugged out the collapsible bowl, dumped a packet of food in it, and held it while she chowed down.

"We got a feed from Command," Watterboy said as he crouched beside them, munching on a protein bar. "There's a village just around the next rise. We'll reconnoiter." He jutted his jaw toward Trinity. "How's she holding up?"

Heath rubbed her head as she sat back, licking her chops. "Better than me, I think, in this freezer of a mountain."

Watterboy nodded with a smile, then clapped him on the shoulder. "She's gotten us this far. Take care of her so she can get us back."

"Hooah." Heath smiled as he buried his hands in Trinity's dense fur and, unbelievably, found warmth.

Someone landed next to him, shoulder to shoulder, leaving no room. Heath frowned, then saw who it was. Haur.

His captain stood over them, surveyed the shoulder-to-shoulder arrangement, then with a grunt he left.

Had that been done on purpose?

"A friend I knew had a dog like her," Haur said over the howling wind.

Heath grinned. "Not possible." He rubbed her ears. "With her pedigree and her training, other dogs don't compare. Besides, she's my girl." As if in answer, Trinity swiped her tongue along his cheek, then leaned against him, closed her eyes, and lowered her snout to his arm. Power nap. *Atta, girl. Get some rest. You've earned it.*

"Do you have family?"

Heath paused before answering. Odd piece of dialogue in the middle of a mission. "Don't we all? How else would we have gotten here?" But the bitter pill of truth caught at the back of his throat. His parents had been dead for years. His only father figure lay in a soldier's home dying.

"Then you have your parents?"

"No, actually." Heath chewed over how much to divulge. "Trinity" — her ears flicked toward him despite her closed eyes — "here is my family. I have an uncle I'm close to, but he's . . . well, one war too many."

Haur gave a slow, curt nod.

Family. Why on earth had he brought up family? To point out to Heath that he'd do anything to help his brother? What about his father, the general?

Something niggled at the back of Heath's mind. Had since the guy first started talking. He looked to the Chinese man. "Can I ask you something?"

Keen, expectant eyes held fast to his. "Of course."

"I've noticed you call Wu Jianyu 'brother,' yet you have never referred to General Zheng as your 'father.' " When he didn't respond right away, Heath resisted the urge to backpedal. "Or am I wrong?"

"No." Haur's face filled with an artificial expression, one that spoke of a deep hurt yet . . . something else. Respect? Maybe, but that seemed too . . . good. "General Zheng has treated me well. I owe him great respect. He is a great man in China. To have him provide shelter for me when I was alone, when my family was not there . . .

many in China say I owe him my life."

Heath cradled Trinity, but his mind was trained on his talk with Haur. "China says, but not you?"

Haur tucked his chin. "I owe him a great deal. I am very grateful."

"But not thankful?"

"China is my homeland. Of course I am thankful."

"But not to Zheng?"

Haur looked to the right, which drew Heath's attention to Bai, who sat staring into the swirling chaos. *Ah. Got it.* "It's obvious with the loyalty you show that Zheng has no reason to doubt you."

An appreciative smile was his reply.

"When one's father betrays your country, it is hard to be trusted." Emotions twisted and writhed through his words. "I have worked hard to ensure that my name and reputation smother any doubt."

"Gather up, people," Watterboy said as he circled a finger in the air.

Heath nudged Trinity up, then hoisted her onto his shoulders in a fireman's carry so she could have a little more rest.

"Okay, round that bend is a flat plain. It stretches out then drops into a valley. The village there is believed to be the site where the woman is being held."

"And my man is there, too."

"Right." Watterboy shifted to Putman, who shook his head. "We've lost coms, so we're winging this. Probably another two klicks to the supposed site of the village."

"Not supposed. It is the last known location of my agent."

"In other words, no shooting the Brit?" Candyman asked. Then shrugged when the spook glowered. "Just making sure I know my priorities."

"Our priority," Watterboy said, "is getting Jia back."

Heath nodded. About time they mentioned that.

"We want our man as well." Steady, Haur met everyone's gaze. "If at all possible, we want him taken into custody, not killed. He will be removed to China and dealt with there."

"This is getting muffed up," Candyman said. "Too many hands . . ."

Watterboy nodded. "Agreed." He towered over the others by a half foot. "Bai and Haur, we understand your concern, but our orders are STK. If we are being fired upon, we will shoot back."

"If we encounter Chinese soldiers, let me or Bai handle it. They are our people, under our command. We can convince them to listen."

Watters and Candyman shared a look that told Heath they weren't happy, but conventional wisdom said the plan made sense. That is, unless Haur and Bai weren't on the right side of convention, which was something Heath did not believe of Haur. He couldn't say the same of Bai.

Camp Loren, CJSOTF-A, Sub-Base
Bagram AFB, Afghanistan

"What do you mean we've lost communication?" Lance pulled himself from the dregs of sleep and off the mattress. Cold shot up through his stocking feet and pinged off his bones. He stuffed his feet in his boots and yanked the strings taut.

Otte, looking like a bloated sausage in his winter gear, shifted near the door. "The weather, that's what they're saying. The storm is interfering with communication."

Lance fingered his hair, glad in this angry weather that he hadn't gone bald like his father. It paid to have Cherokee blood, even on the days that made it boil. Like today. "What was the last confirmed relay?" He threw on a thick sweater, then reached for his heavy-duty jacket.

"The village location."

Shoving through the door, down the hall, and into the bitter night, Lance searched his memory banks, nodding. But against the fog of sleep deprivation — two hours on a sofa prevented minds from operating on all cylinders — he knew something wasn't right. Village . . . what else — ?

He wove around vehicles cluttering the road that separated his home away from home and the command bunker. "Daggummit, where'd all these vehicles come from?"

"They pulled in the teams from FOBs Murphy and Robertson. The storm is going to bury the tactical teams."

"You don't think I know that?" Asking about all the traffic was just his way of venting his frustration. Of off-loading the foreboding that dumped on him as fast as the elements. And playing host to —

"The general." He stopped as an MRAP turned into his path to enter the motor pool, and when the driver saluted, Lance threw him one back, then moved on. "That message about Haur. Did it make it?" Inside the command bunker, he shook off the snow from his jacket and boots.

Papers rustled as Otte consulted his notes. Seconds fell off the clock. Slowly, his semi-balding head swung back and forth. "No, sir."

Lance leaned into the major. "Are you going to sit there and tell me those men don't know Haur is a traitor?" His boots squeaked against the vinyl floor as he trudged through the hall so quiet they seemed partnered with death tonight.

"No, sir." Otte blinked. "I mean, yes, sir — they don't know. Or at least, it's not confirmed."

Half the lights were killed, and loneliness clung to the walls. "Where in blazes is everyone?" When he stepped into the command center and the same eerie silence met him, Lance cursed. He slowed, annoyed at the quiet that draped the room that should've been buzzing with keyboards, coms chatter, and general chaos. Instead, only two of the eight monitors were manned.

He turned to a specialist, her hair pulled back tight. "Where is everyone?"

"The storm," the nervous specialist looked up from her station. "Most of the teams have been called back, and there's little to do, so Colonel —"

His pulse pounded. "Little to do?" He thrust a finger back and to the side, in the general direction of the mountains. "We have a team of twelve men, two Chinese soldiers, a spy, and a dog handler stuck in the mountain tracking down what they believe to be a rogue Chinese colonel, and you're going to tell me there's little to do?"

"With all due respect, sir —"

"Shove your respect —"

"Sir," Otte said. "General Early ordered Colonel Hastings to shut things down, give the men downtime."

"I don't give a rip." Lance waved a hand over the room. "Wake them up. Everyone, including Early. Get everyone in here who can operate a machine. We need to find our men and stop them from getting killed."

Wide-eyed, the woman stared at him.

"Specialist, unless you want an automatic six-month extension added to your tour, get moving."

"Yes, sir." After an obligatory salute, she flew out of the chair and out the door.

"Otte." Chest puffing, Lance moved to a computer. "Find my girl." Misery groped for a foothold with him. "Bring her home. I don't want to have to tell her father China won after all."

Deep in the Hindu Kush
15 Klicks from the Afghan-China Border
Trust. A sliver-thin film that stretched over relationships like food wrap. Flimsy enough to be broken. Strong enough to protect.

Twenty years he had worked to prove his trustworthiness. Twenty years he'd lived beneath the shadow of his father's actions, his father's betrayal. No one bore the brunt of that betrayal more than Haur. Left alone in a country without a mother and father. Left to face the authorities who'd beaten him unconscious several times in the first few weeks. When they finally decided the fifteen-year-old boy left behind didn't know anything, they turned their efforts toward obtaining convincing proof that his father had committed the ultimate betrayal. Soon after, he was shown pictures of burned bodies. His father and sister. Dead. Their betrayal cost them their lives.

"Where is your loyalty, Li Haur?"

Standing before the minister of defense, stripped of honor and name, he'd screamed at Zheng Xin, raged that they'd stolen his life. Demanded to see his father again. Told them he refused to believe the charges. That he wasn't going to turn on his own family. Or believe their deaths.

Not until the officers showed him a video of his father and *Mei Mei* entering a building but never leaving . . . then another image of a man and little girl in London who bore a striking resemblance . . . not till then.

He'd cried. He fought. Then pulled himself together.

The next day, he was delivered to the minister's palatial home. Shown to a bedroom on the second floor. Told to shower and clean. He was then escorted to the minister's private office. In that room in the heart of Taipei City, his life changed. General Zheng said Haur's fire was borne out of anger at being abandoned, at being left behind by his own father. The same father who had betrayed his friends, including Xin.

Haur vowed his loyalty to homeland China. To the Rising Sun. A brutal fight with Jianyu created not a lifelong enemy, but a lifelong brother. They became allies, battle hardened through life and the daunting weight of being in the public eye on a regular basis as the sons of Zheng Xin.

Even now, that film of trust had stretched taut . . . between him and America, but also — and more important — between him and his own people. It did not escape his attention how Bai monitored him, tracked his moves, never gave him more than a few minutes alone with the American elite warriors.

They know. Both the Americans and Chinese doubted his loyalty. Each for different reasons. His father's choice twenty-plus years ago cost Haur more than he could've ever imagined. *I will never escape this black mark on my life.*

"You seem friendly with the Americans."

Haur slanted a glance to Bai, who watched the men crawling up to the crest of the incline. "Keep your friends close, your enemies closer." With that, he crouch-ran forward, then dropped to his knees in the snow. He crawled up to the dog handler, Daniels.

"Down," Daniels said, then returned his attention to the night-vision binoculars he held.

Haur peered over the lip.

A village smiled up at him, its buildings sunk beneath the heavy snowfall. Roofs peeked out, but the road into the village had been beaten down by large-wheeled vehicles that grouped in the middle of the structures. The mountain resembled a cup with one side, the southernmost, missing. To the left of the team, a rocky incline swooped down toward the base of the village. Probably compliments of a landslide during rainy seasons. The rocky slope would be the best tactical entry point. Able to hide among the boulders and use the color variation to their benefit.

Since the snow had let up, the moon peeked through the clouds, bathing the

431

pristine blanket with a blue hue. That aided him in seeing with the naked eye, but not much.

Haur glanced to Daniels with the binoculars. "May I borrow them when you are done?"

Though the man's distrust screamed, he handed them over.

The dog watched the exchange, panting, her breath puffs of blue in the predawn hours. Head down, she jerked her snout back toward the village. Keen eyes locked on the village, as if she'd seen something. She seemed to be processing the scene as much as her handler. With a small whimper, she scooted back.

"Counting at least twenty, maybe thirty, unfriendlies," came Watterboy's report.

"Roger," Candyman said from his left.

Haur saw only stubby figures, then zoomed in, almost able to see facial features. Half of the men on guard were Russians. He just cared that Jianyu was down there. With Russians. That made Haur tremble. China had long been allies with the Russians, but for them both to be here, it meant trouble. Both for China — they would have to deal with the bad publicity that would come out of attacking American forces — and for the Americans, who would have to face two enemies.

He returned the NVGs to Daniels and hesitated. "Where is your dog?"

Daniels glanced over his shoulder. "Call of nature. Don't eat the yellow snow."

Chuckles rumbled through the area, which confounded Haur. Were they not aware of what trouble they were walking into? The buildings were huddled and around them were sentries. "Impossible."

"What's that?" Daniels asked.

"There are too many. How can you get in and get this girl without being seen?"

"We'll get the girl," Candyman said. "Whether we're seen or not is another matter. Besides, haven't you heard? This is our lucky day."

"You will need more than luck." Haur knew the type of man they were facing, the ruthless determination to do what he felt was right, to bring glory to China.

"We've got that, too." Candyman held up his weapon. "M4, M16. Who can stand against us?"

"China. Jianyu. Any enemy who wants you dead."

"God's got our backs." Daniels stilled, uncertainty in his eyes. He did not believe what he'd said. Were the answers so meaningless? Did he not understand?

"That and my M4." Candyman snorted.

"Quiet!" Watterboy hissed. With quick hand signals, he sent four men scurrying to the west and another four southeast. "Putman, how's our coms?"

"Working on it."

"Get it up. We need Command."

Next to him, Daniels propped himself up on one arm and looked around. "Hey . . ." He pushed himself upright.

Haur knew what he was thinking. "Daniels, where is your dog?"

Daniels tugged a whistle out and blew on it. No sound came out.

Watterboy keyed his mic. "Heads-up. Trinity's missing."

"We've got movement in the village," Candyman said. "And the incline."

Eyes snapped to that spot, Haur itched to look through the NVGs, but Daniels had already moved out to find his dog. "It is a good spot for a sniper, yes?"

"My thoughts exactly."

"Moving kind of fast."

"Yeah . . . and agile . . ."

"Got a bead," someone else said.

"Take the sho—"

"No!" Heath shouted. "It's Trinity!"

Rifle fire cracked the darkness.

THIRTY-TWO

Small Village in the Hindu Kush
15 Klicks from Chinese Border

The report of the rifle fire echoed through the valley and bounced back to Heath, thudding against his chest. "No!" He lunged at the Green Beret who'd taken the shot. He tackled him and flipped him over, straddling the guy. "Tell me you didn't hit her! Tell me!"

"I . . . I don't know. I just saw snow dust."

Heath flung himself to the ground, grabbing for his NVGs. *Oh God. Please . . . please don't let him have hit her.* Back and forth, he scoured the pocked slope.

"Anyone got a line of sight on Trinity?"

Heath's pulse roared as the green field blurred. His hands shook with rage and panic. "I can't find her." *Lord, God . . . Lord, God . . .* He zoomed in. Rocks. Shrubs. Snow. Branches. *Lord, I know You didn't bring us out here for her to die on that hill. Please!*

For her, I'll beg.

A sickening feeling dropped his heart into his stomach. The thought of her getting sniped . . . of her bleeding out . . . He was going to be sick.

A flicker of movement.

His heart vaulted back into his chest. He whipped back to the left, where the movement occurred. Rocks. Snow. Heath eased the whistle to his lips and blew. Scanned. *C'mon, c'mon.* He blew it again. Scanned.

Eerie green eyes locked on him.

"Got her!" His heart now flipped into his throat, choking him with elation as she stared in his direction, her sensitive ears picking up the high-frequency whistle. He gave her the signal to return.

"You got her?"

"Yeah." Heath mentally prodded Trinity to head back. Her beautiful head trained in his direction, then flitted around, then back to the village. He blew the return signal again.

Instead, she slunk farther down the slope.

"No," he said to her, knowing she couldn't hear that. "Crap!" He pushed to his feet. "She's broken behavior. Something's wrong." He trudged through the snow, each step dropping him knee-deep. "I'm going after her."

"Whoa, no." Watters caught his arm. "No way, Ghost."

"Back off, Watters. I know you didn't want me on this trip, and if I die going after her, you won't have to worry about us anymore." Everything in Heath pulsed with conviction. "You wouldn't leave one of your men behind, and I'm not leaving her. She's *everything* to me."

"I know, Heath." Watters touched his shoulder. "I didn't want you to come because I didn't want you getting hurt. But you're here. Now, you're part of my team. And I won't let you go into a situation that could get you killed. Let's make a plan."

Pulse lowering, Heath nodded. "You make the plan. I'll meet you down there."

"Look, if she's gone rogue —"

"No." Heath drew in a frigid, ragged breath. "Not rogue. She broke behavior. It's different."

"How?"

"Rogue means she's not responding to commands. She responded to my whistle command, but then — I didn't see it at the time, but she was trying to tell me she caught a scent. It's not normal for her to go without me, but she is trained to work off-lead. That's what she's doing — working off-lead." Realization dawned like the sun rising into its zenith. "She's only done that one other time — with Jia at Bagram. I don't know why, but she's taken a liking to this woman." *Just like me.* "I have to believe she must've seen her or can detect her scent."

"That's a stretch, don't you think?"

They'd worked together enough for Heath to know Watters's words held hope, that he wanted to believe what Heath was saying. "Not as big as you might think." Heath grinned. "I'm going down. Cover me, okay? Then bring in the cavalry."

"Candyman, Java, Scrip, Pops — take the spook," Watters said, never taking his gaze off Heath. "Go with Ghost. Keep coms open. Rocket and everyone else, you're with me. We'll flank the south."

"Hooah," Candyman said.

"Remember, orders are STK." Never doubt that Watters was a soldier. "Let's find the girl and bring her back."

"Lock and load." Candyman's grin never faded.

Heath nodded to the team leader. "Thank you."

"You're wasting air," Watterboy said with a grin.

Heath jogged, as much as the deep snow would allow, toward the place he'd seen

Trinity scaling the jagged terrain. Alive with the mission of finding and securing his girl, he struggled against the elements that impeded speed. An impression in the snow snagged his attention.

"That her trail?" Candyman voiced Heath's thoughts.

"That's her." Heath used her already-carved path down the slope. Sneak of a dog had plowed through this with such speed he hadn't even seen her doing it. Nobody had. And here, he felt like he was trying to wade through a tub of sour cream. Or quick-drying cement. Frigid wetness chomped into his legs, his pants wet and sticking to him. But he plowed on, determined to find Trinity.

And Jia.

He prayed that what had lured Trinity into breaking behavior and going into the village alone was the woman. The two had taken to each other as if they'd met before. Which was ludicrous. Their first encounter had been at the base. He was good with faces. Rarely did he forget one.

As the snow crowded around the first line of defense the rocks formed, Heath slowed. Searched for Trinity's trail.

"It's like she disappeared," Candyman said.

"Or jumped." Heath's gaze hit on a spot to the right. Paw prints on a rock. Then another trail to the left where the snow wasn't as deep.

"It's like she knew it wasn't as deep."

"She did. She's a dog — she can smell the earth beneath the snow easier." Fueled by finding her trail again, Heath maneuvered his way. Behind him, the rest of the team did the same.

"Down, down!" Candyman hissed into the predawn morning. "Movement, ten o'clock."

Heath's gaze went left. Sure enough, a sentry stalked toward a tree, vanished behind it. What would a sentry be doing way out here? A few seconds later, the man reemerged, then slogged back to camp, whistling.

"Clear," Candyman whispered.

Heath used Trinity's tracks through the foot-deep snow to hide his own steps as much as possible, leading the men in the same path to hide their numbers. Moving on, Heath hopped down a two-foot drop. This was where Trinity hesitated, then ignored his whistle call. He searched for signs of blood. Had the shooter hit her?

"No blood," he muttered as he looked around.

"Then I guess that means you're not going to kill Scrip." Candyman grinned to the man behind him.

"I'm sorry, man. I thought it was a sentry or a wild cat."

"As long as she's not hurt, I'll let you live," Heath teased.

"Then let's make sure that's the case."

"Supreme excellence consists in breaking the enemy's resistance without fighting."

Jianyu took in a long, slow breath of the incense on the table before him. He pushed aside the bitter cold. Folded away the anger. Ignored the doubts. He must find a center, find a way to reach that nirvana and quiet he'd once known.

With Meixiang.

The first time he'd ever thought life had smiled on him.

The first time he'd ever be made a fool of. And the last. He would make sure. A kiss shared equaled a life of honor stolen. Love —

With a growl, he leapt to his feet, shoulder-width apart, hands at the side.

Roiling fury stirred the air around him.

No. He must calm himself. Draw strength from sage wisdom.

Curse the wisdom. She was here! In that

hut. Alive, beautiful, and traitorous. She would not divulge which of his men had fed her the information. She could not have accessed their secret military files without that information. Though she'd tried to twist his suspicions back to himself, Jianyu knew better. He only had a part of the codes. No one soldier held them all. The safety protocols were immense. She had to have worked with someone with great power. Or with more than one source.

Jianyu stuffed the incense in the snow, snuffing it out.

He would find out. He would make her spill all of her secrets before he spilled her guts all over that table. It was a waste, of course. A beautiful woman like that.

How had he failed? Should his passions and views not have swayed her?

She had spoken with conviction of her belief in the same values and systems. Were they all lies?

Perhaps he could play on her sympathies. She cared for him — loved him. He saw it in her eyes. He would use that and drag the truth out of her. Then give her one last chance to walk away from the disgraced life of a spy. He would speak to his father, grant a dispensation so she could live.

But would she betray him again? Would

his father believe her? Would *he* believe her?

No, he must never give her the chance to make a mockery of him again.

She had stolen honor from him once. Now he would rip it from her, just like the breath from her lungs. He spun and stalked out of the hut.

A guard snapped to attention as Jianyu stepped into the morning and headed to the hut where they'd held Meixiang. Or Darci. That was the name the British spy had given. Once they got out of this valley and could reestablish communication, he'd contact his father. Give him the name and location. Let them ferret out that filthy pig of a man Li Yung-fa.

Dr. Cho looked up from his work as Jianyu entered. He smirked. "Your meditation did not work again?"

"You should worry about your patient and my patience."

The doctor laughed. "She needs a hospital. The ribs are broken. Moving her, torturing her, will risk puncturing her lungs."

Jianyu stood over her, gazed down at her face. So pretty. Fair skin against her black hair. Just like most Chinese women. But there was something . . . serene, peaceful about Meixiang that had always drawn him. "She only needs to live long enough to give back what she stole."

Cho tossed down a bloodied wad of gauze. "That I cannot guarantee, especially if you continue to brutalize her body."

Fire whipped through him. "Do not tell me how to conduct an interrogation."

Cho's eyes crinkled as a placating smile creased his lips. "Would not think of it. You merely said you wanted her to live long enough to tell you what you want to know. I offered my medical opinion."

"Are you done?" Jianyu snapped, his breath heaving.

Cho drew up straight. "There is no sense in my doctoring her if you are going to undo it." He plucked off the bloodied plastic gloves and slammed them in the trash.

"Then there is no need for you here." Jianyu planted his hands on the table, just millimeters from her long, black hair. Between his thumb and pointer fingers, he rubbed the silky strands. Things could have been so different.

Why? Why did she have to — ?

It did not matter. He shoved himself upright. He would not mope over this woman, no matter how much of his heart she'd trampled.

Jianyu slapped her face. Hot, clammy. Feverish.

Her eyes fluttered, and she moaned but slipped back out of the present.

Again, he slapped her.

This time, her eyes snapped open. Met his — and he saw the fear roiling off those irises that used to sparkle for him.

"Names, Meixiang. Who did you work with? How did you get so far?"

She groaned and rolled her gaze from his.

Gripping her face, he squeezed hard, forcing her to look at him. "Answer me! Who did you pay off? Who did you buy?"

"I told you," she said between his tight hold. "No . . . body."

"I do not believe you."

A breathy laugh rose and fell on her lips. "The one time you should . . ."

He pounded the table and smacked her — hard. "I do not care if you die. You will tell me what you know." He grabbed an instrument from the table.

Her head lobbed side to side as she struggled.

He pressed the scalpel against her throat. "Tell me! Names! Who — was it Ming? Gualing?"

"No," she ground out. A drop of blood slid over the blade, a tear down her cheek. "It was you."

"That is not possible. I never gave you access to that."

"Little by little," Meixiang said. "A piece here, a pie —" She yelped, her eyes wide.

Jianyu realized he'd pushed the knife deeper into her throat.

Blood trailed down her neck faster this time. He could not kill her. Not only because he must bring her to his father.

"I'm sorry," she said, her Adam's apple bobbing as she swallowed. More tears. "I did not mean to hurt you. I . . ."

"Hurt me?" He leaned into her face. "You did not hurt me. You *destroyed* me!"

She shook her head. "No, it wasn't me. They knew. They knew and they used you."

"Lies!" His voice bounced back at him. "You lie."

Pinching up her face, she shook her head, tears and blood mingling in the hollow of her throat. "No. No, I'm not. Your father found out." She drew in a breath, wrought with pain, then slowly exhaled. "He thought you were complicit. It's why I left so fast. If I stayed, they would've blamed you."

Jianyu stumbled back. It wasn't true. Couldn't be. His father said he never doubted his loyalty. "My father trusted me, unlike you."

She met his gaze. "You know better than that. He trusts no one. He's paranoid. He's

446

delusional."

His fist flew before he could stop it.

She lay on the table, nose oozing blood and drainage. Mouth agape.

His breaths came in ragged, difficult gulps. "Sir."

He spun to the door, stunned to find Tao there. "What?" Jianyu snarled.

"The Russians are here. They're ready to talk about payments."

He turned back to the table, to Meixiang. He smoothed her hair from her face. Lifted gauze from the table and wiped the blood from her face. "Have our men been successful?"

"Yes, sir. They are on the bases."

Had his father doubted Jianyu, even then? "What of the devices?"

"The bombs are ready for your activation codes."

THIRTY-THREE

Eyes trained on the nearest hut, Heath waited. Adrenaline wound through his veins, knowing that despite being declared unfit for duty, he was here. In the middle of it.

"Clear." Candyman's word came with a thud against his shoulder.

Heath bolted forward, sprinting across the twenty feet that separated the lip of the bowl-like valley and the hut. Daylight lay in wait, ready to expose them to the soldiers huddled out in the cold and elements.

Pressing himself into the shadows, Heath used his M4 to scope the area. Nothing moved, so he searched for Trinity's tracks. Trailing along the building, they banked right. Out of sight. The swift rustle behind him told Heath the team had moved in.

A soft clap to his shoulder gave him the clear to advance. He hustled forward, weapon up, ears probing for sound, mind pinging with possibilities, expecting every turn to throw trouble into his path. Right shoulder to the wood wall, he tugged the whistle from his pocket and gave the signal again.

He returned it to his pocket and shuffled forward. Candyman slipped in front of him, took a knee as point, and eased into the open to clear the area.

When silence reigned, Heath pied out, stepping into the open. He advanced quickly, sweeping, watching, listening. His head pounded with the rush of adrenaline and the fear that any step could be his last. The fire at the base of his neck warned him of a pending blackout.

Heath shook it off and sidled up to the next building, easing farther into the den of thieves. Candyman was hot on his tail. Shaking off the anticipation spiraling through him, Heath eased forward.

Two claps on his shoulder jerked him back, heart pounding. Spots bled into his vision.

Crap, no. Not now. He couldn't do that now.

"Hold," Candyman whispered.

Over his shoulder, Heath said, "What?"

"Spook is going ape-crazy."

Heath glanced back and sighed as the

spook slipped into a hut. "What — he's going to get us killed."

"Keep moving, Alpha team. Spook's not our problem," came Watters's command through the mic.

Pulling in a breath and blowing it through puffed cheeks, Heath braced himself. Squared his mind with the fact that God must want him here. So, if the Almighty wanted him here, then He had his back. Right? All that stuff he'd spouted sounded good in theory. Out here, in the field, with trigger-happy Chinese and Russians breathing down his neck, it was another thing.

No, it's not. It's theory put to practice. Faith in action.

Hooah.

He stepped out.

A shadow coalesced into a man.

Heath froze. In the two seconds it took to register that the enemy stood before him, Heath saw the muzzle slide up in front of a hardened Chinese face.

Oomph!

The man tumbled forward. Slumped into Heath.

Heath caught the man, stupefied.

"Tango down."

With Candyman's help, Heath dragged the body into the shadows. When he shifted, he saw the blood stains in the pristine white. Toeing the snow, he piled it up over the spots. Recovered, they took a second to reassess their position.

As they did, noise from behind drew them around, weapons up. Prepared to fight.

The spook emerged, a body draped over his shoulders. He swung toward Heath and the others, gave a thumbs-up, and headed back toward the rocky incline but stumbled. Clear indication they were in the right place if the spook found his guy. Thumbs-up meant the guy was alive still, right?

Candyman signaled Scrip to aid the guy, then shrugged at Heath and nodded for him to keep moving.

Right.

Trinity.

Jia.

Heath eased through the narrow space between two huts, where the snow wasn't as deep as the shadows. Grateful for the cover, he took a corner, and through a sliver of huts, he saw — No, that couldn't be right. Haur wasn't here. He was with Watterboy on the south side, wasn't he?

Heath cleared the right, Candyman the left, then they both stepped into the open, sweeping the path that led down then vanished around another hut. How many huts were there? This place didn't seem this dense from the mountain.

"Ghost," a voice skated through the coms. "Line of sight on Trinity. North and east of you. Moving pretty quick."

Heath keyed his mic. "Copy." He rushed forward, in between more huts, cringing as his boots crunched on the snow-and-ice-laden path.

"East," the voice instructed.

Heath went right.

"Ahead — wait, she ducked between the last two huts. She's heading into the heart of the village. Eyes out."

Warmth spilled down Heath's neck and shoulders as he plowed onward. Why did she have to be so mission focused? Get the job done. She was a better soldier than many men he knew. Including him. His vision jiggled, slowing him.

Oh no.

Okay. Faith. Focus on faith.

Lord — my faith in action is believing that I won't pass out doing this.

Things were going in their favor — snow had stopped, wind had gone down a notch, they hadn't encountered but one Chinese soldier — so he didn't need to mess it up by passing out. Or put the men in danger. But even the thought of doing that stressed him. Made things worse.

He stumbled over his own feet.

A hand on his shoulder told Heath they had his back.

He drew himself up straight and pushed on.

Barking clapped through the morning. Followed by gunfire.

"Crap!" sailed through the coms. "Ghost — they got her."

The words threw Heath forward.

"No, back, back!"

Heath pushed on. Wasn't going to leave his girl to die. Wasn't going to abandon her in the midst of chaos.

"Heath, stop. Listen."

"Not leaving her." He hustled, M4 cradled in his arms. Keyed his mic. "Where is she? Tell me!"

"A yard north, beside a truck."

Already in motion, he barreled forward before he heard the rest of the dialogue.

"But there's a mess-load of Russians there." The voice sounded strained. "Heath, she's down. She's not moving. Get out of there. It's not worth it."

"Bull! She's my partner," he growled as he jogged in the right direction. Each footfall sounded as a cannon blast. *Thud! Thud!* Surely, they'd find him. He didn't care as he launched over a pile of wood, his focus locked on Trinity, finding the girl who'd done everything to protect him. Now it was his job to protect her.

As the narrow passage opened up, ahead he could see trucks. Men. Heard laughter. On a knee, he lifted his rifle to his shoulder and peered down the barrel.

C'mon, c'mon. Where is she?

A soft thud to his six alerted him to Candyman's presence. "Anything?" he whispered into the wind.

Heath ignored the question, ignored the thunder in his chest and the whooshing in his vision. He shook his head, trying to dislodge the dizziness. Vision ghosting . . . gray . . . *No!* Not with Trinity down. Gray . . . dark gray . . .

"Help," Heath muttered as the world winked out.

Haze and fuzziness coated his synapses. Weighted, he pulled himself up.

"Ghost, it's okay. We got you." Candyman patted his arm. "And guess what?"

Heath shook his head and straightened.

Candyman handed him a pair of binoculars. "Take a look. At the truck."

Pinching the bridge of his nose, Heath brought the binoculars up. He peered through the lens . . . *Trinity.*

The snow around her a blood bath, Trinity lay on the ground.

"Oh —" Wait! He scanned the body. Wrong size. Wrong color.

"It's not her," Candyman said, his words thick with relief.

"Yeah." The fist-hold on his lungs lessened. "It's a black shepherd." He slumped back and handed off the binoculars, shaking from the adrenaline dump. Then a hefty dose of determination surged through his veins, dispelling the chill the adrenaline left. "Let's find my girl."

Candyman grinned. "Which one?"

Heat swarmed Heath. "Not funny."

"Wasn't meant to be."

A feeling of falling snapped Darci's eyes opened. The room writhed. Ghoulish shapes danced before her. She squinted trying to . . . *Oh, a fire.* That's why the room shimmied and swooned.

She pushed back and tried to lie down again, but her head thumped against something. Only as the haze of sleep faded did Darci realize she was now propped against the center support, hands and ankles tied. Her head drooped as the room spun once more.

Pain seemed to ooze from every pore.

Legs, arms, side — broken ribs. Every breath felt like inhaling fire.

"*. . . awaiting your activation codes.*"

The words brought Darci up short. Had she imagined them? She had no idea how long she'd been here or in this — she looked around assessing her surroundings — wherever it was. The village. That's right. They'd brought her to the village. Jianyu tried torturing her. Though he'd ordered the session and oversaw it, he found no pleasure in it. She'd been at the hands of sadistic men, those who enjoyed watching others suffer, and she'd expected to see those feelings roiling through Jianyu after all she'd done to him.

Instead, she saw her own pain mirrored in his expression.

But not enough to move him to stop the electroshock session. Her fingers throbbed, and she strained to see them. Confusion wove through her as she saw the blooded tips. Her stomach churned. Bloodied fingernails . . . wait, no. The nails were gone. They'd pulled out her fingernails? When had *that* happened? She had no recollection . . .

Nausea swirled and spun with the dizziness.

Stay awake. She'd missed too much already. What if they drugged her and pried the truth from her? Truth serums were more James Bond make-believe. They didn't actually make someone spill her guts, but they did make one very prone to suggestion.

Is that why her head was spinning? Why she couldn't see straight to save her life? Is that why the room darkened . . . even now?

Heat bathed her, cocooned her, tempted her to rest in its arms. But . . . something . . . the heat . . . not right.

Crack!

Darci snapped awake.

What . . . what woke her? How long had she been out this time? Was it hours? Minutes? Seconds? Heart chugging, she shivered beneath the tease of a draft that slithered in through the wood slats twined together.

She couldn't stay awake long enough to break out of her bindings — if she even had the strength to free herself. Rescues didn't happen, not in the middle of the mountains, fifteen klicks or so from the Chinese border.

Horror swooped in and clutched the last of her courage, taking it away on a gust of icy wind. What if Jianyu was planning to take her back to Taipei City?

A round of cheers shot through the atmosphere, chilling and haunting. Darci wondered who'd been killed. It sounded like *that* kind of exultant cheer.

She pulled at the restraints. Her shoulders sagged in exhaustion. *Oh, God, I am in trouble.* Worse than ever before. The realization proved heady, suffocating. She struggled for a normal breath, not one strangled with panic. *I won't make it without Your help.*

But God didn't help her mom. She'd died clinging to her convictions. Her faith.

The missionary who delivered the message had said her mom had been unrepentant about her faith to the authorities. She preached to them. *Like Nora Lam.*

A shudder rippled through Darci. At a youth camp, she'd seen the movie of Nora's firing squad testimony. And Darci had bolted out of the building, sobbing, remembering her mother. It'd been way too close to home. She struggled with anger — why hadn't God given her mother that sort of miracle? And if He wouldn't give her mother, who'd died for Him, why would He work a miracle for her?

A whimper squirmed past her hold. "Please . . . God . . . she believed in You . . ."

Defeat shoved her courage back from where it'd come. She couldn't survive on her mother's faith. Isn't that what she'd been doing all these years? Being a good girl, attending church, reading her Bible — when missions afforded her that luxury — but . . . faith. What was it? *The substance of things hoped for, the evidence of things not seen.*

Well, she sure couldn't see her way out of this mess.

But did she believe God would get her out?

Exhaustion tugged at her, encouraging her to fall back into its sleepy embrace. So tired. So much pain . . . so sleeeeeppy . . .

No!

No more sleep. She had to stay awake. Stay alert. Darci pushed herself up against the wood. Propped her head back. The fire drew her attention. A story . . . there was a story . . . three men . . . Shad', 'Shach, and 'Nego. They'd told the king that even if God didn't rescue them, they wouldn't bend their knees.

Resolve festooned itself around Darci's wounds, inside and out. That's right. *God, You can. Even if You don't, I believe in You.*

The door flapped open. A cold wind snapped into the hut.

Darci hauled in a breath as a dark shape swam toward her. She moaned a single prayer — *God help me* — knowing she was powerless to stop the darkness drenching her mind and body.

Cold pressed in around her, nudging her from the iron-clad grip of sleep. Oh, everything hurt. Hurt so very bad. Each minute, each breath dragging her closer to death's permanent hold.

Again, cold pressed against her.

Moaning reached her drifting consciousness. *That's me.* Though she tried to sit up, a nagging at the back of her mind lured her to the surface of reality. She groaned.

Cold, wet lapped at her hands.

Darci yelped. What was that?

Beside her, the shadow that had chased her into oblivion the last time shifted side to side. She sucked in a breath and pulled away. Wait — what was . . . ?

Tall, triangular-shaped ears lifted into her view and slowly revealed the glow of two yellow eyes. Holding that breath, Darci felt a swirl of warmth coil around her. What . . . what was it? Uncertainty held her fast.

The shape shifted up onto its haunches.

A tongue swiped over her face.

Trinity.

No. Not Trinity. No way she could be here. Just a stray dog. How did a dog get in here?

Darci blinked as the fire flickered and shadows danced over the fur, which in some places sat in wet clusters. "Trinity?"

A slight whimper as the dog scooted forward. Another kiss on her cheek.

"Trinity." Repeating the dog's name firmed in her addled brain that she was really here. Darci's gaze shot to the wood door. A rescue? Could it be? If Trinity had come, then . . . "Heath."

A louder whimper preceded Trinity in lowering herself and ducking out of sight behind Darci. Wet tongue, cold nose. Against Darci's hands.

She tried to glance over her shoulder to see. Gentle but firm pressure, almost a nuzzling type of motion against the sensitive part of her wrist. The ropes binding her wrists slackened. Hauling in a breath, Darci wriggled her arms. Even as she fought free, she wondered how she'd get out of here. Weakness weighted her like a boulder to the earth. Walking drugged . . . that would be interesting. But she'd do it, because with Trinity here, Heath must be, too. And that meant Darci was getting out of here. Even if it killed her.

A thought stilled her. "*She never does that.*" Heath had said Trinity never broke from him. And if he wasn't here . . . was he in trouble, too? Had Jianyu or the Russians found him?

Was he alone? Were there other American soldiers here to help?

Trinity leapt up. Her ears rotated like satellite dishes as she threw a glance over her shoulder, to the right. To the door. A broad chest and long legs hinted at the speed and power of this dog.

Darci couldn't help but lean into the godsend. "You found me," she said, her thoughts jumbled and chaotic, tossed around with relief and fear and a thrill. Tears slipped down her cheeks, renewing her hope that she might survive and encouraging her to tug against the ropes. Her wrists burned, but there was enough give that kept her fighting. *You gave up too fast.*

No, you believed just in time.

Trinity's bark shot into the lightening day like the report of a rifle.

"No," she bit out.

Great. Trinity had no doubt alerted every guard and person within a fifty-foot radius. Darci yanked hard — her right arm pulled free. Shoulders aching from the awkward restraint, Darci dragged her arms around to the front. Ugh. She might as well have telephone poles for arms they were so heavy. So sore. Trekking her fingers along the ground, she slumped to the side against Trinity and dug her fingers into the ropes around her feet.

Shouts outside pushed her gaze to the door.

Footsteps rushed toward them.

"Down," Darci ordered Trinity, praying the dog wouldn't be noticed at first, if at all.

The door flung inward.

THIRTY-FOUR

With a wintry blast, Major Wang lurched into the hut.

Darci yanked her arms behind her back and faked being tied up as he loomed closer. The war dance of flames against his face painted him with a wicked malice that sent alarm spiraling through her veins.

"Stay." Maybe Wang thought she was making an innocuous comment about him.

"Ha!" he said, gloating. "You did not think you would escape?" He produced another needle. "More juice?"

When he knelt at her side and reached for her right arm, Darci rolled, her mind darting over the vibration in the ground — *what is that from?* — and the breathy grunt of Wang coming again.

She flipped over. Out of reach. A scream climbed up her throat. Outmatched.

Air and dirt shifted to her right. In the space of a blink, Trinity flew over her shoulder and nailed Wang in the chest.

He stumbled backward and dropped. Tripped by his own feet.

Trinity caught his arm, growling through clenched teeth.

Darci thrashed against the ropes on her feet, locked on the duel between the beast and the dog. Wang struck Trinity, but she held.

Fumbling, twisting, Darci was unable to loosen the ropes. She searched for a weapon while she dug her fingers in the hemp. Only the logs, half consumed in flames, would work.

She tossed herself in that direction. *Thud.* Her chest slammed into the dirt, spitting the breath from her lungs. She squeezed off the pain that exploded in her abdomen and strained for the log. Dragged it free.

Sparks hissed and popped in protest of being yanked from the fire.

Holding the center tent support, Darci dragged herself upright as Trinity and Wang went at it. The dog proved unyielding, even when Wang rammed the butt of his weapon at her. She yelped but maintained her lock.

Anger tightened Darci's chest. "Hey!" With everything in her, she swung the four-inch-thick log at Wang. It connected with a resounding crack. He staggered, then went down.

Darci thumped him on the back of the head again, hard enough to make sure he was out, but not enough to kill him, even though he'd wanted her dead. He'd helped Jianyu and took pleasure in her torture.

The log began to slide in her hands, the warmed bark raking the pads of her fingers. Darci slumped to the ground on one knee, breath shallow. Trinity nosed her cheek, and she leaned into the dog's warmth. Buried her face in Trinity's neck where dense fur met the stiff nylon vest. Darci's eyes traced the high-tech outfit. She didn't have this on at the base. Where had it come from? She wasn't a certified MWD anymore. And this was a pricey vest. Had someone recruited or borrowed Trinity?

Using the log to hold her up, Darci planted a kiss on Trinity's neck. "Thanks, girl." She rubbed Trinity's ear with the back of her hand. "Couldn't have made it without you."

Her amber gaze flicked to Darci as if to say, "Yeah, I get that a lot." She panted.

"I bet you do," Darci muttered.

"But you should see my handler."

"Oh, I have. He's almost as good-looking as you." Darci smirked at herself. Half dead and having an imaginary conversation with a war dog could get her wrung up for a psych eval.

Time to find out what's going on.

Darci struggled to her feet, the log slipping in her bloodied hands. It was too heavy to carry, and Wang had just donated a fully automatic to her once-empty arsenal. *Ditch the log, try the gun.* It seemed logical. But could she even hold the AK-47?

She bent to release the log.

Movement rustled outside, stilling her.

Adrenaline sped through her veins and tightened her grip on the log. She shot a glance to Trinity, who stood with her ears trained on the door. Ready to attack. Ready to defend . . . *me.* The thought proved a heady tonic to her wounded soul.

Darci took a step back. What would Jianyu do to her if he found her free with his officer out cold? *Nothing good, that's for sure.* Wobbling on her feet, Darci held the log with both hands. Prepped herself. She was not going down. She would not die at the hands of Jianyu or any enemy. Trinity had come for her, and that meant Heath had, too. Staying alive was the best way to thank him for coming after her, putting his life — and partner, Trinity's — at risk.

Again, she looked to Trinity, who spared

her a glance, then everything in the beautiful creature realigned on the door.

Darci braced herself.

With another blast of the winter storm, the door swung inward. Light blinded her but not enough to blot out the silhouette of a man with a fully automatic weapon. Sweat dripped into Darci's right eye as she brought the log to bear with a loud grunt.

"Hey!"

Ignoring the spike of pain in her side, Darci raised it over her head.

"Jia, stop!" The silhouette shifted to the left.

Darci's mind tripped on her name as she lost her balance. *Heath?*

Heath braced for impact as the thick weapon in her hand registered. The log wobbled in the air over her head, then toppled from her grasp. Eyes hooded with exhaustion and pain, Jia heaved forward — straight at him.

Heath stepped forward and hooked an arm around her shoulders as she tumbled into his chest. In a dead faint, she was heavy yet . . . light. There wasn't much in terms of weight to this enigmatic woman.

As he lowered Jia to the ground, Trinity trotted to his side and relief swept him.

"Hey, girl." He petted her as he keyed his mic. "Primary objective located."

"Retrieve and return," came Watterboy's quick response.

Gaze tracking over the unconscious operative, Heath nodded. Right. Sure. How was he supposed to get her back up the side of the mountain he'd just scaled down when she was unconscious?

"Jia?"

Trinity nudged him, then sniffed his face — then sneezed.

He chuckled. "Good to see you, too." She always hated the smell of tactical paint. He leaned his head toward her, but he scanned Jia for injuries, his heart regaining a normal pattern after thinking Trinity had bit a bullet. "Don't scare me like that again." That fried his brain like nothing else. He couldn't stand the thought of losing her.

Trinity lowered her snout to Jia's cheek.

"Jia, hey. You there?" Man, seeing her like this, pale and unconscious, hurt as much as thinking Trinity had bit one, and that was plain weird. How could he feel that way about a woman he'd met a week ago? Wasn't something he could articulate to himself, let alone anyone else. Whatever it was that had snagged his attention, she had it. And she couldn't die on him. He wouldn't let her.

Heath visually traced the lines of her face. A fat shiner puffed her left eye and blood dribbled down her temple. Dried and cracked, her lips proved her dehydration and the split on the left side matched the one on her temple. Whoever had assaulted her must have been right-handed. He searched for injuries or wounds that would incapacitate her. No head knots or gaping wounds there. He tried to sort out why it was so important to him that she survive. Dark hair spilled toward the dwindling fire, its shadows stroking her black strands.

How could a woman look beautiful even when battered and unconscious?

Because she's a fighter. She doesn't take bull.

"Jia," Heath whispered her name as he smoothed his hands down her shoulders, strong biceps, and forearms, and his mind flipped back to the night at the base MWD training field when she'd thrown Trin's ball with a perfect arc. Athletic, intelligent, but those things seemed so minor. The lunch date when he'd held her close, feeling her unsteady breathing, he wanted to seal their attraction with a kiss.

Stow it, Ghost. He shoved his jagged thoughts aside.

"Ghost, report. What's the holdup?"

"Jia, c'mon." He noted movement behind her eyelids as his hands ran across the stiff binding around her waist. Had she been shot? Cut? What was this?

He hit his mic again. "Target is injured and unconscious." He traced a gloved finger along the red welts on her wrists. Not exactly gentle on her, were they?

"Roger. Candyman — get in there. Grab the package and go," Watterboy ordered.

Crossing her arms over her chest to lift her —

Her fist shot up. No time to deflect it. She nailed his jaw.

Heath tumbled backward. As he did, a swirl of cold air rushed him, snapping his attention to the open door. He sucked in a breath as a form filled it, and he pushed himself upright again.

Candyman stepped inside and pulled the door to, holding the catch with one hand and gripping his weapon with the other. "Inside."

A scream rent the air. Another fist.

Heath hauled himself forward and landed hard on his knees as he gripped her arms. "Jia!" Holding her arms was like wrestling an octopus. She writhed, broke free, but he caught her again. "Jia — it's me, Heath, Ghost!" Like she would remember him,

471

coming up out of it. "American. We're American."

She struggled, then went still. Wild eyes locked on him. A whimper. "Heath?" Her taut limbs went limp, her brow smoothing as the fight drained from her expression.

"Yeah." Dawg, that felt good to hear the way she said his name. "Let's get you out of here." He tried crossing her arms again, then bent to scoop her into his arms. As he pushed to his feet, she hooked an arm around his neck and burrowed into his vest with a shudder.

Something strong and powerful tugged at his heart with that simple gesture. A shudder . . . it wasn't like she'd vowed her undying love. Although he'd take that, too. But the shudder told him she trusted him, she felt safe with him.

"Hey, RockGirl, you okay?" Why did he feel shy all of a sudden? No, he'd never been shy. Confident, arrogant — yeah. But shy? He peered down at her, and though she didn't look up at him, she nodded.

"Yeah . . ." Her grip around his neck tightened as she pulled deeper into his hold. "Now."

Hesitation strangled him and held fast. His lightning-fast mind attached a bevy of meaning to that simple statement. Expectation like he'd never experienced before hung in her words. *Oh, Lord, help* . . .

"You're going to be fine. I've got you." Heath firmed his hold, careful of the delicate package in his arms, mindful of the yanking of his heartstrings. Aware he was willing to move heaven and earth to get Jia home safe and alive!

Against his right hand, he felt the vibration of sound through her back and glanced down at her again. Her lips were moving, slowly.

"up . . . ted . . . grace . . . enfolded . . . peace of His embrace."

Ice and fire competed for dominance in his stomach. No, he couldn't have heard that right. But her whispered words unleashed an angel from his past. An angel everyone said didn't exist, that he'd been dreaming. An angel who voiced a prayer that clung to his soul while he lay in a coma at Landstuhl, hovering on the brink of death.

That angel . . . did she lay in his arms now? He watched her lips moving, stunned. "*Finally, I pray you'd be uplifted by His grace, and feel yourself enfolded in the peace of His embrace.*"

"Ghost."

Heath jerked to the entry point.

Candyman shot a look over his shoulder. "Ready?"

Mind singed with the memory, Heath braced her against his uplifted right leg to get a better hold, then nodded. "Go."

"Right, left, left." After the instructions, Candyman peered out the door. Nodded. "Move!"

The door swung open, and Heath rushed into the morning. The steady cadence of his boots crushing the snow beat in rhythm with Candyman's and the soft padding of Trinity at his side. They made the first right without a hitch.

Sidling up against the hut, they came to a juncture. As Candyman took point, his weapon stabbing into the open, Heath again hoisted Jia up farther. In view, Candyman gave a sharp nod.

Heath hustled into the path between the huts and rushed forward, trusting Candyman who moved two paces ahead to guide him to safety. Trinity trotted in between them. This didn't seem right. Hadn't they come — ?

"Back!" Candyman snapped and threw himself at Heath.

Feet tangling with Candyman's, Heath tripped. Instinct tightened his grip on Jia, but he went down on a knee. Crushing her to himself, Heath prayed he didn't drop her.

"Augh!" She arched her back and pulled away.

Heath tugged her closer as he caught his balance. "Sorry."

"Quiet," Candyman hissed. "Base, we need an out."

Leaning against the mud-and-thatch hut, Heath ignored the burn in his arms and legs. Didn't know what he was thinking trying to carry her like this. Fireman carry — only way to make this journey. He shifted. "Jia." She groaned and lifted her head. "Gotta change carry."

Her head bobbed in understanding.

Heath set her down, then hesitated, thinking about the injury in her side before he shifted to the other side, hooked an arm under her leg, tucked his head, and let her slump over his shoulder. A steeled grunt pushed warm air along his neck and cheek as he supported her across his shoulders. Heath had a perfect line of sight through the huts. All the way to the main hub. Two men emerged from a hut. One older and vaguely familiar. The other Zheng Jianyu.

Heath pushed up and backed into the shadows, praying like he'd never prayed before that they hadn't been seen.

A minute later, Candyman swung around,

patted Heath, then pointed a few huts down. "This way."

As he scurried behind Candyman, Heath realized his coms link had come out. Bracing Jia wouldn't afford him a free hand to replace it, so he'd have to trust —

Fingers tickled his ear. He shrugged off the tickle.

"Keep still," came the quiet command — from Jia.

The coms link tucked back into his ear, he eyed her face, so close to his . . . and sideways. He gave a nod and kept moving. Shouts erupted behind them and served as motivation to move faster. They cleared the line of huts and broke into the open. Heath trained his focus on the rocky incline. Remembered slipping and sliding down it. *This will be interesting.*

"Ghost, Candyman, you've got tails."

Okay, make that very interesting.

Halfway up the hill, rocks and dirt peppered his face.

"Taking fire," Candyman called.

Heath stuffed himself behind a rocky cleft and peered up. Huffing, he knelt and looked at Jia. "Doing okay?"

"Sure."

He panted through a quick laugh. "Good." Eying their route, he felt desperation clogging his veins. At least another fifty, sixty feet up to the ridgeline — but they'd still be prime targets. Then another mile or more to the team.

The verse in Proverbs about God making paths straight teased Heath. He smirked, imagining the great hand of God smoothing a path directly to safety. Then again . . . *You are the God who says all things are possible to him who believes, right?*

Trinity barked to the right.

Heath checked . . . and froze as she darted out of view. Tucked behind a stack of boulders, a path led up the side of the mountain. Smooth. Straight. Protected. "No way." He readjusted, looked to Candyman, who already pushed up from his spot and started toward Trinity.

"Hold on," Heath muttered to Jia.

"Ya think?"

He smiled and broke into a sprint.

Gunfire peppered the ground.

Fire lit through his leg.

Jia sucked in a sudden breath.

The ground rushed up at him.

THIRTY-FIVE

"Cover them!" Watterboy's shout sailed through the air.

Peering through the binoculars but unarmed — at least, they believed he wasn't armed — Haur trailed the trio as they hoofed it back up the mountain, mind stricken with what he'd seen and heard. M4s provided suppressive cover.

He let the extended reach of the lens trace the village. Jianyu's elite were there in force. Russians . . . not so much. Odd. If the purpose of Jianyu's presence here was to align with the Russians in order to attack the Americans, wouldn't there be more?

Maybe they were holed up on the other side of the ridge.

Or maybe there was something different, something more sinister going on here.

Haur double-checked on the threesome and the dog. Making good progress. A tiny explosion of blood on Ghost's leg told of a shot. The man hobbled but made it into the passage.

He'd be fine. So would the dog. And the woman. The spy who'd outsmarted his brother and escaped him twice. Haur would like the chance to talk with her, determine her motives, determine if the love she lavished on his brother was real. Or was in fact a tactic to unseat Jianyu. No one had mastered his brother, the master of all.

Except the woman spy. Meixiang. But that's not what the others had called her. Jia, wasn't it? Thoughts rolled around his mind, laden with curiosity and venom, a hunger to know the power she'd exerted over Jianyu.

He'd tried to exert power, to influence the brother whose thirst for power had darkened his outlook. Oh, how Haur had tried. For more than twenty years. And here he was on an icy mountain, staring at the scene before him, distanced. Cold. Left out.

Again.

Haur studied the village, tried to mesh his thinking with Jianyu's. They'd been close, studied together, planned together, passed exams, and soared through the ranks like twins. But there had always been a particular twist to Jianyu's thinking. The awareness of that element in his "brother" had kept

Haur alive.

So, brother, what are you doing here? What madness is behind this mission?

The binoculars hit on movement near the center of the small village. Men ran in all directions. A door spun through the air. Haur trained in on that structure.

A man stepped into the open. His face a mask of indignation and rage.

Giddy warmth slithered through Haur so heated he feared the snow around him would betray his guilty pleasure.

"What do you see?" Bai asked in a low voice. "Do you see Jianyu?"

Haur ignored him, glad he'd kept the smile from his face. "No." The lie was necessary. Especially with suspicions abounding. Especially with loyalties shifting.

"They're clear, but let's keep them safe," Watterboy announced. "Spook, you ready to haul butt out of here?"

"We're ready."

Haur kept his focus on his enraged brother. Who kicked a truck. Punched a private. Knocked a boiling pot from its stand in a fire. Men around it shot up, tumbling backward, away from the spewing maw of the pot and their colonel.

So. Jianyu had discovered the American spy had been recovered. Taken right from his hands. Right out from under his nose. The same operative who'd toppled the Zheng empire.

He should not be so pleased. It was not good to revel in the misfortune of others. His mother had taught him that. But Haur could not help but think even his mother was smiling on this day. Or . . . perhaps not yet. Perhaps soon though.

"Haur," Bai said hoarsely.

"They're almost out," he muttered, hoping Bai would beg off and leave him so he could figure out what Jianyu would do now. He wanted to witness this.

"Pack it up, people. Let's move!"

As Haur was about to pull up, a second man emerged from the hut. Heat splashed down the back of his neck, filling him with dread. He knew that shape. Or did he?

No, it couldn't be . . .

Same height but twice the girth. He placed a hand on Jianyu's shoulder, bringing him around. His brother shoved off the hand, arms flailing as he raged at the man. Yet the other man clamped the hand back on his shoulder, brought him back in line.

This . . . this was too familiar. Unease squirmed through Haur's gut.

At this angle, Haur could not see the

man's face. But something . . . Jianyu shifted.

And with him, so did Haur's world.

General Zheng.

"Ghost!"

His foot plunged into soft snow, shin-deep, the second fire ripped through it. Heath struggled to stay upright, to keep from dropping Jia. The weight of the world rested on his shoulders. She was an American operative with information that could put a lot of people in danger and countries at war.

Heath trudged out of the deep snow, staring at the path where Candyman stood with Trinity, each step felt like trying to plunge into a vat of glue.

"Sorry." Jia's apology warmed him.

"For what? This" — he grunted as he pushed up and over a crevice — "walk in the park?" She sucked in a breath that slowed him, worried he was hurting her with the ragged, jerky movements.

"Bomb."

In the split second after she said that word, Heath's gaze hopscotched over the terrain, a blast — literally — from the past still ringing in his ears. "Where?"

"Don't know." Jia moaned. "Jianyu . . .

bombs . . . bases."

He braved another step. "But not here?" He couldn't help but assess the ground with more caution now. With the sun about to peek over the tips of the mountain, the pristine snowfall would soon be blinding.

"No . . . bas . . ."

Hands pawed at him. Candyman tugged him into the safety of the passage. "Want me to take her?"

"No." Heath surprised himself at the vehemence of his response. *Easy, chief.* "We're good."

"Tell him," Jia wheezed out, then drooped.

Candyman's gaze darted to him. "Tell me what?"

Thwat!

Heath ducked and went to a knee — which hit hard because of the incline.

"Move!" Candyman shouted as he zig-zagged farther into the passage and up the mountain.

Heath pushed himself, ignoring the sweat sliding down his neck and back despite the chilling, bitter wind and the frigid temps. His nerves bounced, wishing he could stop and reassess Jia, but even though they had the protection of the passage, this walled-in passage would provide a perfect ambush point.

He propelled himself up the narrow path and focused on getting back to Watters and the others. It took a minute before they reached the top. Candyman crouched at the opening, Trinity too. She came to Heath and licked Jia's face.

"We'll go up some more, then beeline it for the team. They're waiting and will cover, but going up over the ridge and down a little will provide cover."

"Got it."

Candyman's gaze tracked over Heath and then Jia. "You okay?"

"Sure."

"Let me take her the rest of the way."

"I'm good."

"Bull." Candyman's dogged determination held fast. "Your head's hurting, isn't it?"

"No," Heath said as a thump inside his head argued with his answer. "Okay, a little." Little? The thing felt as if it wielded Thor's hammer. He hadn't noticed.

"Your leg . . ."

Heath glanced down to where blood seeped into the snow. "Just a graze." But standing here, not moving, the muscle contracted and squeezed, sending shards of fire up past his knee and into his thigh.

"You willing to risk her life on that graze

and little headache?" Candyman stepped closer, his tone softer. "Ghost, listen — dump the pride. Work with me. We can move faster. You slowed down. You're tripping. Let me take her."

Heath considered the offer. But three things made him hesitate: They had less than a mile to go. The incline had been hard and completely in the open. The other element was Jia's trust in him, her saying she was okay "now," *now* that he was here, now that he held her. And third, jostling her from his shoulders to Candyman's might inflict unnecessary additional trauma.

Then again, if he passed out, went down for five seconds like he had days earlier . . .

Heath nodded. "Okay." He went down on a knee again, angling his back to his combat buddy. Weight shifted from his shoulders and unbalanced him.

Heath swiftly turned and aided Candyman with adjusting and getting back on his feet. "Got her?"

Straightening, Candyman nodded. "Let's go."

Only as he moved free of her weight did Heath notice the burn in his leg, the pounding in his skull, and the aches in his legs and arms. He couldn't help but make the comparison to the moment of surrender . . .

with God.

A month ago, he would've been too stubborn and filled with pride to admit that he needed Candyman to share the burden. Just as Heath needed to now admit he needed God's help. He didn't belong here. As much as he'd said he wanted to get back into combat, into the fray . . . he didn't. His pride had been wounded by that blast. Shoved out the back door by the Army, his self-worth and identity took a hit, center mass.

He'd been so focused on proving he still had what it took, he nearly caused more harm than good. No wonder he hadn't qualified for the chaplaincy.

"Do it," Candyman grunted.

Heath turned to his beautiful partner, invigorated by the life lesson that had just dumped down his nerve network. "Trinity, go!"

She threw her muscular body around and launched along the ridgeline. Heath gauged the incline, making sure they were out of sight. Keying his mic, he reported in. "Base, Ghost and Candyman en route. One klick."

"Roger. We have you in sight. Covering your six."

And wasn't that just like God, too? Surrender the load, admit you can't do it alone, and He's right there, ready to fight. *"The Lord will fight for you; you need only to be still."* The verse from Exodus sailed across his mind and propelled him toward the team.

Help me be still, God. Not literally, of course, but in heart and mind, in attitude. The fight wasn't his. He needed to surrender the dreams, the hopes, the yearnings . . . God would defend his honor. God would prove the mettle buried deep within Heath Daniels.

A shape rose from the snow.

Heath's breath backed into his throat.

"Ghost!" the form waved an arm.

Heart stuttering, Heath let out the breath. "Watterboy!" He spun around and guided Candyman into the safety of the team's embrace.

Scrip and Doc rushed forward and took Jia. In a two-man carry, they lowered her onto a thermal blanket and litter. Candyman and Watterboy joined the others in lifting it. The spook and his objective were there helping — even though the other man's face looked as beat up as Jia's. A white bandage covered the guy's neck as the team made a quick turnaround and got moving again. They navigated the treacherous terrain for about another klick before pausing near an outcropping.

Scrip and Doc knelt around Jia, probing, assessing. Scrip slid a needle for an IV into her arm.

"How bad is she?" Heath shifted to alleviate the throbbing in his leg.

Doc looked up, then dropped his gaze to Heath's calf. "Let me see that."

Heath tugged the leg back. "I'm good."

"I didn't ask, and I outrank you." Doc wrapped a firm hand around Heath's knee and ripped his tactical pants open around the wound. He grabbed a packet from his field kit, tore it open, and squeezed the clear contents onto the injury. Then he pressed gauze and tape around it. "Just a graze. You're good."

"Except now it stings." Heath couldn't resist the taunt and smirked when Doc glowered at him. "How's the girl?"

"Can't tell — messed up," Scrip said. "Broken ribs for sure."

"Means this hike could make this journey a killer."

Scrip shook his head. "Watterboy, we need an extraction. She can't make the hike."

A curse stabbed the tension.

Heath looked at the team leader. "What's wrong?"

"No coms." Watterboy huffed. "Okay, pack

her up. Let's get moving. Putman, keep trying coms. First signal, I want to know."

"Roger."

Heath squatted beside Trinity and held her face in his hands, rubbing each ear between his thumb and forefinger. "Good work, girl." Nose cold but dry, she panted and gave him that squinted "You betcha" look. Heath tugged the bite valve of his CamelBak and took a draught of water. Icy cold, but at least it hadn't frozen yet. He sucked hard, then aimed it at Trinity. She lapped the water, but he could tell she didn't have the stamina she'd had twenty-four hours ago.

Heath dug his hand into the fur along her chest, feeling for her pulse. Had she been injured and he hadn't noticed? No noticeable bullet holes. No blood. "You just tired, girl?"

As if in answer, she lowered herself to the snow, pink tongue wagging with each rapid rise and fall of her chest. He slipped on the insulated doggie mitts.

"Let's move. Last established coms was two klicks out."

Heath lifted her onto his shoulders. Though she tensed at first, it wasn't her first rodeo, and she settled into the hold.

The journey proved treacherous and

laborious. Heath watched the path in front of him, head tucked, gaze down to ensure he didn't step off the path and plummet to his death. When Trinity whimpered, he wondered if she'd be better off walking. At least down among their legs, her back and ears weren't exposed to the frigid air. Gently, he brought her around and lowered her. As he patted her head and took a step — his foot plunged downward. Stomach went with it.

Something tugged him back.

"Easy there, Ghost."

Steadied and moving again, he glanced back. "Thanks, Haur." Shaken that he could've plummeted to his death, Heath mulled over who'd saved him. The Chinese man. The dichotomous one. Whose words always seemed to have double meanings. Or maybe that was just Heath's imagination.

Thanks to the narrow path covered with snow, every cell in his body felt frozen through. Howling winds tore at their clothes and exposed flesh. Heath's head pounded in cadence with each step. He eased two tablets out of a packet tucked into his pocket and dumped them in his mouth. With a dry swallow, he hoped that would cut off the thumping in his skull.

Minutes bled into what felt like hours. In fact, two hours. Still no communication.

Shadows overtook the team, drawing Heath's gaze upward. Gray, heavy clouds shielded the earth from the sun. Thick, fat snowflakes swirled and danced on the tendrils of icy air. As Heath's gaze roamed the sky, it hit the foot-deep ledge of snow that stretched over the mountain passage.

A foreboding wormed into his gut and took root.

"All quiet," came the hissed words from the front.

Watterboy, too, had noticed the shelf of snow.

And the danger it posed. They didn't need a missile. Or even a bullet. Just a sound. Just the right frequency, and the enemy could wipe the whole grid off the map and into an icy, suffocating grave.

Thirty-Six

They're going to die because of me.
The thought strangled her as the sky twisted into a cauldron of white and gray fury. Darci appreciated the warmth of the thermal blankets and the less-jarring method of carrying her. But that these men were placing their lives on the line. For her. Unacceptable.

In all, she counted four men carrying her, at least four others and Heath closely trailing her. Had he been carrying Trinity? *I thought he carried me.* Two men, shoulders burrowed and heads tucked, trailed Heath. A couple more behind them. A dozen? Why were a dozen men searching for her? Too many! She didn't want to be responsible for that many lives. She'd seen the weight her father bore after her mother's death and being separated from her brother. She didn't want that burden.

She shifted her left arm and felt the

familiar pinch of a needle. For what? Darci searched her mind for coherency. She didn't feel addled. That told her they hadn't given her morphine. Saline, most likely. Maybe antibiotics. She was, after all, missing a few fingernails.

Down the length of her body, at the foot of the stretcher that bore her, Darci locked onto Heath. He'd stormed into the hut, all bravado and good looks. Face still streaked with tactical paint, he maintained that grim determination. But beneath it . . . something else spoke. A certainty. A . . . knowing.

What was that? He'd done that at Bagram, too. One thing remained clear to her: When that man decided something, he went after it with war dog-like tenacity. Or was that just a one-day fluke? Would he press her again? Funny enough, it hadn't bugged her the way he'd gotten into her face about hiding her feelings. She liked it. Felt drawn to it. Nothing fake there.

It reminded Darci of her parents. Especially her mother. She'd been so strong, right up to the day she never came home. Friends said she'd been taken from the street on her way home from a Bible study. It still happened today — Christians vanishing into the penal systems of countries like China, Afghanistan, Iran. And the world looked the other way, right into the mind-numbing, moral-erasing conscience of entertainment: television, movies, Internet. Anything to anesthetize their minds to things they didn't want to deal with. Things they felt were out of their control and power. And so . . . they let it continue.

Then there were the men like those around her. They'd sacrificed time with their families, some sacrificed everything — even their lives — to make a difference. Fight wars nobody wanted to fight. Again, more of the same that most of the world didn't want to face.

The sense of justice faded. But not for all. Darci felt the call burning in her from the moment her mother vanished. What put the burning in Heath to be a soldier? To fight battles? To live a brutal life? Who was he, really? What family did he leave behind? Parents? Siblings? A girlfriend?

Darci swallowed. Did he have one? Why wouldn't he? Handsome, funny, inspiring . . . But he hadn't mentioned one at the base when he took her into his arms and all but demanded she admit she liked him. And he hadn't diverted her obvious interest.

"*Thought so.*" At first, he'd come across as cocky. But it wasn't that. He was confident. He knew how to read her. And he called her on her attraction to him. "*I see it in your eyes.*" Then he nearly kissed her. But she'd pushed him away. And now, she was afraid she would die before they made it home. Heath would never know how much she wanted to see what would happen between them, how much she regretted pushing away that kiss.

This is crazy.

Voices drowned against the roar of the wind. The team slowed and stopped, her stretcher jarring, sending spikes of pain through her side and back.

One guy shouted to the others, but by the time his words hit the icy din, the sound was lost. Darci tried to read their faces.

Heath's gaze skidded into hers. The left side of his lip slid upward. Then he shot a look to the man who stood shouting. An argument ensued. When he looked back at her, she mouthed the word *bomb*. Had he told them? They were up here in the swirling anger of a winter storm, but down there . . . at the bases . . . was Jianyu finally exacting his vengeance?

The thought of people losing their lives . . . because she'd angered a beast of a man . . .

One of the men supporting the side reached toward her. His large hands bathed in black gloves, he retrieved something near her shoulder. He gave her a firm nod, then slipped an oxygen mask over her mouth and nose. Only as he did that did she realize what he planned. Her gaze cut to Heath's just seconds before a blanket blacked out her visual.

No, no! Blind. I'm blind.

At being covered, head to toe, to protect her from the driving wind and snow, Darci lifted her chin and tried to avoid the suffocating pressure that built in her chest.

No, not your chest. Your mind. It's in your mind. You have oxygen. You're warm.

Being able to talk herself off the ledge was part of the reason Burnett had said she was a prime candidate for an operative. Those who didn't fear were willing to risk too much. Fear kept a healthy balance. Maintained an awareness.

And her awareness now was that this was a smart move, to cover and protect her face and nose from the freezing elements. But she couldn't see what was happening. Couldn't be prepared.

Darci tried to focus on where she knew Heath to be — right at her feet. She trained her ears to listen for his steps. Wind, wind, and more wind pawed at the blanketed environment, rustling out any ability to detect noise.

Faith. Have faith.

A swirl of panic laced through her chest. *I don't have faith! My mother had faith.*

The thought strangled her hope. If she didn't have faith . . .

No, she had to have faith. She'd grown up in a Christian church, her father's attempt at keeping the spirit of her mother and their faith — there was that word again — alive. She'd gone through VBS, memorized the Twenty-Third Psalm, faithfully — ack! would that word not leave her alone? — attended youth group. Dated John Byrd, the most spiritual teen in their group.

When had she needed to stretch herself as she did now? Most likely she had broken ribs, and one wrong move and she'd puncture her lung. Which could be fatal without proper medical treatment. Which was impossible up here in the mountains during a storm.

"With God all things are possible."

Okay, she knew that verse. Matthew 19 . . . something.

Darci groped for a tendril of hope, of faith. *What is faith?*

Faith is the evidence of things . . . the substance . . .

Augh! Why were all the verses tangling in her mind?

I get it, God. I get it. I've been doing it all in my own power. Living off my mom's faith, not letting You in deep enough to risk vulnerability.

Weightlessness clawed at her, as if she were falling.

Darci started.

The blanket pulled back. Heath hovered over her. "You okay?"

"Where . . . ?" She tried to look around but felt pinned to the ground.

"The storm's raging. We had to take shelter." Heath pivoted in his crouched position, looking around. "Not much of a cave, but it'll give us some protection for a while."

Her mind chambered the volatile round. "The bombs. Have you told them?"

Dragging the heavy scarf off his head and neck, he shook his head miserably. "No time. Storm wouldn't let us talk."

"Tell them. It might not be too late."

He nodded. "Okay, tell me what you know."

She eased back, tracing the crooked lines of the granite-looking ceiling a foot above Heath's close-cropped, sandy blond hair. "Just . . . bombs. At the bases." She wet her dry, cracked lips and grimaced. She must be quite the sight. Then again, God had

498

given her the chance to do this, to tell them so they could stop the attacks. *Not in my power, in Yours, Lord.* "They're planning to hit the bases, and they're waiting for Jianyu's activation codes."

"Rest, I'll talk to Watterboy first chance I get."

"First chance?"

Another nod, this one slower, less confident. "They're scouting positions, trying to reestablish contact. He's not here."

"Are we alone?"

"That a problem?"

Her cheeks tingled with unexpected warmth. "I just meant . . ."

"Relax, Jia. We'll be fine. Trust me."

"How do you know?"

He shrugged and pursed his lips. "I . . . just do. Trust me, okay?" Was his face red? "I won't —"

"Beg."

He smirked. At least she thought he did. With the shadows and rogue snowflakes that took shelter with them, she couldn't tell for sure.

He patted her shoulder. "Rest. Hopefully, our time here will be short."

The chair sailed through the air, straight toward the rounded wall. *Crack!* Wood splintered and shattered, raining down in a heap at the feet of Major Wang. The man had enough gall not to flinch. Blood and swelling disfigured his face.

"Is this supposed to stay my anger?" Jianyu stormed toward him. "You are already disfigured — no Yanjingshe allows a prisoner to escape. You have failed!" He raised a hand and struck the man. "You have dishonored your family and your name."

"There was nothing I could do! I was knocked out."

Jianyu's temper trembled beneath the cauldron of fury. "Would you bring this excuse to your father, General Wang, and tell him you have allowed the great enemy of China, the one who stole his life work to walk out of this village — alive?"

The man lowered his head.

Hand on his weapon, Jianyu glowered. "I thought not." He lifted the gun from its holster, aimed it at the man's temple, and fired.

Satisfaction thrummed through his veins as he took in three large, deep breaths. Teeth

500

ground, he stared at the lifeblood spilling out just as the man had bled Jianyu of the right to strip Meixiang of the victory she'd stolen from him, his fathers, and his ancestors.

"Feed him to the dogs," Jianyu said as he holstered the weapon and turned back to the table and chairs.

Behind, he heard the scraping of the body as his colonel dragged it into the bitter storm. Jianyu dropped into one of the chairs and stared at the map adorning the wall. He traced the line the Americans would take, the trail he'd sent four of his elite along to track them down and kill those who had stolen from him.

"Be extremely subtle, even to the point of formlessness. Be extremely mysterious, even to the point of soundlessness. Thereby you can be the director of the opponent's fate."

Sun Tzu might have succeeded in that, but Jianyu still had yet to master that tactic. Perhaps he should have withheld his anger, been more forceful with Meixiang's questioning.

"She still holds power over you."

Jianyu kept his gaze locked on the map. On where he imagined her to be. She was badly injured. How did she expect to survive out there, in this, the last of winter's fury unleashed on the mountains? Why would she not listen to him, work with him, let him help her? He'd even summoned a surgeon, who had arrived with the helicopter.

"She will die in the mountains with her American counterparts." But he hoped not.

"Do not underestimate her."

"I have not." Jianyu pushed out of the chair and strode to the map, hands behind his back. "Four Yanjingshe — four of the best — are on their trail."

"A wise decision."

Annoyed with the patronizing tone, Jianyu moved to the soiled earth. He smeared the spot with his boot, then strode to the small serving table and dumped steaming tea into a mug. He stirred honey into the warm brew.

"Honey will not sweeten what is about to happen."

Words meant to reduce him no longer held sway over him. "Retaliation against the ones who dishonored us is sweet enough."

"Do not take pleasure in pain."

"I take pleasure," Jianyu said as he returned to the table, "in delivering justice where it has gone unmet."

"You take too much glory upon yourself, Jianyu."

Seething at the antagonism, he settled in the chair and blew across the top of the ceramic mug. In the hot liquid, he saw his own anger. His own sense of indignation. And like a cool wind, the bitter herb of revenge sailed across it. Sated it. Reminded him to be patient in the journey. To let the leaves settle, the flavor imbued in the hot water, filling every cell of flavor, till the drink was consumed.

The door swung open.

Colonel Tao entered and strode to the table. "It is done. The Russians are dead."

And dead do not talk. Jianyu sipped. Savored. "Enjoy some tea, Colonel."

With a curt bow, he pivoted and served himself.

The man seated at the head of the table pushed to his feet, towering over the colonel, who relinquished the steaming tea to the giant behind him. And bowed.

Jianyu seethed. But he coiled the disgust into a ball and swallowed it with the last gulp of tea. It burned . . . all the way down.

"Any word on Meixiang?" the colonel asked.

Jianyu glowered at him.

"Do not worry about the traitor." The voice still bore the annoying taunt. "She will receive her reward in time."

Their plans were eerily similar yet very different. Jianyu kept his peace, determined not to be undermined in front of his first officer.

"I will deliver that reward — in person."

"No." Jianyu came to his feet. "I put this together. I worked out the details, contacted you —"

"And would you like to answer what you were doing here in the mountains, away from the mine as instructed?" The giant loomed, scowled.

Jianyu swallowed. He would *not* look away. Would not yield his power. "I fed the information necessary — we agreed. Do not take this from me."

Large and powerful, not in size but in the enormity of presence the man wielded, a hand rested on Jianyu's shoulder. "The fight in you is large, but you must master it. Temper it with patience enough to see the mission through. She is out of your reach — for now. But it does not matter. She cannot stop what is already in motion."

"I want her." Jianyu's voice and being shook.

"And you will have her." The man squeezed his shoulder. "In time. We have an agent with the Americans. In time, he will be revealed." He turned and strode to the

504

table where his emissaries stood in the shadows. "As I have waited twenty-one years, nine months, and fourteen days to have my victory" — he drew up his chin, the resemblance undeniable to even Jianyu — "so will you have yours." Age lines crinkled at the corners of the man's eyes. "But much sooner."

"Are you sure?"

Radio chatter ate up the ominous silence. One of his father's officers stepped into the light. "Sir. They're in place."

A smile creased his father's face. "Completely, my son."

THIRTY-SEVEN

Tunnel 5 Miles outside Parwan Province, Afghanistan

It did strange things to Heath's heart to see Trinity cuddled up next to Jia on the stretcher. Jia had even lured Trinity into the warmth of the thermal blanket, and the two were fast asleep. Trinity's amber fur complemented Jia's fair skin.

Okay, that's a weird thing to notice.

Sitting against the wall, legs bent and elbows on his knees, Heath ran the back of his knuckles along his lips. It scared him, what he was feeling and thinking about Jia. She was an operative. Sure, she'd had lunch with him, laughed and talked with him. She'd wanted that missing kiss as much as he had that day. But was he anything more than a player in a mission to her? When this was over, would she skip along her merry

506

way? He'd have Trinity and a lot of heart-ache.

He tilted his head back, thudding it against the cave wall.

Getting way ahead of the game, Ghost.

First priority: get off the mountain. And there wasn't a single guarantee in attempting that. The storm had unleashed its fury. *Why, God? Why now? When Jia needed a doctor and surgical bay like nobody's business, couldn't You have held off the storm?*

And if God had, would the enemy have found them sooner?

Jia had antibiotics. Color returned to her complexion. And she was sleeping — peacefully.

Peace.

Bomb.

Heath jerked. He hadn't told Watters. Pushing to his feet, he noticed Trinity open her eyes. Her head slid along the blanket to track him but didn't lift. Her "eyebrows" wobbled as she looked up at Heath.

"Not getting up, are you?"

She looked away.

"Traitor." *But I don't blame you.*

Heath bundled into his jacket and inched along the outer edge of the cave toward the others.

Watters stood. "You okay?" he called over

507

the howling wind.

"Yeah, can I talk to you?" Heath bobbed his head to the side.

Watters nodded and followed him, pointing. "Guess she had business to take care of."

Heath caught sight of Trinity squatting in the snow but then focused on Watters. "Hey, listen." He stepped back, away from the others. No need to cause panic with half-baked information. "Jia believes there —"

Boom! CRACK!

Ice dumped down Heath's spine. Watterboy's eyes bulged. Heath whirled toward the cave opening. Saw Trinity tearing up snow toward the cave.

ROAR!

A shadow appeared in the opening. Jia! Propped against the wall, frowning as she aimed those eyes heavenward.

His heart dropped into his stomach. Then vaulted into his throat. He pushed himself, feet skidding on the ice. Gaining traction, he shoved himself toward her. Waving. Hard. "Get back!" Why did it feel like he'd hit slow motion? "Back!"

Ice and snow slowing him, Heath sprinted. Snow and ice rained down.

The great fury of the winter storm bellowed in his ears. Though he shouted, he heard nothing. Felt only the thunderous vibration of the avalanche.

Snow thumped against his legs. Heath spiraled through the air.

Collided with Jia, whose face said she'd caught up with what was happening. Her arms closed around him as they flew backward. Hard earth scraped and clawed at him as they slid deeper. Heath ducked closer to her.

Darkness. Roaring. Tumbling. Cracking.

Whoosh!

Light shattered. Darkness prevailed.

THIRTY-EIGHT

Heath rolled off Jia. "You okay?"

"Yeah," came her weak, soft voice.

He glanced to where daylight and snow raged through the opening. The one that was no longer there. Only darkness existed.

"Trinity?" His voice bounced back at him. "Trin!" He pushed off Jia, careful not to injure her any more than he had. "You okay, Jia?"

"Yeah." Quiet but trembling, her voice skated through the darkness. "Are we alone?"

"You really have a thing about being alone with me."

"No."

At the frantic word, Heath reached through the void for her. He caught her shoulder, surprised when his fingers tangled in hair. It must've come loose when they impacted. "Hey, it's just a joke."

"The darkness —"

"Hang on. Got it." He reached toward his shoulder lamp. "Watch your eyes." He twisted the barrel and light exploded around them. "Trinity?" He turned and checked the corners and crevices. "Crap." Other words filled his mind, imagining his girl trapped, buried in the snow.

The team! Did they get buried. Were they lost?

"So . . . we *are* alo— on our own." Her eyes sparkled, the light of his shoulder lamp glinting off the mahogany irises. Wide. With fear.

"Don't worry. We'll get out."

"How?"

He didn't have the answers, but he wouldn't accept that they would die in this cave. Could they dig their way out? How much snow had heaped on them?

"We'll get out."

"Where are they?"

Ignoring the question, Haur clambered over the mound of snow that had dumped down the mountain, narrowly avoiding him and the others who took shelter beneath the lip of the overhang. Hands plunged through soft, shifting snow. Cold seeped up his sleeves and made his bones ache. Balancing on a boulder that had made the journey

511

with the snow, Haur wobbled. Weak knees, trembling hands. The terror of being buried alive had choked off any bravado or confidence he'd held a few seconds earlier.

That and the conviction that he knew what caused the avalanche. But revealing that would get him killed.

Soldiers skittered back and forth. Dropping to their knees, digging with gloved hands. A couple produced collapsible shovels, then went to work.

"Anyone got them?" Watterboy threw himself over one mound after another, searching. Shouting.

Haur slid a glance to Bai, who stood back, staring. No, not staring. Watching. Enjoying. Haur had had his suspicions about his captain, but the movement out of the corner of his eye in the seconds before he heard the loud crack — which was really a *boom* — could only be one thing.

A grenade. Thrown by Bai up onto the shelf.

Which triggered the avalanche.

And buried Meixiang.

The soldiers rushed around. Frantic. Scared. His stomach churned. Meixiang had more information on Jianyu and the Chinese government than anyone else. He must be certain that information was protected. Kept from the wrong hands.

"Storm's letting up." Watterboy's voice boomed over the unsettled area. "Candyman, we got coms?"

"No coms," Rocket announced from his position.

Just as the storm had let up, the avalanche slowed them.

"Then get it! We need coms — *yesterday!*" Watterboy's face was red, his posture rigid.

"There's no signal," said a shorter, black-haired man who sat on a pile of rocks.

"Then get off your lazy butt and get me one." Watterboy's shout echoed through the narrow valley as he stabbed a finger in a southern direction.

Haur shifted. Glanced up. South? Or was he pointing west? With the sun hiding behind the clouds and storm, there was no telling.

"Hey," Candyman spoke with a hiss. "Lower your voice. Anything could trigger another one."

The dog bounded around the area, sniffing, whimpering. The spook and the man he rescued — a man named Toque — trailed the dog.

A stream of curses mingled with the fluttering snow. "I want them found!"

Candyman knelt beside Trinity. "Where

are they, girl? Find Ghost!"

Nose up, she sniffed. Leapt over upturned debris. Sniffing. Bounding.

It was hopeless, was it not? They would not find Ghost or the spy. Not with the way the snow heaped against the opening. Most likely they were buried anyway. That much of the mountain surely filled in the hole.

Watters went to his knees with a shovel and started digging. "They were right here. Let's get them out."

"Think that cave had another way out?"

Haur considered the question spoken with a British accent. "It is possible."

"How would you know?"

Haur understood the animosity, even though he now knelt to aid in digging. "These mountains lead to the Wakhan Corridor and river in China. There are many tunnels and caves there."

"Remember, Jia said she and that little girl found a way through another tunnel."

"That's right."

"But we don't know there was a way out. I went into that cave — there wasn't anything but walls."

"Keep digging," Watterboy ordered.

Candyman shook his head. "What do you think about sending me, Scrip, and Putman on ahead to try to gain radio contact, get us help up here?"

Watterboy hesitated. Pushed back on his knees, sleeves soaked from digging. "Do it."

Haur did not miss that Bai had not taken up the task of trying to find the Americans. He stood to the side. "We should help," he said in their tongue.

"You saw how little regard they had for our people," he replied back in kind. "How can I help save the life of a woman who betrayed and violated all of China?"

"Because you value life, not politics!"

He saw it. For a fraction of a second, Haur saw the sneer bleed into his captain's face. And just as fast, it was gone.

Haur went back to digging, both figuratively and literally. His time was short. To accomplish his mission, to carry out his intentions, he must not let himself be sidetracked by anyone else's leanings. "You will give them the wrong idea," Haur muttered to Bai.

"As you are Colonel Zheng."

He would not be goaded, not by this man, no matter how much he once trusted him. " 'Know thy self, know thy enemy. A thousand battles, a thousand victories.' " Slowly, Haur came to his feet. "It is prudent not to forget the ways of old, the proven tactics of our ancestors." He let his gaze drift to Bai's.

"I see your doubts, both the spoken and unspoken. And I see more." He let the words hang in the air. "We have our mission."

"Why did you not go with them into the village to confront Jianyu?"

The moment of truth. Could he convince his captain? "Because the girl has become a higher priority. Do you realize who she is, Bai Ling?"

Question glittered in the man's gaze. "You know?"

"Yes, I know. And do you see my brother here?" Vehemence streaked his words. "I will return her to General Zheng. I will restore honor to the Zheng name."

Bai's head tilted up slightly.

"Do *not* question me again, or I will make that your last."

THIRTY-NINE

"Find anything?" Lonely and hollow, her voice skipped along the curves of the cave.

"No." With that blinding light on his shoulder, Heath returned and crouched. His gray eyes bounced over her face. "You've got a sheen."

She didn't want him worrying about her. They had bigger obstacles to tackle. So, despite the pain and the fire dousing her courage, Darci managed a smile. "If that's your best pickup line, you've got a lot to learn."

"Ha. Ha." He swiveled and went to one knee and tugged off his gloves. Heath pressed the back of his icy hand to her cheek. "You're hot."

Another smirk.

"Don't," he warned.

Darci couldn't help but laugh at him stopping her comeback line. "What? It's okay for you to be direct and forthright, but not me? You shouldn't worry so much."

"Easier said than done." He smoothed out the thermal blanket. "Lie back down. You should rest. Who knows what's ahead. I'll pack ice around your fingertips. They're bleeding again."

"I can do that."

"Don't get all modest on me after making every comment into an innuendo." Heath's smile trickled through his words as he bent over her. "How're your ribs?"

"Some guy just dove into them."

"What a jerk."

"Yeah." Darci turned her face toward the wall, not out of modesty, but so he wouldn't see her face tighten at the pain. She could still breathe, so he hadn't done further damage, but holy cow, it hurt.

Cool air swept up her shirt as he lifted the blanket and took her hand. He hissed.

"That pretty?"

"As beautiful as you are, there's no way something like this can be described as pretty."

Darci's pulse ricocheted off his words and thumped against her chest. Had he really just said she was beautiful? Was he being sarcastic? Only one way to gauge that — the eyes. She glanced back. Thick browridge — a sign of intelligence — hung over eyes laden with concern.

No sarcasm. Did he mean that?

Why was she wishing so hard that he had?

He angled around, then pushed on to his haunches, reaching for something. He turned back and his gaze collided with hers. Softness filled his features. Handsome, rugged, yet . . . soft.

"You just have to complicate things."

White-hot fire shot through her. Then icy cold. She would swear she heard sizzling and realized he was packing snow and ice around her fingers to stop the bleeding. The pain blazed up her digits, through her wrist, and into her arms.

Darci squeezed her eyes and groaned.

A pause was followed by another application.

"Infection's trying to flare up," he said as he pressed a hand to her cheek. Awareness flared through her, but the pain and the severity of the situation doused that tremor of longing.

"I always wonder what my mom's last days were like."

Heath stilled, his somber gaze coming to hers.

She knew what he was thinking — that she shouldn't be talking about last days. But . . . this is how she dealt with things, talking or thinking about her mom. "She was martyred." Why did she want him to know everything about her all of a sudden? "Taken in the middle of the day while my father was out of the country. We never saw her again."

Heath eased down and drew up a leg to his chest. "In China?"

With a nod, she gave away a key piece of information. Weird. Darci didn't mind. She trusted him with this. Besides, if they died . . . "She was a Christian. And my father was very influential and powerful, and of course that couldn't be tolerated. They'd tried to convince him to do away with her, but he loved her too much. He'd been trying to make arrangements to move her back to the States, but . . ."

"Jia —"

"Darci." Oh no. Had she just done that? Okay, well . . . it was okay. "I want you to know my real name."

Something slid through his expression. "Darci. I like it." Though small, his smile was thousand-watt power. "Thank you."

She smiled. *Oh good grief. Can we say "schoolgirl"? Stick with facts. Those I can handle.* "I was born Jia, but when my father and I fled China after they murdered my mom, I took her name for safety's sake."

He nodded.

"Anyway . . . sorry . . . don't know why I'm rambling." Heat again soaked her cheeks.

"I like it."

She rolled her eyes. "Don't get all romantic on me, cowboy."

"How'd you know?"

"What?"

"That I'm a cowboy — well, not really, but I grew up in Texas." He shrugged and looked so adorable and boyish, she couldn't help the smile. "Doesn't that make me an honorary cowboy?"

"Do you mean ornery cowboy?" The laugh made her stiffen, then she relaxed out of the fiery breath. "I'd love to see you in a cowboy hat."

"Nothing doing." He looked sheepish and ran a hand along the nape of his neck. "My head's too big."

Darci threw her head back and laughed. It made her insides hurt, but it also made her insides giddy. Curling an arm around her waist, she pulled herself up.

"Whoa." Heath's smile vanished as he reached for her. "Where are you going?"

"Nowhere. I'm sick of lying down."

"Lying down gets you better."

She cocked her head at him. "It gets me dead."

His lips flattened. "Not on my watch."

A strange twisting and warming melted through her frozen exterior. Was he feeling what she felt when they were together? Did it matter? Burnett would go ballistic if he knew she hadn't severed their connection. She'd lose her job.

"Why do you do it?" he asked as she propped herself against the wall.

"Do what?" Wow, sitting up hurt like crazy. On second thought . . . She slumped a little, alleviating the pressure on her ribs.

"Be a spy."

Darci frowned at him. "Why are you a soldier?"

"I felt called."

"Felt?"

"Exactly." He nodded. "Your story first."

She smiled again. It felt so good. When had she smiled so much? A real smile, not one to get what she needed? "My mom."

Heath watched her, his amazing gray eyes penetrating her barriers. And strangest of strange things — she let him. "Justice. You wanted justice for her."

"Yeah."

"Have you gotten it?"

She let out a soft snort. "Several times."

Arm dangling over his leg, he didn't let up. "And has it worked? Has it given you what you were looking for?"

How had he seen straight to the dark chamber where she kept that secret buried? She hadn't thought it possible anyone would understand that mission after mission left her only with more emptiness. Not a sense of justice. Doing this — spying, intelligence work — had driven her to fill the hole. To somehow give to others what nobody had given her mother — a chance, a way out. She didn't blame her father . . . much. He'd been out of country when the police snatched her off the street.

Heath gave a breathless laugh. "I see . . ."

Why did she feel like clawing that smile off his face? "Shouldn't you be looking for a way out?"

With a stiff shake of his head, he pushed onto his haunches. "Point taken." He angled toward the back, darkness drenching her vision and mood.

Panic swooped in on her. He was gone. Gone! "Heath?"

"Don't worry." Boots scritched over hard earth. "I'm not going far."

Darci laughed at his joke — there wasn't *anywhere* to go. Had he said that because he knew it'd scared her? As stillness and quiet vied for her sanity — pulling at her common sense that there was nothing to be afraid of, that Heath wasn't going to vanish and leave her alone . . .

"Hey."

She sucked in a quick breath at his voice.

"Might'a found something."

"What?" A way out? Would it be that easy, that quick?

"A whole."

"A whole what?"

"No — *hole*. At the very back. Missed it when I looked before. It's not much bigger than me. And . . ."

"And what?"

"It goes straight down."

Heath stretched his arm into the space and wagged his arm. Nothing but icy air, but . . . was that a breeze? Or was that just him stirring up the air? He aimed his SureFire down, hoping to see how far it was.

His stomach flipped when the darkness ate up the light. No bottom? There had to be. Nothing was infinite. Except God.

Lying on his side, he scanned the area around himself for a rock. He dragged a golf-ball-size one within reach and flopped back onto his belly. SureFire aimed over the chasm, he dropped the rock. It whipped out of sight. The darkness ate it, too. Finally, a plunk — distant and almost inaudible.

C'mon. Don't do this to me. They needed to get out of here.

Heath eased away from the chasm, mind chugging. Trapped in here, did they have much of a choice? He roughed a hand over his chin and cringed at the stubble.

"Down how far?"

In a squat, he eased himself out from the compressed space and strode back to Ji— Darci. "It seems bottomless. As far as I can tell, there's nothing but emptiness down there."

"That's not possible."

"I know." He lowered himself to her side, noting she was once again upright. "I told you, you should be lying down."

"Yeah," she said, wrinkling her nose at him. "I never have done too well under orders."

"They weren't orders." Man, she got under his skin fast and deep. "Just strong suggestions."

She grinned, and Heath looked away before his mind could wander. *Could* wander? It already had. What was he . . . ? Oh yeah. The hole. Chasm. No way out. Heath ran a hand along his neck and scratched it. They were out of options, but if the gentle stirring of air *was* a breeze, at least they wouldn't run out of air.

Ice could be melted for water.

Three days. They'd be okay for three days.

Food . . . that was another thing. What was in his pack? Heath turned, and the light cut through the darkness to where his pack . . . *had* been. Now lost to the avalanche. Maybe it wasn't buried too deep and he could reach it. On his knees he moved to the barricade of snow, ice, and rocks. Crap. He couldn't even dig — his shovel was in his pack.

Tension wrapped a vise around him. Heath balled up his fists. Couldn't a guy just get a break? He punched the ground. Everything for survival was in that pack. His shovel, his ammo, MREs . . . His fist impacted dirt. Pain spiked through his elbow and shoulder. Jammed into his neck.

"What now?"

"Nothing." He wouldn't fail her. As he bent forward, it felt like his entire brain dumped into his forehead. Heath swung out a hand to steady himself. Pounding returned with a voracious roar.

Hands cradling his head, he clenched his eyes shut. *Father in heaven . . . please.*

Heath . . . Heath . . .

Was that God calling?

Rolling out of the pain, he wriggled his shoulders and neck as his eyes opened — he jerked. Darci knelt in front of him. Her face wrought.

"Heath . . . you there?" She tucked her chin and peered up into his eyes.

Did she have any idea how beautiful she was? How her concern for him felt like a warm salve over his wounded heart and mind?

But it was embarrassing. Humiliating. He edged away. "Yeah. Just . . . a little pain."

"I think you need to go back to kindergarten and learn what *little* means."

"Funny."

"It's killing you, isn't it?"

Cowed beneath the intense pressure, he slumped against the wall.

"Let me try something." She touched his shoulder again. "Okay?"

Heath waved a hand. "Sure." Whatever. It wouldn't work. He'd hoped the chiropractor would help. And it did. But obviously it was limited. Would he ever be pain-free again?

"This won't be fun," Darci said. "But you're a tough guy, so . . ."

Iciness draped his neck. Heath tensed and hissed against it. Waited for it to wear off. Instead, it grew stronger. Colder — was that

527

even possible? He ground his teeth and hissed.

"Grit through it," Darci said, her voice weak.

"You should be —"

"Quit being the boss."

Heath snorted — but quickly lost his humor as the frigid ball of ice bit into his muscles. He fisted a hand. Tight . . . tighter.

"Relax, Heath."

"Why don't you drive a stake through my skull?"

"Would it help?"

Freezer burn had nothing on this. Heath clamped his teeth again. Watched his knuckles whiten. The icy fire streaked through his shoulders.

"How's the head?"

The what? Heath let his shoulders slump . . . searched . . . "It's . . . gone."

"Wimp."

Arching his eyebrow, he faced her full-on. "You just turned my neck into a deep freeze."

"I thought you were a tough Green Beret."

"*Former* Green Beret." The truth hurt. A lot. Former in so many meanings of the word. Mentally, physically, emotionally. Jabbing his fingers through his hair, Heath sat back against the cave wall. But here, with

Darci, maybe he knew why he was here. Not just to let go of what he'd lost, but to cling to something he'd found — new faith and . . . Darci.

"Don't think about it too hard or long."

He flicked his gaze to Darci, who curled a protective arm around her side. She was right. Thinking got him stupid, depressed. "Ya know, I think God brought me out here just to show me how wrong I was."

"About what?"

"Everything." Heath breathed a laugh. "Life, myself, what I wanted —"

"What did you want?"

"Action. Adrenaline. The beret. The whole shebang."

"You don't want that now?"

Why did her voice hitch on that question? He rolled his head back and forth. "Not the way I thought I did. It cut me to get side-lined. Injured more than my thick skull — hit my pride."

"You still have a lot left over."

With a smile, Heath nodded. "Ouch."

"You ready?"

Heath frowned as he looked at her. "For what?"

"To go down that hole."

FORTY

"We are not going down that hole." Heath pried himself off the cave wall. "We don't even know where it leads — if it leads anywhere."

"So . . ." Darci motioned to their surroundings. "We just stay here? And die?" Her head cocked. "I know you're a *former* Green Beret, but even I thought you had more fight in you than that."

"What I have is some common sense." He poked a finger at her. "You're injured — you can barely sit up — and you expect to rappel down a chasm? Our rope won't even reach the bottom."

"It doesn't have to."

He knew where this was going. "You don't know how far it is from the end of the rope to the bottom. You could break your legs — and that's the bright side."

"You're all sunshine and roses, aren't you?"

"Darci." Heath pushed up onto his knees. "Please, I've made a dent using my fingers, but let's give them time."

"What if they don't make it, Heath? What if they were buried?"

"I can't accept that." He swallowed that bitter pill. "Please — let's just wait."

"Only if you beg."

Heath glared at her. "Not funny."

"Why can't you accept that? It's completely within the realm of possibilities."

"Because if they didn't make it, then that means the men are dead. And so is my girl. I'm not going there. Not again." He remembered those men, their funerals he'd missed, the fading in and out, the PT learning to walk, and the scars from Trinity's bite. "I can't lose a team again." This time it was his heart thundering, not his head. All the same in the grand scheme of things though.

Fierceness rosied her cheeks. "That bomb wasn't your fault. You couldn't have known."

Heath stilled. "I should've been more alert."

"It was an ambush. You have to move on and stop letting it color your past."

Heath angled his head, gaze locked on her. "How . . . how do you know about that?"

For a fraction of a second, Darci's eyes widened, then slid shut. And to Heath, it felt like the light in his life blinked out. She hung her head.

He inched closer. "How do you know about that ambush? I never told you. It was above top secret. No reason for you to know."

"*. . . uplifted by His grace, and feel yourself enfolded in the peace of His embrace.*"

The fragments came together in that moment as if the bomb that had exploded into shards two years ago flew back together. They were in the mountains. Just like right now. Then the angel who stood over him —

"You . . . it was you at Landstuhl, wasn't it?" They'd told him he was crazy. Whacked on painkillers as he came out of surgery. They vowed over and over that nobody had been with him in the days afterward before he regained consciousness.

"I felt responsible." Darci's words were small as she stared down at her hands. "I didn't know what to do, but I couldn't just walk away. So I stayed there until they convinced me you were going to live."

"You prayed over me." Awe speared him.

"I found it in my mom's Bible — a little gift card with a prayer stamped on it." With a sad smile, she shrugged. "It was all I had to offer, to undo the pain I caused."

Heath tilted his head, confused. "*You*

caused?"

Again, her eyes widened. She looked away. Then down.

Realization dawned on him. His gut twisted, and his mind warred with the gravity of what she had just revealed. "You provided the bad intel."

"*Not*" — she jerked her gaze to him, her eyes watering — "on purpose. It was blowback."

Blowback. His ragged pulse lumbered to a slower pace. "Unintentional consequence of spying operations . . ."

"Not just unintended but designed so that when the retaliation comes — the ambush — the public doesn't understand why it happened, can't connect X to Y."

"Amazing." He'd lost his career due to bad intel, provided by her, but then God brought it full circle. Brought them together. Ya know, for the first time, Heath didn't mind the scars so much, if that's what placed Darci in his life. In fact, he'd take a few more for her.

She swallowed. "I am so sorry. Please. You have every right . . . but please . . . don't . . ."

The brokenness in her voice tugged at his heartstrings. "Don't what?"

Big, brown watery eyes. "Don't hate me."

Aw man. She was as bad as Trinity when

she tucked her tail and head, then sidled up to him with that pathetic whimper. At least it had the same effect on his heart.

Emotion. Too much emotion.

"Hate you?" Needed some testosterone injection here. "I'm about to go down a rabbit hole for you."

Shhhink. Grind. Whoosh. Thud.
Shhhink. Grind. Whoosh. Thud.

Peter Toque shoveled hard, determined to do his very best to find the girl who'd spearheaded efforts to take down one of the most powerful men in China. And that had drawn the sleeping dragon from his den.

No way was Jia Li going down now. Not this way.

He rammed the shovel into the snow again. Again. Again — *thud!*

Peter cursed.

Another dead end, solid rock.

Shouts from the right drew his attention as he repositioned in a new spot. This was where the opening had been. Would they ever break the two out of the cave?

Watters, Candyman, and the one they called Rocket huddled up, talking. Something was going on. He wasn't sure what, but Peter trained his ears and eyes that way as he started digging again.

"What's going on?"

Peter eyed his handler, Bright. "Not sure." He dug. Thrust, toss. Thrust, dig, toss. "Maybe they got coms back up."

"That'd be nice." Bright grunted. "Our ride should be here soon."

"I'm not leaving till they have her back."

Bright stilled. "This isn't the time to get romantic."

"You're right. And I'm not." Peter rammed the shovel into the hard-packed snow. "It's about respect. About protecting one of my own."

"She's American."

"She's an *operative*. She covered my back before. I'm covering hers."

"We don't have time for this."

"Then leave." Peter glared. "I know where you live."

Bright shook his head with a laugh and rejoined the effort. "D'you see it?"

Peter tossed another load over his shoulder, sweat sliding down his temple. "What?"

"I'm not sure." Bright's ruddy face twisted beneath the labor. "I thought I saw one of the Asians throw something seconds before the avalanche."

"A grenade." Which is why he wasn't letting the men out of his sight.

"Which one?"

"Don't worry about it."

"What are you going to do?"

Peter smirked.

Bright shook his head and held up a hand. "You're right. I don't want to know." He shoved his hands into the snow, no doubt to alleviate the burn from the blisters. Peter had them, too. But what's a bit of blood and blisters when racing to save a life?

Shhhink. Grind. Whoosh. Thud.

"This is senseless, you know." Bright wiped the sweat from his brow. "It's been too long."

"Unless the cave has an air source."

Bright sighed.

Shhhink. Grind. Whoosh. Thud.

"But if it doesn't . . ."

"If you want to stop digging, then stop. Otherwise shut up and let me work."

With another grunt, Bright drove the shovel into the snow. "I'm going to see what they found."

"Please." Peter tossed rocks and snow. "Go."

Foul became his mood. The thought of not getting to her in time. She was a good operative. A kind woman. She didn't deserve this. Nobody did. And he had that mantra, the "do unto others as you would have them do unto you" that he tried to live up to.

Of course, while on a mission, all bets were off. But as a regular citizen, he practically wore a halo.

Another thrust. With it . . . a strange noise.

Peter looked to the side, listening. Nothing. He lifted the shovel.

There — again. Behind him. He twisted his upper body and looked back. Who would be over there? It was nowhere near —

A bark sailed over the still air.

The war dog!

Peter threw down the shovel. "Where's the dog?"

Heads popped up as the others turned their attention to the barking.

Peter jogged around the incline. Oddity of oddities — this stretch was pristine and white, undisturbed, save a trail that snaked down . . . down . . .

A black-and-amber form. "There!"

"It's Trinity. She's found them," Watterboy shouted.

"Not possible," Peter called as he pointed back up over the ridge. "They were up there. In the cave. We didn't make it down this far."

Watterboy hesitated, his gaze bouncing around the area.

"He's right," Scrip said. "It doesn't make sense."

Watterboy raised gloved hands. "That dog is trained to protect her handler at all costs." He looked back down the mountain to the plain where she dug with fervor.

"She's got a hit!" Candyman threw himself down, half sliding, half jogging.

Watters went with him, and so did the Asians. Peter rushed after them, hoping against vain hope that they weren't making a big mistake.

Bright joined him. "This is asinine."

"Did you guys come up this way?"

"Hanged if I know." Bright sighed. "It was dark half the time and the pass so narrow . . . but no, this doesn't . . ." He looked around. "The snowfall changed the face of it. I wouldn't know if I'd lived here."

Toque's face hardened. "Well, let's check it out."

"I have got to be out of my mind." Heath swiped a slick palm down his pants as he adjusted the rope around his hips and waist.

"Maybe for once you're in your right mind." Darci sat at the edge of the hole with him, her voice confident and calm.

"Are you always this annoying under pressure?"

Her smile amplified the beam of his lamp. Then fell as if she'd jumped off a ledge.

What replaced it yanked so hard on his heart, he jerked. "Hey." He frowned as he took in her overwrought expression. "What just happened?"

"I . . ." She cringed and held her side. "I just . . ."

"Darci." Heath shifted on the ledge to face her better.

"Do you like me?"

Feeling like a Ping-Pong ball caught between her thoughts, Heath blinked. "Huh?"

"Because if you like me, I can die happy."

Whoa no. No talk of death. "Darci."

"No, seriously. I know it sounds crazy —"

"Yeah, it does."

"I've faced death before —"

"Darci." Heath hooked a hand around the back of her neck. "Stop." He tightened his hold. "Stop talking about death. We're not going to die. You're not going to die and —"

"Will you kiss me?"

Heath blinked. "*What?*"

"You wanted to kiss me at Bagram, but I pushed you away. So kiss me before you go down there."

What ledge had she just jumped off of? His pulse chugged through his veins. God forgive him, but his gaze bounced to her lips. His yearnings betrayed him, but he finally pushed out a response. "No."

"Why?"

"Because . . ." Heat clawed his face. Two years ago, he wouldn't have hesitated. He liked her. She liked him. But it felt like something bigger, greater was happening here. "Because you're thinking I'm going to die, so you want no regrets." He shook his head, his chest feeling like a mortar range. "And because a kiss would mean something to me."

"It would mean something to me, too. That's why I asked." She shoved the black hair away from her face. "I don't need romance, Heath."

"Maybe." He couldn't believe she was dead serious. "But it's kind of nice. Know what I'm saying?" Taking things slow. Not rushing.

"I just need to know if you're feeling the same thing I am."

Now his brain felt like it was attached to the bungee cord on the ledge she'd just jumped from. His head hurt — and it wasn't the TBI. "How did we just go from death to talk of romance?"

"If I'm going to die —"

"Stop!" He cupped the back of her neck with both hands. "Darci. Slow down." He tugged her in closer, determined she believe him. "Nobody's going to die. I'm going down this hole — doing it for you, remember?"

"You're right." Shoulders sagging, Darci shrunk back. "I don't know what I'm thinking. I'm just . . . tired." She lowered her head. "Sorry. I . . ." Her gaze darted over his face, mouth open about to say something, then she pulled herself inward, crashing down as she pressed her lips into a thin line. "Never mind."

"Hey," he whispered, still holding her neck. "What's going on inside that pretty head?"

Looking up, out from under her eyebrows, she considered him.

"What's wrong?"

"I've never been this scared." A weak smile quivered on her lips as she worried the cuff of her jacket. "Not like this."

Heath nudged her up so he could look into her brown eyes. "Maybe it's because this time you have something to risk."

"Yeah?" Her voice went crazy-soft. "What?"

"Staying alive to make good on that request for a kiss." Heath angled around, bracing himself on the edge before she could see how much that line just embarrassed him. Why did she have to go and get all mushy on him as he was lowering himself into oblivion? It was good incentive, true, but it also made jelly of his iron stomach that someone like her was scared.

Shoulder light fracturing the black void, Heath eased himself down, toes braced against the wall in front. With one hand threading the line, he glanced down. Nothing but pitch black.

Why had he watched all those horror movies? Too many images flashed into his mind, holding him in a vise grip of hypervigilance.

"See anything?"

Her voice already sounded miles away. Heath glanced up at the top. How had he descended that far? "How much line do I have left?"

"Plenty."

Right. Heath considered the depth below . . . waaaay below. He plucked the Sure-Fire from his shoulder and aimed it down. The light danced along a slick wall where snow melted and trickled down.

His beam reflected off something.

Heath angled it again, this time over his shoulder as he strained to see what was down. Unable to see anything, he adjusted his balance so he could turn.

"Why aren't you moving?"

"Thought I saw something."

"No sightseeing."

Heath smirked as he lifted his arm and pointed the beam straight down.

His toe slid free.

His body swung to the right.

He slammed into the wall, his head thudding hard. He flung out a hand to stop the move — in that instant he realized his mistake. "No!"

The *clank-clanky-clatter* of his SureFire tumbling to the bottom — if there was one — reverberated through his mind.

Heath pounded an arm against the wall.

"What's wrong?"

He watched the beam twirling, tumbling —

Splat!

Darkness gulped the beam in a wolfish devour.

"You gotta be kidding me." Heath wanted to punch something. Kick the wall. But he had to keep it together. *Stay upright, calm . . . for Darci.* For her to get frantic, want to cut to the chase when she was all avoidance and distance at the base — panic had its talons dug deep into her courage. And too much distance already separated them.

"Heath." Her voice strained. "What's wrong?"

"Nothing. Everything." He cursed himself for being so careless. He was so far out of his element, off his game. When Darci was depending on him.

And I'm dangling in a shaft with no light.

His studies for chaplaincy rained down verses, one after another, about Jesus being the Light of the World. A staunch reminder that Heath wasn't a shining example of trusting God.

He peered up, no longer able to see Darci's hope and expectation gouged into her face. No longer able to see where he'd come from. And below . . . unable to see where he was going.

Just like my life.

He knew God had a twisted sense of humor, and though he didn't find it funny, the poignancy struck center mass. Hand fisted on the cord below, Heath glanced up and down again. Should he keep going? Or return? The slight tremor in his arms warned him of his weakness.

In more ways than one.

He knew, in his own strength, he could go back up. Get to the top. Be with Darci. But that would get them nowhere. But going down, exploring the unknown . . . hadn't he done the same thing with his life? Familiar with combat and military life, he'd pushed and pushed till he got what he wanted.

And how's that working for you?

Okay, God, enough with the stark parallels. Despite his playful thought, he was wide open to whatever God was doing here. He could sense the life-altering shift. He just wasn't sure how it was connected to this shaft.

Going down was a matter of faith. Exploring the unknown, being vulnerable, was putting action behind his faith. *Faith without works is dead* . . .

Okay. That was beyond stark.

Heath released the belay and lowered himself more.

"Heath?"

Was this stupid? Going farther down, risking getting stuck or never reaching bottom? He continued down.

"Heath?"

Water gurgled below, drawing his gaze downward. A strange glow swirled . . .

The SureFire!

On the surface. About ten feet below.

Heath let out the tension and glided down . . . down . . . to the end of the rope.

Still hadn't hit bottom.

"Heath!"

Her frantic call jerked him out of his focus. "Sorry." If he let go and dropped, he could go straight into the freezing water. With the rabid temperatures, he'd have fifteen minutes — max — before his body temperatures dropped to critical.

So did he feel the way out was there, with the icy water and certainty of death?

"Hang on." His voice bounced off the walls and thudded against his mind.

He stared down at the beam. He couldn't be more than six or seven feet from the bottom. He'd jumped from greater heights in training. The fear that had him clinging to the rope was the question of the water. It'd swallowed the flashlight. Then spit it back up. Deep enough to go down, but not enough for it to vanish.

Noise filtered through his senses. Heath looked left. What was that? To the right? Crazy. There wasn't anything here to make noise.

Again, he felt his toe slipping against the wall and reached out.

Hollow and distant the noise actually sounded closer.

How was that possible?

Thwat. The soft sound registered like a sonic boom. He jerked up, barely able to see the multistrand rope fraying. A strand snapped free.

Playtime over. He had to get down. Now.

Heath quickly lowered himself. The cord snapped taut. *Ploink!* Another snapped.

Do or die, he had to take this literal leap of faith. Heath released himself from the harness. Dropped. Straight down.

FORTY-ONE

"Heeeeaathh!"

Gravity yanked hard.

Straight down. Though it happened in seconds, the fall felt like an eternity.

Icy water clapped its painful talons on his ankles. Calves. Knees. Thighs. Waist. *God, help me!*

He hit bottom of the well. Jarring pain darted up his legs as he impacted. Threw him backward. His head banged against the cave wall. "Augh!" He jerked forward and steadied himself, frigid water cocooning his body.

Seconds. He had just a few minutes to get out of this water before hypothermia set in. But how did you get out of a well that's little more than shoulder-wide with no way out?

The hollow noise he'd heard earlier reverberated again through the water. *Trinity?* No. Now he was imagining things. He shook his head and looked up to where he knew Darci sat. "I'm at the bottom. Chest high in water."

"That's . . ." her voice faded. Quiet. Still. "Not good."

"Ya think?" Heath plucked his SureFire from the water and scanned the walls. The beam stroked the climbing rope . . . too far up to reach.

"What're you going to do?"

Again, the hollow sound — so much like a bark. He had to be going crazy. Hypothermic symptoms included unclear thinking. But he hadn't been submerged long enough for that . . . right?

"Uh . . ."

Water stirred to his right. What on earth would be swimming in ice-cold water?

"What's wrong?"

"I think . . ." He kept his legs and upper body as still as he could, swiveling a bit to look around him.

Darkness rippled through the water.

"Something's in the wa—"

A dark shape stirred a heavy wake.

Augh!

Heath plunged his hand into the water, aiming for his holstered weapon.

Erupting water splashed his face.

He flinched away, but in the seconds where his heart rate hit catastrophic, his mind latched on to the attacker. Who wasn't an attacker. "Trinity!"

Her bark roared through the shaft.

Heath pulled her into his arms. She lathered him with drool, icy water, and elation. His heart chugged as he laughed and hugged her tight. Laughed again. "How did you find me, girl?"

She barked.

"Your dog? How did your dog get in there?" Darci asked, her questions filled with a nervous laugh.

"There must be a hole or something." Heath beamed the light, his body trembling from the cold. "Hang on." Man, to find out where she'd come from, he'd have to submerge — all the way! *Better to lose a few digits than a whole life, I guess.*

He stuffed the SureFire back in place and lowered himself below the surface, ignoring the stinging water. He angled in the direction Trinity had come and sure enough — a hole!

He burst back up. "There's a passage. Let me check it out."

Quiet amplified the cold.

". . . okay."

"Don't worry. I'm not leaving you." Heath willed her to trust him. "R–remember — you owe me a k–kiss."

550

"Very funny, Daniels."

Her voice sounded lonely but hopeful. He could live with that. For now. He smoothed a hand over Trinity's head. "Ok–k–kay, g–g–girl. Sh–sh–sh–show m–m–me."

Heath again submerged. Swam for the hole. Hauled himself through the opening. A steep rise made it hard to wiggle up. Panic clenched him in the narrow space. This was their only way out. A blast of cold air stung his face. He slumped to his knees, still partially submerged.

"Hooah!" The shout pervaded the tunnel.

It took a few seconds for Heath to see in the semidarkness. Backlit by pure, beautiful daylight, two silhouetted forms hunkered close by. Watterboy and Candyman.

Hands hauled him up the slope and onto the passage floor.

"We thought we'd lost you."

Teeth chattering, Heath chuckled. "If I d–d–d–don't" — the clatter of teeth on teeth hurt — "g–get warm quick, you w–w–w–will." He hated the way his lip wobbled.

"Where's the girl?"

Heath bobbed his head back. "The t–t–tunnel" — he bit down to stymie the shivering — "leads to a well . . . w–w–water." Violently, he shook. "Twenty- or thirty-foot shaft in the cave we were in. Sh–sh–she's at the t–t–t–top."

Someone cursed. "How are we supposed to get her out?"

"F–fast," Heath said, teeth banging. He bit his tongue and tensed. His arms felt heavy, stiff. Legs, too.

A dark shadow sucked out the light. "Chopper!"

Heath smiled. "This just . . . gets better." Why wasn't he shivering? He slumped against the wall. Felt like an MRAP sat on his chest.

"Hey, get out there." Watterboy shoved Heath's shoulder.

"Get off, man," Heath growled.

Watterboy stilled. "Scrip — get him out of here. He's hypothermic. Do we have extra clothes?"

"Negative." Scrip bent closer.

Heath swatted him off. "Not leaving till . . ." Till what? Where'd that thought go? What was he saying? "Darci." Why couldn't he breathe?

"Scrip, get a litter." Watters angled himself closer to the water, nudging Heath away from the mouth of the shaft, from Darci. "Candyman!" Watters pointed to Heath. "Now!"

He dragged himself past Heath, keying his mic. "Command, this is Candyman. Need warming blankets and prep the medical bay for hypothermia."

"Heath?" Her voice bounced back, empty of promise and void of response. This must be what it was like for the first man on the moon — to look out across the pitch black and know he was utterly alone, save the few on the ship. Heath was . . . somewhere. Down the shaft. He'd said he wasn't leaving.

Then he did.

Water had stirred, then nothing.

Darci lay back and drew her legs from the ledge. Hand over her forehead and another resting lightly over her side injury, she closed her eyes. A moot point since the pitch black closed in around her, bringing with its totality and desperate isolation suffocating panic.

She swallowed. *Relax. Don't think about it.*

As she had during interrogations, she looked for something recent and pleasant.

Heath and Trinity filled her mind.

Okay, maybe that wasn't the best place to put her thoughts. She had no idea what had happened to him down there. What if he didn't find an out? What if — water . . . he'd mentioned water. In this winter storm? It'd be freezing. What if . . . what if he froze to death first?

The thought punched through her tough exterior, fisted its thorny tendrils around her heart, and squeezed. Hard.

Her eyes burned.

She gritted her teeth. She'd never been a baby. Never been a *cry*baby. She had to get it together, keep it together, until . . .

Until what? If Heath was dead, she had no way out. Already she felt the sharp teeth of frostbite gnawing at the top of her nose, her ears, her fingers, and her toes.

I'm alone. Completely alone. Wounded. Freezing. Dying . . .

Darci felt the odd warmth of her tears against her chapped cheeks. She closed her eyes. *God, I gave my life to You . . . extended my faith . . . my faith, not Mom's. I believe You can get me out of here, but even if You don't . . .*

Just like Shadrach, Meshach, and Abednego.

She recalled her earlier thoughts about the three, but now the story felt personal. They were thrown into the fire. She was thrown into the earth's freezer.

Whatever Your will . . . I want it.

But if she survived this, then . . . where would things go with Heath? Could they work something out, so . . . ?

So, what?

Was she seriously thinking of making a life with him?

A giggle leapt from her chest. *Yeah, I am.*

Idiotic. They didn't even know each other. Although, at the same time, she knew a lot about him, knew the mettle in him, knew the goodness that made him a man of character, knew the tender and funny side . . .

Jianyu had never been funny. She hadn't seen his demons until it was too late. Jianyu's patience had hidden his poison. DIA wanted more information, so she had to buy time by selling her soul. She'd sacrificed everything trying to distract him. Thanks to a CIA operative, she escaped — barely. And spent the next six months in counseling and begging God to forgive her.

And trying to forgive herself.

Splash!

Darci stilled, stifling the tears, ears trained on the shaft below. Heath . . . he'd gone . . . told her he wanted her to live, to make good on that request for a kiss.

Did she really ask him for one? The cold must be getting to her brain. She'd never done something like that. And after they got back, after she recovered, Heath would be on to his next speaking gig with Trinity.

And Burnett . . . sent her . . . away . . . to focus.

Her hands hurt. Her legs. The cold dug into her shoulders, down her spine.

I am focused. For the first . . . home, want . . . home. I want to see my father. I want . . . a life.

Where was her thirst for vengeance? The determination to see justice done?

It's quenched.

Sleep . . . cold . . . it hurt . . . alone . . . so dark . . .

Swooshing dragged her out of the sluggish thoughts.

"Heath?" she barely breathed his name.

No, she was alone. With God. She closed her eyes.

Darci Kintz.

Yeah. Me. Tired . . . pain . . . cold.

"Darci Kintz!"

She opened her eyes. Darkness. Cold. But . . . *my name . . .*

"U.S. Special Forces. Are you alive?"

Yes.

"Can you hear me?"

She realized she didn't put voice behind her answer. "Yes." It came out a mere breath. She coughed — pain! Her ribs. Curled onto her side, she shifted around, dragged herself to the edge of the shaft.

Peered down.

Bright light vanquished the darkness.

She grunted and withdrew. "Here." That was louder. But not enough. She pushed herself to shout. "I'm here!"

"Hooah!" Came his response. "Ma'am. Move away from the ledge."

Darci wiggled back, unable to push back.

A strange thwipping sailed through the air . . . louder . . . closer.

Thunk! Clank!

Pebbles rained down, and a snake coiled down from the ceiling. Darci shrunk away — at least, she thought she did. But she squinted. Not a snake. A rope dangling from a grappling hook.

"Thank God," she whispered, her thoughts clinging to her Maker.

In minutes, light and the powerful form of the special-ops soldier loomed over her. Darci relaxed, knowing she was going to make it.

"We're going to get you out of here. Just relax." He shrugged out of a pack and dropped it beside her. He lifted her arm, a small pinch . . .

"Hea . . ."

He said nothing as he wrapped another thermal blanket around her, and then slid her into some type of cocoon. Another soldier appeared beside him. Together they assembled a litter, then lifted her into it.

"We're going to strap you onto me. We'll go down, then into the water, and into the tunnel," the first man said as he drew her toward him. The other secured harnesses around them.

Darci grimaced against the pain roaring through her side. But she'd endure it. To get out of here. To get home.

But the first shift over the ledge jarred. Hard.

Darci tensed and held her breath. Each length he dropped felt as if someone rammed a hammer into her back and side. She dropped her head against his shoulder, unable to withstand the fire eating her up from the inside out.

"Easy," he muttered.

Water trickled and gurgled. Darci felt it encircle the insulated cocoon they'd placed her in. Then her knees. Her waist.

She endured the suffocating feeling as the oxygen mask tightened.

"Hold on and hold your breath."

She nodded.

They went under, her back arching. She reminded herself to breathe, not to scream against the knife being driven through her spine. Within seconds, thrashing water and hands pawed at her. Drawn up out of the water, she heard Trinity's bark . . . somewhere.

"Let's move," Watterboy shouted.

They carried her out of the lower cave, and Darci strained to see into the brilliance of the day. Black and dirty against the pristine white, the UH-60 Black Hawk thrummed with life. Rotors whipped the powder-fine dusting of snow. The rescue team huddled around the helo. Two men in flight suits stood at the foot of a gurney, easing into the chopper.

Heath . . .

"Make a hole," Candyman called as they hurried toward the bird.

They slipped her through the opening the team made — and her gaze struck Heath. He gave his "Ghost" moniker new meaning with his deathly pale skin and lips. The medics worked to wrangle his hands. He was punching. Thrashing — but in a slow-motion way. Like he was drunk. He almost flopped off the litter.

Darci's heart backed into her throat. Such a strong man. Seeing him combative, confused, clumsy . . .

Others crowded into the chopper around her just seconds before it dipped, then rose into the pale blue sky. She grabbed Watterboy's sleeve. "How long to the base?"

His gaze hit Heath for a fraction of a second, then her. "Twenty."

Twenty *minutes?* Heath didn't have twenty. If he was combative, he'd already entered the severe stage. But at least he was fighting. And not in a coma.

Heath's arm slid down. His other swung wildly, then flopped.

His eyes rolled back into his head.

FORTY-TWO

Aboard Helo, En Route to Bagram

Intubated, Heath lay on the precipice of death.

Darci lured a whimpering Trinity into her lap and wrapped her arms around the seventy-pound ball of fur, whose only attention lay on her handler. Her partner. Though Darci couldn't hear it for the wind and rotor noise, she felt a whimper rumble through Trinity.

Pale. Heath was so pale. Darci covered her mouth. It pained her to see that thing sticking out of his mouth. The medics hovering, working. Death had never felt so close and violent.

How long had Heath been drenched and icy cold? He'd gone down that shaft for her, to save her. Was it going to cost him his life?

"Pupils dilated," a medic shouted.

"Unconscious."

Wary, Darci shivered uncontrollably,

watching Heath slip from this world. *You can't. Please . . . don't leave me when I just met you. Heath . . .*

"Drink." A sergeant stuffed a thermos straw toward her.

She shook her head. "No . . ." Couldn't drink with Heath fighting for his life.

"Drink," he shouted over the roar of the wind and rotors, his expression cross.

She sipped, surprised as sickly sweet warmth slid across her tongue and down her throat. Painful yet . . . better. She took another draught.

"Two minutes," came a shout from the cockpit.

"He doesn't have two minutes!" the medic shouted back.

Warmth tumbled into Darci's stomach, and she wasn't sure it was the drink. Was he breathing? *Heath! Don't do this to me. Not when I found someone worth knowing. Please . . .*

"He's going V-fib!"

Heath looked dead. His chest wasn't moving — or was it?

The next two minutes felt like an eternity. Darci looked away, terrified Heath wouldn't make it. *You owe me a kiss.* Warmth slid down her cheek as she felt the descent of the chopper. She glanced out the door, where three men sat in the opening. Buildings dotted the terrain a few miles out.

Even as they lowered to the ground, Darci saw the medical teams waiting. And a lot of soldiers.

Before the skids touched down, the three men launched out of the way. Settled on the ground, the chopper wound down as the medics hopped out, unlatching Heath's litter.

Behind him rushed a team of six. They transferred Heath to a gurney.

A doc stood on the side of the gurney as the others shoved it away. They shocked Heath. Once. Twice. Three times. CPR. They were doing CPR.

That meant Heath wasn't breathing.

He was dying.

FORTY-THREE

A window peeked out into the night. Snow, falling thick and angry again, drenched the compound. Little movement and even less traffic stirred throughout the American base. Walls creaked and groaned beneath the strong wind, pounding the building with its mighty fists. The last attack of the storm would slow Jianyu's Yanjingshe fighters.

Hands behind his back, Haur stared into the dark night at the mercy of the blizzard. With the fighters delayed, he had more work to do. The bars and lock on the cell, the cuffs on his hands — they were impediments he must figure out how to overcome.

"It sounds bad."

Haur kept his face impassive at the sound of Bai's comment about the weather. On the surface it sounded benign, but when mentioned in light of recent events, he knew they referred to the situation.

"Did you hear, they got the girl out?" Bai's bunk groaned as he shifted onto his side.

Haur said nothing.

"You are planning something," Bai whispered as his dark shape drew closer to the bars on the right that separated them. "Why did you not go into the compound to capture Jianyu?"

Beyond their holding cell, voices rose and fell. The sound of someone approaching pushed him away from Bai. Away from the window. But further into the arms of the storm.

"It is time."

Inside, Darci tried to locate where they'd taken Heath. She heard a flurry of voices and could see shadows and personnel hustling at the far end of the hall, but her team wheeled her into a bay. They laid warming blankets across her chest. Sitting upright a bit, she was ordered to consume more of the all-too-sweet and warm liquid.

"Heath."

"Your core temperature," a doctor attached a probe to her temple, "is just around ninety-three degrees."

"Ninety-four," a nurse announced.

"Good, but we need that higher." He nodded to the thermos in Darci's hand. "Keep drinking."

"I want to see Heath. Where is he? Is he okay?"

"Don't worry about him. If your temperature drops, you'll run some very serious risks. That's what you need to focus on right now."

An orderly rushed in with a machine, which he set up beside her. A steady whirring filled the room, along with warm, moist air.

They were working and moving so fast that Darci took a moment to savor the fact that she didn't have to move at all or jar her ribs. But her mind and heart were with Heath . . . wherever he was. Had she really gone mental on him, asking for a kiss? He'd taken it in stride. During her moment of panic, he helped her haul in the tattered edges of her courage.

The warmth burned a bit, but Darci knew it was just the bitter bite of the frigid temperature wearing off. She closed her eyes and focused on Heath. On seeing him again. Getting warm fast so she could scurry down the hall to where he was warming up, too.

"That's it," the nurse said. "You rest. I'll be right back."

Darci let the quiet descend . . . only, it wasn't quiet. A bevy of noises a few bays down captured her attention. The *tsing* of a curtain jerked her gaze to the side. A nurse rushed down the hall and around a corner. When he did, the curtain slung aside. Just enough . . .

Heath!

Even from here she could see how white he was. Her stomach churned.

Drawn to him, she eased off the gurney but held the blue warm water blanket around her shoulders and trudged closer.

The doctors looked frantic. Nurses, too.

IV bags hung over him. Several tubes snaked into his arms and abdomen. What . . . ?

"Get that heart-lung bypass ready."

Hand to her throat, Darci stilled. Bypass? What did that mean?

"Up to eighty-four-point-two."

Degrees?

"That's progress."

"The only progress we've had."

"His heart rate is dropping."

"Losing him!"

Darci dropped back against the wall, hand over her mouth. Tears streaming.

A nurse started out of the bay and stopped. "Oh."

Blinking the tears away, Darci shook her head. Her knees wobbled.

"Help!" The nurse rushed her.

Arms caught Darci as she slid backward. Lifted her — pain stabbed her side — and hurried her back to her bay.

But nothing — *nothing!* — would gouge from her mind the image of Heath dying.

Back on the gurney, the man who'd carried her stood over her.

She looked up into green eyes. The dog handler owner who'd brought Heath over. In his gaze she saw her own pain reflected. Something pinched her arm.

Her vision swooned.

FORTY-FOUR

A blurry white image loomed over her.

Darci jerked.

"Ah, you're awake."

She straightened, her head feeling like a thousand pounds. "I didn't know I fell asleep."

"Yeah, sorry about that. We had to put you under for your own sake."

Though she should feel ashamed for taking matters into her own hands, Darci didn't. Heath was dying — or dead. "Heath. How is he?"

"I'll let the general know you're back with us."

"Wait."

The nurse left, and in her place came the doctor.

Glowering, he moved to her charts. "You were very foolish to get out of that warming bed."

Darci took the beating. "How is he?"

"Haven't you heard of doctor-patient confidentiality?"

"Can I see him?"

"Not till you're stable and your temperature's much higher." He yanked the curtain around her bed, and outside he ordered the hall cleared, stating it was for medical personnel only.

The nurse returned with a steaming mug and some warm food. "Keep drinking and eating. Get your insides warmed up so you'll stop shivering."

Shivering? Darci glanced at her hand, surprised to see tremors.

"You're doing good. Once you're warmer, we'll take a walk. Exercise is good to get the body heated up."

"A walk?" Darci's yearning to see Heath latched on to those words.

The nurse arched an eyebrow. "Well, not to see anyone. Just to walk around."

Surely she could find a way to convince the nurse. Then a thought struck her — hard. What if Heath hadn't made it? What if he'd died after she fell unconscious?

"Heath — is he alive?"

"Just relax. I can't give out information on other patients. Now, drink."

"Wait." Darci took an obedient sip, more thoughts assailing her exhausted mind.

"Have there been attacks?"

The nurse laughed. "You're in Afghanistan."

"No." Darci swallowed. "I mean, bombs — here. On the bases."

Confusion rippled through the older woman's face. "No, not here. Things have been pretty quiet." She tapped Darci's arm. "Ninety-four degrees. Keep that coming up and you'll be out of here in no time."

The nurse disappeared, leaving Darci alone with the chill that seemed to have clung to her bones and the mental fog that made it hard to think straight. No attacks, so . . . Heath had kept his word. He'd told them. But . . . how had they stopped the attacks so fast? Had the rescue team notified Command, and they in turn found the bombs? It seemed too fast.

"Well, 'bout time you came back. Don't you think you've had enough playtime?" General Burnett's voice boomed before he entered the sick bay. His stern features, his gruff voice, felt like the warming jacket she still sported. Then it faded as a smile seeped into his rough exterior. "You should take better care of yourself, or your dad will wring my neck."

Darci couldn't help the smile. "Yes, sir."

He bent over the bed and peered down

into her eyes, no personal space between them. "How you doing, kiddo?"

He'd been general first, friend second. But it was a really nice arrangement that provided Darci a base from which to operate in more ways than one. She recognized the concern in his eyes even amid the gruff voice and exterior. "Been better."

"I could've told you that." He straightened and folded his arms across his chest. "That's what you get, trying to take down the entire Chinese army by yourself."

"So, you stopped them — got him?"

Burnett smiled, eyes crinkling. "Thanks mostly to you."

Darci let out a long breath. Exhaustion plucked at every sinew. "Good."

"Get some rest."

"Wait. Heath."

Something indiscriminate flashed through his face. "Don't worry about him. You need to get rested and better."

"I'm fine."

He scowled at her.

"Okay, a little pain — they broke my ribs, but I'm fine otherwise."

"You're an ice cube."

"Water freezes at thirty-two degrees." She pointed to a small box readout. "I'm at ninety-four, so technically . . ." She swung her legs over the side of the bed.

"Whoa." Burnett's large hands steadied her. "Where are you going?"

"I already told you, I want to see him." Even as she moved, the cold temperature made her ankles throb. "Besides, the nurse told me exercise would warm my body."

Burnett squatted in front of her bed, peering up into her eyes. "Darci. Please. Your body isn't ready for you to do this."

"My body isn't, or you aren't?"

"Kiddo, I don't think *you* are ready for this."

Alarm spiked. "What do you mean?"

"It doesn't matter. You can't go in there anyway. Even I couldn't get in there." General Burnett sighed. "Just . . . rest. Okay, Darci? You've been to hell and back. We thought we'd lost you —"

"You did. To the Chinese who captured me."

"Which is why I talked with your dad. He's worried, wants you to go home for a while."

Avoidance. "I want to know how he is, General."

"Your father's —"

"You know who I mean." Though she fisted her hands, her stomach squirmed under his scrutiny. "Heath — how is he?

Why can't I see him?"

"Darci —"

Not the tone she wanted to hear. "No. Please don't —"

"Darci, he's not good."

Fire sped through her veins. "What do you mean?"

"He went into full cardiac. Twice."

Darci drew in a hard breath. "How . . . they got him . . . he left . . ." Those gray eyes . . . the strength . . . he'd saved her . . . gone down that shaft . . . *for me.* Tears stung her eyes. "What are you saying?"

"He's in a coma. They don't know why he hasn't woken up. They're arranging to take him to Landstuhl."

"But he'll make it." She looked to the nurse who came back in and stopped cold. "Right? He'll wake up, won't he?"

The nurse shot a glance at General Burnett, then hurried back out.

With her went Darci's frantic hope for Heath. "Why won't she answer me?" A tear broke free.

"With the TBI, they just aren't sure what to expect. It doesn't look good."

She threw off the blanket. "I want to see him."

"Darci —"

"Don't." She froze, her heart stamping

574

out his objection. "I know you don't want me involved with him, but . . ." She looked him straight in the eye. "It's too late. I'm invested."

Burnett hung his head as he pushed back to his feet.

"Take me to see him, General — Lance. As my godfather, as my favorite 'uncle.' "

He shook his head. "That's not fair."

"Please."

Escorted by the general, Darci slowly — very slowly — made her way down the hall, each step heavy and awkward. They trudged around a corner, and when they passed through a door, three people came to their feet from the chairs huddled by another door. Heath's dog-handling team.

Trinity. How was Trinity doing? Was she okay? A renewed ache wormed through her chest.

"General." Green eyes bounced to Darci as the team leader greeted her. "Ma'am."

"You're . . . you brought him over here?"

He extended a hand. "Jibril Khouri."

"Darci Kintz. Thank you."

Confusion rippled through his handsome face. He checked with the two women with him. "Thank you? For what?"

"For bringing him. He saved my life."

Sorrow crossed his brow, but he quickly

tried to conceal it. "He is a good man, a hero." Jibril put an arm around the blond, whose hair hung in short spirals around her face. "This is Aspen, and also Timbrel." The brunette with a long ponytail.

"How is Trinity?" Darci asked, hands shoved in the pockets of her jacket.

The brown-haired girl jutted her jaw. "Going nuts."

Sweet relief! Darci let out a labored breath. "But she's okay?"

They nodded. Kindness and gentility marked Jibril's face as he inclined his head. "As best as can be expected without Heath."

"Any news?" General Burnett cocked his head in the direction of the door.

"They are . . . tending him now," Jibril said.

It all sounded morbid — and hopeless. She couldn't take it anymore. *Wouldn't* believe that Heath was taking his final plunge. Not when she'd finally set her heart on him. Darci shifted and pushed through the door.

"Hey!"

The loud calls came from behind and in front.

"You can't be in here."

Darci lumbered toward the bed. Lights gaped at him as the doctors and nurses moved around the bed draped with several puffy warming blankets that looked like clear rafts. The same warm moisture that had coated her room filled this one. Heath, tubes running into his mouth and nose, looked peaceful.

Too peaceful.

The thought ricocheted from her chest to her stomach and back. She shuffled closer, surprised when they did not stop her.

"General . . ."

"Let her have a minute."

Relief warred with her panic.

Panic? At what? Heath . . . never opening those warm, caring eyes again.

At his bedside, she leaned against it, using it for support against the tidal pull of emotion. Darci smoothed a hand through his short, sandy blond hair. At least he had some color now. When she'd seen him before . . . death. Not even warmed over. Just icy, cruel death.

"Ghost . . ." she whispered as she drew herself up and sat on the edge of his bed, taking in his large frame beneath the humming warming blanket, which looked more like giant bubble-tube packing, and the warming fan. "You said you'd come back . . . for me." Stubble coated his angular jaw and chiseled features and tickled her fingers as she dragged her finger along it, avoiding the tubing. "Remember?"

Behind her, murmuring. But Darci felt all twisted up and turned inside out over what Heath had done to save her. Again, she touched his face, noting it still was cool. Even with the chill in her own hands, his skin felt icy.

"Remember," she breathed through a clutter of tears and angst, "I owe you something." The general would go through the roof if she mentioned it.

"Let's give her some time," the general's soft words filtered through her awareness.

Soon, the soft thump of the door came.

Darci released the hold she had on her emotions. "Heath," she said, her voice hoarse. "Please . . . come back. Let's figure things out, just like you said. Okay?" She pressed her lips to his temple. "I'll give you a real one if you'll just wake up." A tear slipped over her cheek and landed on his.

"*Thought so.*" She could just hear him saying it. Challenging her. And the weird thing was, he just seemed . . . lonely . . . without Trinity.

Darci looked over her shoulder, not surprised to find the dog team watching her through the window. Darci nodded the brunette in.

Timbrel eased into the room. "You need something?"

Waving her over, Darci eased onto her feet. "He looks lonely."

Brown eyes widened. "Don't expect me to help with that."

Smiling, Darci leaned closer to the mid-twenties girl. "Can you get Trinity?"

Timbrel's face brightened. "I like the way you think." She spun on her heels and jogged out of the room.

Alone again with the man who had infiltrated her heart, mind, and life, Darci slipped her hand under the warming blanket and coiled it around Heath's. "C'mon, Soldier. Snap out of it." She had no vehemence behind it, but everything in her ached for him to come to attention. "I won't let you die for me, Heath."

Minutes later, Timbrel hurried into the room, accompanied by the soft click of nails. "She went ape when she saw me."

Trinity wagged her tail as she scampered to Darci, then went up on her hind legs, sniffing the bed. Darci drew Heath's hand to the side.

Trinity whimpered, licking his hand as if it were a Nylabone. Digging her claws into the bed, she tried to haul herself up onto the mattress. Darci bent down and gave her a boost.

"Trinity, down," Timbrel said in a firm command that wasn't loud but authoritative, ordering the dog onto her belly.

The dog complied instantly, stretching out next to her handler. She swiped her tongue over his face, then rested her snout on his shoulder and let out a sigh.

Darci ran a hand over Trinity's fur. "Thank you, girl. For everything."

"Hey." Timbrel pointed to the other side of the bed. "There's room for one more."

One more dog? Darci frowned at the girl. Wha— ? "Oh, no. I couldn't."

"Oh, for Pete's sake. We're in a hospital. Nobody's going to get the wrong idea." She nudged Darci's shoulder with a fist bump. "Besides, everyone knows body-heat transfer is the best at rewarming others. And we all know you and Heath are into each other."

Heat flushed through her face.

"He needs a reason to come back." Timbrel's expression went soft. "Be that reason."

FORTY-FIVE

"I pray you'd be uplifted by His grace, and feel yourself enfolded in the peace of His embrace . . ." Angelic and soft, like a murmur against his soul, the voice drifted out.

Darci's ivory-pale face, almond-shaped eyes, and pink lips dusted his mind. Smiling, laughing . . . leaning forward for a kiss, then pulling away with another laugh.

Stop taunting me.

Then wake up, Ghost.

Wake up? Was he sleeping?

A bark jolted through his hearing. Wet and warm, a tongue slid along his cheek. Heath tried to touch the fur ball but couldn't move his arm. He dragged it out from under Trinity. He wrapped his arm around her as she greeted him with more kisses.

When he tried to lift his other arm, he realized it was pinned, too. But beneath what? Tugging his arm free, he angled to the side, aware of two things in that instant — tubes feeding him oxygen and snaking down his throat, and the blue halo of light against a crown of silky black hair.

Darci? Curled up next to him, in the bed?

No, that had to be a dream.

More like a fantasy!

He wanted to wrap an arm around her, make sure she didn't fall off the bed, but he was afraid to touch her. Afraid to burst this dream bubble. He liked it, a lot. Liked her next to him. Heath coiled an arm around her and closed his eyes. It was so right, so perfect.

"See you finally decided to join us." The voice, though gruff, was quiet.

Heath looked in its direction and grimaced.

Arms folded over his broad chest, General Burnett simmered. "I asked the doc not to remove that tube so you couldn't talk."

Darci still hadn't moved. What was she doing here?

"That woman next to you is very important to me."

"Sh—" *Curse this stupid tube!*

Burnett grinned. "I'll have your neck, back, legs, every piece of you if you hurt her."

Understood, Heath conveyed with a lone nod. In more ways than one. The general was accepting that things were happening between Heath and Darci. He wasn't giving permission, but he wasn't going to interfere either.

"She's been like that next to you for nearly twenty-four hours. The docs ain't happy, but I ordered them to let her and that stinking dog of yours be."

Heath let the glower seep into his eyes. *That "stinking dog" saved your asset!*

"All right, Doc." The general motioned to Heath.

A man moved in and reached toward him. He removed the breathing tube, turned off a machine, then returned. "This will make you gag."

Heath braced himself as the tube — and his lunch — retracted. He coughed. Gagged.

Darci stirred, but Heath firmed his hold on her. She straightened, then jerked upright. Her mouth formed a perfect O when she looked up at him, sleep prying at the edges of her eyes.

"Hey," he managed, and what an effort it took!

"You're awake." She laughed and came out of his hold, but he caught her hand. She stilled for a moment, then kissed the back of his hand.

"Cheater," Heath rasped. She was out of

her mind if she thought that kiss would settle her debt.

With a shy laugh, she held his hand next to her face. Tears glimmered in her eyes. His fingers itched to touch her cheek.

"Give me a minute to check his vitals, then I'll be out of your way." The doctor took Heath's pulse, checked his heart rate, listened to his chest, recorded the information in his chart . . . all while Heath watched Darci. She'd stayed with him? Why was he laid up in bed and she was up and moving around? Genuine concern carved a hard line in her face.

"Wha . . . happ'n?" Talking felt like passing razor blades over his windpipe instead of air.

"You went into cardiac arrest twice," the doctor said. "We've had a tough time getting you to stabilize, then a harder time getting you to come out of it."

"Thickheaded," Darci said, her light brown eyes glittering.

He grinned and felt punch drunk with the way she gazed down at him. Wow, he'd risk his life every day of the year if she was the prize.

"They were prepping you for Landstuhl."

That was the last place he wanted to end up again. "Good thing I woke up." *With you in my arms.* That was amazing. Incredible.

"This young lady and your dog have kept your body temperatures stable. You should be thankful." The doctor perched a straw between Heath's lips. "Sip."

Nasty-sweet and syrupy, the drink squirted down his throat. Though too sweet for him, Heath was glad for the way it soothed the dry, cracked plains of his throat and esophagus.

"Sip this and keep sipping. I'm leaving the saline solution till you down a meal."

Nurses descended on him and over the next fifteen minutes examined, tested, checked — all as Heath kept his fingers entwined with Darci's.

"This doesn't make sense," a nurse mumbled as she recorded information.

Darci looked at her. "What?"

"His electrolytes, blood gases . . . repeat EKG are all perfect." She shared a glance with the doctor. "Like the severe hypothermia never happened. I guess because you were in top shape before, save for the TBI."

Jabbing a finger over his shoulder, the doctor grinned. "That man in the hall has been praying since we brought him in. Maybe it's a miracle."

"Yeah." Heath glanced to the hall where

he spotted Jibril. "Definitely — a miracle. That's what it feels like." He downed more liquid. "Amazing. I'm tired but otherwise fine." Weird enough. He even pried himself off the bed. Okay, so his body was a bit sluggish, but they could work with that.

The doctor nodded to the general, then turned to leave. "He's all yours."

Trinity pushed up onto her haunches, panting down at him, those amber eyes sparkling. Heath dug his fingers into her fur and massaged the side of her face. "Thanks, girl."

She swiped another kiss.

Speaking of a kiss . . . Heath turned his attention to Darci, who suddenly seemed gun-shy and wanted to wrest her hand free. He frowned, but before he could say anything, she leaned down. Her lips aimed for his forehead, and his hopes crashed against her modesty.

"Still cheating."

She smiled. "I'll be right back."

"Where are you going?"

"To tell your team you're awake."

Heath couldn't help the smile. Already watching out for him. "You're the bomb —" Heath's eyes widened. "Did you tell him?"

Darci nodded. "Everything's taken care of."

Heath glanced at the general, who seemed peeved, probably over the PDA. "You got the bombs?" Wait. He hadn't had a chance to tell the doc. "How'd you find out about them? Was Haur connected?"

"What do you mean?" Darci asked. "Didn't you tell him?"

"Daniels was DOA. He couldn't tell me nothing." The general went all military on them. "What didn't he tell me?"

Darci hauled in an audible breath. "About the bombs!"

"*What* bombs?"

FORTY-SIX

Panic and fury erupted in his chest. Lance surged forward, aware of the bleeping that monitored Daniels's blood pressure and other vitals. Aware the increments were shortening. "What bombs, Darci?"

"Wu Jianyu," she breathed, confusion marring her young features. "When I was at the village, his captain said the bombs were ready and waiting for his activation codes." She blanched. "I thought you said you got him. I *asked* you!"

"You asked if I got *him*. And I did — Colonel Zheng is in custody."

"His son?" Her question shrieked as she stabbed her fingers through her black hair.

"Wait," Daniels asked. "That guy you sent with me on the mission?"

Lance nodded.

Darci's voice pitched. "Why is his son in custody?"

"General Zheng came here, told me Haur

had gone rogue."

"The minister of defense came here?" Darci's brow knotted. "And that didn't ring fishy to you?"

"Watch yourself, Lieutenant." Lance felt the steel grip of guilt. "Everything was fishy at that point. When a man like that comes into a hostile situation and claims one of his sons is rogue, I listen."

"Wait."

Darci spun toward Heath.

"I think I saw him — the general," Heath said, his voice weak. "At the village. When I was leaving with you, I saw Jianyu with an older man, talking."

"Zheng went back to China." Lance's blood chugged to an achingly slow pace, clogged around his brain, around the brutal information Daniels had just delivered. "He couldn't have been there."

Daniels's gaze lit with challenge. "You verified that?"

What was going on? Nothing made sense. Except that he needed to do as Daniels had suggested. Lance spun and jogged out of the room. Otte pulled to attention. "Get General Early. Call an AHOD of all officers in ten."

"Yes, sir."

"Put SOCOM on high alert. We have a

589

direct threat against military personnel in the region."

Bagram AFB, Afghanistan

"Go!" Heath said to Darci. "Stay with him. I'll get dressed and meet you there." He stumbled out into the hall with Trinity at his side.

Jibril came off the wall. "What — ?"

"Help me get to the bunk. I need to dress. Gotta help . . ."

They rushed to the building where his bunk offered him clean clothes, boots, and a jacket. He stuffed himself into the warm garments, savoring the delicious heat coiling around his body. Thank God he lived in Texas, because one thing he never wanted to be again was cold.

"You really gave us a bad scare, Ghost."

On the edge of his cot, Heath stuffed his foot in a boot and shot a grim expression to Aspen. "I'd love a reunion, but there's a very real, very tangible threat right now."

"I'm hearing rumors," Aspen said.

"No rumors." Heath shook his head. "It's real. Chinese have placed bombs on bases."

A voice careened through a loudspeaker, rousing everyone and warning them to grab their gear and get into formation.

Darci appeared with a vest, lead, and harness. "Here."

Man, just the sight of her . . . "Thanks." Heath threaded his arms through the vest — the thing felt like a hundred pounds with the exhaustion from two heart attacks and hypothermia — and secured it before he put on a heavy jacket.

On a knee, he rested his gloves there and donned the harness vest and lead on Trinity. "What're you hearing?"

"Burnett has put the word out." She looked good in clean clothes, even with the bruise and busted lip. She moved stiffly as she handed him an HK USP. "The other dogs are being pulled from their kennels. Ordnance is clearing buildings as we speak."

"EDD. Smart." Heath nodded.

Explosive Detection Dogs were the best at tracking down chemicals and powders. While Trinity could hunt down bad guys like nobody's business, she didn't have the intense training EDDs had. On a base three square miles in size, they had a lot of territory to cover. "This is crazy. No way we'll locate the bombs in time."

"Let's find Burnett." Darci started walking, her movements slow in the thick coat and with broken ribs.

"He's not going to tell us anything."

She eyed him. "I want to talk to Colonel

Zhen —"

Crack!

Heath stopped. "That was weapon's fire." He darted toward the building it'd come from. The same building where Zheng Haur was being held. Heath jerked open the door, and Trinity lunged in ahead of him. Weapon at the ready, he moved down the too-quiet halls.

"Don't like it," he whispered to Darci, who bounded and covered with him, her Glock held like a pro.

She shook her head. Sweat beaded on her forehead. The pain from her ribs must be excruciating, but he knew better than to suggest she rest. Or not engage in the hunt.

Bang!

The sound pounded Heath's breath into the back of his throat.

"Door," Heath said, as much to himself as to her. The squeaking and swishing of tactical pants warned them of the incoming flood of soldiers.

Sure enough. Around the corner, a sea of uniforms.

Muzzles swung toward them.

"Whoa!" Heath raised his hands. "Friendly."

The men banked left, so Heath and Darci went right. Down the hall. Clearing one room after another, his heart pumping harder and faster, sensing they were closing in on their quarry. The last room. Heath shoved a foot against the handle. It burst inward. As it flapped back, his heart thudded.

"Hands in the air," he shouted. "Hands in the air!"

Zheng Haur stood over the body of his captain, gun in hand. A guard lay to the side, unconscious . . . but coming to. And still armed.

"Haur, what happened?" Heath shouted, praying the others heard. "Who killed him? Where'd you get the gun?"

Absolute calm shrouded the man. "I want to speak with General Burnett."

"Fat chance." Heath eyed the weapon. "You just killed a man and took out another. Do you really think they'll call Burnett here?"

"Bring Burnett." Haur did not relinquish the gun.

"Not happening," Watterboy's firm voice cut into the room.

"If you want to live, if you want to stop the bombs, bring Burnett here." Way too calm. "I suggest you do it now. Time is short."

FORTY-SEVEN

"You are Meixiang?"

Daniels stepped in front of the woman, cutting off Haur's line of sight.

Haur gave a halfhearted smile. "I am no threat to you or to her."

Unfazed and undeterred, Daniels held his aim. "I'll be the judge of that."

But Meixiang edged back into view, living up to her reputation as the skilled, bold operative Jianyu had said she was. "I am Meixiang," she said in perfect Mandarin.

With a respectful nod, Haur smiled. "It is a pleasure to meet you at last." She was much paler than he'd expected for his brother's tastes, but her beauty could not be denied. "You created quite a stir in the Zheng dynasty."

Though she said nothing, Meixiang studied him. Intently. She flicked a finger to the body at his feet. "Why have you done this?"

Haur smiled again. "In time, Meixiang."

Shouts and thudding boots reverberated through the building. More military police poured into the room, weapons at the ready, in full tactical gear.

General Burnett stood there, shielded by two MPs. "What is this, Zheng?"

Haur raised both hands, the gun dangling from his thumb. "Thank you, General." Eyes on those before him, Haur dropped the magazine. Expelled the chambered round. Slid the barrel off. A few more quick flicks, and the weapon lay on the table. "There are times we implicitly trust those who work close with us. We come to believe so fully in their identities, we do not question them." He glanced at Meixiang. "Sometimes that is a mistake."

She eased to the side. Eyes locked with him, she retrieved the barrel from the floor.

"What's your point? Why is Bai dead?"

"Captain Bai is dead because I killed him." He straightened and held his head high. Not that he was proud of his actions, but there was no point in denying the obvious. "I discovered not too long ago that he was not my ally, but my enemy."

Burnett stepped past the guards. "Is that supposed to enlighten me?"

"I was sent to the mine to check on Jianyu. General Zheng ordered me into this country to find Jianyu and bring him home." He tilted his head. "But as the mission progressed, things became less certain." His gaze shifted to Heath. "At the village with your team, I saw something that told me I had been betrayed."

"What was that?"

"I saw my brother *and* General Zheng there. Together." The image burned into his memory. "They hugged. Father and son, happy. Not as the bitter rivals they had pretended to be."

General Burnett planted his hands on his belt. "Why would they do that?"

Haur snorted and shook his head. "I think you, of all people, know why, General."

The older man took another step into the room. "Zheng Xin came to me after you were knee-deep in this mission."

It should not have surprised Haur to hear this. The twists, the betrayals were enough to solidify his determination.

"He said you were the rogue son, Haur."

Words held the power of life and death. And in that moment, a piece of Haur died. The piece of flagging courage that had fallen into the trap of a man he thought he'd made proud. Yet the wound from those words cut deep.

"Now, why would he do something like that?"

"*It was time.*" Three beautiful words that would allow him to keep a promise. "When I was fifteen, my father left China. Defected — with your help, I believe, General Burnett."

The man yielded nothing.

"In the days before my father's escape, I learned of Xin's suspicion of his oldest friend, my father, so I chose to stay behind." Haur tried to steady his palpitating heart, noting the stunned expressions but also the unaffected ones. Meixiang was hardest to read and yet, somehow, he felt he had an ally in her. They'd both been burned by the Zhengs.

"I played the abandoned, grieving son, allowed Zheng to take me in and adopt me so his anger and attention would be deterred. I knew the man would find greater pleasure by drawing me into his camp than by killing me. Making me his son was an act designed with only one purpose — to destroy my father.

"I have endured more than twenty years under the mental and verbal abuse of General Zheng Xin." Haur let out a heavy breath, so relieved to unload that knowledge. "When I realized Bai was not my captain, not my friend, but an asset of General Zheng himself, I knew I had been betrayed."

"How'd you know it was him?" Daniels asked.

"Little things along the way, but the two most revealing — when he threw the grenade that set off the avalanche. He was trying to bury you all alive."

"And the other thing?"

"He had too much information to be a man *under* my authority."

"What does Zheng gain by betraying you to us?" Daniels asked.

"Irony." The word hurt. Stung. "He believed you would kill me . . ." Haur let his gaze linger on the weapons still aimed at him. "My father defected to America, and there would be no greater satisfaction for Zheng than if the Americans killed me —"

"We'd be killing the son of one of the greatest Chinese assets we've ever had."

Peace swarmed Haur as he reveled in the words of the general. "Thank you." He confirmed his secret thoughts, that Burnett was the one who'd helped his father. And the words encouraged him to hope that his father was still alive. "The bombs — I believe it is close to lunch, is it not?"

Burnett hesitated. "I'm warning you, Haur. If those bombs aren't found, I'll feed you to Zheng myself!"

Anticipation hung rancid and thick as they waited with Haur, while the teams searched for the explosives. But something just felt . . . off. Heath glanced at Trinity, but she had curled into a ball in the corner, uninterested. Poor girl had been through enough to sleep for a week. And if she was zoning now, then there was no threat.

Then what was eating at Heath's internal radar? He glanced to the side —

Darci.

Hand to her stomach, she eased to the back of the room.

What was that about?

Burnett advanced. "You expect us to believe you spent twenty years under that man and never tried to escape?"

"There was no need to escape." Haur shifted, as if the words made him uncomfortable. "My father — my *real* father — was safe. Do not mistake my outstanding service record for loyalty to evil men. I did what could be done to keep them from hunting down my father." Serious and tense, Haur held his ground. "I have no regrets."

"Ya know," Heath offered, "I wondered why you never referred to General Zheng as 'father.' " He inched closer, determined to ferret out what was needling him. "You were vague in the mountains when I asked you about your relationship."

Haur nodded as soldiers removed Bai's body and aided the wounded guard to sick bay. "It takes more than a name to make a father. Zheng is a cruel man, who bred a cruel son."

"But you called Jianyu 'brother.' How is that?"

"We grew up together. After my father left and I went to live at the general's home, Jianyu and I were inseparable. I looked up to him — he was fierce, a fighter. Respected. Admired." The man's gaze slid to someone in the back. "He was a ladies' man, which is why I was especially intrigued with Meixiang, the legendary woman who took my brother down."

"Jianyu's weakness took him down," Darci said.

"It is evident, is it not, that while Jianyu and the general accepted me in name, they never accepted me in heart." Haur's smile was genuine. "As I never accepted them. Not fully."

Darci came forward. "Why? Why did you

not accept them? You had that beautiful home, wealth, fame . . ."

Haur glanced down. "Those are poor replacements for family."

"We found them!" Candyman's voice boomed through the room. Burnett glared. "Just like you said."

Heath glanced at the general, who seemed peeved. "Then what's wrong?"

"It's too easy." Burnett pressed his knuckles to the table and leaned toward the thirtysomething colonel. "What's your game, Haur?"

50 Yards outside Bagram AFB
"Go ahead."

"It's done," the voice said. "Ordnance found and disabled the bombs — and Burnett doesn't know, but locals have reported the bodies of the Russians. It's about to blow wide open."

"As expected."

"There's been a small complication though."

Jianyu ground his teeth, feeling the jaw muscle pop. "What?"

"Haur and Bai were arrested upon returning to the compound. Haur killed Bai."

"Understood. Well done."

"I do my job well and count on people

like you to make sure I'm never found."

"It will be so." Jianyu ended the call, rubbing his thumb along the spine of the phone as he stared out over the dark night. The final betrayal had come.

"What news?"

Jianyu lifted his gaze from the darkened interior to the wash of moonlight reflected over the blanketed road. "It is done."

"All of it?"

"Bombs have been found, disabled." Still, it unsettled him that Haur had taken extreme measures. "Bai is dead."

A belly-jouncing chuckle filled the interior of the camouflaged vehicle. "Just as we planned." His father pushed open the door. "They're distracted. Let's move."

FORTY-EIGHT

Camp Loren, CJSOTF-A, Sub-Base
Bagram AFB, Afghanistan

"You're my brother."

His expression — eyebrows tense, lips firm, a slight dimple in the chin — was so like her father's that Darci couldn't pry herself away if she tried.

The boulder of truth hit him. "Meixiang —" Haur's eyes widened. "Oh — how did I not see it? All those days in the mountain . . . even your name . . ."

He pulled her into a hug. It felt right. It felt wrong. She didn't know what to think or do. She'd last seen him as a teenager. But he knew she was alive. Knew their father was alive. And he didn't search for them? She stood stiff in his arms, not sure what to feel.

Growling pervaded the room. Several loud barks.

"Release her," Heath said in a firm voice.

Mind whirling, Darci eased back and looked at Trinity, who was primed on Haur, hackles raised. "It's . . . okay."

Heath eyed her, then Haur. "Trinity, out."

The dog turned a circle, then sidled up next to Heath, panting as she watched Darci.

With a nervous laugh, Haur shook his head. "You were five the last time I saw you."

"And you, so big . . ." Tears stung though she fought them. "I . . . was so mad at Ba for leaving you. I couldn't understand why he'd leave you. He wouldn't talk of you or Mom. But you — why didn't you find us?"

"Didn't he tell you?"

She frowned. "Tell me? What?"

"He told no one," Burnett said. "He never betrayed you, which makes me wonder why you betrayed General Zheng. What's the game?"

"No game."

Darci swung around on the general. "You *knew*? You knew that my brother stayed of his own free will, and you never told me?"

He shrugged those broad shoulders. "You never asked. Look, there's a lot to sort out, but not right now. Later." Burnett focused on Haur. "What's going on, Haur? It was too easy to find the bombs — Ordnance isn't even sure they were viable."

Haur frowned. "I do not understand."

"That makes two of us." Burnett growled. "It's like they knew this would happen."

"But . . . that's impossible."

"Unless they were counting on you to finally switch sides," Heath said, his hands tucked under his armpits, probably stealing warmth. "But to what end?"

Haur looked to Darci. "Would he do all this for you?"

She laughed. "Never."

A thoughtful knot formed at the center of his brow as he nodded. "You're right. The general would want to inflict a big wound —"

"Merciful God!" Burnett banged a fist on the table. "He couldn't have known."

"What?" Darci asked, breathless at the fury on the face of the most stoic man she knew.

He looked at Haur. "They were coming after that greatest Chinese asset."

Haur's eyes widened. "He's *here*?"

A curse sailed through the air as Burnett barreled out of the room, MPs and ODA452 on his heels.

It took two seconds for Darci's mind to catch up with the fact that Haur sprinted after the general. They were going to save someone. The greatest Chinese asset.

"Ba!"

FORTY-NINE

With Trinity bounding ahead, just feet from Burnett and Haur, Heath ran after them. His heart spiraled into his throat. The infamous Li Yung-fa was here? On this base? Why on earth had Burnett brought the man here?

Beside him, Darci struggled — the ribs, no doubt — but she ran heedless of the pain that had to be punching the breath from her with each step.

As they bolted into the command bunker, Heath slowed at the ominous silence that hung in the building.

"What's wrong?" Darci spun to him.

"It's too quiet."

Burnett hesitated. "He's right."

Candyman and Watterboy were right with them. "Everything okay, General?"

"Lock it down," Burnett shouted as he rounded a corner. "Nobody gets out!"

Heath threw himself after the general as a

grinding siren punctured the air. Emergency lights swirled.

Around another bend, Heath barreled over a body. He skidded and glanced back — just in time to see Watterboy and Candyman jogging toward them, armed and serious.

"Got him." Candyman dropped to a knee beside Otte, who groaned.

"Got another one here," Rocket called from the far left. "It's General Early — unconscious." He planted a hand over a wound and dug in his pocket.

At the sound of pounding boots, Heath spun. Darci vanished to the left. "Darci!" He propelled himself after her, praying harder than he'd ever prayed. His body wasn't moving as fast as he'd like, but after being technically dead twice today . . .

Shouts and thuds reverberated through the hall.

Heath pushed himself. Trinity lunged ahead. A corridor stretched before him. Four doors, two on each side. All closed. No Darci. No voices.

"Trinity," Heath said, looking over his right arm at her. "Seek!"

She zigzagged from side to side, checking doors. At door three, she sat and looked at him. A pat on his shoulder alerted him to the stacked team of ODA452. Heath nodded. He slid up to the jamb and took point.

Watterboy kicked the door in.

Heath stepped in. His split-second recon dumped ice through his veins. And that made him mad. He vowed to never be cold again. To the right, an older man he hadn't seen before sat with a gun to his temple, compliments of the older man he'd seen at the village earlier: Zheng Xin. In that whipped-cream chaos of a moment, Heath couldn't shake the haunting peace that filled the first man's face. Was that Darci's father, Li Yung-fa? Greatest Chinese asset?

A yelp hauled his attention and weapon to the left. Wu Jianyu held Darci in a stranglehold. Eyes ablaze and locked on Heath, he flared his nostrils. By the reddening of Darci's face, Jianyu was squeezing with his arm muscles. Strangling her.

"Let her go." Man, that sounded like a bad line from a B movie. Heath lined up the sights with Jianyu's beady eyes. "*Don't* move."

Trinity's snarling and snapping fueled Heath's anger. Amazing how she'd taken to Darci, ready to defend her.

The hushed rustle of ODA452s swift filing into the room gave Heath little reassurance, especially with Jianyu strangling

Darci and his father about to put lead into her father's head.

"Get the dog to stand down," Jianyu said, shielding himself behind Darci.

Coward.

"Nothing doing," Heath said. Crazy. Confusing. So much happening. Burnett and Haur faced off with Zheng, who held Yung-fa captive. Heath kept his focus on Darci.

"Unlock the door," Zheng commanded.

"Not happening," Burnett said with a growl.

"I will end this happy reunion if you do not."

"It's already over, Zheng." Burnett held fast. "No matter what happens, you're not walking out of here alive."

Heath knew ODA452 had lines of sight on the tangos . . . or at least they would if he wasn't blocking Jianyu from them. He eased to the side, keeping his weapon on him, determined to place a bullet in the guy if he escalated.

Only as Heath weighed options did he notice Burnett's hand. Signals. He was giving the SOCOM team signals. "You know this isn't going to end the way you want it to, Zheng."

"It will. Twenty years! I have waited

twenty years."

"You should have let it go nineteen years ago," the man in the chair said, his voice strong, sure.

"Shut up, Yung-fa! This is my victory. You will not steal it from me." The man's face reddened. "Are you ready to die?"

The question drew Heath's attention.

Jianyu looked around Darci to his father.

Her gaze locked with Heath's. Meaning spiraled through those beautiful eyes. She blinked. Once. Twice. Three times.

"Trinity, go!"

Darci bent forward, hard and fast, driving her elbow into Jianyu's gut.

Trinity lunged, between Burnett and Haur, straight at Jianyu. Grabbed the man's arm and yanked hard. As soon as Darci was out of the way, Heath fired. Winged Jianyu. He was not going to let this guy take anything else from Darci, especially not her life.

Another shot rang out.

Darci dropped, pulse rapid-firing.

ACUs filled her vision. Swarming. Shouting. Taking over.

She had one goal — Ba. She shifted. Backed up. Where was he? Why couldn't she see him?

"Darci!" Heath plowed through the scene and slid to his knees. "Are you okay?"

"My father!" She scrabbled around the others toward her father. A tangle of bodies made it impossible to figure out what was happening. Shouts. Thuds of fists against bone. One colossal whoosh of action. Then quiet fell over the room.

Boots stepped aside.

Her father looked straight at her and smiled.

"Ba, what are you doing here?" As she scrambled to him, she saw the dark stain on his chest. "No!" She pressed her hand against his wound. "You're shot!"

He held her hand, his goatee trembling. He reached past her. Darci glanced to where he reached and stilled. Haur squatted behind her. She looked back to her father, years falling off his face. "My children," he said with watery eyes and a weary voice. "Together. At last."

"Ba." Haur knelt and bent down, embracing his father. "It has been too long." Tears streamed down his face. "I kept my promise, Ba. I found a way home."

Hand clapped around Haur's neck, their father managed a smile. "Thank you." He sobbed. "Thank you, my son."

Choked at the scene, at the memory of

their last time together, Darci let the tears slip free. Her father pulled Haur's forehead to his, murmuring "my son, my son" over and over. Her heart melted at all the horrible things she'd believed of her father, when in fact, she hadn't understood a single thing. His sacrifice — for her. For them. So huge.

A father's love is great.

In that moment, Darci felt an eternal love sprout in her heart. She realized what her mother believed held such depth, such beauty, such truth. Faith. Darci had believed to get out of the tunnel, to see her father once again . . .

And God made it happen.

Medics nudged into the room, taking over. Darci relinquished her first aid to the medics who pressed gauze to her father's shoulder, then lifted him onto a stretcher. "We'll be waiting for you, Ba."

But something warm and sinister swept across her mind. How had Zheng and Jianyu gotten onto the base? Who helped them? A subtle move on the other side of her father's stretcher ensnared her mind. The next few seconds ground to a slow but painfully fast pace. Someone held a gun along his leg. Her gaze traveled up his ACUs to his face — Otte!

He lifted the weapon toward her father.

Darci dropped to a knee and swung her other leg under the stretcher, catching the legs of the man on the other side.

Thud!

Shouts collided with her movement as she whirled around and dropped her elbow hard on the man's face. A resounding crack shattered the noise.

Soldiers dove on top of them.

Flattened on top of Otte and under the special-ops soldiers, she saw the medics scurry her father to safety. Hands pawed at her, drawing her out of the fray and up onto her feet. Swung her around into the arms of Heath Daniels. She clung to him, trembling. "He was going to kill him."

"I know."

"He had a gun."

"Shh."

"But he was General Burnett's personal aide!" She knew him. Trusted him. Talked to him. How . . . ?

"You sorry piece of —" Burnett slammed his fist into Otte's nose.

The man crumpled beneath the punch.

"Get him out of my sight," General Burnett shouted, drawing Darci around. She looked over her shoulder as MPs cuffed and dragged Otte out of the room.

"Mei Mei."

Tears blurred her vision at the "little sister" nickname. She tilted her head and looked at her brother. "I have not heard that name in a very long time." She went into his arms.

Haur held her tight.

"I have missed you." Clinging to him, to the piece of family she'd been without, she regained what she lost with her mother's death.

He kissed the top of her head. "You look so much like our mother. How could I not know?"

"And you look like him." She laughed. "You even sound like —"

Crack!

The sound of the shot swung Darci around.

Eyes wide, face taut, Heath stared down the barrel of his gun — aimed in their direction. Slowly, he lowered it, his chest heaving.

"He overpowered me," someone behind her said.

Darci turned around. Propped against a wall, lay Jianyu. Dead.

Shaken, she looked back at Heath. She hauled in a breath that was undeterred when he gave her a halfhearted smile.

Heath winked. "I promised myself he wouldn't take anything from you again."

He saved her. Again. She eased away from her brother — *my brother!* — and went to Heath. "I owe you my life."

A lopsided grin tugged at his face as he stared down at her. Warmth swirled through her belly at the way he looked at her, with those beautiful gray eyes, that crooked smile.

Cupping her face, he stroked her jaw. "You owe me a kiss."

Darci stretched up on her toes, ignoring the fingers of pain scratching at her ribs. They were outmatched by the nervous jellies as Heath's arm encircled her in a firm but gentle hold. She stiffened for a second, darted a look into those steely eyes, then pressed her lips to his.

His kiss was light . . . tender, searching . . . firmer.

Darci melted into his arms as he deepened the kiss.

Applause erupted, along with shouts.

Trinity barked.

"Jealous," Heath murmured against her lips to his partner, then leaned in again.

EPILOGUE

A Breed Apart Ranch,
Texas Hill Country

It'd been four long, excruciating months. No calls. No letters. No texts. No nothing.

Heath sat on the edge of the cliff overlooking A Breed Apart. He had a lot to be thankful for, the most important one that he could put genuine belief behind those talks he'd give at the bases. And there were more than a dozen gigs lined up since returning from Afghanistan, but he'd asked Jibril to give him a few months off.

He had hoped to spend that time with a certain woman.

But she hadn't reconnected since they'd had to go their separate ways — her, home to D.C. with her recuperating father and her newfound brother. Him, to Texas to reinvent himself, accept God's path, no matter the journey.

No matter the journey.

"Beautiful," came the gruff voice from behind.

Heath nodded, his gaze caressing the cloud-streaked sky. "Better than the view from your room at the Soldier's Home, don't you think?"

"That place was depressing!"

Heath climbed to his feet and moved to his uncle's all-terrain wheelchair. Heath had bought the contraption when he returned to an uncle who'd found his second wind. Crouching beside the old general, Heath sighed.

God had his back. No doubt. That he got some more years with his uncle . . . "Sure am glad you're better so we could share this."

Emotion rippled through Uncle Bob's face followed by a trembling lip, then a jutting jaw. "Bed was uncomfortable."

"Hardened veteran like you? They should've given you a cot."

A smile danced along the weathered lips.

"I'd better get you back down before Claire has my hide."

"I'm fine. She's not my CO."

"No, she's your wife now."

"Same difference."

Heath chuckled, thinking through the whole wife thing. By the time he'd returned, his uncle was up and barking. Claire ordered him to the altar within a month. His uncle complained loud and hard all the way to the chapel, but Heath had never seen the light in the man's face so bright. Claire was good for General Robert Daniels.

Would Darci have been good for Heath? Did it matter? Four months and no sign of the woman. What if Darci didn't want to be part of his life? What if she decided their time together had been too fraught with action and drama? Too risky to risk love?

Because that's where he was. He loved that woman. No question about it.

Trinity trotted to his side, a branch in her mouth.

"Goof," he muttered, tugging it free. "I've got your ball right —"

Trinity went rigid. Radar-ears swiveling as she struck a "seek" pose, aimed in the direction of the house. Heath followed her lead. Sunlight glinted against a white luxury SUV as it wound toward the ranch.

Heath couldn't help the hiccup in his chest. He wanted it to be her. *Please be Darci* . . . But he'd done that for three months with no luck.

The car turned into the drive.

Heath pushed to his feet, watching. "It

could be anyone. Another speaking gig request."

"And you called me the fool?"

"Not to your face."

His uncle chuckled.

Trinity wagged her tail.

"Guess we should check it out."

Trinity sprinted down the path.

"Cheater!" Heath released the brake and aimed his uncle back to the jogging path, trailing after Trinity. Ironic how a little hypothermia had somehow corrected — no, that wasn't the right word — warded off? No, not quite right even still — well, whatever. The TBI hadn't manifested since his return, no matter how rigorous his workouts. His physical therapist suggested the good freezing through he'd gotten might have alleviated the nerve pressure that made his brain fry.

Whatever happened, Heath was glad. The symptoms could return, but he was done wrestling God. Clearly, the Lord had a plan for his life. And he would spend the rest of his days figuring it out, one day at a time.

"Slow down before you kill me!"

Heath complied as he broke through the clearing. Two women stood at the foot of the home, talking.

"See?" Pride shone in his uncle's voice as

Claire waved and started toward them. "Commanding officer."

"Well, someone has to keep you in line."

His uncle smiled and pointed a shaky finger toward the other woman. "Yeah? Well, she's got your chain."

Heath's blood chugged at the words as he relinquished control of his uncle's wheelchair to Claire, who smiled but said nothing. She didn't have to. Women had *that* look that seemed to say they know everything. Heath slowed at the vision before him. Man, she did crazy things to his pulse.

In a pair of jeans and a white sweater, Darci smiled at him, accepting Trinity's kisses. "I think she remembers me."

"You're hard to forget."

Darci's smile grew. She straightened and strode toward him, her gaze traipsing over the valley. "So, this is the ranch."

After killing the man who'd devastated her, he'd thought of nothing but that kiss at Bagram. And now, he couldn't think of anything else again. "Figured that out all by yourself?"

Quiet wrapped around them as they strolled across the property, driving him crazy, but the comfort of her presence kept his anxiety at bay. She'd come. That meant something. And he hoped it meant something *big*. Heath kept pace, enjoying the simple fact that she was here. With him. No matter how long she stayed.

"I'm sorry it took me so long."

Heath snapped off a branch from a leafless tree. "Did you have doubts?"

"No, I had family." Darci sighed. "I resigned my commission with DIA."

"What . . . why? I thought you liked it. You were good as all get-out."

A pained expression stole over her beautiful face. "It took too much of me already." She surveyed the surroundings, then slowly brought her gaze back to him. "I think I'm ready for a slower pace."

Rapid-fire had nothing on his heartbeat.

Darci turned. "Haur is taking over my commission. He hasn't accepted it officially, but . . ." She scrunched her shoulders. "He's staying with my dad in D.C."

What a heady statement. "And you aren't?"

The prettiest color seeped into her cheeks.

He couldn't breathe. *Please, let this mean what I think it means.* "Does that mean you're here to stay?"

"Well." Darci turned and looked back at the house, still blushing. "Jibril offered me a job as assistant manager." Squinting to avoid the sun behind him as she peeked up at him, she shrugged. "His sister invited me to stay with her until . . ."

Heath grinned. "I like where this is going."

"Where, exactly, is this going? I mean, we don't really even know each other. We spent two weeks together, on and off, in the mountains."

Chuckling, Heath stared down at her, dead certain he wanted to spend the rest of his life with her. "That two weeks took about two years off my life. I died for you, remember?"

Playfully, she punched his gut.

Hooking a hand around the back of her neck, Heath tugged her closer. Kissed her. "I have no doubts I love you, Darci. Some day, when you're as sure as I am, I hope you'll marry me."

Both hands pressed to his chest, she leaned into him. "Are you asking?"

"No." Loving the disconcerted look she gave him, he kissed her again. "I'm begging."

LOYAL PROTECTORS

What follows is a true account written by an Air Force handler. I hope you find Elgin and Max's story as inspiring as I did, and that perhaps, we all will realize our military heroes come in many shapes and sizes, especially the four-legged kind.

God bless our troops, veterans, and MWDs, abroad and at home!

Ronie Kendig

"MAX" J216

"MAX" J216

During my Air Force years, I had the pleasure of being selected and trained as a Military War Dog (MWD) handler. Over the course of my twelve-year Air Force career, I handled and trained many dogs for law enforcement and force protection. Out of all the dogs I ever worked with, MWD Max will forever be my favorite. Max was a 65–68 lbs Australian shepherd–pit bull mix. He was a beige lean-and-mean machine with a heart of gold and truly loved his handlers and all children. The Department of Defense had trained Max as a Patrol

Bomb dog.

The month and year was January 1987. Max and I were assigned a graveyard patrol on Fairchild AFB (Spokane). As part of our duties, we were required to do random common-area building checks in search of illegal explosives and weapons. During the completion of one such common-area search, Max and I began to walk across a parking lot to our patrol car. Suddenly and without warning, both of my feet went flying out from under me and down I went, with a crack, onto the frozen asphalt. My head impacted the ground, and I lost consciousness.

I later awoke to the sound of Max standing across my middle torso and growling at my buddies and fellow patrolmen as they were trying to check on me. Max knew his role was not only as my partner, but also as my protector, and Max knew I was hurt. Max was in no way, shape, or form, going to let further harm come to me.

As soon as I had enough faculties to realize what was occurring, I told Max "Out" (the command to cease aggression) and began to talk with him in a normal tone. Max touched his wet, cold nose to my face and then "permitted" a fellow patrolman to lead him back to our patrol car. As I sat up,

I looked across the parking lot and saw Max looking directly at me without so much as a flinch. Fortunately, the injury I sustained that night was a bump to the back of my hat holder (head). Nothing very bad.

By Max's actions that night, his undying love for and loyalty to me, I knew no harm would ever come to me as long as he was at my side.

MWD Max J216 lived to be thirteen years old. Postdeath the base flag at Fairchild AFB was flown at half-staff. I later received Max's flag as a gift, and to this day it is proudly displayed in my office in a shadow box inscribed with his name, service number, and dates of service.

God bless you, Max. I miss you, buddy!
Elgin Shaw
U.S. Air Force 1982–94

JOHN BURNAM MONUMENT FOUNDATION

John Burnam, a Vietnam-era dog handler, formed the John Burnam Monument Foundation (JBMF) to raise an estimated $950,000 needed to build and maintain this long overdue National Monument to honor the heroic U.S. military dog handlers and their incredible working dogs.

Please consider making a donation in honor of the four-legged heroes who have protected their human counterparts and hundreds of thousands of troops throughout history.

ABOUT THE AUTHOR

Ronie Kendig grew up an Army brat and married a veteran. Her life is never dull in a family with four children and three dogs. She has a degree in psychology, speaks to various groups, is active in the American Christian Fiction Writers (ACFW), and mentors new writers. Ronie can be found at www.roniekendig.com, on Facebook (www.facebook.com/rapidfirefiction), Twitter (@roniekendig), and GoodReads.